Justin Thyme

Justin Thyme – The Tartan of Thyme – Part One
Published in Great Britain by Inside Pocket Publishing Ltd.

A CIP catalogue record for this book is available from the British Library.

ISBN: 978-0-9567122-8-8

10 9 8 7 6 5 4 3 2 1

Illustrations by Adrian Poxmage
Cover graphics by Paxman O'Gradie

Printed and bound in Great Britain by
CPIBookmarque, Croydon, CR0 4TD

Visit www.justinthyme.info

The TARTAN of THYME
Part One

Justin Thyme

THYMUM SEMPITERNUM

by
Panama Oxridge

INSIDE POCKET

CAST of CHARACTERS

The Thymes

Justin Thyme – 13 year-old inventor and billionaire
Robyn – his older sister
Albion – their baby brother
Sir Willoughby – their father, Laird of Thyme
Lady Henny – their mother, a celebrity explorer
Lyall Austin Thyme – their long-lost grandfather

The Staff

Verity Kiss – the nanny
Professor Gilbert – Justin's private tutor
Mrs Kof – the cook
Angus Gilliechattan – the gardener
Moray Gilliechattan – the housekeeper
Peregrine Knightly – the butler

Outsiders

Jock – a postman
Hank and Polly – Lady Henny's film crew
Sergeant Awbrite and PC Knox – local police

Pets

Eliza – a computer-literate gorilla
Burbage – Mr Gilliechattan's parrot
Tybalt – Mrs Gilliechattan's cat
Fergus – Jock's Scottie dog

O thou, my lovely boy, who in thy power
Dost hold Time's fickle glass, his sickle hour;

William Shakespeare

A paradox? A paradox!
A most ingenious paradox!
We've quips and quibbles heard in flocks,
But none to beat this paradox!

W S Gilbert

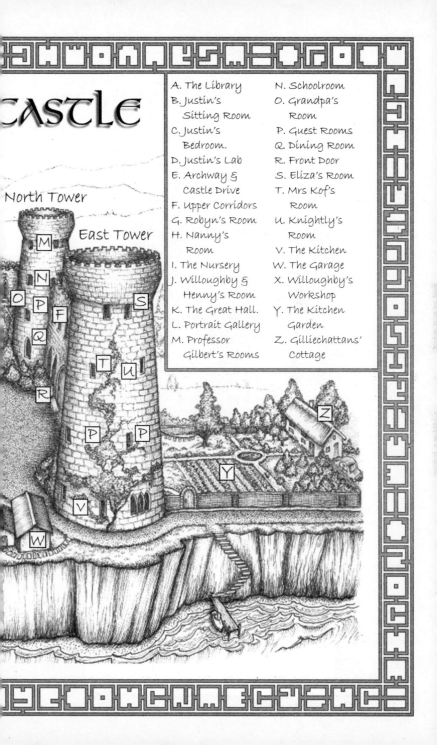

CASTLE

A. The Library
B. Justin's Sitting Room
C. Justin's Bedroom.
D. Justin's Lab
E. Archway & Castle Drive
F. Upper Corridors
G. Robyn's Room
H. Nanny's Room
I. The Nursery
J. Willoughby & Henny's Room
K. The Great Hall.
L. Portrait Gallery
M. Professor Gilbert's Rooms

N. Schoolroom
O. Grandpa's Room
P. Guest Rooms
Q. Dining Room
R. Front Door
S. Eliza's Room
T. Mrs Kof's Room
U. Knightly's Room
V. The Kitchen
W. The Garage
X. Willoughby's Workshop
Y. The Kitchen Garden
Z. Gilliechattans' Cottage

North Tower

East Tower

*If you come across
any words you don't
recognise, the appendix
(a mini-dictionary at the
back of this book)
might help.*

CHAPTER ONE

Once Upon a Thyme

Justin Thyme chose not to celebrate his birthday. No cards, no gifts, no fuss. So when he awoke that morning and found a small, neatly wrapped package on his bedside table, he couldn't decide whether he felt excited or annoyed ... or both.

With a deep sigh, he wandered off to the bathroom, leaving the parcel untouched. After all, he *knew* what it was; the ticking was a dead giveaway. It was either a bomb or yet another wristwatch ... and since his parents had started grumbling about his lack of punctuality – *again* – it was hardly a case for Scotland Yard.

'I can't help it,' he told the pale, spiky-haired boy in the bathroom mirror. 'When I'm busy I just sort of ... lose track of the time.'

Justin told his parents the same thing a dozen times a day, explaining how, when inspiration struck, he became oblivious to everything: lessons, meals, bedtime – even the deafening chimes of the old tower clock. Time seemed to move at a different rate; Einstein had proved that. But, being parents, they refused to accept Relativity Theory as a valid excuse.

'They just don't get it,' Justin grumbled to the mirror. 'And now ... *another* watch!'

The reflection shook its head sympathetically, then grinned as Justin remembered the fate of all the previous wristwatches. He could never resist prising them open and tinkering inside. Within weeks, each had been dismantled, their cogs and wheels used in one of the strange contraptions whirring and puttering away in his lab.

Justin dressed mechanically, his eyes fixed on the parcel. There would be no debate this year, he decided. He was thirteen now; old enough to be treated like an adult. He would return it unopened, politely pointing out that he'd stopped celebrating his birthday four years ago.

A deep, resonant chiming rang out from the top of the south tower, reminding him that breakfast had already started.

'Bother!' he gasped, stuffing the package into his pocket. Seconds later he was hurrying along the castle corridors, hoping, for once, to avoid the annual joke about how he'd been born *just in time* but had been late for everything ever since. He pushed the dining room door open and stepped inside.

Robyn, his older sister, stood at the sideboard, helping herself to cereal. Their parents were sitting at the far end of an impossibly long rosewood dining table. Justin gazed at them, astonished as ever that an American TV celebrity and an absentminded Scottish Laird were so perfectly matched. They seemed such an unlikely couple. Lady Henny had returned from her last expedition a week ago, yet still wore a khaki shirt and jungle fatigues. It suited her, complementing her tanned skin and short, sun-bleached hair. Sir Willoughby, on the other hand, looked every inch the country gent in his old green jacket, faded and crumpled, its worn elbows patched with leather. Neither had noticed Justin enter. Sir Willoughby had his nose buried in a newspaper, while Henny gazed out of a window, a faraway look in her eyes.

Once Robyn returned to the table, Justin reached for the parcel and took a deep breath. But before he could utter a word, the door swung open behind him and a middle-aged woman in a crisp nanny's uniform bustled in. She had rosy cheeks, and dark hair pinned beneath a starched cap. In the crook of one arm she carried a baby and, as she swept past Justin, the aroma of freshly ironed nappies and talcum-powder wafted in her wake.

'Good morning Sir Willoughby, Lady Henny,' she called, bobbing as she spoke. 'Come and sit down, Justin. Och, don't *slouch*, Robyn; we don't want to be a hunchback now, do we?'

Nanny Verity Kiss beamed at everyone, her eyes twinkling like rain-washed blackberries. She settled the baby in his highchair and fetched him a bowl of porridge and a spoon.

'Did Albion have a good night's sleep, Nanny?' enquired Lady Henny.

'Bone-dry all night, your Ladyship,' Nanny Verity replied, with her sunniest smile. 'Then a tiddly-widdly the size of Loch Ness two ticks before upsy-daisy time.'

Sir Willoughby guffawed, inhaled a toast crumb and coughed until his eyes bubbled.

'Never you mind, I told him,' Nanny continued, tickling Albion's feet. 'You're just thirteen months old. Even the family genius wet the bed at that age.'

Robyn exploded with laughter. 'I think he must've wet it again this morning; he isn't usually down this early.'

Justin blushed a fiery red. 'For your information, I thought I heard someone in my room. When I woke up I found *this*!' He tossed the package onto the table and looked at each of his family in turn. 'I thought we'd agreed to put a stop to all this gift nonsense.'

'What gift?' asked Sir Willoughby, peering round his newspaper.

'Duh ... the *WATCH!* Honestly Dad, you couldn't act your way out of a paper bag; you might at least *try* to be convincing.'

Sir Willoughby looked at his wife, eyebrows raised quizzically. Lady Henny shook her head – and from her puzzled frown, Justin felt sure she was genuinely mystified.

'Do *you* know anything about this, Robyn?' she asked.

'*Fffhuhhh*! You've *got* to be joking. The last Rolex you gave him ended up as part of that miniature robot-thingy Dad stood on.'

'Microbot,' Justin mumbled. 'And I ...'

Robyn picked up the parcel and shook it vigorously; Justin winced, then immediately tried to look as if he couldn't care less.

'Aren't you going to open it, Poppet?' asked Nanny Verity.

'No Nanny. I've told you a hundred times; I want the 1st of May to be like any other day.'

A moment of awkward silence followed while the adults

exchanged baffled glances – then Lady Henny spoke brightly:

'Why, if you hadn't inherited your dad's brains, I'd swear I'd brought the wrong baby home from hospital. You Brits! I guess I'll never understand your eccentricity.'

'Scots,' muttered Sir Willoughby, looking faintly irritated.

Lady Henny shrugged. 'Scots, Brits, whatever. You're a Thyme; that's what matters,' she said, ruffling Justin's hair. She took hold of a narrow silvery tuft and gave it a playful tweak. 'Here's the proof. And you *know* how much your sister envies it.'

Robyn snorted like a carthorse. 'As *if!* That Goth look is *so* five minutes ago.'

'Five minutes?' gasped Sir Willoughby. 'Five centuries more like! The Thyme streak's been a distinguishing feature of every male Thyme since ... since ...'

'... Thymes began?' concluded Robyn. She paused, pretending to stifle a yawn with her fingertips. 'I *know* Dad. I walk through the portrait gallery a dozen times a day and there's not a single Laird without it. But why not us girls?'

'Genetics, of course,' said Justin, spying an opportunity to steer the conversation away from his birthday. 'Y-linked inheritance. Females – well, female mammals that is – have two X chromosomes, whereas the gene for this particular form of poliosis is always carried on ...'

The sound of tearing paper interrupted him, and everyone turned to stare at Robyn, calmly unwrapping her brother's present.

'HEY!' yelled Justin. 'Who said *you* could open it?'

'Somebody had to shut you up before one of us died of boredom. Anyway, I thought you didn't want it.'

'I don't.' Justin poured himself a cup of tea, feigning complete disinterest as his sister opened a small velvet-covered case ... but her gasp of admiration made it impossible.

'WOW! This *rocks*! It's even got your name on it.'

Justin gave the watch a desultory glance. 'It's written upside-down.'

'No it isn't.'

'Yes it is; I can read it from here ... unless ...' He reached across the table and turned the case around. 'Cooool! It's an ambigram.

4

They're amazing. Look ... my name reads exactly the same even when it's upside-down.' Justin pulled the watch out and gazed at it admiringly. Despite his aversion to birthday presents, he felt himself weakening. 'Thanks Dad ... if I could custom design my own watch, this is how it would look.'

'I've told you,' said Sir Willoughby, frowning. 'It's not from me.' He took the watch and examined it closely, running his thumb around the edge of the face. 'Dashed odd! That ambi-whotsit must be brand new – but I'd swear the casing's antique. See how worn this engraving is on the back. I can hardly read it.'

Justin peered over his father's shoulder. '"*Everything is Connected to Everything Else.*"'

'Whatever happened to good old *Tempus fugit*?' muttered Willoughby, turning the watch over again. 'And look at that X.'

'You mean the ten? What's wrong with it?' asked Justin.

'Well, er ...' Sir Willoughby hesitated, his brow deeply furrowed. 'It's ... it's in a circle; none of the other Roman numerals are. *Most* peculiar! Is there a card with it, Hen?'

Lady Henny rummaged through the wrapping paper. 'No, nothing. I'm sorry son ... I really don't think you oughta wear it until we know who it's from.'

Now it was Justin's turn to scowl. Typical parents, he thought. Continually nagging me to wear a watch – and when I finally get one I won't be tempted to dismantle, they want to confiscate it. 'Stop overreacting,' he groaned, taking it out of his father's hands. He draped the bracelet around his wrist and fastened it hurriedly before anyone could stop him. 'It *has* to be from *somebody* living at Thyme Castle.'

'Hhmm ... that only leaves the professor,' murmured Sir Willoughby. 'I wonder ...'

'Mystery solved,' Nanny beamed, slicing Albion's toast into soldiers. 'Now, young man, you'd better be on time for your lessons and say thank ...' She broke off mid-sentence and stared at the dining room door, cringing as the thunder of enormously heavy feet pounded towards it. 'Brace yourselves!' she shouted.

The door crashed open and an immense gorilla stood in the doorway, roaring and beating its chest. Dropping onto its knuckles, it prowled towards the sideboard and delicately lifted a priceless silver plate-cover off a dish of fresh fruit.

Nanny Verity frowned, and cleared her throat to attract the creature's attention. '*Really* Eliza! How often do I have to remind you *not* to slam doors?'

'Don't fuss, Nanny dear,' drawled Lady Henny. 'She's an ape – what do you expect? There are no doors in the Kisangani rain forest.'

Sir Willoughby sighed and retired behind his newspaper. After shooting a wary glance at his father, Justin slid his sleeve over the watch, and helped himself to an oatcake.

Meanwhile, the gorilla carried the fruit to the far end of the table and sat down. She bit into a banana and tore off the skin, casting Nanny a look of withering scorn. Nanny Verity stared back, her lips pinched tightly together. Eliza crammed the whole banana into her mouth, and then carefully opened a laptop computer fastened to a harness around her waist. She flexed her fingers a few times, and then moved them over the keyboard, activating a synthesised voice: 'Eliza very hungry,' it said, as she continued chewing her banana with evident relish.

'And please don't speak with your mouth full,' grumbled Nanny. 'You know it sets a bad example for baby Albion.'

Eliza's fingers flickered over the laptop again. This time it spoke with quite a different voice. In condescending regal tones it said, 'Eliza not speak. Computer speak for Eliza.'

A fleeting grin hovered on Justin's lips. The gorilla's knack of always picking the ideal voice from her repertoire never failed to impress him. The Queen was her current favourite. Once Eliza discovered that she and the "*lady-with-big-shiny-hat*" shared the same name, she'd spent hours watching satellite news broadcasts, determined to record a viable sample of her royal speech pattern the computer could replicate. Now, whenever she selected QUEEN from her voice menu, somehow, you couldn't argue with her any longer.

Justin tidied his plate, pressing leftover oatcake crumbs onto the tip of his forefinger, and then poured himself a second cup of tea. As he sipped it, he wondered why he hadn't realised the watch was from Professor Gilbert straight away. The professor was punctual to a nanosecond, and had never understood why someone so fascinated by time was always late for their lessons. Justin smiled into his teacup, remembering their good-natured arguments about what made the universe tick. For the last few months he'd been unable to concentrate on little else. However, something was lacking – some inspirational spark that, like the missing piece of a jigsaw puzzle, would allow all the other pieces to slot into place.

If only I could crack the enigma of time, Justin thought, that really *would* put my name alongside the likes of Newton and Da Vinci. Then his shoulders slumped. But why, oh why, he wondered for the billionth time, did Mum and Dad have to call me Justin? No one's ever going to take my inventions seriously with a name like Justin Thyme.

This wasn't true. When Justin was eleven, someone stole his mobile phone, which inspired him to invent a minuscule device you could attach to a phone's SIM card. Dialling a PIN number from another phone activated a continual ring-tone at full volume, making the stolen mobile useless; only by keying in the same PIN on the phone itself could the deafening alarm be stopped. He approached all the major networks with his prototype and, within six months, had become Britain's youngest multimillionaire.

Justin wondered if that was why he felt so awkward about accepting birthday presents; or maybe it was just that he hated all the fuss. He gazed round the table, relieved to see his parents slipping back into their daily routine: Sir Willoughby left toast crumbs and smears of butter in the whisky marmalade, while Lady Henny attacked a rasher of bacon as if it was a python. Nanny, however, had other ideas.

'Och, I've just remembered,' she gasped. 'You're a teenager this year.'

Stating the obvious was one of Nanny Verity's special talents;

being totally irrational was another. 'Watch out Robyn,' she added, 'or he'll catch up with you.'

A stranger would have naturally assumed that Nanny Verity was trying to be witty, but Justin knew better. Verity Kiss lived in a parallel universe all her own, where the conventional rules of science and logic didn't apply. No one minded. For some reason Justin couldn't quite fathom, it made him love her all the more. But Robyn ...

Robyn had been a teenager for twenty long months, and considered herself too grown up for Nanny's amiable dottiness. She groaned and rolled her eyes towards the ceiling. 'Yes Nan, and I'll catch up with *you* ... if we keep you cryogenically frozen for the next thirty years.'

Nanny's attention remained fixed on Justin. 'If the professor's given you a present, then I don't see why I can't too.'

Justin shook his head, shuddering at the thought of Nanny's hand-knitted bedsocks.

'There must be *something* you'd like,' she wheedled.

He looked round the table at the eager faces of his family. 'Well ...'

'Go on,' whispered Lady Henny. 'If you could make a wish – what would it be?'

Sir Willoughby folded his newspaper, Robyn leaned forward – even Albion stopped smearing egg over his highchair and appeared to listen.

'The things I *really* want ... well, they're not the sort of things you can buy,' explained Justin. He paused to look at his sister. 'I know what Robyn would like me to wish for; that Grandpa Lyall was still alive ... but ...'

He stopped, hoping he hadn't said the wrong thing. Sir Willoughby had never entirely come to terms with his father's death. Exactly one month before Justin was born, Sir Lyall Austin Thyme had vanished while mountaineering. An avalanche had swept him away, and his body was never discovered. Robyn's most treasured possession was a photograph of herself, aged one and a half, sitting on her grandfather's shoulders.

'That doesn't count,' sighed Lady Henny. 'You can't bring

people back from the dead.' She reached for her husband's hand but, for once, he drew back. From the pain in his father's eyes Justin knew that, for some inexplicable reason, he still blamed himself for the old laird's accident – and the two tragic deaths that preceded it.

Sir Willoughby ran his fingers through his untidy hair and took a deep breath. 'The Thyme Curse!' he muttered. 'The one thing I *can't* forget. There's irony for you.'

Justin shuffled uncomfortably; he *had* said the wrong thing. Sir Willoughby had once been a brilliant scientist, but something mysterious had happened that nobody ever spoke of. All Justin knew was that there had been a terrible accident at work, damaging his father's memory. Vast chunks of his past had been erased, and the bewildering gaps still haunted him.

'I ... I wish there was nothing wrong with Dad's memory,' said Justin, the words tumbling out in a rush.

Lady Henny stifled a gasp, and glanced at her husband, wondering how he would react. Sir Willoughby loosened his tie. Then, after undoing the top button of his shirt, ran a long forefinger around the inside of his collar.

'Well, er ... hrrm,' he faltered, his husky voice breaking the uneasy silence. 'I erm ...'

Justin's face burned. 'Sorry Dad – that was insensitive ...'

'Wow!' sniggered Robyn. 'The brain of a boffin; the tact of a triceratops.'

'That's *quite* enough, young lady,' Nanny scolded, then turning to Justin, added: 'Maybe you could try a slightly less serious wish, Poppet. Something, well ... a bit of fun, perhaps.'

Justin gazed at his nanny, fussily straightening the broad band of petersham ribbon that secured a cameo around her throat. Dear, sweet Nanny Verity, who frequently believed six impossible things before breakfast. If you told her you had just seen the Loch Ness Monster, she'd simply murmur *that's nice dear*, and carry on tidying the nursery. Nanny *thought* she'd seen it scores of times, but it always turned out to be nothing more than driftwood.

'I'd like to see Nessie,' said Justin. 'That's what *you'd* wish, wouldn't you Nanny?'

'Ridiculous!' snapped Sir Willoughby, his voice suddenly angry. 'How many times do I have to tell you? It's nothing but hype to attract the tourists.' He rose abruptly, tossing his newspaper aside, and then strode towards the door. 'I'll be in my workshop ...'

'Chill out, Willo Honey,' Henny called after him.

The dining room door slammed shut.

Justin blinked. He knew his dad refused to believe in the Monster, but he'd *never* seen him get so angry about it before. 'Wow! I ... I didn't mean to ...'

'Forget it,' said Henny, giving his arm a reassuring squeeze. Then lowering her voice added: 'I'd like to see Nessie too – but it's never gonna happen, is it?'

'S'pose not.'

The logical left side of Justin's brain knew that the possibility of a plesiosaur surviving in such cold waters since the Jurassic period was remote to say the least. And his Mum should know. Her TV show, *Thyme-Zone*, wasn't just about *endangered* wildlife; in their latest series, Henny and her film crew had searched for every cryptid imaginable: giant anacondas, Sasquatch, Kongamato, thylacines ... even the Yeti.

'So much for wishing,' sighed Justin. 'I should know better at my age.'

'Don't be silly,' said Henny. 'Now, those didn't count. Wish for *yourself* this time. And if you *really* want it to come true – you have to wish silently!'

Justin laughed. Then, as he gazed at his adventurous mother he realised that, more than anything else, he longed for a real adventure of his own. He knew wishing was illogical, childish – but what harm could it possibly do? He closed his eyes – and wished.

'Baby has pooped,' announced a computerised voice from the depths of Albion's nappy.

Nanny Verity sighed. 'That thing would be more useful if it told me before he ... *went*.'

'Try adjusting the hydrogen-sulphide setting on the flatulence sensors,' suggested Justin.

'Hhmmph!' Nanny scooped Albion up and, after giving Justin a look that told him she'd do nothing of the kind, hastened off to the nursery. Breakfast over, Robyn trickled away next, claiming she needed to get changed for lessons. Eliza stayed put – still devouring bananas. Meanwhile, a polyphonic rendition of *Thyme-Zone*'s theme tune reverberated from Lady Henny's pocket. She reached for her cell phone.

'Hi ... oh, it's you Polly. No, I haven't got your letter ... but the mailman's due any minute.'

A faint, tinny voice replied, but Justin was unable to decipher what it said.

'Don't be such a drama queen,' Henny continued. 'It's probably just a silly rumour. Anyway, we're leaving for the Congo in twenty-four hours. That tribe of BaAka pygmies promised to help us track the Mokéle-mbembe ...'

Justin stood up, sliding his chair back quietly. As far as he could remember, Polly did Henny's make-up and either sound recording or filming; he could *never* be certain which.

He wandered into the entrance hall. His mum was right; the post *would* be arriving shortly. Sure enough, as he opened the castle door a red mail van rattled through the archway into the courtyard. As it came to a halt, the postman wound down his window.

'What Thyme is it?' he asked, pretending to peer at Justin short-sightedly. Then, chuckling helplessly, added, 'Oh ... it's Justin Thyme.'

Justin forced a polite smile. Jock's conversation was duller than the Scottish weather – and just as predictable. He'd been cracking the same dreary joke all year.

He wore a regulation GPO coat and cap, and once you'd said that there was little more you *could* say. Beside him, however, sat a firecracker: a Scottie dog as black and shiny as a lump of coal, bristling with mock ferocity.

Justin delved into his pocket. 'Here, Fergus – catch,' he said, tossing him his favourite treat: a stick of Edinburgh rock. The Scottie caught it with ease and crunched it to atoms, his tail thumping. Meanwhile, the postman handed Justin a wad of about forty envelopes.

'Thanks,' said Justin, wondering which of his stock phrases Jock would use next: *grand weather*, *it looks like rain* ... or ...

'Almost twenty years I've driven round this loch, and never *once* have I seen the Beastie.'

Justin struggled to keep a straight face. 'Me neither,' he said.

'Aye,' sighed Jock, with a shake of his head.

'I'd like to though.'

'Aye,' Jock replied, nodding this time. 'Aye.' He touched the brim of his cap, which meant the strain of keeping up such a demanding conversation was rapidly becoming unbearable and he would have to leave. Fergus put his paws on the dashboard and pressed his nose against the windscreen. With a cheery wave, the postman drove through the archway and down towards the castle gates.

Before returning indoors, Justin flipped through the envelopes. Most of his business enquiries zapped straight to his e-mail address, but a few still dawdled by snail-mail. Today they were all for him, except for one letter addressed to Lady Henrietta Thyme, its flamboyant flowery writing standing out amongst the plain typewritten bills.

Justin had taken over the family's finances about eighteen months ago. His father earned next to nothing. Fortunately he spent even less – content to either potter in his workshop or read the daily newspaper. After his accident, Henny had become the primary breadwinner, but her earnings did not stretch to the upkeep of a fourteenth century castle. Justin not only managed the daily running costs, but had been able to afford extensive renovation. He was proud to think that by the time he became *Sir* Justin, the twenty-fifth Laird of Thyme, the work would be complete and Thyme Castle not merely restored to its former glory, but modernised to withstand the onslaught of several generations to come.

The last envelope contained Robyn's credit card bill. She had more than enough money to pay it herself, but Justin had it sent to him, and paid it as he did everything else. He scanned the list of avant-garde fashion designers his sister had patronised, his eyes widening at the last itemised transaction. He couldn't help wondering what their mother would say if she found out Robyn had just spent £117.00 at *Big Jimmy's Tattoo Emporium*.

Justin closed the castle door and trudged across the entrance hall, searching for a tactful way to broach the subject with his sister. It wouldn't be easy. He glanced down at his new watch and groaned. Lessons started in ten minutes and he needed to collect his school things.

After wedging his mother's letter beneath the old millefiori paperweight on the hall table, Justin dashed along the portrait gallery. He ran up the west staircase, his footsteps echoing on the worn, stone flags, then sped along the upper corridor to the clock tower. Apart from the library on the ground floor, he had the entire south tower to himself. As he approached the only door, he saw a small brown paper package leaning against the oak panelling.

'So *that's* why Nanny was twittering about presents,' he groaned. 'She must've crept up here with it straight after breakfast.' He turned the hourglass gift tag over and read the inscription:

To my favourite pupil.
I know gifts are
against the
rule

but every
rule should have
an exception. Best
Wishes, Prof Gilbert.

'The professor!' gasped Justin. 'So he *couldn't* have given me the watch.'

He tore back the paper and withdrew a small notebook. It had a Thyme tartan binding, combining all the colours Justin loved best: the vibrant purple of freshly blooming heather; the crisp, dark green of the ancient, noble pines; the deepest blues of an unfathomable loch and the coppery orange glow of sunset. In the centre of the book was the Thyme clan crest: a scythe and an hourglass surrounded by sprigs of thyme. Above, he read the clan motto:

Thymum sempiternum

As Justin stared at the notebook, he suddenly felt very silly. The professor would *never* have bought something as expensive as a watch. But who had? Lost in thought, Justin hurried up another spiral staircase, then, after passing his bedroom door on the next landing, breathlessly clambered the last few steps to his laboratory at the top.

The huge face of the old tower clock dominated the left side of the lab. Pale morning sunlight slanted through its mosaic of opaline glass, bathing the clockwork mechanism in a dappled patchwork of light. The whole room seemed alive. Apart from the industrious cogs and wheels rotating amongst the rafters, dozens of Justin's own inventions rattled or hummed, or belched pungent smoke. A shimmering tangle of wires buzzed like a beehive, a weird holographic eyeball hovered over a stack of blueprints, and swarms of insect-like robots scaled the walls or scuttled over tool-covered work benches.

Still wondering about the watch, Justin scoured the lab for his schoolbooks. A well-thumbed copy of "*Advanced Quantum Mechanics*" evaded discovery for several minutes, half hidden beneath a flask of tantalum and a Harrison chronometer, but his ancient edition of "*The Copernicus Chronicles*" lay open on the windowsill beside his telescope. As he reached for it, something attracted his attention: a faint movement at a fork in the road just beyond the castle gates. Unable to resist, he put his eye to the lens and adjusted the focus.

At that precise instant, the tower clock started to strike. As the first chime reverberated along the shelves of chemical bottles, a dazzling shaft of sunlight burst from behind a cloud, illuminating the stooping figure of an old, old man. He had snowy-white hair, a flowing beard, and appeared to be wearing long linen robes. Justin blinked. For a split second he saw a golden hourglass in the man's right hand, and a scythe carried over his left shoulder. *Old Father Time – surely he was imagining things*? He leapt back from the telescope, putting both hands on his stomach. It felt as if someone was tossing the caber inside it.

Justin readjusted the focus. His eyes must have deceived him, the sudden ray of light creating an optical illusion. Now, he saw nothing but a raggedy stranger carrying a shabby bundle over his shoulder, tied to the end of a long stick. He looked like some elderly shepherd who'd lost all his sheep. From the vacant expression on his face, Justin assumed he'd probably lost his marbles as well.

The old man stood peering at a sign by the roadside, deciding which fork to take: left towards Drumnadrochit, or right, leading directly to the castle. He withdrew a coin from his pocket and tossed it high into the air, leaving chance to plot his course. The tower clock continued striking as the coin somersaulted skywards. Gleaming sunlight glanced off its facets, and the illusory image appeared a second time, shimmering around the old man like a fragmented hologram. Then, as the tenth chime faded, the image flickered and died.

Something clicked deep within Justin's brain: like the turning of a long lost key in a well-oiled lock, instantly liberating a million thoughts, letting them erupt into life and hurtle around his synaptic race track. He felt within him the power to defy gravity, soar into the heavens and explode into a billion particles of the purest light. It was the sensation that Justin loved beyond all others: that exhilarating thrill of discovery that centuries earlier had prompted Archimedes to shout *Eureka – I have found it*.

But as Sir Isaac Newton once said, *"To every action there is an equal and opposite reaction."* When Justin *found* inspiration, he invariably *lost* track of the time.

In a daze of spectacular ideas, he reached for his new notebook. Below the clan badge was a rectangular brass plate containing a piece of parchment. Justin withdrew a fountain pen from his breast pocket and slowly removed the lid. After thoughtfully considering the three lines available, he wrote the title of the book that would, one day, secure his place in history:

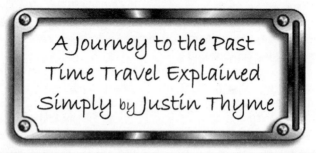

A Journey to the Past
Time Travel Explained
Simply by Justin Thyme

Justin turned the tiny brass key in the notebook's miniature lock, and pulled back the strong leather clasp. Meanwhile, the old man had pocketed his coin and turned towards the castle. His face looked lined and weary, and his footsteps faltered, but as he stepped through the castle gates, he smiled, and a ray of hope shone out from the depths of his eyes. He walked faster, like a man who after many years had finally found his way back home.

Blissfully unaware, Justin turned to the first page of his notebook and started to write ...

Logical people believe that time travel is impossible - though a few centuries ago most logical people believed that the world was flat, and anyone travelling too close to the edge would fall off. Just because a thing seems beyond all possibility now, does not necessarily mean it always will be.

Probably the first step in accepting the prospect of time travel is to realise that WE ARE ALL TIME TRAVELLERS - travelling through time in the same direction; minute by minute, hour by hour, day by day and so-on. We assume that time cannot be speeded up or slowed down, but in reality, this is not entirely true.

Einstein's Theory of Relativity shows that space and time are comparable to a tossed coin - with time on one side and space on the other. It is perfectly possible to either stretch or squeeze this spacetime, and, in certain circumstances, time may even be exchanged for space, as long as the overall balance remains unaltered.

Experiments show that subatomic particles moved at speeds close to that of light inside particle accelerators, have a longer life span than those that remain stationary. This all seems rather technical. So consider a situation a little more personal: the relentless rate at which we humans age ...

CHAPTER TWO

The Operatic Tutor

'Flux! It's gone ten-past.'

Justin leapt to his feet, dropping his fountain pen and splattering a half-written page with ink. He raced around the lab, frantically gathering his school things.

'Better late than never, I suppose,' he sighed, wondering how long he'd have kept writing if he hadn't happened to glance at his new watch.

Justin knew lessons wouldn't start without him; after all, he was usually the only pupil. Still, he hated to keep his tutor waiting now Robyn was home. He imagined the professor sitting at his desk in the schoolroom, drumming his fingers impatiently ... and Robyn, wearing a smug grin. She'd been uncharacteristically early for lessons since getting back from boarding school; probably doing it on purpose to make him look bad.

He frowned for a moment, exasperated by his sister's unscheduled return from St Columba's in the middle of term. What had prompted it this time, he wondered. Sneaking out to a pop concert? Missing her Latin exam to check out the Harpy Nyx Spring Collection? Giving her uniform a grunge makeover?

As if by way of a reply, his subconscious search engine retrieved a crisp mental image of her credit card bill, zooming in on the last transaction: *Big Jimmy's Tattoo Emporium.* Justin erased the thought rapidly – but an invoice for her school fees materialised in its place. He sighed; the money he'd lavished on

Robyn's education would feed a small country.

Finding the right school for his sister was harder than splitting an atom, and with her volatile personality to factor in, twice as hazardous. Options were running out – and allowing her to share his private tutor wasn't working either.

Justin hurried towards a shiny fireman's pole in the centre of his lab. It had been installed during the south tower's recent renovations, and certainly helped when he was in a rush. He grabbed it, took a deep breath, and let gravity do what it did best.

Clutching tightly with his arms and knees, he stopped at the first floor, and then ran along the upper corridor. As he dashed across the west tower landing he heard his sister's footsteps clattering down from her bedroom. A pair of boots came into view and then stopped.

Robyn stamped a shiny purple heel. 'I thought you'd *be* there by now, busy thanking the professor for that watch he didn't give you.'

'*Hey* ... how did you know *that*? I've ...'

'Only just twigged? *Fffhuhhh!* Some genius; I can't *believe* you fell for it.'

'What?'

'The old reverse psychology trick,' groaned Robyn, then impersonating her mother's American twang, added: '*I'm sorry son ... I really don't think you oughta wear it.*'

'You mean ... it actually *is* from Mum and Dad?' Justin gave his head a swift, shuddering shake, as if trying to rid himself of the thought, but it was useless. As much as he hated to admit it, his sister was probably right. 'But ...'

'Sharp as a sausage! I thought I'd give you chance to embarrass Professor Gobbledygook, then razz in and finish the job properly ... wearing *this*.'

Robyn stepped onto the landing dressed in an incredibly short acid-green kilt and a metallic tangerine-coloured top that appeared to be several sizes too small. Justin drew a sharp breath through clenched teeth and pretended to shield his eyes.

19

'Did it shrink in the wash? Or is there an international mohair shortage?'

'Very funny,' replied Robyn, flashing a sarcastic smirk. 'For your information, it's retro seventies glam with a millennial twist of chic.'

'If mum sees it, you'll be retro seventies glum with a terminally twisted neck. And as for poor Professor Gilbert ... in the last three days your fashion statements have wrecked two and half years of therapy.'

'*Therapy?* Since when has bursting into an operatic aria been therapy? Insanity more like.'

'I've told you,' said Justin. 'It relaxes his vocal chords.'

'It doesn't relax *me!*'

Robyn turned sharply and marched towards the north tower.

'He's not *that* bad,' Justin called, hurrying to catch up. 'He was a member of the Harvard Operatic Society. Last week he taught me how to memorise the elements in the periodic table by singing them to the tune of "*The Modern Major General*."'

'Wow,' gasped Robyn, her eyes wide with mock admiration. 'A couple more nerds and you've got yourself a boy band.'

'Once he's calmed down the stuttering stops. But I've *told* you: the more you embarrass him, the longer he'll keep singing.'

Robyn's smirk stretched to dangerous proportions. 'Then be prepared for an aria and three encores.' She clutched a pile of books to her semi-bare midriff, and Justin realised that the worst was yet to come. Robyn was not the scholarly type. If she insisted on carrying books it was for another reason altogether.

'*Please,* tell me it's not a tattoo. Mum'll go berserk!'

'It's not a tattoo. Happy?'

'Ecstatic,' said Justin. 'Does the name *Big Jimmy* ring any bells?'

Robyn didn't flinch. 'He does a *lot* more than tattooing,' she replied coolly.

As Justin's mind explored the alternatives, she slid the books to one side revealing a topaz stud in her navel. For a full five seconds, he bit his lower lip, trying to think of a suitable remark. It was decidedly awkward. Part of him, (a microscopic part, admittedly), admired her defiant independence, but he'd no intention of saying so. Teasing, of course, was another matter entirely:

'Legally speaking, Big Jimmy is on pretty dodgy ground. Parental consent is compulsory for minors.'

Robyn's eyes flashed with undiluted fury. Minors indeed – that was below the patent leather belt. 'Let's get one thing clear,' she hissed. 'I don't need *your* permission, *little* brother. I'm older than you – and always will be.'

'Mmm ... not *strictly* true,' said Justin. 'If *you* travelled at light-speed while *I* remained stationary, you'd....' He stopped short; Robyn's eyes had glazed over.

'Oh, great! Time Dilation – *again*,' she said. '*Do* go on ... it's as fascinating as earwax.'

Justin clenched his lips.

'Anyway, *Dustbin*,' Robyn continued. 'For your information, I had *written* authorisation.'

'And I can guess who wrote it ... or should I say *forged* it?'

Robyn widened her dark eyes and puckered her lips, assuming an expression of saintliness. The face of a Botticelli angel, thought Justin, yet deep inside ticks the calculating brain of a Moriarty.

He halted suddenly, clutching his sister's arm. 'You needn't look so innocent. Admit it: that letter to Dad from your headmistress was another forgery. "*Poor Robyn has been overworking and is in desperate need of an extended holiday.*" As if! You've been expelled again, haven't you?'

Robyn shrugged, her angelic features morphing into an impish grin. They stared at each other, their eyes locked in silent combat; Robyn's sparkling with mischief whilst Justin's struggled to retain their frown of disapproval. He was fighting a losing battle – and knew it. After a moment or two, he turned away, determined to conceal his smile.

'Honestly Bobs, what *is* it with you and schools? If I was Dad,

I'd ...'

'Well, you're *not*,' Robyn whispered. She tried to lace her words with resentment, but they came out sounding oddly wistful. At least Justin noticed her, worried about her, cared enough to nag; whereas their father was on another planet.

They plodded up the north tower staircase side by side.

'Well,' Justin continued, 'Mum's off on another expedition tomorrow, and seeing as Dad wouldn't spot your stud if it glowed in the dark, you might just live to be fifteen after all.'

Robyn grinned.

Justin found himself grinning back. 'Please Bobs ... I need the prof's brain firing on all cylinders this morning – *not* terminally traumatised. I know his stammering irritates you ... and his dress sense is a bit behind the times, but ...'

Robyn snorted. 'You mean Out-Dated Tweedy-Nerd with a twist of the Old School Tie? And what's the deal with that chalk dust on his cuffs? There hasn't been a blackboard in the schoolroom since we were toddlers.'

Justin shrugged. He had to admit that Professor Wilfred S Gilbert was something of an enigma. Like Henny, he had a soft American accent, but that was where the resemblance ended. Whereas Lady Henny could cheerfully face a herd of stampeding elephants, the professor looked as if he had a morbid dread of bacteria. Describing him as fastidious was an understatement; everything from his precision-trimmed beard to his symmetrically aligned shoelaces screamed perfectionist – which was why the chalky cuffs were so incongruous. He claimed to be a similar age to Willoughby, though Justin wasn't convinced. The beard made it difficult to estimate, and there were times when a deep sadness etched in the lines surrounding his eyes, made him look considerably older.

Intellectually, of course, the professor couldn't be better suited for the post. Prior to his appearance, Justin had sent several well-educated tutors gibbering into early retirement, unable to cope with his desperate thirst for knowledge. But in Gilbert, he discerned an intellect not merely similar to his own, but one that had ripened with the benefit of experience.

'Please be gentle with him,' begged Justin. 'If he walks out I don't know what I'll do; after all, it's not every day an ex-Harvard professor turns up on your doorstep begging for a job.'

'If he's so over-qualified, what's he doing here – miles from anywhere?'

Justin lowered his voice: 'Nervous breakdown, Dad says. Doctors recommended plenty of invigorating fresh air.'

'Wasn't the air in America fresh enough for him?'

Justin couldn't answer. His tutor was a strictly private person, and had revealed little more about himself than on the day they'd first met.

They paused outside the schoolroom. Justin caught a second glimpse of Robyn's stud and rolled his eyes. 'You *know* what he's like. Do you *want* to give him another breakdown?'

'Nanny could knit him a nice Fair Isle straightjacket.'

Justin groaned and pushed the door open; Robyn flounced past, looking mutinous.

'Perhaps today, he'll notice he's got *two* pupils,' she hissed.

She marched to her desk and slammed the books down, deliberately attracting Professor Gilbert's attention. He turned hurriedly from the window, and the instant he glanced at Robyn, she swaggered into a shaft of sunlight, gyrating her midriff like a belly-dancer.

The professor jerked his head away, looking anywhere but the stud. He said nothing, but Justin knew he'd seen it. His eyebrows twitched a fraction and his ears turned an interesting shade of cerise. He scuttled behind his desk, sat down, and arranged his pencils in a neatly serried row from 2-B to triple-H. Still, he said nothing. He coughed a few times, and then cleared his throat forcefully, like a man who'd mistaken a beaker of H_2SO_4 for a glass of H_2O. Finally, when the tension became utterly unbearable, he took a deep breath and gripped the arms of his chair, steeling himself to speak.

'Mm ... Mmm ...' he began. 'Mmm-m-m ...' Then suddenly, without the slightest warning he burst noisily into song: '*"M-m-my gallant crew, good morning. "'*

'"Sir, good morning!"' Justin sang back, saluting smartly. H.M.S. Pinafore – ACT 1 – Captain Corcoran's first entrance, he thought; a very bad sign indeed. It had been several months since Professor Gilbert had resorted to opera *this* early in a lesson; a sure sign he was feeling discomposed.

'I warned you,' Justin whispered, turning to his sister.

'*"W-w-w-whispering, I've somewhere met. Is contrary to etiquette,"'* sang Professor Gilbert, wondering if he'd need to conduct the entire lesson operatically.

Justin glared at Robyn. The professor hardly ever told him off – especially in song.

Robyn grinned back. All this pandemonium caused by one little stud, she thought. Money well spent – and the fact it wasn't *her* money made it sweeter still. She contemplated her next move: an original improvisation entitled *The Bellybutton Rap,* perhaps. Robyn considered a few choice lyrics whilst mentally choreographing a dance routine guaranteed to singe the professor's eyebrows. The teachers at St Columba's had never been *this* easy to wind up.

The moment Robyn thought of her old school, she slumped down in her chair, allowing a curtain of glossy raven hair to obscure her scowl and protruding lower lip. She forced herself to focus on the things she'd hated about it: the petty rules, the poxy uniform, the control-freak teachers with oral hygiene issues and the fashion sense of hobbits. But at least there had been boys, she thought. Okay, most were blighted with acne, while the rest believed soap was an annual option, or could belch the alphabet – but anything was good enough to practice on. A bewhiskered boffin old enough to be her father seemed a lousy substitute.

Meanwhile, Justin apologised and then thanked his tutor for the notebook: 'It's brilliant. I've started writing in it already. My head's absolutely bursting with ideas; I can't wait to tell you about them.' He hesitated, not wanting to embarrass his teacher into performing further solos. However, the professor just smiled. Either he was still recovering from the shock, or couldn't think of anything appropriate to sing. For a moment, Justin was tempted to show the professor his new watch, but the prospect of further gloating from Robyn stopped him.

Professor Gilbert rose and started writing on the whiteboard. As soon as he turned his back, Robyn reached over and silently traced the word *SWOT* across Justin's desk with a glittery fingernail. Once the professor had set several complicated algebra equations, he took a deep breath and asked Robyn to take out her exercise book and try solving them. He spoke clearly and calmly, though Justin noticed he remained facing the board. After returning to his chair and satisfying himself that Robyn appeared to be busy, he focussed his full attention on Justin. Gradually, the professor's tension subsided and his dark brown eyes twinkled teasingly.

'S-s-so, what's that amazing brain of yours d-devising then?' he asked. 'Not teleportation again, I hope.'

Robyn sniggered – then made a strange guttural purring noise whilst the fingers of her right hand crept along Justin's sleeve in a pseudo-arachnid crawl.

Justin ignored her – or tried to, but it was like trying to ignore toothache. Quantum teleportation had been his one failure. But a failure so dismal and monumentally spectacular, that the effects still continued to haunt him and every other inhabitant of the castle. He stubbornly maintained he'd taken every possible precaution, although Sir Willoughby had never believed him.

Justin frowned, and brushed his sister's scuttling fingers aside, determined to dispel the unhappy associations. Looking on the bright side, he realised that Professor Gilbert seemed to have recovered from the effects of Robyn's stud. Taking full advantage of the opera-free hiatus he told his tutor what he'd seen.

'I was looking through my telescope at this old man,' he explained. 'He was standing at that fork in the road outside the castle gates. As the tower clock struck ten he tossed a coin into the air and ...' Justin stopped, realising that if he described how, for a moment, the man had looked like Old Father Time carrying his scythe and hourglass, it would sound crazy. '... And er ... it sort of gave me an idea,' he concluded.

Robyn sniggered.

'Go on,' said the professor. He leaned forward, guessing this was about to lead somewhere interesting.

'As you know, I've been trying to understand time lately,' said Justin. 'I mean ... *really* understand it. I've read everything: the theories of General and Special Relativity, quantum mechanics – and then a few weeks ago I found an amazing book in the library with all the latest thoughts on the Casimir effect, cosmic strings, antigravity and wormholes. Yet for some reason I couldn't get it all to mentally gel together.'

'Wormholes?' gasped Robyn, wrinkling her nose. 'Boredom *cubed!*' She gave a loud theatrical yawn. 'So ... what's this cashmere effect? That sounds more my style.'

Professor Gilbert concentrated on the male half of his class. 'Listen Justin,' he said. 'This is seriously complicated stuff. Even M Theory can't successfully combine those ideas into one united theory working consistently throughout nature. Why, in a few years' time, even strings might seem too intractable for phenomenological applications; they'll probably end up just being utilised to discover new properties of quantum gravity.'

'*Urghhh* ... like anyone cares,' groaned Robyn. 'Get a *LIFE!*'

Neither Justin nor the professor so much as glanced in her direction. For a moment, Robyn wondered if she'd dematerialised or slipped into parallel dimension. But no such luck.

'It all seems so needlessly complicated,' Justin continued, his eyes burning like twin supernovas. 'For ages now, I've suspected a fundamental pattern is being overlooked; something that would explain the whole stream of time in a way anyone could understand. When I saw that old man tossing a coin at a fork in the road, it came to me in a flash: FORKS! Time isn't in one single stream ... it forks, then forks again ... and again ... *and*

AGAIN. But the beauty of it is its simplicity; at each fork there are only two choices, making it possible to plot the whole fabric of time on a simple binary scale.'

Justin leaned over, his face glowing with a luminous inner energy. He grabbed a worksheet and began scribbling equations at light-speed. Robyn watched him, her shoulders drooping. When the sun rises, the moon fades, she thought. He can't help being brilliant – but once he starts shining, Professor Gobbledygook forgets I exist.

Robyn checked her watch and shook it. Each minute seemed like an hour – yet to her brother, still poring over his calculations, she guessed they were zapping by like seconds.

She *tried* joining in, offering her own brand of helpful observations whenever the opportunity arose, but eventually she gave up and snuck online, stealth-boxing her way through the first nine levels of *Dead-Brainz II* instead. After expiring in a puddle of radioactive cogito-plasma, she unearthed some black ink from the back of her desk and spent the next twenty minutes creating a fake tattoo on one knee. As she worked, she half-listened to the bewildering babble beside her. Bored rigid and unable to grasp more than one word in five, she finally cracked, shoving a huge atlas onto the floor to see if anyone noticed. It landed with a resounding crash, sending up an attractive plume of dust motes. Professor Gilbert lifted his head and blinked like a moonstruck owl.

'G-g-g-good heavens Robyn. W-what was that?'

'Oh, was that me?' Robyn replied dangerously. 'I'm *so* sorry. I *do* hope I didn't disturb you two gentlemen.'

The professor seemed confused by the sarcasm, until Justin pointed out it was almost half past twelve. Instantly, a flux of blood surged to his ears.

Whistling tunelessly through her teeth, Robyn tore a page out of her exercise book, folded it into a plane – and, after taking careful aim, launched it at her tutor.

'Not that you take much interest in my work,' she sneered, putting the rest of her books in her desk and banging the lid three times for emphasis.

Professor Gilbert unfolded the paper and glanced quickly at the rows of algebraic calculations. They were neat and tidy, and above all – completely correct. It amazed him. He was about to commend her when she stood up, and his eyes found themselves drawn to the newly completed skull-and-cross-bones design on her kneecap.

'F-f-ff-fff,' he stammered. But when the words *fine work* refused to come, he gloomily resorted to something more operatic: '*"F-f-f-feast we body and mind as well, so merrily ring the luncheon bell."*'

Robyn gave him a look of purest pity, which did nothing to boost his self-esteem whatsoever. She walked to the door and opened it. 'I'm a lot smarter than you think,' she remarked. 'Unfortunately, I always get compared to my younger brother, and next to him, Einstein looks thick. And in case you hadn't noticed,' she added, pausing in the doorway to give her words maximum impact, '*that's* Relativity!'

The door slammed. The windows rattled. Professor Gilbert trembled.

'W-w-well Justin,' he stammered, after what seemed like an interminable silence. 'You've certainly made a splendid start at cracking the basic enigmas of time. Forks indeed ... who'd've dreamt it? But I've a sneaky suspicion this is just the beginning.'

'Precisely! I haven't made all the calculations yet, but I predict that forks and loops will be an underlying mathematical pattern replicating on every scale ... like fractals.'

The professor's brow creased. 'Actually, there's a similar hypothesis suggested in "*Multiversal Time-Flip Theories*," by Janus Rangler,' he murmured, withdrawing a slim leather-bound book from his inside jacket pocket. He held it close, his fingers tracing the embossed gold letters along its spine.

'Sounds fascinating. Strange I've never heard of it.'

'Mmm ... hardly s-s-surprising,' returned Gilbert, his frown deepening. He thumbed through a few pages – then stopped abruptly, hurling the book at his desk. It landed face-down, like an injured bird, a scrap of torn paper nestling between its crushed pages. 'So, what are you going to call *y-y-your* theory?'

'I haven't settled on a name yet,' said Justin. He tilted his head and tapped his fountain pen against his front teeth. 'I'll let you know as soon as I've decided. Meanwhile, I'm going to write everything down in my new tartan notebook and ...'

He paused – aware that his tutor's attention had drifted. The professor gazed out of the window and across the loch, a far-off gleam in his eyes. Sensing his pupil's probing stare, Gilbert lurched to his feet, blindly grabbing the little book as he stumbled towards the door.

'That's enough for this morning,' he whispered, his voice catching on the last syllable.

Like an out-sized snowflake, the scrap of paper fluttered to the floor.

The schoolroom door creaked shut. Justin sat perfectly still for a moment, uncertain what to do. The torn parchment lay beside his desk. Despising himself for being unable to resist, he twisted his neck to read the professor's spidery handwriting:

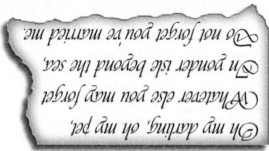

①Oh my darling, oh my pet,
②Whatever else you may forget
③In yonder isle beyond the sea,
④Do not forget you've married me.

Justin rubbed his forehead. It didn't make any sense. The professor had never mentioned anything about marriage.

'I'd always assumed he was a confirmed old bachelor,' Justin whispered to himself, 'and likely to remain so.'

At the top of the west tower, Robyn kicked her purple boots across the room and flopped back on her bed, grinning and hugging herself. Men were *so* gullible. Amazing, she thought, how even the most intelligent shared a mutual blind-spot. Their focus on one thing made them completely unaware of anything else. Nerds! Copying those equations from one of Justin's old exercise books had been child's play – and, just as she'd suspected, old Gobbledygook never noticed they were different from the questions he'd set.

There were two types of intelligence, she decided: the all-in-the-head stuff the geeky types thrived on, naively thinking their theories would actually be of some use in the big bad world; then there were the streetwise types, resourcefully handling all life threw at them, with nothing to depend on but their wits. When the going got tough, the tough were the real survivors – not owlish dweebs who could recite the three laws of thermodynamics, yet barely cross the street.

'So *what*, if the moon can't outshine the sun,' Robyn whispered to herself. '*It can eclipse it.* Look out genius-boy ... I might surprise you after all!'

An astronaut travelling through space at only a fraction of the velocity of light, ages less rapidly than those of us who remain on earth. If he could travel much closer to light-speed, we can logically assume that his ageing would slow still further.

Now imagine that he finds himself beside a sizeable black hole. He needn't enter it to feel its effects, but could position himself within its strong gravitational field and allow the surrounding universe to go by at a faster rate. Although we are unlikely to find ourselves travelling at light-speed or beside a black hole, both examples show our imaginary astronaut experiencing time more slowly than others; in a sense, travelling into their future. This is known as TIME DILATION, and occurs even at aircraft speeds - though unfortunately, our ageing is only reduced by a few nanoseconds!

As long as certain key 'ingredients' are an integral part of the process, this type of time travel is possible. But travelling into the past is problematic and only feasible in certain spacetime configurations. If a chrononaut could only travel forwards, he may become trapped in the future, unable to travel back against the flow of time.

While many scientists claim that time merely exists, others believe it flows inexorably onwards. Why?

CHAPTER THREE

Eavesdropping at Story Thyme

Justin tucked the little scrap of paper in his pocket. He felt terrible, but there seemed no alternative. Returning it to Professor Gilbert would embarrass both of them, but leaving it on the schoolroom floor would be asking for trouble. If Robyn found it, a complete performance of "*The Mikado*" wouldn't fix the professor's stammer.

After packing his books away, Justin trickled downstairs. As he meandered across the entrance hall, he heard footsteps, and turned to see his tutor hurrying towards him. His eyes were still downcast, though his ears had faded from crimson to a delicate fuchsia pink.

Justin tried to act natural. 'Off bird-watching?' he asked, instantly realising the question was nothing short of idiotic. Apart from his tweeds, the professor now wore a deerstalker, carried a walking stick and a haversack, and had a pair of binoculars dangling round his neck. What *else* could he be doing, thought Justin. Synchronised swimming?

Professor Gilbert gave him a sheepish glance. 'Thought I m-m-might get an hour or so in before lessons start again.'

'Why don't you take the whole afternoon off?' said Justin. 'I've got to talk to Dad about something – but don't worry, I'll get on with my writing later; we can pick up where we left off tomorrow.'

'F-f-fine,' said Gilbert, confident he could trust his pupil to work conscientiously.

Strolling into the kitchen, Justin took a sideways peek at his tutor. He seemed a little calmer now; the promise of an afternoon's ornithology never failed to cheer him. Rain or shine, he trudged off at every opportunity, always content to be alone.

The kitchen was empty, though a trail of whisky marmalade blobs proved that Sir Willoughby had been foraging. Justin opened the fridge and recited the contents to his tutor: 'A red pepper, fourteen eggs, a pack of butter, ten bottles of highland spring water, nineteen cloves of garlic and a large jar of Dad's favourite marmalade. Any appetising recipes spring to mind?'

The professor peered over Justin's shoulder. 'Mmm ... M-M-Miss MacCipiter could've whipped up a five course banquet from that lot. Pity she's gone. I can't think why she suddenly ran off with that alarming butler; I thought they loathed each other.'

Justin shrugged. 'I *know*! Herr Ingred's note said he was taking her back to Germany and they planned to get married. But I still think it was odd of them to leave in the middle of the night without taking their final week's wages.' He closed the door and tapped an e-mail wedged under a fridge magnet. 'Anyway ... read the good news ...'

To:	justin@thymecastle.co.uk
From:	napkinsdomestix.com
Subject:	Your New Cook & Butler

Napkin's Domestix are delighted to inform you that we have on our books a highly qualified cook willing to relocate to the north of Scotland. By an odd coincidence, she has been searching for a situation as far north as possible. We have passed your name & address on to her and anticipate that you should hear from her shortly.

Yours faithfully,
Hubris Napkin – Napkin's Domestix.
PS. We are still looking for a suitable butler and will contact you as soon as we have located one.

'W-well ... it's about time,' remarked Professor Gilbert, resigning himself to whisky marmalade sandwiches. 'Seven nights of eating Chinese takeaways has played havoc with my digestion. I wonder when she'll arrive.'

'Later today,' said Justin. 'At least ... I *think* so.' He reached into his trouser pocket and offered his tutor a grimy, dog-eared envelope. 'This arrived this morning. '

Disinclined to touch the envelope, Gilbert used the tips of his fingernails and reluctantly withdrew an old shopping list with a brief note scribbled on the back:

> Dear Sir,
>
> I am Nadezhda Przolwamiczenkof.
>
> I am job for you. I am cook job.
>
> I am train in London next day for job.
>
> Thank you good buys.

'Ummm,' said the professor, rasping his beard with his index finger. 'I wonder if she's travelling by train, or still being trained how to cook?'

'Who knows?' Justin groaned. 'That's it – no references – nothing. A homicidal maniac with her own set of butcher's knives could be on her way here right this very minute.'

Hearing a muffled gasp of alarm, Justin silently reproached himself for allowing his mouth to bypass his brain. 'She's er ... probably very nice,' he blustered. 'I ... I'm sure she wouldn't harm a fly ...'

The door flew open and a pair of purple boots clacked over the tiles. The professor hurled his sandwiches into his haversack and scurried off like a startled rabbit. Robyn seemed oblivious. After slamming the fridge door, she headed straight for the kitchen computer.

'I suppose ordering more stuff never occurred to you?' she drawled, shooting her brother a look of cool disdain as she flicked the on switch.

But Justin wasn't listening. He was too busy thinking about what he wanted to ask his father. After the teleportation disaster, Sir Willoughby had insisted his son always asked for permission before starting any dangerous experiments ... just to be on the safe side.

Justin wondered whether to tackle his dad about the watch first and make him admit it was from him, then, remembering his sudden outburst at breakfast, decided not to mention it.

Best let him think he's fooled me, Justin decided, placing his sandwich on a plain white plate. I'm going to need him in a really good mood. He poured himself a glass of sparkling water, and turned to leave. Then, noticing a pair of binoculars on the table, shouted: '*Arghh* – the prof's forgotten his field glasses.' He grabbed them and dashed outside, but Professor Gilbert was nowhere to be seen.

Justin hung the binoculars around his neck for safekeeping and headed towards the old stables. The largest housed the Thyme family's cars; the other had been converted into a workshop for Sir Willoughby. Behind it was a pleasant suntrap, and once the Laird of Thyme had leafed through his daily newspaper, he could usually be found snoozing in a deckchair. Today, however, he was poring over a stack of old photograph albums. Justin edged forwards, stomach churning, but when Sir Willoughby glanced up, it was clear that all traces of moodiness had evaporated. Justin hadn't seen him so animated since he first thought of inventing electromagnetic bagpipes.

'Hi Dad,' he mumbled. 'Look – about this morning ... I er ... I'm sorry if ...'

'What?' asked Sir Willoughby, looking momentarily puzzled. 'Oh ... *that*!' He gave an awkward grimace. 'My fault entirely; got out of bed the wrong side, eh? Listen: I've got something *amazing*

35

to tell you.'

'That makes two of us,' said Justin. 'Hang on a tick; I'll get another chair.'

He opened the workshop door, wondering how long it had been since his father had actually *worked* there. It was dark and gloomy inside, and the endless rows of tools were coated in a thick layer of dust and cobwebs. The remaining deckchairs smelt of mildew, so Justin settled for a moth-eaten beanbag instead. He hauled it outside and flumped down on it, effectively firing out a barrage of polystyrene pellets and a disgruntled mouse. He set the binoculars beside him and took a huge bite of his sandwich.

'' ou 'irst.'

'You're *never* going to believe this,' said Willoughby. 'I think there's a pretty good chance your grandfather's asleep in one of the spare bedrooms.'

If Sir Willoughby hadn't looked so pathetically earnest, Justin would have burst out laughing. 'But Grandpa's been missing for thirteen years,' he said. 'Don't you think Mrs Gilliechattan would've noticed him while she's dusting?'

Willoughby snorted. The idea of their nosey old housekeeper missing *anything* was nothing short of ludicrous. 'I don't mean he's been in the spare room the *whole time*. I'm not explaining properly; it's the excitement. After breakfast I came out here as usual. I was just settling in my deckchair when an old man wandered through the archway.'

'Carrying a raggedy bundle over his shoulder?' asked Justin, guessing this was the man he'd seen outside the castle gates.

'That's right. I was going to tell him this was private property, but he looked so desperately tired and hungry, I thought I'd feed him up a bit first. He had no idea who *I* was. In fact, I suspect he thought I was just a gardener; he said the *oddest* thing.'

'What?'

'As we headed towards the castle, he suddenly asked *where's Old Wallace*.'

'So?'

'Of course, you wouldn't remember. Old Wallace was the gardener way back when I was a boy,' Willoughby explained. 'After him, came young Wallace, then Livingstone in ninety-two. Finally, Gilliechattan replaced him about three years ago.'

'Wallace *is* a clan name, Dad; they've been around for the last twelve centuries. I bet there's been a Wallace on every estate in Scotland.'

'I guess so,' said Willoughby, looking crestfallen. 'But when we walked through the front door he turned right and headed towards the kitchen, as if he knew the way.'

Justin shook his head. 'Still not convinced. Most people know the kitchen and servants' quarters are usually at one end of the castle. Anything else?'

'Only the most important thing of all: I recognised him. The moment I clapped eyes on him, I knew there was something familiar about him – even the way he walked. The closer he got the more convinced I felt. While he was eating I took a good, long look at his face. It was unquestionably thinner than I remembered; certainly older; and Pops didn't have long hair and a beard. But, I know that face. I'd know it anywhere.'

His certainty made quite an impression on Justin, though it didn't convert him. Sir Willoughby had a distressing habit of discovering his lost father at least once every few months, and some bore about as much resemblance to the family as Eliza.

'What happened next?' Justin asked.

'Once he'd eaten, he thanked me and said he'd best be on his way. Well, I couldn't have that, could I? Poor old chap looked totally cream-crackered. No – I insisted he had a nap. Took him up to one of the spare bedrooms, and he was asleep before I could draw the curtains. I'm hoping if we all try really hard we might persuade him to stay.'

'Oh, I'm pretty sure we'll manage *that*,' replied Justin. 'The *real* problem will be getting him to leave. We practically needed a crowbar to dislodge the last one.'

Sir Willoughby's face clouded over. 'I thought it might be

37

difficult for you to accept; you never met your Grandpa. That's why I've been searching for some snapshots of Pops. Once you see the resemblance for yourself, you'll *have* to admit it: it's him. The Thyme Curse is broken!'

Justin started to say he'd seen the old photo that Robyn kept on her bedside table about a zillion times already, but decided to keep silent. He didn't want to risk upsetting his dad again, especially when he was looking so buoyant for a change. He'd been decidedly fidgety of late, obsessed by this ridiculous fixation that the Thymes were cursed. According to Willoughby's calculations, a family member died tragically every thirteen years. First, his mother, Lady Isabel, had drowned; next, his brother, Deighton, got thrown from a horse; and finally, Sir Lyall had been swept away by an avalanche. Now, thirteen years later, he was convinced that yet another member of the family was doomed to perish. Justin dismissed the idea as unscientific; the human urge to find pattern in chaos. Three deaths in twenty-seven years wasn't a curse – it was a coincidence.

'Uncanny him turning up like that, after you wishing he was still alive,' remarked Willoughby. 'You know ... I think that's what convinced me.'

'Honestly, Dad! It's just a fluke; nothing but random chance.'

Sir Willoughby turned on Justin sharply. '*Never* say that,' he whispered, with a sudden note of panic in his voice. '*Nothing* happens by *chance*.' He sat hunched over, his brow deeply furrowed. Then, determined to change the subject, muttered, 'So ... what's *your* news?'

Justin's eyes lit up. 'I want to build a time machine.'

Willoughby gasped, turned deathly white and sat bolt upright. He looked both galvanised and petrified at the same time. '*What?*'

'I want to b–'

'Shhhhh ... don't say it again. Wait there a minute.' Willoughby crept round to the front of his workshop, his eyes darting in every direction. Angus Gilliechattan, the gardener, was dead-heading daffodils beneath the gallery windows, well out of earshot – and

38

Eliza prowled majestically through the archway, pushing baby Albion in his pram. Willoughby returned to Justin. 'All clear,' he said, with obvious relief.

'What's wrong?' asked Justin, baffled by his father's behaviour.

'Nothing – I hope. Better safe than sorry. Now, two important things: firstly, you must promise *never* to say the words *time machine* again, even to me .... *Well?*'

'I promise.'

'And secondly ... have you told anyone else your plans?'

'Not exactly,' said Justin. 'I think Professor Gilbert might have guessed. We *did* spend the whole morning plotting conceptual timelines.'

'Well *don't* tell him. And if he asks any questions, say it's only the hypothetical theory that interests you. You don't take any of it seriously ... *right?* And never, *NEVER* tell him you're planning to build a ... a ... *contraption.*'

'Okay,' said Justin, wearing a bemused frown. *Most* peculiar. The words *time machine* appeared to distress his father deeply. Yet, unless Justin misunderstood, he hadn't been forbidden to build one. After a few moments' deliberation he asked: 'Am I still allowed to construct the ... er ... device, as long as I keep it a secret?'

Sir Willoughby closed his eyes and groaned. 'You've no idea what you're letting yourself in for,' he murmured. 'No idea at all.'

Justin felt a delicious shiver of excitement surge down his spine like a row of toppling dominoes. He peered into his father's eyes.

'Is there something you're hiding from me, Dad?'

Willoughby shuffled in his deckchair, avoiding his son's gaze.

'I *knew* it,' said Justin. 'Come on ... tell me the worst.'

'Very well,' Willoughby relented. 'I guessed I'd have to tell you sooner or later; no point in letting you walk into this blindfolded.'

Justin settled back on his beanbag and raised his eyebrows expectantly.

'You see,' sighed Willoughby, 'you're not the first Thyme with ambitions to become a ... er ... *chrononaut.*' He stared across the loch and took a deep breath:

'As you know, your grandmother, Lady Isabel Thyme, drowned the year I turned four. When you're that age you soon forget people. After a year or two, I barely recognised her face in photograph albums. She was nothing more than a headstone in the family plot. That's what started me thinking about time travel. Even if I couldn't alter the past, just seeing her again would give me a real memory to hold on to. Your grandpa was a wonderful man ... but such an eccentric. He was an explorer at heart, like your mum, and the problem with explorers is they can't stay put. It's as if they get, er ...'

'Itchy feet?' laughed Justin.

'That's right, son. Pops *certainly* had itchy feet. His ambition was to climb every Munro and catalogue the experience in his Highland Journal. When he came home he'd read excerpts out loud to me, and I'd listen, enthralled. But a day or two later he'd be off somewhere else.

'During my early years it didn't seem to matter. My nanny, dear old Nanny Fluff, was kind but terribly strict. She believed a boy my age ought to be out in the fresh air – not sat in the library, reading. Out you go Master Will, she'd say, and don't come inside until you've got some roses in those cheeks.

'When I was five, she arranged for me to attend the village school. She said a nice ordinary place would keep my feet on the ground, but being the Laird's son made it difficult at first. There was only one class; children of all ages from the local farms. I could read and write better than the oldest, but I tried to fit in and not look too clever.

'Pops disapproved. When I was eleven he sent me off to Gordonstoun. I loved it; serious study at last! I boarded of course ... just coming home for a few weeks each summer, but even then, I was far too busy to daydream about time travel. I only thought about it twice: the year Deighton died ... and one other occasion ... four summers earlier.

'As it turned out, science was my best subject. At university, all my professors predicted a successful career in physics. Then something unexpected happened. In my final year, a shifty-looking man wearing mirrored sunglasses approached me and promised to change my life. He had curly hair, long sideburns, and a droopy moustache. He said he recruited for a top secret organisation that designed high-tech gadgets used in the field of *espionage!* And they urgently needed people of my outstanding calibre.'

'He wanted you to be a spy?' gasped Justin, his eyes gleaming. 'You've *got* to be joking!'

'I thought it was a joke too – but I soon realised he was deadly serious. He said that *TOT Enterprises* had authorised him to offer me a job. If I accepted, I had to start immediately and leave university without taking my final exams.'

'Cool!'

'Yep, it seemed pretty cool to begin with. He even assigned me my own code-name. I imagined myself making wristwatches that became satellite receivers, and sports cars that fired nuclear missiles or converted into submarines. I was young and innocent ... but I soon learnt that reality bears no resemblance to the movies. I'd made the biggest mistake of my life.

'The following morning, the chap with the sunglasses collected me from college and drove me to *TOT* Headquarters. The first thing I had to do was sign a watertight nondisclosure agreement which basically said four things: Firstly, I was never to talk to anyone about my work ... *ever*; secondly, all copyrights and patents for everything I invented, belonged to them; thirdly, I must agree to submit to random polygraph tests any time without warning. A polygraph is a ...'

'A lie detector,' said Justin. 'I know ... carry on.'

'Finally, I had to give *TOT* permission to erase my memory if they ever had reason to doubt my integrity – and sign a medical release document stating that if I died during the memory-wipe procedure, I absolved them from all responsibility.'

'But that would virtually give them permission to kill you,' gasped Justin, his face turning pale. 'Why didn't you just turn around and walk straight out?'

'It wasn't that easy,' explained Willoughby. 'Mr Sunglasses called me *the man who knew too much*, and said I was a threat to national security. If I declined their offer, *TOT* would simply wipe my memory without permission. All those years at university wasted; I'd be no smarter than your average five-year-old. They had me trapped and they knew it.'

Justin shuddered. He was beginning to suspect his father's memory loss had *not* been an accident after all. *This* explained why his dad could only recall the last dozen or so years, plus a few vivid memories from childhood – whereas almost everything in between seemed to be missing. No wonder mentioning it at breakfast had made him so edgy. But that didn't explain his paranoia. Did he seriously believe he was *still* in danger after all these years?

Justin's lunch felt like a ball of lead in his stomach. The sudden raucous cry of a gull made him start. It sidled along the workshop roof, staring at the remains of his sandwich. No longer hungry, Justin threw it to the ground. As the gull swooped down, two others flew up from beneath the cliff top. All three squabbled noisily, the disturbance attracting others.

'Surely no one's watching you now,' said Justin. 'Not with your memory ... the ... the way it is,' he faltered, unsure how to finish the sentence.

'I suspect there's one individual keeping me under constant surveillance,' snarled Willoughby through gritted teeth. 'I can almost feel his eyes scrutinising my every move.'

'Why?'

'He's biding his time. But he won't catch me out. No, I was always one step ahead of him from the start. I outsmarted him years ago, and there was nothing he could do to prove it; nothing but watch and wait.'

'What for?' begged Justin.

'For me to build another *time machine!*'

The moment the words passed his lips, Sir Willoughby could have bitten his tongue. With a look of horror on his face, he clamped one hand over his mouth, and pointed with the other towards the birds. Justin thought the gesture absurdly melodramatic; they were just gulls after all. But as several flew off, he saw the reason for his father's alarm. Hidden amongst the sleek, snowy bodies of the gulls was another white bird, with shorter legs and a powerful hooked beak. It regarded them with bright boot-button eyes and raised its sulphur yellow crest.

'*Men of few words are the best men,*' it cackled.

'Burbage!' cried Justin, jumping to his feet.

The parrot cocked its head on one side and screeched with laughter. Willoughby groaned, holding his head in his hands. 'That dratted bird's a living piece of recording apparatus. He'll be squawking *time machine, time machine* all over the castle. I might as well get it broadcast on the News at Ten.'

'Honestly, Dad,' said Justin. 'I know he's an uncanny mimic and can recite the complete works of Shakespeare – but so what if he *does* say time mach ... *umph.*'

Willoughby's hand smothered his son's mouth. 'Spies take many forms,' he whispered fiercely, his eyes shooting in seventeen directions per second. 'Gilliechattan can't be far away.' Dragging Justin with him, he rushed to the front of his workshop – and sure enough, they found the gardener weeding a convenient flowerbed. He knelt with his back to them, a pair of mud-encrusted wellies protruding from beneath his kilt. Burbage flew to his shoulder and nuzzled his bushy ginger beard.

'Did you hear anything, Gilliechattan?' Willoughby snapped.

'Tha wee bairn's bin cryin',' replied the gardener, nodding at the empty pram abandoned beside the workshop. 'That big ape just carried 'im indoors.'

'Anything else?'

Angus Gilliechattan hauled himself to his feet and turned to face them, a pair of muscular arms folded across a dirty white singlet. With his craggy eyebrows and mane of flaming red hair, he looked like a highland warrior who'd lost his sword.

'Are ye callin' me an eavesdropper, Jimmy?' he roared.

Justin winced. His father was the easy going type, and *never* insisted on being called *Sir* Willoughby – but Gilliechattan's perpetual habit of calling everyone Jimmy tended to rile him. Unfortunately, the gardener – despite being in his fifties – had the physique of a lumberjack who indulged in a little amateur wrestling; not someone to start quarrelling with. Justin calculated the driving time to the nearest hospital.

'What Dad means...' he began, desperately trying to think of something his father *didn't* mean. 'What he means is ... did you hear the gong for afternoon tea? We wondered if we'd missed it.'

Mr Gilliechattan deflated visibly. 'Och, sorry Sir Willoughby,' he muttered. 'Nae, I didna hear the gong, but I did hear her Ladyship clatterin' aboot in the kitchen as I wheeled ma wee barra to the compost heap. Aye, I ken yer tea'll be ready any time noo Sir.'

'Thank you, Angus,' said Willoughby, casting a grateful sideways glance at his son. 'We'd better hurry indoors.'

As they plodded to the east tower, Justin watched his father sink into a trough of depression. Sir Willoughby paused outside the kitchen garden, leaning against the arched gate.

'The blighter was spying on us,' he insisted, his voice dull and flat. 'Years of constantly being on my guard, and the first time I slip up Angus Gilliechattan's big ears are flapping. Never trusted him. That stagy outfit, that preposterous accent – he's more Scottish than any Scot I've ever met. Too damn theatrical! Nobody wears a kilt for gardening; it's just *asking* for haemorrhoids.'

He trudged up the kitchen steps, wringing his hands.

Justin kicked a lump of turf and kept silent. Poor Dad, he thought; past trauma – present paranoia; cause and effect. But believing the gardener's a spy – that's *crazy*. He'll be suspecting Professor Gilbert next.

Thinking of the professor triggered a mental image of his field glasses languishing beside a moth-eaten beanbag. 'Bother ... I'll catch up with you in a tick, Dad,' Justin called, as he turned and sprinted back to the cliff top. 'Forgot something.'

As he bent to retrieve the binoculars, Justin noticed a distant movement on the surface of the loch. It was driftwood of course; probably a log – a log with a hump. He raised the binoculars and adjusted the focus, mentally measuring the distance between himself and the humped log while calculating its approximate size. Seconds later he found himself trying to estimate its speed – and he had to admit it was going pretty fast for a log. It accelerated north by north-west towards Brackla, then all at once, raised an enormous glistening neck, and, with a rapid twist, disappeared below the surface of the water, leaving barely a ripple.

Justin froze in shock. The whole sighting had lasted no longer than four or five seconds. And that's what it was: a sighting. *Nessiteras rhombopteryx.* No log would be capable of those lithe, graceful movements, reminding him simultaneously of both a swan and a gigantic seal.

Unable to contain himself, Justin yelled for his father: '*DAD – DAAAAAAAAAD!*'

Bother, he thought. If only he'd stayed a minute or two longer, *that*'d have cured his scepticism. Hype indeed! That was a living, breathing, prehistoric dinosaur. I've got to get Dad out here – quick – in case it resurfaces.

Dragging his eyes away from the loch, Justin turned and ran back towards the castle.

Meanwhile, Angus Gilliechattan trundled his wheelbarrow through the castle archway and turned right. He stopped by the west tower, withdrew a sharp pair of secateurs from his sporran, and started to trim the ivy growing round the window. Burbage flew to his shoulder.

'*Time travels in diverse places with diverse persons,*' he

murmured.

Gilliechattan smiled and scratched the parrot's head with a large grubby forefinger. 'Clever old bard,' he said. 'As You Like It?'

'*All the world's a stage*,' Burbage cackled, '*And all the men and women merely players*.' He hopped onto the windowsill and sidled in through the open window. Gripping alternately with his beak and claws, he climbed one of the tapestry curtains, and settled himself snugly behind the pelmet.

Moments later, the hall door opened and Lady Henny swept in carrying a large silver tray laden with hot tea and warm buttery scones. She placed it on a little table then walked over to the gong and rang it. The tumultuous noise echoed along the corridors and through the windows, summoning the family to afternoon tea.

Angus Gilliechattan heard the deafening clamour and glanced up from his work. A flash of silver caught his eye as Henny tipped the teapot, and the scent of freshly brewed Earl Grey drifted towards him.

'Jolly good show,' he whispered, without the slightest trace of a Scottish accent. 'Spiffing! Absolutely capital!'

Some scientists claim that whatever its speed, time only moves ahead. The programming of our brains influences us to accept the logic of 'cause and effect'. First someone writes a book; then we read it. We cannot read a book before it is written - that would be illogical. And any process that makes it possible would have to be equally illogical. Or would it?

Consider again our hypothetical astronaut. Special relativity states that nothing can accelerate beyond the speed of light, but if he COULD travel at light-speed, would his ageing stop? By taking these thoughts to their logical conclusion, we begin to see that time is a lot more flexible than we have previously believed.

Fictional time travel appeals to the imagination of many readers, offering the enticing prospect of either stepping back in time to right some past wrong, or moving forward to see what the future holds. In books and films, the path that most story-tellers take is a predictable one, littered with asinine clichés, the most common example being the notorious MOTHER PARADOX: a time traveller who while visiting the past, accidentally kills his mother, or prevents her marriage, thus rendering his own birth impossible.

But how could he travel back in time if he had never been born?

CHAPTER FOUR

The Hypnosis Experiment

'Dad ... *DAD!* You'll never guess what I've just seen.'

Justin hurtled through the kitchen door, and stood a moment, gasping for breath. The room was empty, but a line of drips from the huge stone sink to a crumpled towel showed he'd missed his father by seconds. After a flicker of disappointment, Justin grinned. *Good*, he could tell the whole family together. He washed his hands, and then drying them on the seat of his trousers, raced along the corridors, following the delectable scent of freshly baked scones.

His brain teemed with a tangle of random thoughts all vying for his attention: Nessie, Old Father Time, his plans for a time machine. It was almost too much to comprehend. Then, in a flash, he recalled the words engraved on the back of his new watch: "*Everything is Connected to Everything Else.*" But if that was true, how did Sir Willoughby's mysterious past fit into the equation?

His strange story had left Justin with more questions than answers. Was his dad's amnesia the result of a mind-wipe? Why, after all these years, was he still plagued by wild conspiracy theories? And oddest of all: how had he suddenly remembered so much of his past?

I'll have to talk to him again, Justin decided – but right now ...

'*GUESS WHAT!*' he shouted, bursting into the great hall like a teenage tornado.

Nobody answered. Justin's face fell; he half expected to hear it land with a resounding thud on the polished oak floor.

The atmosphere in the great hall reminded him of a dentist's waiting room. Sir Willoughby sat hunched in an armchair, still furious about his slip of the tongue. A quick glance at his deeply furrowed brow and Justin knew this wasn't the time to mention Nessie. No way. His father had been grouchy at breakfast time, but now his dark mood had intensified. A gloom hung over the family like a thundercloud; one wrong word and lightning would strike.

Robyn – wisely attired in one of her less controversial outfits – kept her knees tucked under her chin, and scowled like a gargoyle with a grievance. Nanny Verity perched on the edge of a sofa jiggling Albion on her lap. Even Lady Henny looked unusually worried – and Justin wondered whether the letter she'd been expecting from Polly had contained bad news. Still dressed in khaki, Henny poured steaming Earl Grey into delicate china cups – which Eliza handed out to each family member in turn.

'Well?' Robyn drawled, not even bothering to lift her head.

'Well, what?' asked Justin.

'You burst in yelling *guess what*. What have you done this time? Solved global warming? Invented a cure for pimples? Discovered a new element and called it justinium?'

'Erm ... never mind,' Justin murmured.

He imagined Robyn's contemptuous expression if he told her the truth. He scarcely believed it himself. First some old codger strolls down the drive and has Dad believing he's Grandpa Lyall – then the Loch Ness Monster surfaces and waves a cheery flipper. Weird! Weird *cubed!*

'*NEVER MIND?*' snorted Robyn. 'Guess what ... erm ... never mind. *Fffhuhhh!*'

Justin feigned deafness. 'Thanks Eliza,' he said, taking a cup and saucer from the gorilla, and politely ignoring her huge black thumb across his teaspoon.

Her hostess duties complete, Eliza settled herself down on the hearth rug. With rapt concentration she emptied the contents of her cup into its saucer and blew upon it vigorously, sending little waves over the rim. Henny made no comment; she needed to ask the gorilla a big favour shortly, and wanted her in an agreeable humour. Eliza slurped her milky tea.

'Very nice drink,' she said, her computer replicating the queen's cultured tones. Then leaning back, she rubbed her stomach and gave a resounding belch of satisfaction.

Albion giggled, and bit into his scone. But his enthusiasm didn't last; with a new tooth almost through he preferred hard food and the floury softness was a major disappointment.

'Yigoo!' he cried, dropping it as if it had bitten him back. The scone landed jammy side down on his sister's strappy suede sandals. Robyn leapt up in dismay, spilling half the contents of her teacup across her father's knees. Willoughby yelped like a scalded puppy and hopped around, upsetting Henny's plate.

Justin saw a family argument looming on the horizon.

Eliza saved the day. Oblivious to the ensuing chaos, she ran her fingers over the laptop's keyboard. 'Who old man in bedroom?' demanded the strict voice of a TV quiz show hostess. It was Eliza's favourite voice for asking important questions, and rarely failed to grab everyone's immediate attention.

Henny was especially curious, and glanced at Willoughby with her eyebrows raised. To Justin's enormous relief, a wide grin spread across his father's face.

'Good heavens ... I clean forgot,' he said. 'Absolutely wonderful news everybody: Grandpa's turned up.'

'*Arrghh* – not *another* one,' groaned Robyn. 'That's three this year. Tell him, Mum.'

Henny remained calm. 'You're still in denial, Willo. You can't alter history no matter how many senile old hobos you rescue. Ahhh well, I suppose we'd better meet him.'

Willoughby bounced to his feet. 'Of course! What *is* wrong with me? He's bound to be awake by now. I expect he'll want to meet all of you.' He rushed out of the room, pausing for a moment in the doorway. 'You'll have to make allowances for his appearance.

His clothes are in a pitiful state, and he can't seem to remember who he is. Justin – you explain while I fetch him.'

Justin acquainted the rest of family with the situation, trying not to sound as doubtful as he felt. 'I think what I said at breakfast might've put the idea in Dad's head,' he muttered apologetically. 'He's pretty certain about this one.'

'What do *you* think?' asked Robyn.

'Well,' Justin replied, torn between brutal honesty and loyalty to his father. 'I haven't met him, so it wouldn't be fair to say. But the evidence I've heard so far doesn't convince me.'

'He *can't* be Grandpa,' said Robyn. 'He's probably just a con man determined to swindle Dad out of a fortune.'

'What fortune?' asked Henny. 'Willo hasn't got a cent. Okay, he's inherited the title, but the property's entailed – and you know what *that* means!'

Robyn scowled. She knew only too well. 'If Dad dies then everything goes straight to Dustbin here, and I get diddly-squat! It's medieval and totally unfair.'

'Don't worry, I'll try to resist the temptation to boot you out,' Justin laughed. 'Anyway, we male clan members have our problems too. We inherit the estate whether we want it or not. The inheritance tax can cost millions, but we can't sell the property to recoup our loss. That's why Dad's penniless. After Grandma Isabel died and Grandpa disappeared, the inheritance tax knocked him base-over-apex. Even if this old chap proves he *is* Grandpa Lyall, all he'll get is a financial millstone round his neck.'

'So what does the old fossil hope to gain?' asked Robyn.

'To be honest, I don't think he's claiming anything,' said Justin. 'It's all Dad's idea.'

'When I first met your father I was warned that insanity ran in this family,' groaned Henny. 'It doesn't run; it gallops! Don't worry ... I'll make him see sense. We can't have this guy wheedling his way in.'

Justin shrugged. 'There's no point in upsetting Dad. If the old chap's a fraud, he'll slip up eventually, unless he's a really

51

incredible actor. Best let Dad discover the truth for himself.'

Henny nodded. 'I certainly couldn't identify him. After your Dad and I got married we lived in Edinburgh. I was always jetting off abroad, so we didn't visit Sir Lyall that often. I guess I met him less than a dozen times. We moved into Thyme Castle the month after he disappeared. Nanny honey, you've been here donkey's years. Apart from Willo, you must be the only one who can remember what he looked like.'

'Och, that's right dear,' said Nanny Verity. 'No impostor will be able to pull the wool over *my* eyes. I guarantee it.'

This failed to reassure anybody. During the awkward silence that followed, they listened to the sound of approaching footsteps along the portrait gallery. Henny arranged her face into a fixed smile, Robyn prepared her most obnoxious frown, and Nanny Verity looked anxious.

Justin pondered over the strange story his father had related. It had seemed far-fetched an hour ago, but now he wasn't so sure – and Sir Willoughby's mercurial mood wasn't helping. One minute he seemed paranoid about spies, the next minute happy to invite a total stranger for afternoon tea. Well, at least the old fellow couldn't have overheard anything about the time machine, Justin thought ... not if he was asleep.

Willoughby strode into the room, followed by the elderly gentleman. Once again, the stranger's resemblance to Old Father Time struck Justin forcibly. His clothes were dishevelled and far too big for his emaciated body. His long, white hair stuck up in sparse feathery tufts and a beard hung almost to his waist. He looked like a scrawny prehistoric scarecrow and smelt pleasantly of highland rain and windblown bracken.

Henny rose, and stepped forward with her right hand outstretched. 'Pleased to meet you, er ... Mr ... er ...' she wavered.

'Just call me Austin, ma'am,' murmured the old man with an exaggerated courtly bow. 'Can't be certain that really *is* my name ... not *absolutely* certain, if you know what I mean ... but, it feels as if it is. Whether it's my surname or Christian name I couldn't say ... no recollection ... but, as they said at the hospital, we've got to call you something ... so, as one name's as good as another, I thought ... well, why not ... and from then on ...'

Willoughby could barely contain his excitement. Austin was his father's middle name; it couldn't be a coincidence. He must have survived the avalanche and ended up in hospital, with amnesia brought on by the shock and exposure. If only he could just remember something – some little detail, it would prove his identity beyond all doubt. Could the location of the hospital provide any useful clues, he wondered.

'Tell me about the hospital,' he said, cutting through the endless blether.

The old man looked round the room uncertainly. Willoughby's agitation appeared to confuse him. 'It seems a very good hospital,' he faltered. 'You mustn't worry ... they'll have you right again in no time. The nurses are very kind here ... very kind ... and a polite young doctor settled me in my bed ... one of the private wards, with a splendid view of ...'

'No ... *no*,' snapped Willoughby. 'This isn't a hospital. I think you must have had some sort of accident ... about thirteen years ago ... up a mountain perhaps?'

'*Accident?*' said the old man, rubbing his forehead. He peered at Henny and Nanny Verity. 'Which one? They both look fine to me. What are they doing here? This is private property.'

Willoughby ran his hands through his hair in sheer frustration.

Henny took control: '*Do* sit down Mr Austin,' she cooed. 'Perhaps you'd like some tea.' No point distressing the poor guy, she thought. He's just some dotty old tramp who, by chance, happens to bear a certain family resemblance.

The piping hot tea seemed to help. Mr Austin settled back in his chair with a bemused smile. 'What a charming room,' he said. 'It reminds me of ...'

Exactly what the great hall reminded him of, no one ever found out. Eliza, eager to exhibit her good manners, appeared at his side and offered him the plate of scones.

53

'Hello old man,' she said. 'You want nice cake with drink?'

The effect was startling to say the least, and nearly removed *all* worries about him being an impostor, by transforming him from a very old man to a very dead one. His face turned an ashen grey and he clutched his chest. Eliza looked quite put out. She had taken considerable pains to choose a bright, friendly air hostess voice, and had even managed to operate her laptop with one hand, whilst holding the plate in the other.

'Good grief ... she's killed him,' groaned Willoughby.

'Nonsense,' said Henny. 'He's just fainted.'

Eliza prodded Mr Austin with a huge toe. 'Why old man sleep?'

'He's er ... not feeling well,' explained Henny, placing her hand on Eliza's arm. 'Perhaps you'd better leave until he's strong enough to cope with seeing you. I'll explain that you're perfectly safe as soon as he wakes up.'

Eliza marched huffily out of the room slamming the door behind her. She'd experienced adverse reactions before – though never inside the castle. After adjusting the computer's volume to as loud as it would permit, she chose the clipped voice of an old-fashioned radio announcer.

'Eliza good gorilla,' it blared. 'Eliza not frighten old man. Silly old man not like cakes.'

Meanwhile, Nanny Verity had been rummaging in her handbag and found a bottle of lavender cologne. She dabbed some onto a lacy handkerchief and wafted it under Mr Austin's nose.

After inhaling the merest whiff, Justin had a brainwave: if the old man *was* genuine perhaps the lavender could help unlock his past. Some months ago he'd read a fascinating book about hypnosis. He'd felt sceptical at the time, but the book explained how scents were the greatest stimuli to our memories. As Mr Austin's eyelids flickered, Justin spoke softly:

'Just relax and breathe deeply. Keep your eyes closed and let your mind wander until you see a clear picture.' He took the tiny bottle from Nanny Verity and shook a few more drops of lavender onto the handkerchief. 'Drift back through time,' he whispered in a gentle monotone. 'Keep searching and eventually you'll find it; some special picture in your mind's eye. When you do ... focus on it ... zoom in ... see every little detail.'

The old gentleman smiled and a single tear trickled down the side of his nose.

'What can you see?' murmured Justin.

'A beautiful young woman.'

Justin's voice became sharp and incisive. 'What's her name?' he demanded.

A furrow of concentration puckered the old man's brow. Then all at once, his eyes flew open with an expression of pure bewilderment. 'I know her name! I haven't the foggiest idea *how* I know ... it just popped into my head out of nowhere. It doesn't mean a thing to me, yet ... yet somehow it feels vaguely familiar, almost as if ...'

'*WHAT'S HER NAME?*' shouted everyone.

The old man gazed at them, his eyes brimming with hope and unshed tears. Finally, he spoke in a hushed voice:

'Lady Isabel.'

Nobody spoke.

After what seemed like an eternity, Robyn broke the silence:

'That's grandma,' she whispered, her voice scarcely audible. 'So ... so you must be ...'

'Grandpa Lyall,' shouted Willoughby. He grabbed Henny by the shoulders. 'I told you so! My long-lost father ... I knew it the minute I clapped eyes on him.' Well done, son,' he added, turning to slap Justin on the back. 'You're a genius.'

'It was just a matter of triggering nerve impulses to the olfactory bulbs, prompting subconscious images in the rhinencephalon,' said Justin, flicking a wary glance at his sister. 'Anyone could do it.'

Henny snatched a quick hug. 'Not *quite* anyone,' she said. Then in tones of mock resignation she added: 'Ah well, I suppose I'll have to get used to having another man in the family.'

Robyn, the hardened cynic, buckled in spectacular fashion. She flung her arms round the old man's neck, murmuring 'Grandpa, Grandpa,' over and over again. Nanny Verity just smiled and jiggled Albion up and down on her lap, singing *Hickory Dickory Dock.*

The old gentleman himself looked dazed, and more than a little alarmed at Robyn's histrionics. But most of all he looked desperately sad.

'If only I could remember who she was,' he said, tears streaming down his wrinkled cheeks. 'That beautiful face ... it's faded already.' He lowered his head and broke into a spasm of uncontrollable sobbing.

Henny and Willoughby exchanged a hurried glance.

'Change the subject,' Willoughby hissed. 'Get his mind onto something else – *quick.*'

Henny frowned for a moment, then nodded. Her manner became breezy, and she slid into the brisk, confident voice of her TV persona. 'Have another scone Mr ... er, Grandpa. Now, you mustn't be frightened of that gorilla you saw; Eliza's perfectly civilised. I rescued her eight summers ago when poachers killed her mom, and she's been part of our family ever since. Hasn't she Willo?'

Sir Willoughby took up the cue: 'That's right,' he said, rushing forward to refresh the old man's tea. 'Henny's been studying gorillas since ... well, since childhood. Her father was the head keeper of the Bronx Zoo Ape House and her mother was a simultaneous translator at the United Nations.'

'I was plain little Henrietta Higgins back then,' Henny laughed. 'Never imagining that years later I'd get chance to study them in their natural habitat.'

'But it talks,' gasped the old man, wiping his cheeks on a threadbare sleeve. 'I heard it.'

'All gorillas communicate,' Henny explained. 'They use a complex language of sounds and gestures. Some primatologists have even taught them sign language ...'

'But Mum kept muddling the signs,' said Robyn. 'So brain-box over there, designed a special computer programme that used symbols Eliza could memorise. Once she'd learnt that computers didn't bounce, she was talking in no time at all.'

The old man nodded and gave a pale, watery smile – his grief forgotten.

The perfect family group, Justin thought – yet when he mentally stepped back to observe the scene, something – or *someone* – looked wrong. He peered at each person in turn until he spotted the odd one out: Nanny Verity Kiss. He'd never seen her look so preoccupied. She *seemed* happy, but her smile reminded him of a greasepaint grin on the face of a sad clown.

'What's up Nanny V?' he whispered.

In an instant, she snapped out of her distracted mood and gave him one of her customary smiles, oozing genuine warmth from every dimple. 'Och, nothing at all, Poppet,' she said. 'Splendid. Lovely. I can't remember when I last saw Sir Willoughby looking *so* happy.'

'You can tell me.'

Nanny Verity dithered, as if some internal struggle prevented her from speaking the truth. After a minute or so, she stood up and excused herself, announcing to the room in general that it was time for Albion's afternoon nap. As she passed Justin, she leaned over and whispered in his ear: 'Give me time to get Alby settled ... then follow me up to the nursery.

Justin felt puzzled. Nanny Verity wasn't the secretive sort at all; she was normally an open book – a book about knitting probably ... or cures for bunions.

Nanny's abrupt departure seemed to signal the end of afternoon tea, and after Justin's exit the rest of the family started to drift as well. Henny asked Robyn to take the tea things back to the kitchen while she went to console Eliza. Willoughby took Grandpa Lyall, as he now insisted everybody called him, to see the painting of Lady Isabel in the portrait gallery.

Once the room was deserted, Burbage, the cockatoo, peeped over the pelmet and raised his sulphur yellow crest. He unruffled his crisp, white feathers and fluttered to the floor in search of leftovers. Beneath the sofa he spied Albion's rejected scone, and promptly dug his beak into its delicious strawberry-jamminess.

'Things sweet to taste prove in digestion sour,' he cackled to himself – and then flew out of the window in search of the gardener.

Justin climbed the west tower staircase to the nursery. The door was slightly ajar, so he peered through to check whether Albion had dozed off. Nanny Verity caught his eye, put a forefinger to her lips, then beckoned him to enter. Justin crept in, and in total silence they both tiptoed into Nanny's adjoining bedroom.

It was a fussy room, full of crocheted cushions and pottery robins; it smelt of peach potpourri, mint humbugs and Elliman's embrocation. Justin sat in the creaky old rocking chair by the bed. For as long as he could remember, Nanny had always called it her special story-telling chair, but it had been several years since he'd sat spellbound on her lap, listening to tales of brave knights and fire-breathing dragons.

Nanny crossed to her writing bureau and pulled down the lid, revealing two dozen little pigeon holes overflowing with letters and bundles of envelopes. After a brief rummage she extracted a package of pink notepaper tied in a narrow blue ribbon. She sat on the bed and turned to Justin.

'When I first came to work here I wasn't much older than your sister. Och, that's almost thirty years ago,' she sighed. 'How time flies! I started as a trainee housemaid, and Fluff, the old housekeeper, took me under her wing; she even gave me this cameo I always wear. She'd been Master Willoughby and Master Deighton's nanny – but by the time I came to the castle, your father had been attending Gordonstoun for a couple of years, and Sir Lyall had promoted Fluff to ...'

Justin stifled a yawn, wondering whether Nanny would reach the point before one of them died. Dear old Nan, he thought; it was beginning to feel like nursery story time all over again.

'... she retired years ago, but we still keep in contact,' Nanny twittered. 'I'm visiting her in Brighton next week. She's ninety-nine years old, bless her – but still as sharp as a needle. I got this from her yesterday. I shan't read it all. She's rather fond of reminiscing I'm afraid, and she does tend to ramble.'

Chuckling at the irony, Justin watched Nanny shuffle through several sheets of notepaper.

'Ah, here it is,' she said, holding one aloft and adjusting her spectacles. 'Listen ...'

Her Ladyship was always so particular about perfume; she never wore anything but jasmine. I remember once, Sir Lyall buying her a bottle of lavender cologne. "Lavender is for grannies and spinsters," she said, and told me to pour it straight down the sink. You should have seen his face. But I had to laugh ; she never once persuaded her husband to call her Isabel during their entire married life. He always insisted on calling her Izzy, even though it drove her to distraction ...

'There you *are*,' said Nanny, positively bristling with suspicion. 'I warned you no one could pull the wool over my eyes. Without a shadow of a doubt ... that man is a fraud!'

'Are ... are you *sure*, Nanny?' Justin whispered. His heart felt like it was pounding in his throat. He normally took everything Nanny said with a huge pinch of salt, but who knows, he thought – she could just be right. 'We've got to tell Dad,' he gasped, tugging her starched sleeve. '*NOW!* If you're right ... he ... he could be in terrible ...'

Nanny raised a finger to silence him, and spoke again in her strictest voice: 'I won't have you upsetting Sir Willoughby; he wouldn't believe you anyway. Neither would Robyn. And there's no point telling her ladyship. She's jetting off to *heaven-knows-where* tomorrow, and there's something troubling her ... I can tell.'

'But, what if ...?'

'Och, calm down Poppet,' Nanny continued. 'Remember: he doesn't know we suspect him. We must keep our eyes peeled ... then, once we've got proof ...'

She stopped short, but narrowed her eyes and gave a knowing nod.

Justin nodded back.

Nanny Verity Kiss bustled over to her bureau, and returned the little pink bundle to its own particular spot, nestled amongst her lifelong accumulation of letters.

The fictional time traveller preventing his own birth is usually unable to return to the present – or may even cease to exist. Such notions may appear clever, but when compared to real time travel their spurious logic swiftly unravels. Sadly, such nonsensical scenarios cause many to dismiss real time travel as rapidly as its literary counterpart.

Although paradox is an inherent part of time travel, this doesn't prove it is impossible. One resolution is to accept that we can never defy logic or break the laws of physics, whatever the circumstances. If this seems too hidebound, we can still solve the 'Mother Paradox' – but it requires a new perception of reality. A good starting point is to accept that ACTIONS IN THE PRESENT CANNOT ALTER HISTORY, because the past has already happened. It logically follows that a journey through time, once taken, is part of history too. Therefore, our actions in the past cannot erase that journey, or alter our present day existence.

Time travel appears to resolve every bewildering paradox it engenders, but these resolutions are only visible to those with truly creative imaginations. Try for yourself: While visiting a time before your birth, you accidentally cause your mother's death. What do you do? You can't travel further back in time and stop the accident; her death is now a historical event, as unalterable as your own birth. So, what is the solution?

CHAPTER FIVE

Willoughby's Incredible Secret

'Ridiculous!' grumbled Nanny Verity. 'Fancy her Ladyship agreeing to head an expedition at the same time as my annual vacation. What about Master Albion? That's what I want to know.'

Robyn grimaced, holding both hands up like someone warding off a vampire. 'Don't look at me. Anyway, Mum's got plans.'

'Hhrrmph ... plans indeed! We all know what *that* means.' Nanny cleared the kitchen table without another word, slamming the plates one on top of the other.

'Here Nanny, let me take those,' offered Justin, wondering whether the Crown Minton dinner service handed down for the last seven generations, would survive an eighth. 'Why don't you make yourself a nice pot of tea and leave the clearing up to us?'

The mysterious cook with the unpronounceable name hadn't arrived, so the Thymes had been reduced to takeaway pizzas followed by leftover scones and jam. Henny insisted she was far too busy packing to make a proper meal; probably just as well, as scones were about the limit of her cooking skills – apart from pan-fried witchetty grubs.

Suddenly, the door crashed open and Eliza pounded across the kitchen sending chairs toppling like skittles. Lady Henny followed, exuding patience.

'Now Eliza, be reasonable. You adore Alby, and I promise he won't be any trouble.'

Eliza opened her laptop, but its vast vocabulary lacked suitable words to convey her true feelings. She pursed her lips and blew several long, wet raspberries instead.

An hour or so later, Henny's film crew arrived in their ancient, battered Land Rover. Eliza had been watching out for them. She swung down from the east tower and pounced on Hank, pinning him to the ground. Hank was a gentle giant of a man, with gleaming black skin and a permanent smile. He shrugged Eliza off with careless ease, and tickled the big gorilla until she begged for mercy. Polly giggled uncertainly, then, tucking a loose strand of hair into a blonde ponytail, trotted indoors. After a long chat with Lady Henny, they whiled away the rest of the evening in the library. Hank played billiards, while Polly found an old book by H. G. Wells, and sat in a secluded corner, eyes glued to the pages.

Sir Willoughby and Grandpa Lyall spent their evening sifting through piles of old photographs, but without success. Grandpa failed to recognise anybody, and nodded off in his armchair. This was awkward. Justin desperately wanted to continue the *top secret* chat with his father and, hopefully, get his permission to start building a time machine. But Willoughby wouldn't leave the old man alone, in case he woke up and couldn't remember where he was.

'I'll meet you in the library once everyone's gone to bed,' he promised. 'Let's say, er ... about half past eleven.'

Justin slipped off to his lab, eager to jot down a few more temporal theories in his notebook. At about eight-fifteen he spied Professor Gilbert clambering up the steep path from the loch side. He looked flushed, breathless and uncharacteristically cheerful. When Justin waved to him, he pointed to the kitchen and mimed taking a long, cool drink. Justin got the picture. The professor would collect his supper tray and a beer from the pantry, then escape to the solitude of his rooms. He *never* dined with the family.

The tower clock started to strike and, out of habit, Justin counted the chimes under his breath as he strode across the lab. From inside, the clock face looked back-to-front, and it was only during the day that its hands cast visible shadows across the opaque glass.

'... eight ... nine ... ten ... eleven,' he whispered, cupping his hands to his eyes, and peering through one of the tiny panes of clear glass that encircled the face; there were sixty of them, each no bigger than a credit card.

Across the courtyard, a light shone in one of the north tower guest rooms, which probably meant that the old man had stirred at last, and Sir Willoughby had taken him upstairs. Otherwise, the castle looked uninhabited. A faint bluish haze glowed from the depths of Robyn's bedroom. Justin guessed she was online. Most nights the highest windows of the west tower flashed and reverberated with explosions from her X-Box. But tonight, it was the east tower that sounded like a war zone. He could hear Eliza stomping about, repeatedly hurling her empty banana bucket from one side of her room to the other.

It was obvious what was troubling the gorilla, but Justin decided to e-mail her anyway, hoping to quell her tantrum. About six months ago he'd programmed her computer to automatically convert incoming text into pictogram symbols, and vice versa. He strolled over to his PC, typed the words '*What's wrong?*' and pressed SEND.

Despite the rumpus, Eliza heard the soft melodic chime from her laptop, and instantly became calm. She ran a huge black finger over the mousepad and clicked the envelope icon:

To:	eliza@thymecastle.co.uk
From:	justin@thymecastle.co.uk

Eliza frowned at the screen, her lower lip protruding as she read. She rattled her fingers over the pictogram keyboard, opening menus and highlighting vocabulary symbols, until she finally clicked SEND, automatically transposing the outgoing e-mail to standard text:

To:	justin@thymecastle.co.uk
From:	eliza@thymecastle.co.uk

Eliza look forward Congo expedition long time. Last expedition meet hunky silverback. Probably has brain size kiwi fruit but Eliza not interested size brain. Now Henny change plan. Henny want Eliza care human baby. Sad Eliza left campsite. Not meet any cute boy gorillas.

Justin grinned. It was bad enough having one teenage sister without Eliza starting to sound like another. Inevitable really, he thought. Gorilla puberty came early. Despite being six years younger than Robyn, their similarities were uncanny: both loved being the centre of attention; both were prone to dramatic mood swings; and both had Henny to hamper their pursuit of male company. Unfortunately, the Glen of Thyme had about as many eligible boyfriends as it did silver-backed mountain gorillas: absolutely zilch.

Oddly enough, they both handled the problem in exactly the same way: chatrooms. Eliza had a wicked sense of humour and was smart enough to work out that if she concealed her identity, no one would ever suspect she was *not* a human. Many a teenage boy had spent an enjoyable evening chatting to her, unaware he had been flirting with a 267 pound mountain gorilla. Like Robyn, Eliza considered anything was good enough to practice on.

It was almost eleven-thirty, and there was still no sign of Sir

Willoughby. Justin stared abstractedly at his new watch, then, for the umpteenth time that day, ran his forefinger around the outer case, pressing each of its function buttons in turn. The first button froze the time like a stopwatch; the second altered the date; the third, (probably for setting an alarm), seemed to be jammed; but it was the fourth button that baffled him most of all.

He pressed it again, and watched the three hands glide around the face until they all pointed directly to the ten; he let go, and they drifted back to the correct time. *Weird.*

What was the point, he wondered. Was it just to draw his attention to the X in the circle?

Justin strode to a workbench and held his left wrist under a powerful arc lamp. Now that he looked closely he could see that the circle wasn't a single line, but a chain of minuscule letters. He opened his tool drawer, pulled out a watchmaker's eyepiece and put it to one eye. As he adjusted the magnification, two words slid into focus:

'*Beware Procrastination*,' he whispered.

The phrase sounded strangely familiar, yet he couldn't remember where he'd seen it before. He knew it was on a clock, of course – but that didn't help much. There was scarcely a corner of the castle that didn't harbour some historic timepiece ticking away; most of his ancestors had been avid collectors.

'Never mind,' he sighed. 'I'd better get down to the library; Dad'll moan if I'm late.' He stopped abruptly and frowned. 'Hmm ... the *library* clock; I wonder ...' Marching to the centre of his lab, Justin grasped the fireman's pole and slid down to the ground floor.

Except for a crackling fire, the library slumbered in silent dimness. Bright golden flames danced over the pinecones, casting elongated shadows that flickered over the bookshelves like the fingers of a ghostly librarian.

Justin drew back a heavy tapestry curtain and peered across the courtyard. Lights glimmered through the long stained glass windows of the portrait gallery.

Looks like Dad's on his way, he thought; there's just enough time to check ...

He hurried across the library and stood on the hearthrug.

The old Thyme Clock was so ornate it dominated the mantelpiece. Its face was the size of a dinner plate, and had the Thyme clan motto written across it in elaborate copperplate. Behind the gold filigreed hands were four smaller dials – counting the seconds, days of the week, months of the year, and showing the phases of the moon. The outer case was solid gold encrusted with jewels. Emeralds carved into sprigs of thyme grew around the right half of the face; tiny playing cards made from ivory, rubies and jet bordered the left.

To the right of the clock stood Old Father Time. His sinister hand carried a scythe over one shoulder; his dexter hand held a golden hourglass, smaller than an egg timer and filled with a minute's worth of sand. As the last grain fell, it flipped over to measure the next minute. To the left of the clock, leaning back against it, sat a jester. He glanced mischievously over his shoulder at the hourglass. In one hand he held a theatrical mask; in the other, he twirled a pair of dice. Each mechanical figure was a work of art, exquisitely crafted in gold, ivory and platinum, studded with diamonds.

Beneath the clock, between the two figures, a polished pendulum swung to and fro with the words ...

TIME & CHANCE
— XXI-IX-XI —

... engraved upon it. A small arched bell-tower stood above the clock – and etched across the bell were the words Justin was looking for:

Beware Procrastination

Justin rubbed his forehead; it was a coincidence of course – but a most peculiar one. Glancing down at his wristwatch again, he remembered how, at breakfast, his father had drawn his attention to the X after they'd read the motto on the back about *everything being connected to everything else*. But he *must* have known about the tiny message hidden in the circle, Justin thought, unless ...

Suddenly, an unsettling idea occurred to him: what if the watch *wasn't* from his parents after all? They *had* denied it. Maybe Robyn was wrong. For a moment, Justin felt tempted to ask his father outright, then he remembered Sir Willoughby's paranoid behaviour earlier that afternoon, and pushed the thought out of his mind.

'If the watch isn't from Dad, he's sure to panic,' Justin told himself. 'He might even confiscate it. And if I upset him again, I'll *never* get permission to build a time machine.'

Looking back at the clock, Justin marvelled again at the uncanny resemblance between Grandpa Lyall and the figure of Old Father Time. The jester reminded him of someone too, but he couldn't for the life of him think who. It almost seemed to be laughing at him. He leaned forward and gently prodded the carved ivory face with the tip of his finger, then leapt out of his skin as a log in the grate cracked loudly, spitting a glowing ember of coal between his feet.

Faster than a particle in an atom-smasher, he grabbed the tongs from beside the fireplace and tossed the smoking nugget back into the flames. He stamped on the smouldering rug and pushed the brass fireguard over the mouth of the blaze. Finally, he crouched down to examine the damage. He rubbed the sooty scorch mark with his fingers and, to his astonishment, saw that it resembled a perfectly formed capital X. At that precise instant, the clockwork figure of Old Father Time swung his scythe forward and struck the bell once.

The library door creaked open and Sir Willoughby stepped inside wearing his pyjamas and dressing gown. '*Dead* on half past,' he remarked, glancing at the clock. His dark hair stood up in

68

untidy tufts, and he looked perturbed.

Justin, who'd been hoping to put his father in a good mood by being punctual, rose hurriedly and placed one foot over the scorch mark. 'What's up, Dad?'

'Pops,' Willoughby groaned. 'When I put him to bed, he kept rambling on about his granddaughter, saying that she was nothing but trouble to the whole family.'

'How perceptive of him.'

'That's the odd thing. When I asked if Robyn had upset him, he just shook his head and said: *No, no ... I'm talking about Roxanne.* At least, that's what it sounded like; it might have been Sandra. He'd taken his teeth out by that time. And that's another thing: I don't remember Pops having false teeth. Dash it all ... I *have* done the right thing, haven't I?'

Justin frowned. He knew what his father *wanted* him to say: that he believed the old man really *was* Grandpa. Great! That'd blow Dad's crazy curse theory to smithereens, he thought. But I *can't* say that; not after what Nanny told me. But if I tell him the truth, he'll start droning on about the curse, prophesying death or imagining spies round every corner. *Arghhhh* ... if it wasn't for his memory problems, I'd tell him he ought to stop behaving like I'm the father and he's the ...

Justin stopped short, his cheeks reddening as he recalled Willoughby's story about *TOT* and their sinister mind-wiping threats. Dad can't help it, he reminded himself; just let him believe whatever makes him happy ... like Nanny said.

'Are you certain he's Grandpa?'

'Yes.'

'*Definitely*?'

'One hundred and one per cent; I'd know that face anywhere.'

'Then you've done the right thing,' Justin assured him. 'Stop worrying.'

Willoughby gave a sheepish grin. 'Thanks son, I really appreciate that. So, what did you want to talk to me about?'

'I should've thought that was obvious,' said Justin, a little taken

Jusτιn Ͳhyme

aback. 'This afternoon, Burbage interrupted us at a rather important point. In view of my latest project, I think I have a right to know what happened when you built the ... er ... *thing-I-can't-mention!*'

'S'ppose you do,' sighed Willoughby. 'Now, where did I get up to?'

Realising this was a rhetorical question, Justin settled in an armchair by the fire and waited for his father to begin. Sir Willoughby opened the library door; once he seemed satisfied no one was lurking in the shadows, he shut it again and checked the windows. Finally, he drew a second armchair towards the fire, and sat opposite his son. After a deep breath, he recommenced his story:

'I didn't start designing the er ... contraption ... until I'd been with *TOT* three or four years. At first, I was so angry at being trapped by them I invented very little. Oddly enough, they didn't seem bothered – or half expected it. Perhaps all new employees responded like that ... though I never met any to ask. They tried to help me settle, sending me on all manner of amazing trips to field test new equipment. At times it felt more like an exotic holiday than work. That's how I met Henny. She was studying how animals sensed impending earthquakes; I was checking the effects of seismic vibrations on satellite communications equipment. We hit it off right away, and when I got back to Edinburgh, I invited her out to dinner.

'Eventually, I stopped moping and realised what incredible opportunities lay at my disposal. I had my own private lab – and most of the time *TOT* left me entirely to my own devices. Mr Sunglasses called once a week with my wages, but that was all. Money and resources were limitless, and they encouraged me to work on anything I chose ... no matter how bizarre. Suddenly, it came to me: I could build a ... *you-know-what*. After researching it thoroughly I submitted a written proposal, expecting them to turn me down like a page corner. But to my astonishment, they gave me the green light instantly. Furthermore, they assigned me an

70

assistant; someone working in the same field from one of their other labs.

'He was a pleasant enough chap; older than me by a good few years ... and to my surprise, not an intellectual. I wondered how he'd got himself recruited by *TOT*, and assigned to work on something so high-tech. Sheer charm, I guessed – and he *was* fascinated by ... er, our project. I'd worked alone for years, so it was great to have company. What he lacked in brains, he more than made up for in good humour. He was a real joker; at the time I mistakenly considered he was the best friend a chap could ever have.'

'So what went wrong?'

'My initial calculations proved that while it was possible to visit the past and return to the present, it was impossible to travel to a *definitive* point in the future. This infuriated my colleague. In every time travel story he'd ever read you could always visit the future and bring back all manner of advanced technology. I told him he was confusing science fiction with science fact ... but he accused me of lying. After a while, I suspected he was tampering with my experiments behind my back.

'Three years later we were ready to build the prototype. My assistant seemed determined to test it out first. Naturally I disagreed, but he insisted that *TOT* couldn't risk losing me if the machine malfunctioned. As the less valuable of the two, *he* should be the guinea pig. Somehow he managed to convince me; like I told you ... by hook or by crook he always got his own way! Oddly enough, it was fortunate he *did* try it first; the machine had a fatal flaw. We set the destination coordinates to take him back forty-five years, but time altered *inside* the capsule at the same rate as on the outside. The further back he travelled, the younger he became, until he was less than one year old. If we'd set the coordinates any earlier he'd have regressed to a time before his birth and ceased to exist.'

As Willoughby paused, a sudden thought occurred to Justin:

'If ... if *you*'d tested it first ...'

71

'I wouldn't have survived,' said his father sombrely. 'Not to *those* coordinates; too young. Let that be a warning to you, son: you're embarking on a dangerous mission.'

Justin nodded. 'Did you manage to get him back okay?'

'Yes. I'd included a number of safety features in case he lost consciousness. Unless the capsule door opened within two minutes of arrival, the machine automatically returned to its original coordinates. No sooner had the machine vanished ... when it instantly reappeared. Fortunately, he grew older again during the return journey. I'd no idea anything had gone wrong until he climbed out of the pod, ashen faced and yelling that unless I fixed his time mach ... whoops ... I mean his *contraption*, he'd make my life a misery.'

'So he remembered getting younger?' asked Justin, his eyebrows rising.

'That surprised me too,' Willoughby continued. 'I later discovered that although our faulty pod altered the physical appearance of the body, the memory always remained intact. A good job too! He knew to stay calm and wait for the automatic safety mode to return him to the present.

'It took me months to work out where I'd gone wrong. Once I knew, I could've adapted it easily ... but I hesitated. His words kept haunting me; he'd called it *his* machine. Something smelled fishy ... so I told him I couldn't fix it; I'd tried everything and failed. He looked so dejected I thought I'd fooled him.

A few days later, I arrived at the lab especially early. The previous night I'd er ... well, I'd been worrying about the device falling into the wrong hands; the consequences were unthinkable. I'd made up my mind to destroy it and go on the run. I hadn't been in the building more than five seconds when the phone rang. It was Random Chance, head of *TOT*. Mr Chance was a gruff, whiskery old gent I'd only met a couple of times. He said he had reason to suspect I'd completed my invention weeks ago, and was stalling for time. I kept telling him it wasn't true, but he knew I was lying.

'I panicked, left the phone on my desk and biffed off. While his irate voice ranted and raved, I crept down the fire escape to the car park. As I mounted my motorbike, I noticed a man in the car beside me, shouting into his mobile. To my dismay, I realised it was the shifty chap with the sunglasses. Worse still, I recognised his phoney gruff voice. He was impersonating Mr Chance ... or perhaps he *was* Chance.

'I started my bike, but it was too late. He leapt out of the car and hit me across the head with his phone.'

'His *phone*?'

'In those days, mobiles were as big as house bricks ... and just as solid. He knocked me out cold. When I regained consciousness, I found myself back in the lab ... with tape across my mouth, and tied very securely to a chair. Once my vision cleared, I realised I wasn't alone; my assistant sat opposite me. But my hopes sank when I saw him holding a curly wig, a fake moustache and a pair of mirrored sunglasses. He wasn't some lowly assistant ... or even a mole planted to spy on me; *he* was the head of the whole organisation. Then I began to wonder if there *was* an organisation. Apart from my so-called assistant in various disguises ... I'd never met anyone else at all. How *could* I have been so gullible?

'With a sinister smile, he unlocked a cupboard behind his desk and lifted out a polygraph machine. While he connected the various wires to my chest, wrist and middle finger, his voice droned softly, almost hypnotically, about how I'd betrayed him. Then, he yanked the tape off my mouth and bombarded me with questions. Did the machine work? Had I fixed the fault? Had I travelled in it myself? On and on he went, obsessed by the rows of needles jerking spasmodically over the paper.

'Fortunately, I had a trick up my sleeve ... or down my sock to be precise. If you silently drum your toes as you answer, it alters your heart rate, making the readings unreliable. He couldn't learn anything – and furthermore, he couldn't work out how I was thwarting him. He ripped the wires off my body and smashed the polygraph machine against the wall, snarling that I was no longer any use to him. He stormed out of the lab. I held my breath, listening to his hollow footsteps echoing down the hall.'

'What happened next?'

'I thought he'd gone to fetch a gun. I struggled for all I was worth, but moments later I heard a squeaking noise as he wheeled something heavy back along the corridor. Then I realised: he didn't intend to kill me ... he'd returned with his electroencephalocuter.'

'The memory-wiper?' gasped Justin.

'That's right. No amount of toe-wriggling could help me now. I was about to have every single thought wiped clean out of my brain.' Willoughby stopped, seemingly lost for words. He gave a sad, desperate little shrug that tore and twisted his son's heart, leaving him, for a moment, unable to reply or meet his father's imploring eyes.

A pinecone shifted in the grate. Justin stared at it, watching a constellation of sparks spiral up the chimney like miniature comets. So, his dad's brain damage *hadn't* been an accident ... just as he'd suspected. At its peak, precious few brains could have rivalled Willoughby's potential for genius: da Vinci, Galileo, Mozart, Newton, Einstein – and a handful of others ... yet, at the flick of a switch it had all been obliterated. What a tragic irreplaceable loss! Justin closed his eyes, mentally projecting himself into his father's shoes – but the horror of having his memory erased made him feel physically sick. He'd rather lose a limb ... all his limbs ... than lose his mind. I'd have done *something*, he thought ... anything ... *anything* at all.

Then it struck him like a meteorite: there'd been nothing his father *could* do. This wasn't some comic book adventure story with a predictable happy ending, but the truth ... pure and deadly.

Yet there *was* something peculiar about the story. How had his dad managed to recall what had happened that night? Wouldn't those memories have been erased with the rest?

Willoughby leaned forward, placing his right hand on his son's knee. They glanced at each other, their eyes meeting for a split-second, then Willoughby turned away. In a voice drained of all emotion, he addressed his remarks into the heart of the fire:

'At last, you know my secret: I built the world's first working time machine ... but paid a terrible price. Maybe now you'll understand my explosive reaction when you told me your plans this afternoon.'

Justin winced. His dad was getting careless and had uttered the forbidden words again. He hadn't noticed. Perhaps it was best not to bring it to his attention.

'Do you want me to abandon my ... er ... project?' he asked.

'*Would* you?'

Justin remained silent; unwilling to say yes, unable to say no.

Willoughby didn't need an answer. 'I can't say I blame you,' he sighed. 'Well, at least you know what you're letting yourself in for now ... and if anyone *is* watching, they'll probably be watching *me* not my thirteen year old son.'

'But ... won't it be risky?' gasped Justin, unable to hide his surprise. He'd been fully prepared to argue if necessary; getting his dad's permission was the last thing he'd expected.

'As long as we take every precaution to keep it a secret ... you should be okay,' said Willoughby. 'This is your opportunity to make history; I can't deny you that. I had my chance and er ... well, let's just say I won't let things go wrong a second time. I'll support you the only way I can; whilst you're busy working I can keep a sharp eye out for any signs of danger.'

'One final question.' Justin paused a moment, his brow furrowing as he searched for the right words. 'You've remembered an amazing amount tonight, Dad. Your memory ... has it ... er ... is it ...?'

A single bead of perspiration trickled down Willoughby's forehead. 'Not entirely,' he whispered. 'This last week or two, I've erm ... started having flashbacks ... nightmares. A few disjointed memories have resurfaced. Gradually, I've pieced the whole fragmented muddle together, until ... *AARGHHhhhhh!*'

Willoughby leapt to his feet, pointing to the window behind his

75

son. Justin swung around quickly, and what he saw made him grip the arm of his chair until his knuckles turned white. A huge, hulking beast stood with its fleshy face squashed against the glass, distorting it into the shape of a hideously deformed gargoyle.

Willoughby grabbed the poker, and roared 'GET BACK.'

The figure edged away, its face sagging into something a little more human.

'I am bang on door. No bodies come,' said a deep guttural voice. 'See light. I come window.'

'WHO ARE YOU?' shouted Willoughby.

'I am Nadezhda Przolwamiczenkof.'

Justin flopped back in his armchair. '*Ohhhh*,' he sighed, 'it's the new cook.'

'Is that her name, or was she having a sneezing fit?' asked Sir Willoughby, opening the window. The cook still loomed like a vast menacing ogre. Then, to their utter astonishment, she flung a large bare leg over the windowsill and hauled herself in. She wore an enormous grey duffel coat with the hood up, and carried a sack over one shoulder that sounded as if it was full of pots and pans.

'Ahoy!' she said, her voice gruff and oddly masculine. 'I am cooking job. Please to take me kitchen.'

'Fair enoughski,' replied Willoughby.

Justin cringed. 'I'd better fetch Mum,' he said, nudging his dad firmly in the ribs. 'Meanwhile ... stick to English. *Please!*'

Lady Henny could speak at least three dozen languages fluently, and claimed to be able to communicate with anyone from the same planet. Justin pounded up the stairs and ran to the west tower. He knocked on his parents' bedroom door, then pushed it slowly open, expecting to find his mother asleep. But to his astonishment, she was sitting up in bed frowning anxiously over a sheet of lilac notepaper.

'What's up, Mum? You've been looking gloomy all day.'

Henny gave a deep sigh. 'Hank's heard rumours the BBC are planning to axe *Thyme-Zone*,' she muttered. 'Polly wrote to me with all the details. Listen to this ...'

These days, TV films about cryptid or extinct wildlife rely heavily on CG-FX. Just searching for evidence isn't enough. They liked the idea of using Eliza to communicate with Bigfoot, but ratings plummeted when you discovered nothing more than footprints!

'Computer generated effects!' groaned Henny. 'The three of us have been discussing it this evening. We'd need a fully equipped studio, programmers, animators. I wouldn't know where to start. And it'll cost a fortune ...'

'Money isn't the problem,' said Justin. 'It's time! It'd take months to set up. And CG animation's a time-consuming process; the first programme wouldn't be finished until next year at the earliest. I'm sure it *is* just a rumour,' he concluded, sounding more confident than he felt.

Henny nodded and forced a smile. 'Now, what did you want me for?'

Justin explained about the new cook.

'I'd better get down there quick and rescue your dad,' she said ruffling her son's hair. 'Off to bed with you, and don't be worrying about *my* problems; you look shattered.'

Justin had to admit he *was* feeling pretty exhausted. It *really* had been the *oddest* day imaginable. Plodding to his room a startling thought occurred to him: during breakfast he'd wished for four things – and now, three of his wishes appeared to have been granted.

Suddenly, he remembered a story Nanny Verity had once read to him, the motto of which had been: be careful what you wish for – it might come true. It was alarmingly apt. Grandpa Lyall might be a cunning impostor; no one would have believed him if he'd told them about the Loch Ness Monster; and although his father's lost memory had started to return, the flashbacks he suffered sounded so terrifying, Justin half wished it hadn't.

'And what about that fourth wish,' he murmured. 'After listening to Dad's adventures, I've lost all enthusiasm for embarking on one of my own.'

But it was too late; his adventure had begun.

It had started the way it was meant to start – the pattern as regular as tartan: a young boy watching as an old man paused at a fork in the road and tossed a coin, allowing chance to determine his course.

Odd, thought Justin, that at that precise instant I should've witnessed the scene through my lab window and grasped the complexities of time travel in a nanosecond. Justin Thyme – just in time. A cosmic coincidence or what?

He closed his eyes, mentally negotiating a fork of his own making. I don't *have* to build a time machine; I could still change my mind. I could ...

Justin shook his head, his intuitive right cortex seeing at once the futility of his dilemma. The first domino had already been pushed; the fuse had been lit; the countdown had started. He'd passed the point of no return, and was trapped in the adventure of a lifetime with absolutely no way out.

When a journey to the past results in a major disruptive event – such as an accidental death – you open a fresh possibility plane, requiring a totally new perspective. You must now imagine your mother being both alive and dead, and yourself being born and not being born. Your actions have created a TIMEFORK into an alternate history. The universe you left remains securely intact in your own present - but you have created a whole new universe, with a unique timeline parallel to your own.

If you travelled forward along this new timeline to a period equivalent to the present, you would be a stranger to all you met, because you have never existed in this universe. However, travelling along your original timeline you would return to your own present, which remains unchanged.

This resolution of the paradox sees time as something infinitely variable, with endless possibilities opening up constantly. The choice we make at each fork allows us to advance into just one future of countless billions. We have total control over our lives and everything is possible. Furthermore, everything will happen, somewhere on one of the numerous timelines, in the endless multiplicity of universes.

With an infinity of parallel worlds, nothing is impossible; but even in a single, isolated universe there is a surprising alternative ...

CHAPTER SIX

Early Starting Thyme

Justin thumped his pillow and turned over. He lay still and breathed slowly, trying to ignore the multitude of thoughts ricocheting round his brain like pinballs.

Although his mother had told him not to worry about *her* problems, he couldn't help it. Then there was his father's strange paranoia, the perfectly-timed arrival of Grandpa Lyall, Nanny's insistence he was an impostor, and that tantalising glimpse of Nessie. But it was the mysterious connections between his watch and the library clock that plagued him most of all. The fact that both warned him to "*Beware Procrastination*" could be a coincidence – but as he'd removed the watch, he'd noticed that the bracelet links were engraved with a sort of playing card pattern. And what he'd assumed was a simple hook and eye catch when he'd fastened it at breakfast, he now saw was shaped like a miniature scythe and hourglass.

'"*Everything is Connected to Everything Else!*"' he whispered, unable to shake the feeling that the watch had been left to deliberately direct him to the old Thyme Clock. *But why?*

Turning again, he tossed the stifling covers aside – only to pull them back minutes later. High above, the tower clock struck three. Justin groaned. Usually, he was oblivious to its constant noise, but tonight, each tick sounded like the shot of a gun.

He flipped on his back and started to calculate Fibonacci

numbers, hoping it would calm his mind. As he reached 433,494,437 he heard the creak of his bedroom window, and his eyes snapped open to see a pale hand snaking between the curtains. A jolt of panic convulsed his body, but when he tried to shout, his lips seemed pasted together and his lungs felt paralysed. Frozen with fear, he watched the intruder clamber inside, a cold finger of moonlight illuminating the parrot-like colours of his costume; his every movement accompanied by an eerie jingle of tiny bells.

Justin heard a harsh metallic thunk as a heavy sack dropped to the floor, followed by the sound of a cable being dragged to an electricity socket. He struggled to move, straining every muscle – but it was useless. The figure danced towards the bed, singing an odd, haunting little tune.

'... Well, you get some repose in the form of a doze, with hot eyeballs and head ever aching, but your slumbering teems with such horrible dreams that you'd very much better be waking ...'

With a wolfish grin, the intruder leaned over the bed and fastened a row of electrodes to Justin's forehead. Still unable to gasp a single breath, Justin stared into his mirrored spectacles; two terrified distorted faces goggled back. Beneath his sunglasses, the man's features were as elusive as smoke; shifting imperceptibly, one moment almost recognisable, the next, utterly unfamiliar.

The door flew open with a reverberating crash and Sir Willoughby strode in. He pointed a gun at the man, who jumped back with exaggerated mock alarm, holding both hands above his head. Then, as Justin watched him, he removed his sunglasses – and winked.

Justin felt the hairs on the back of his neck prickle. Now, the intruder looked exactly like his father; a perfect clone. But it couldn't be – lack of oxygen was making him see double. Confused, he glanced back at the other Willoughby, and saw that beneath his dressing gown, *he too* wore the multi-coloured garb of a jester. Both Willoughbys laughed hysterically, then the one holding the gun aimed it casually at Justin – and fired.

Justin woke with a start, gasping for breath, perspiration running down his forehead. A ray of sunshine filtered through the fluttering curtains and encircled his alarm clock in a golden halo of light. The LCD showed 06:13 precisely; almost two hours before he normally woke up.

For a while, Justin lay perfectly still, hoping sleep would reclaim him – but his brain refused to cooperate and commenced its relentless ticking. The nightmare – or what he could remember of it – disturbed him deeply. Yet surely that was illogical, he thought. Dreams were simply the electrophysiological activity of a few million neurons shuffling random images like playing cards. It didn't mean anything ... *couldn't* mean anything, unless ... unless ...

With a sigh of resignation, he rose, washed and dressed, and, feeling surprisingly hungry, pottered downstairs, planning a raid on the fridge. But judging from the laughter and delicious cooking smells wafting along the corridors, it seemed as if there was some kind of party going on in the kitchen already. When he opened the door Justin discovered he was not far wrong.

The new cook was removing banana fritters from a fryer and dusting them with powdered sugar. Coffee was percolating; eggs were scrambling; a string of sausages and about thirty rashers of bacon sizzled in an enormous frying pan; rows of newly baked croissants were cooling on a wire tray, and a stack of at least two dozen pancakes oozed with maple syrup; there was porridge with clotted cream and heather honey; a huge bowl of fresh pineapple and mango sprinkled with ginger; and a tall jug of ice cold, freshly squeezed orange juice.

Justin could barely recall seeing so many people round the kitchen table so early – and all far too busy boosting their calories to notice him. Nanny Verity shared her porridge with baby Albion; Lady Henny sipped coffee and ate fresh fruit; Sir Willoughby, (wearing his usual beige pyjamas, Justin observed with some relief), smeared whisky marmalade on warm buttered croissants; Hank tossed hot button mushrooms into the air, catching them in his mouth, while Polly nibbled delicately on a humungous sausage; and Eliza ... well, Eliza kept a *very* close eye on the banana fritters.

'Careful you not burnings lip,' warned the cook, handing her a whole plateful. 'Cold blowings first.'

Justin could hardly believe his eyes. The way the new cook took Eliza in her stride was astonishing. The mere sight of her terrified most newcomers, yet here she was chatting away to the gorilla as if she'd spent a lifetime in the company of gigantic wild animals. Eliza carried the fritters to her place at the end of the table, and then blew them so vigorously that she engulfed Albion in a cloud of powdered sugar. He coughed and sneezed, chortling in good-natured amusement at the funny sounds he was making.

'Yaggle-oo,' he squealed, and held a chubby hand out towards the gorilla.

Eliza broke her banana fritter in half and handed Albion one of the pieces. After carefully licking her fingers clean, she rattled them over her laptop until it said, 'Cold blowings first,' in a perfect reproduction of the cook's guttural voice. Everyone roared with laughter – including the new cook herself.

Beneath the halogen spotlights, Justin realised she was nowhere near as fearsome as he first thought. She was still enormous, but now looked more like a friendly giantess than a psychotic troll. She wore a vast, shapeless, sludge-coloured smock, and a plain white apron. Her face was as rough and red as a brick, and on her head she wore a fringed gypsy scarf, tied in a big, lumpy knot at the nape of her neck. Her arms and legs were bare, incredibly muscular – and slightly hairy; her feet were bare too, and were the biggest feet Justin had ever seen. As she plodded round the kitchen she left damp, sweaty footprints on the tiles, like the glistening trail of a gigantic slug.

Glancing up from her work, she spotted Justin hovering by the door, and gave him a welcoming grin, displaying several slab-like teeth and one big gap.

'Ahoy! What 'ungry lookin' boy wants for 'is fast-break?' she called, beckoning him in with a hand bigger than a joint of pork. '*Come-come-come*,' she added when Justin hesitated, and pointed with a large sausage finger towards an empty stool.

Justin sat down, mumbling: 'Pancakes please,' whilst everyone shouted *good morning* with their mouths full. Normally, Henny would have disapproved of such behaviour, but as she was jetting off to the Congo shortly, nothing could spoil her good mood. Even worries about the future of her TV show had been pushed aside in the excitement.

'You're up early,' she remarked. 'Excellent new cook, by the way. How *did* you find her?'

'Oh, it was surprisingly easy,' replied Justin, not wanting to admit he'd had no choice.

'Well, she's a gem,' said Henny. 'Pay her whatever she wants – she's worth every cent. She says her last job was head chef at *Cafe Roman à Clef* in Paris.'

Justin nodded, as if he knew already, though he couldn't help wondering why she'd left France in search of a job in Scotland – and as far north as possible. However, he abandoned all speculation the moment breakfast arrived: three golden pancakes layered with fresh mango slices, smothered with toffee sauce and fudge crumbles, topped with a generous scoop of mango sorbet and whipped cream. It wasn't what he normally chose for breakfast – but he wasn't going to argue.

'She's from Prague,' Henny continued. 'We talked for hours last night. What an incredible life – but you'll know that already. I expect she told you everything during the interview. Thank goodness you're such a good judge of character. With a record like *that*, most people wouldn't have given her a second chance.'

Justin almost choked. He tried to say *record like what*, but discovered his last spoonful of fudge crumbles had glued his teeth together.

'Perhaps you'll have found a new butler by the time I get back,' said Henny, glancing at her digital travel watch. 'Hey, we'd better get a move on, you guys. There may be traffic.'

'No worries,' laughed Hank, hurrying after Lady Henny as she swept out of the room. He turned to wink at Polly. 'If I get the Land Rover, can you and Eliza manage the bags?'

Polly grumbled about his lack of chivalry and gulped down a final mouthful of sugary coffee. The cameras and recording equipment were already in the Land Rover; that just left their overnight bags, Henny's suitcase and the baby's stuff – not much of a problem when you've got a gorilla to help you. 'Fancy giving me a hand, Miss Muscles?' asked Polly. But before Eliza could reply, Hank reappeared looking dismayed.

'We've got a flat tyre.'

'*Dash and blast!*' exclaimed Willoughby. 'You'll never fix it in time. Oh ... this is terrible. We'll have to use my car ... I'd better go and get dressed.' He pushed his chair back and leapt to his feet, accidentally spilling a full glass of orange juice right across the table.

'I wouldn't bother if I were you, Sir Willoughby,' yawned Polly, mopping the tide of juice with a napkin. 'He's lying. Hardly up to your usual standard, Hanky-panky. *I'll* fetch the Land Rover *and* see to the bags, if it's all the same to you. I suspect you're up to something.'

Hank shrugged his shoulders and smiled. The plan had gone like clockwork. Willoughby's perfectly timed diversion had allowed Eliza to remove the passport from the back pocket of Polly's jeans and replace it with a counterfeit one. And *that* certainly *was* up to his usual standard.

'Honestly, can't you two *ever* be serious?' groaned Justin.

Hank waited until Polly had trotted out before answering. 'No way,' he whispered. 'That bespectacled little stick-insect put pepper on my toothbrush, so ...'

'So you've got to get your own back?'

'Sure thing.' Hank laughed, his white teeth gleaming against his ebony black skin. 'We've been at it twenty-one years – since our very first day at school. Polly tied the teacher's shoelaces together and released a dozen white mice. I got the entire blame, of course – Poll just blinked those big denim-blue eyes and looked innocent. Typical! Ten minutes later I accidentally flicked a well-chewed wad of bubblegum in all that straggly blonde hair ... and we've been the best of enemies ever since.'

'Well, I wish you wouldn't rope Dad in,' said Justin. 'If Mum finds out she'll be furious. She still hasn't forgiven you for teaching Eliza how to pick pockets.'

Justin glanced through the window behind Hank, and grinned. Polly appeared to be taping what looked like a large rasher of bacon to the bottom of Hank's suitcase – a treat, no doubt, for the airport security sniffer-dogs.

By seven forty-five, all members of the Congo expedition were ready to leave. Hank took the driver's seat; Henny sat beside him to navigate; the other three squeezed along the back seat – Eliza taking up most of the room. Albion squirmed in his baby chair, contentedly chewing the end of Polly's long, blonde ponytail.

Justin, Sir Willoughby and Nanny Verity stood on the castle steps to wave them off. Nanny seemed especially flustered, and kept giving Henny last minute instructions about Albion:

'Remember to use his chamomile bottiwipes. It gets ever so humid near the equator. The last thing Alby'll want is a rash on his wotsit.'

'I'm his Mom, you old fuss-pot,' laughed Henny. 'I know the rules: diapers changed hourly and no candy at bedtime. Stop worrying and enjoy your vacation. Promise?'

'Oh ... very well then, dear,' replied Nanny, not promising anything of the kind. 'Have a safe journey. See you a week tomorrow.'

Hank released the handbrake and pressed the accelerator. The old Land Rover lurched out of the courtyard, its spinning tyres leaving deep ruts in the gravel. Justin, Sir Willoughby and Nanny traipsed back into the castle feeling rather hollow – the sort of feeling you get when you know someone else is embarking on a thoroughly good time while you're not.

'Your turn tomorrow, Nanny V,' said Justin, astonished to see her looking so down-hearted. 'Just think: a whole week with your grandchildren.'

Nanny Verity brightened at the mention of her favourite topic. 'Little Beowulf was one in April,' she prattled, rummaging in her handbag. 'Leopold and Tristan had a party for him; I've got a photo of all three of them dressed as pumpkins.'

She withdrew a satin-bound baby album. Justin groaned inwardly at the prospect of innumerable photographs, all with Nanny's hand-written captions beneath, such as: *Hurrah – my first tooth*, or *Oh, how I love my fluffy blanket!*

'Ooooh, lovely,' he said, mentally disconnecting within seconds. He flipped through a few pages then added: 'Adorable, Nanny ... you must show them to Dad.'

Sir Willoughby shot him a look of dismay and then bolted off upstairs with Nanny Verity in hot pursuit.

Justin glanced at his watch. No mail for another hour and a half at least, he thought. Plenty of time to see what I can learn about the cook's mysterious past.

He found Robyn in the kitchen, hunched over a mug of coffee, chatting to Mrs Whatsername. The breakfast crockery was stacked in the dish-washer. A pair of old-fashioned scales and at least a hundred packets of ingredients covered one half of the kitchen table; the other half lay hidden beneath a drift of finely sieved flour. The cook stood beside the pantry, grumbling about its inadequacies:

'No walnut, no artichoke, no nectarine, no tofu, no endive, no date,' she grunted. 'No barleys, no yam, no chilli, no onion, no paprikas, no sultana ...'

As she seemed unlikely to stop in the immediate future, Justin decided to interrupt:

'Er, Mrs ... er ... Pr-zol-wammi ... er ...' he faltered, realising he'd never attempted her name out loud before.

Robyn sniggered into the collar of her dressing gown, but the cook grinned at him good-naturedly and daubed in the flour with one enormous finger: SHOLVA-MI-CHEN-KOF she wrote. Justin tried again – to her immense amusement. She gave a deep, guttural laugh and prodded him in the chest, leaving a large white fingerprint in the middle of his black tee-shirt.

'You calls me Mrs Kof. You wants I make you special chocolate cook chippies?'

Justin kept his face straight. 'Thank you, Mrs Kof,' he said. 'Chocolate chip cookies would be great ... but right now, I thought you might ... er ...'

'Bizzy-bizzy,' Mrs Kof grumbled. 'I needings more greedy-ants; walky to shops with many big baskets.'

Justin shook his head.

'I strong as rhinocerpotamus,' she assured him, banging both fists on the table with a deafening thud.

'That's not how we do things here,' said Justin. 'The nearest village is miles away; there's only a few shops there and they won't sell half the things you need.' He walked over to a chrome monitor set into the tiles beside the pantry, and pressed a switch beneath it.

'I'll show her,' said Robyn, pushing past. Seconds later, she was online and had accessed *Fortean & Mayhem*'s website. She showed Mrs Kof how to shop virtually by clicking on the items she wanted.

'It should all be delivered by lunchtime,' explained Justin. Then thinking this might be an opportune time to broach the subject of her past, he added, 'If you don't mind, Mrs Kof ... erm, there's a question I'd like to ask you ...'

At that precise moment, the back door creaked open and Mrs Gilliechattan stepped in. Her timing couldn't have been worse, but this didn't surprise Justin in the least; the gardener's wife and her hideous cat had a nasty habit of materialising in unwelcome places at inconvenient times.

88

Morag Gilliechattan was a wee, scrawny woman with coppery hair and a pinched face. Her eyes were sharper than gimlets, and Justin half imagined them capable of boring right through him to read the washing label in his underpants. She wore a tartan shawl fastened with her clan badge, and a tam-o'-shanter topped off with a spray of moth-eaten grouse feathers. She had vast quantities of cairngorm beads strung around her neck and wore several knobbly rings. Tybalt peered from beneath her voluminous kilt, like her green-eyed inky-black shadow.

'This is Mrs Gilliechattan the cleaner,' said Justin, planning a formal introduction.

'Castle hoosekeeper, dearie,' said Mrs Gilliechattan reprovingly. 'And you arrr ...'

'Nadezhda Przolwamiczenkof,' replied the cook, holding out a massive hand.

'Och, bless you dearie,' said Mrs Gilliechattan, pressing a handkerchief into Mrs Kof's hand. 'Say it ... doon't spray it! Keep those nasty wee cold gerrums to yourself.'

'That's her name,' Robyn explained, pointing to the phonetic spelling in the flour. 'But we can call her Mrs Kof.'

Mrs Gilliechattan gave the cook a sharp, sideways look, and then peered at the kitchen table. After a few feeble attempts at Mrs Kof's full name she muttered, 'Koff'll doo faine dearie,' and wrote GILLY-HATTEN underneath, to rule out any impertinent abbreviations of *her* name. 'The C is silent,' she added, and bustled off to the utility room where she billeted her regiment of mops and feather-dusters. Tybalt scuttled after her.

'*Good gravy!*' gasped Mrs Kof. 'Did my eyes conceive me, or does kitty-puss have eight leggings?'

Justin cringed. Tybalt was always kept hidden from outsiders, but sooner or later, all castle residents had to learn the truth.

'Are *you* going to explain?' Robyn enquired. 'Or shall I?'

Justin gave a deep sigh, and spoke in a husky voice: 'It's almost three years exactly since I first developed my teleportation theories. Scientists around the globe were racing to take the lead in quantum technology, but unbeknown to them I ...'

'*Urrghhh* – not the boring version,' groaned Robyn. 'Leave it to me. During the Gilliechattans' first summer at the castle, Brainbox here built two teleport-pods: one in his lab, the other in Dad's workshop. He managed to zap several inanimate objects from one pod to the other – but some articles vanished and, even more bizarre, a few items appeared spontaneously in the lab pod.'

'A bottle of Fogarty's Brown Ale, a screwdriver and a lightly boiled egg,' added Justin.

'Like it matters,' said Robyn, rolling her eyes to the ceiling.

'Well, it mattered to me,' Justin retorted 'I thought Dad was playing a trick on me, but he strenuously denied it. He said he disapproved of my experiments.'

Robyn gave a derisory snort. 'I think his exact words were: *it's dangerous and unethical you little maniac.* He begged Dustbin not to teleport anything living, but since when do geniuses ever listen to their dads?'

'On October 1st I teleported a petri dish of staphylococcus albus,' said Justin, a trace of pride in his voice.

'Dad became tense.'

'Two days later I transferred a single-celled amoeba.'

'Dad started slamming doors and biting his fingernails.'

'Then catastrophe struck.'

Mrs Kof frowned. 'What this cat's-ass-trophy?'

'Disaster,' explained Justin. 'Calamity, tragedy, cataclysm ...'

'Thank you, Thesaurus Rex,' snapped Robyn. 'I think she gets the drift. The fact is, Mrs Kof, what happened to Tybalt was entirely the housekeeper's own fault.'

'Mrs Grill-a-kitten not keepings castle clean?'

'*Waaaaay* too clean,' said Robyn, giving the cook a conspiratorial look. 'Dusting diaries, tidying out locked cupboards, straightening piles of confidential letters ... not to mention how conscientious she is about polishing keyholes.'

Mrs Kof chuckled.

'It's true,' said Justin. 'She never dusted the south tower

without trying my lab door, hoping to find it unlocked. Finally, after months of torment, her patience was rewarded.'

'Wherr's ma feather-duster?' cackled Robyn, in a perfect imitation of the housekeeper's highland accent. 'Dearie me, there'll be dust-bunnies as big as crocodiles.'

'Unfortunately, she wasn't alone,' sighed Justin. 'Wherever Mrs G goes, Tybalt follows. He probably spied a warm pool of sunlight inside the pod, perfect for a catnap, and crept inside.'

'But Tybs wasn't alone either,' added Robyn. 'While following his mistress through the garden, a tiny spider must've fallen on his fur.'

'To save on fiddly switches, I'd designed the quantum-subatomic-particle-dematerialiser to activate automatically when the pod door closed. We assume Mrs G must've accidentally knocked it shut. Tybalt – *and* the spider – would've vanished in a fizzle of sparks.'

'To make matters worse, Dad just happened to be standing in front of the second pod in his workshop; the arrival of an evil-looking eight-legged cat nearly unhinged him completely.'

'The arachnid and feline subatomic particles reconstituted concurrently,' explained Justin, 'fusing the two creatures into one hideous mutation. Dad was livid. He grabbed a sledge hammer and smashed both pods to atoms. I was *certain* I'd closed the pod and locked the lab door when I'd left, but Dad didn't believe a word. He forbade me to rebuild them. It was very disappointing, but when I saw the result of my experiments, I promised anything – including apologising to Mrs G.'

'Oooh,' gasped the cook. 'I bet she abslutty infumigated.'

'Not as much as we expected,' said Justin. 'Now we all feel obliged to turn a blind eye to her prying. Otherwise ...'

'I was only searching for ma wee lost kitty,' said Robyn, mimicking Mrs Gilliechattan again. 'You know dearie ... the one with *all* those legs.'

'She's banned from the south tower now,' said Justin. '*And* I've had special locks fitted.'

'Special clocks?' asked Mrs Kof.

'No, *locks*,' said Robyn. 'All three doors to Dustbin's rooms have the latest fingerprint recognition sensors. Only the touch of his right thumb can open them, while his left thu ...'

Justin nudged his sister sharply in the ribs. Mrs Kof didn't appear to notice.

'Poor little Octo-puss,' she said.

'Octo-puss! What a perfect name,' laughed Justin. 'Don't worry, he seems quite happy.'

'Yep – evil, malevolent and insidious – but happy,' snickered Robyn. 'A mutant super-cat, able to run the full length of a narrow fence whilst simultaneously grooming his whiskers, swatting a fly and scratching his bottom.'

Mrs Kof laughed so hard her stomach wobbled like a blancmange. 'Now if you infuse me, I gets bizzy,' she said, rolling up her sleeves. 'I makings nice bread-and-butt pudding.'

For a moment, Justin stood transfixed – but it wasn't the vomit-inducing image of Mrs Kof's dessert that disturbed him. No, it was something else entirely.

'You still wants ask me quetzal?' asked Mrs Kof.

Justin shook his head. 'It doesn't matter,' he said, with a slight frown. He *had* wanted to ask about her past and why she needed a second chance; now he thought he knew the answer. When she'd rolled up her sleeves he'd observed a row of numbers tattooed on the inside of one wrist. As far as he knew that could only mean one thing: Mrs Kof had been in prison.

Another crisis, he thought. Since turning thirteen, life certainly hasn't been dull. Mum's on what might be her last ever film-shoot, Dad's developed a spy fixation, Nanny insists there's an impostor in the castle, I've just had the freakiest nightmare ever, and now *this* ...

Can you ever really trust an ex-convict with access to a drawer full of meat cleavers, he wondered. If anything goes wrong I'll never forgive myself – though on the other hand, dare I risk giving her the sack?

With a deeply furrowed brow, Justin turned and trudged out of the kitchen, racking his brains for a way out of the predicament he now found himself well and truly stuck in.

⊗bviously, in a solitary universe, it would be impossible for your mother to die before your birth. Therefore we can logically assume something else happened. Perhaps she had an identical twin accidentally killed by a mysterious stranger before you were born. Or, maybe you were adopted, and your biological mother is still alive. Things needn't be exactly as they appear.

This alternate resolution to the paradox sees each timeline as unalterable. We are merely players acting out fixed roles. At each timefork we appear to choose our direction, but this is an illusion. We exist on the only timeline available. Even a journey back in time is predetermined. The apparent death of your mother happened because you have always lived in a universe where a traveller from the future killed someone resembling her, before your birth.

These two resolutions seem poles apart. Neither is ideal. Multiple parallel worlds appeal to many, especially as they appear to explain the uncanny reality of dreams or feelings of déjà vu. Perhaps you have dreamt of someone who died, or that you still lived in a house you left many years ago. Some theorists suggest that on a parallel timeline that person never died, or you never moved house. Such dreams are leaks from an alternate universe, through the fabric of time into our subconscious.

Unfortunately, the MULTIVERSE theory has a flaw ...

CHAPTER SEVEN

Sir Lyall's Eccentricity

Robyn decided to skip school that morning, chatting to Mrs Kof over a leisurely breakfast of eggs Benedict and spicy apple muffins instead. Like her mother, she had a natural talent for language, though she rarely bothered to exercise it without considerable incentive.

Grandpa Lyall had *his* breakfast in bed, (porridge, kippers and Earl Grey tea). Then Sir Willoughby showed him round the estate, pointing out various sights in the hope he would spot something familiar – but he didn't even recognise the castle as they ambled back towards it.

'That *proves* he's genuine,' declared Willoughby. 'An impostor would've pretended to recognise *something*.'

'I *guess* so,' Justin replied, not entirely certain this was logical. 'I'll surf the web later; check out the latest data on amnesia.'

Willoughby shook his head. '*No*, no ... don't waste your time son – it's Pops alright.'

The timely arrival of the mail van saved Justin from answering.

'Grand weather,' Jock mumbled, handing him a huge wad of envelopes.

They stood in silence watching Fergus crunch his daily stick of Edinburgh rock. Then Justin rushed upstairs, hoping to answer at least some of his mail before lessons. The top envelope looked decidedly ominous; it was addressed to Lady Henrietta Thyme and had the BBC logo printed across it. Fervently hoping it contained good news, he tucked it in his pocket, planning to read it to his mum when she got in contact that evening.

Now that he had permission, Justin could hardly wait to start designing his time machine. Up in his lab, he pushed the previous night's worries aside, determined that nothing would distract him. Even the cryptic words on his watch were dismissed as unimportant, and it was only when the tower clock struck eleven that he realised the time. Apologising profusely, he dashed into the schoolroom, loaded down with books and Professor Gilbert's binoculars.

The professor's eyes lit up as he saw them. 'Aha, I w-wondered where those got to,' he said. 'Wish I'd had them with me yesterday; I saw n-n-n ... n-nothing without them. I was hiding in a little cave just below the cliff top, watching some seagulls feeding their young.'

Justin half listened, but Mrs Kof kept invading his thoughts. He longed to ask the professor's advice about her, but imagined he would resign, pack up and leave, if he learnt the truth. Perhaps it was best to avoid mentioning the cook altogether.

'I w-w-wonder if the new cook'll arrive today,' remarked the professor.

Typical, thought Justin. Absolutely classic. 'She's here,' he said. 'Arrived late last night.'

'Oh. W-w-what's she like?'

Justin chose his words with care: 'She makes the best pancakes I've ever tasted.'

'That's hopeful,' said Gilbert, stroking his beard. 'What's her name again? I suppose I'll have to m-m-meet her at lunchtime.'

Justin laughed nervously, and then turned it into a coughing spasm. 'Kof,' he said.

The professor patted him on the back. 'So I see. And the cook's name is ...?'

'Mrs Kof,' said Justin. 'K-O-F. At least, that's what she says we can call her. Her full name's a bit of a mouthful.'

Professor Gilbert's eyebrows twitched, as he recalled the cook's note in its grubby envelope. He pushed it out of his mind, fully intending to conduct today's lesson without singing. After verifying the perfect symmetry of his bowtie and flicking an invisible speck off his lapel, the professor cleared this throat a few times and took a deep breath.

'As it ap-p-ppears to be just the two of us today, let's get straight down to some w-w-work then,' he said. 'How are you getting on with your time-fork theories?'

Justin sighed. It was going to be one of *those* mornings. Professor Gilbert seemed intent on asking awkward questions. After careful consideration Justin gave an evasive reply, and then glanced discreetly at his watch. Lunchtime looked a long way off.

At twelve-thirty Justin packed up his books with a feeling of relief – an emotion he'd never felt before at the end of a morning's work. He decided to request another afternoon off.

The professor broke all records by smiling on a second consecutive day. 'That's fine by me,' he replied, rubbing his hands together. 'Looks like another afternoon ... er ... b-b-bird-watching then.'

As Justin headed downstairs, he imagined his mother nibbling her complimentary peanuts at fifty thousand feet and tried calculating her ETA, but the deafening racket from the kitchen made it quite impossible. In perfect time to the resounding clamour of saucepans, Mrs Kof sang in a lusty baritone voice. Justin heard the clatter of boots behind him. It was Professor Gilbert, dressed in his hiking gear, complete with haversack and binoculars.

'You didn't tell me she was a musician,' he cried, a fanatical gleam in his eyes. 'Isn't that the Anvil Chorus?'

More like the Croaking Chorus, Justin thought, seriously doubting anyone but a tone-deaf frog would classify it as music. Was there to be no escape from the world of opera?

Looking on the bright side, (and Justin discovered there *was* a bright side when he looked *really* hard), Professor Gilbert didn't seem as nervous of the cook as he'd expected. She made him a huge mound of his favourite sandwiches and packed his haversack with a feast of delicious, wholesome goodies.

'No forgettings big binkle-nocks,' boomed Mrs Kof. She hung his binoculars around his neck and slapped the poor man on the back. Justin could see the danger signs: Professor Gilbert's ears reddened and he started to stammer. Determined to avoid further operatic outbursts, Justin opened the kitchen door and propelled him gently but firmly outdoors.

After a lunch that defied description, Justin decided he didn't give two hoots about the cook's questionable past.

So what if she *has* been in prison, he thought. She must be from one of those ridiculously strict countries that imprison people for keeping goldfish without a licence. Or maybe she hasn't been in jail. A few tattooed numbers don't prove anything. Perhaps she's got a really bad memory and that's how she remembers her favourite aunt's telephone number.

He mentioned the matter to his sister as they wandered along the portrait gallery.

'But she *was* in prison,' said Robyn. '*Honestly* Dustbin ... I thought you knew.'

'Oh,' said Justin. 'What for? Whipping the cream? Beating the eggs? I'll bet it was nothing worth worrying about.'

Robyn grinned to herself, and walked a few steps in silence to maximise the effect of her forthcoming bulletin. She kept her reply as casual as possible: 'Murder.'

'Oh.'

'She got life ... for strangling a man with her bare hands,' she added, relishing every phase of her brother's anguish.

'Oh,' said Justin for the third time, his voice sounding flatter with each repetition. 'But she's free now. I suppose the police discovered she was innocent and let her go.'

'Nope. She escaped.'

'Oh.' It was his fourth and flattest *oh*. After Robyn informed him their new cook was both an illegal immigrant and a wanted fugitive, he racked his brains for something intelligent to say. Utterly lost for words, he resorted a fifth time to what was rapidly becoming the most popular word in his vocabulary: 'Oh.'

'Of course, she *says* she didn't do it – and for what it's worth, *I* believe her.'

'*Oh!*'

Justin felt as if the bottom had fallen out of his world – or as Nanny Verity said when she got anxious and muddled – *as if the world had fallen out of his bottom!*

At 9:30 that evening the Thymes gathered in the south tower sitting room. Nanny bustled in, smoothing her apron, Sir Willoughby sprawled on the sofa, and Robyn waited by the window, fiddling with her mobile. At the last minute, Justin slid down from his laboratory.

'Come *on*,' grumbled Willoughby. 'Your mum'll be waiting.'

Unperturbed, Justin connected his AppleMac to the huge plasma wall screen. Communication with the Congo was surprisingly straightforward, and during the summer they were only an hour ahead of Greenwich Mean Time. He gazed at the blizzard of static, visualising his mother opening Eliza's laptop and setting up her web-cam.

The screen blinked a few times and then Lady Henny flickered into focus. She was sitting in a hotel bedroom, with an apoplectic expression on her normally serene face.

'Hen, darling!' gulped Willoughby. 'Whatever's the matter?'

'What's the matter?' Henny fumed. 'I'll tell you what's the matter! I'm stranded here with a mountain of equipment, a baby, a talking gorilla, and no darn film crew.'

'How come?'

'They're still in Prestwick. Polly got arrested for travelling with a forged passport. You should have seen it: a cartoon rabbit with long blonde hair and big eyelashes, instead of a proper photograph. It didn't amuse the security guards one scrap. Minutes later, the airport sniffer-dogs almost ripped Hank's suitcase apart. As a result, I ended up travelling without either of them. *Idiots!* I swear their next practical joke will be their last. I'm sick and tired of the endless trouble those two are always causing.'

'Don't worry, Mum,' said Justin. 'Dad can drive down to Prestwick first thing, and get them bailed out and booked on the next flight. Meanwhile, just relax.'

'*RELAX*,' snapped Henny. 'You can tell those two scoundrels from me: one more joke and I'll fire the pair of them. They should know better when our careers are on the line.'

'Ah, that reminds me,' said Justin, withdrawing an envelope from his pocket. 'You've had a letter from the BBC. Do you want me to open it?'

Henny groaned. 'Go ahead. How bad can it be?'

Justin tore the envelope open and withdrew a sheet of ivory paper. 'Pretty bad,' he said. 'I'm afraid the rumours Hank and Polly heard were true. It says, "Unless the next episode of *Thyme-Zone* surpasses all expectations we regret to inform you that ..."'

'Say no more,' interrupted Henny, her voice dull and dispirited. 'I get the drift.'

'How's my precious little Albion?' asked Nanny Verity.

'Oh – *fine*,' Henny replied. 'Eliza hasn't let him out of her sight.'

They took turns chatting with Henny until she looked calmer. Then after wishing each other goodnight, Justin promised to get in touch early the next morning with an update.

'Poor Mum,' he remarked, the instant they were offline. 'There must be *something* I can think of. But computer animation ... it's simply out of the question given the timescale.'

'Perhaps I ought to cancel my vacation,' murmured Nanny. 'I should be here with you and Robyn in case anything else goes wrong.'

'Don't be silly, Nanny,' said Justin, giving her arm a quick squeeze. 'Nothing's going to go wrong – I promise.'

The following morning, Justin plodded up the west tower to fetch Nanny Verity's luggage. When he reached the top of the stairs he found old Sir Lyall dragging her suitcase onto the landing, his face an unhealthy shade of purple.

'Leave that to me, Grandpa,' he called, momentarily wondering whether the old man's wheezing was genuine or part of an elaborate scam. Justin peered through the open nursery door and saw Nanny scuttling round in her usual pre-travel flap, stuffing last minute panic-items into a large handbag.

'Cough drops, clean handkerchief, postage stamps, spare reading-glasses, safety pins,' she recited to herself. 'Och, now where did I put those photos of wee Alby?'

Justin passed her a blue satin baby album. 'Dad's just phoned,' he said, as she tucked it in her bag. 'He's been delayed at Prestwick. We'll have to order a taxi to take you to the station.'

Nanny sank onto a chair, her face puckering fretfully. She was wearing a chintzy frock instead of her starched uniform, and the unfamiliar colours made her face look pale and drawn. '*Gracious* – I knew something like this would happen!'

'No need to panic m'dear,' panted Grandpa. 'I'll teck yer m'self. I *can* drive, y'know.'

'Impossible, I'm afraid,' said Justin. 'Dad's taken the Beetle we keep for everyday use; Mum's Porsche is a two-seater; and the Bentley only gets driven on *very* special occasions.'

'What about *Enigma*?' Grandpa asked.

Justin's heart missed a beat. How could the old man possibly know, unless ... unless he really *was* Grandpa Lyall? Perhaps Nanny had been wrong after all.

As he carried Nanny's suitcase downstairs, Justin's thoughts drifted back to the day his father first showed him the old car:

'When I was a boy, Pops – in a fit of wild extravagance – treated himself to *this*,' Sir Willoughby had said, whisking back the dustsheets to reveal a claret-coloured vintage Rolls Royce with

101

distinctive number plates:

Sir Lyall had christened the car *Enigma*. After he disappeared, Willoughby entombed the old Rolls at the back of the garage under several sheets. He never drove it – but he adamantly refused to sell it. Each April 1st, on the anniversary of his father's mysterious disappearance, he unveiled Enigma for just one day: to be washed and polished, sent to the local garage for an MOT and full service, then lovingly enshrouded for another year.

Justin peeled back the moth-eaten dustsheets and put Nanny's case in the boot. Next he checked the old car's fuel gauge; there was enough to get them to the nearest filling station. He hoped his father would approve. Nanny Verity *disapproved*. While Grandpa Lyall manoeuvred Enigma out of the garage, she took Justin to one side and begged him to phone for a taxi.

'How do you know he can drive properly?' she whispered. 'I don't want to miss my train.'

'Stop worrying, Nan,' said Justin, glancing up at the tower clock. 'There's bags of time.'

But there wasn't – and Grandpa stalled the car twice even before they reached the castle gates. By the time they stopped for petrol they were already running ten minutes late.

During the drive, Nanny sat beside Grandpa Lyall, frowning out of the passenger window at the traffic; arms folded, lips thin. Robyn and Justin shared the back seat – it was the first time either of them had been inside the old Rolls.

'Verity *Kiss*!' Grandpa remarked, trying to make polite conversation. '*Very* Glamorous; it makes you sound like a Bond Girl! Is there a Mr Kiss?'

102

'I'm a widow,' Nanny replied. 'And I fully intend to stay that way,' she added primly, hoping to quash any impertinent romantic notions the old man might be harbouring.

'I'm sorry,' said Grandpa.

Justin wondered whether he was sorry Nanny had lost her husband, or sorry she wasn't looking for another. Undeterred, the old man tried again:

'So ... three grandchildren! You really don't look old enough. What's your secret?'

'Twins,' Nanny snapped, and refused to elaborate any further.

Robyn turned to her brother and grimaced. 'Poor Grandpa,' she whispered. 'The atmosphere's so frosty it's a wonder he can't see his breath.'

'We'll explain on the way home,' Justin replied.

Nanny had told them scores of times. She'd got married when she was about nineteen. Her first daughter, Kitty, was born nine months later, and then the twins, Hathaway and Henslowe, arrived the following year. They were all in their early twenties now, with babies of their own.

'It's not Grandpa's fault the roads are so busy,' hissed Robyn.

'She thinks he's a fake.'

'But he knew about Enigma. How much proof does she need?'

'Maybe Dad mentioned it ... or took him inside the garage and showed him,' Justin muttered. Then after a moment's thought added: 'Or Grandpa could have sneaked out last night while we were talking to Mum. Perhaps he found the old car and realised what the number plates spell.'

'Oh, *surely* you don't believe *that*?' said Robyn, sounding quite disgusted.

Justin sighed. He wasn't sure what he believed any longer.

'What are you two whispering about?' asked Nanny, peering over her shoulder.

'Nothing, Nan.'

'Well, start thinking of some short-cuts or we'll never get there by ten to.'

At 12:47 they sprinted into Inverness Station, tumbling through the ticket barrier onto platform two just as the Northern Express glided to a halt. Verity Kiss burst into floods of tears, and hugged Justin and Robyn as if she would never see them again.

'Honestly, Nan,' said Justin. 'You do this every single year, but a few days later we always get a postcard saying what a wonderful time you're having.'

'I know,' sniffed Nanny. 'You should see the state I get in when it's time to leave Brighton. Kitty and the twins bring the little ones to the station. They all wave me off, and I weep buckets!'

'I can imagine,' said Robyn.

'I just wish Sir Willoughby could've brought me as usual,' Nanny whispered, glaring at Grandpa Lyall's back as he hurried over to a kiosk selling sweets. 'It's *so* uncomfortable having to rely on a stranger.'

'Oh Nanny!' groaned Robyn.

Nanny Verity pressed her lips together and gave Justin a knowing look. She *said* nothing, but Robyn guessed what she was thinking.

'Now *do* try to be sensible while I'm away,' Nanny told Justin. 'Promise me you won't get too engrossed in your work and forget to keep an eye on the time; if you don't get enough sleep you're like a zombie the next morning. And as for you young lady,' she continued, turning to Robyn. 'You spend far too long sitting in front of that computer of yours. Chat rooms indeed! For all you know, you could be talking to a dangerous criminal.'

'And for all *you* know, I might have had breakfast with one,' replied Robyn, half-tempted to shock her with the truth about Mrs Kof.

Justin nudged his sister sharply. Nanny looked most alarmed, and seemed to be about to ask what on earth she meant when Grandpa Lyall returned carrying a box of chocolates.

'For you, dear lady,' he said, presenting them to Nanny.

Verity Kiss looked taken aback. Despite suspecting he was a conniving impostor, her sweet nature prevented her from refusing the gift – or perhaps it was her sweet tooth.

'Thank you,' she said. Then, after a brief hesitation grudgingly added, 'Sir Lyall.'

Justin and Robyn exchanged glances. It was the first time anyone had called Grandpa *Sir*. His reaction was not at all what they expected.

'Who?' he asked, glancing round uncertainly.

Nanny gave a reverberating snort and climbed into carriage number seventeen. Justin handed up her suitcase, and Robyn gave her a big white envelope.

'Open it later,' she said, giving Nanny a hurried peck on the cheek.

The guard blew his whistle and Justin slammed the door. Seconds later the train rumbled out of the station with Nanny waving her handkerchief. Once Robyn and Justin were distant specks, she searched for an empty compartment; she hated being stuck next to strangers on a train.

'Breakfast with a criminal,' she sighed, flumping down in a seat. 'Dearie me ... I wonder if Robyn meant ...' she stopped mid-sentence, wearing a deeply puzzled frown, then, seconds later she shook her head and murmured 'No, of *course* not.'

Nanny opened the envelope and several theatre tickets fluttered onto her lap – enough to treat her whole family. The writing inside the card said:

Bon Voyage

Have a wonderful time.
Lots of love, Justin & Robyn

Verity Kiss burst into tears again, then opened the box of chocolates to console herself.

As they stepped out onto Academy Street, Grandpa Lyall clung tightly to Robyn's arm. He suddenly seemed frail and confused, and kept asking where they were going.

'Back to the Rolls,' Justin explained. 'As soon as you feel up to driving home.'

'Me?' gasped Grandpa. '*No*! I can't drive a big car like that ... that's the chauffeur's job.'

That was a problem no one had anticipated. Justin chewed his lower lip as he considered their options ... or lack of them.

'Perhaps he just needs something to eat,' suggested Robyn. 'What about that trendy potato cyber cafe on Oxingam Parade?'

Justin couldn't remember ever hearing the words *trendy, potato* and *cyber* in the same sentence before, but he nodded anyway. Inverness was one of Robyn's regular shopping haunts and she knew all the best places to eat. 'How far is it?'

'Just round the corner, next to the Jamaica Inn,' said Robyn. 'It's astral *cubed!'*

Robyn was right. It was weird but wonderful. Each customer collected a giant baked potato from the counter and filled it with absolutely *whatever* they wanted. You then had your choice of sumptuous leather couches to sit on, each with its own flat-screen monitor and keyboard. Justin grinned; the name over the door was "*COUCH POTATO*" – clearly someone's idea of a joke.

Grandpa Lyall filled his potato with baked beans; Justin chose cream cheese and smoky bacon; and Robyn had peanut butter, bananas and chocolate chips – which sounded disgusting but was surprisingly delicious, especially when the chocolate melted. They sat either side of Grandpa on a huge leather sofa, and as they munched, reminded him about driving to Inverness that morning.

'You must remember Enigma,' said Robyn.

Grandpa looked perplexed. 'Is he your boyfriend?'

Robyn groaned.

Once the meal was over, Grandpa Lyall looked much better – but still stubbornly insisted they needed a chauffeur.

'What now?' asked Robyn.

Good question, Justin thought – though the answer depended on whether Grandpa's sudden memory lapse was fake or genuine. He leaned over and starting typing at a keyboard.

'I found this really good website last night. The latest research on short-term memory dysfunction suggests ...'

The icy glint in his sister's eyes stopped him abruptly.

'Research?' she snapped. 'Is that your answer to everything?'

'Well ...'

'Analysis? Theories? Hypotheses?' continued Robyn, spitting out each word. 'How's that going to get us home?'

Justin screwed his eyes closed for a moment – then reopened them. 'Okay,' he sighed, glancing at his watch. 'Meet me back at the car in quarter of an hour.'

Ten minutes later, he emerged from a large department store carrying several bags, containing: three cushions, two coffee mugs, a grey wig, an eyebrow pencil, a pair of shoes, some strong glue, scissors, a stapler, a packet of drawing pins, a sheet of white card and a marker pen.

Back at the car park, he piled the cushions on Enigma's front seat. Then he glued the coffee mugs to the soles of the new shoes, and left them to dry. Next he opened the car boot and pulled out an old chauffeur's uniform he'd noticed earlier. He stuffed it into one of the carrier bags and ran back to the station.

A quiet voice from somewhere deep within his brain politely pointed out that he was about to do something very, very silly – but Justin ignored it.

When no one was looking, he pinned the sheet of card to the door of the gents' toilet. Finally, he took out the marker pen and wrote the words:

OUT OF ORDER!

eflect for a moment how many parallel universes there must be if each decision we make results in a different timeline. At our first decision or timefork, we face two alternate routes or timelines. Along our chosen route we soon encounter a second timefork; but an equivalent fork exists on our previously rejected route. Therefore, two decisions create four alternate timelines. Each fork DOUBLES the possibility planes. After only six simple decisions there are sixty-three universes in existence, parallel to our own.

How many decisions do we make daily? Twenty-five decisions creates more than thirty-three million parallel worlds; one more decision increases this number to more than sixty-seven million, and so-on. These numbers continue escalating with every decision, every day of our lives, swiftly surpassing anything we can contemplate. And these are only OUR parallel worlds!

Multiply this by the number of people on earth today, those who have lived in the past, and those yet to be born. The sheer volume of possible parallel worlds would make a googolplex* look infinitesimal.

---

* A googol is one followed by a hundred noughts; a googolplex is one followed by a googol of noughts. To write this number in full, you would start by writing a 'one' on the first page of a book this size, and then continue by writing noughts along *every* line of *every* page until you have filled approximately 100,000,000,000,000,000,000,000,000,000,

000,000,000,000,000,000,000,000,000,000,000,000,000,000,000,000,000,000,000,000,000,000 books!

CHAPTER EIGHT

Unexpected Trouble

Although Justin had never driven a Rolls Royce before, he reckoned there was a first time for everything. Driving wasn't a problem. He'd beetled around the courtyard in the VW once or twice when no one was looking, but negotiating traffic was something else entirely – though *not*, he hoped, beyond his considerable capabilities. No, the main problem was that he'd be breaking the law, and having Inverness Police Station directly across the street from the car park, didn't make things any easier; hence the disguise.

First, he shortened the legs and sleeves of the chauffeur's uniform, hemming them with the stapler; then he put them on over his own clothes. The cap fitted surprisingly well once he was wearing the grey wig. Next, he used the eyebrow pencil to add a few artful wrinkles around his eyes and mouth. With the aid of the scissors and glue, he fashioned himself a moustache and matching sideburns from hair trimmed off the wig. Finally, he examined the overall effect in the mirror.

Ho-hum, he thought, squinting through half-closed eyes. I look like ... well, like a 13 year old boy in a wig. Maybe from a distance I'll get away with it. He removed the OUT OF ORDER sign from the toilet door, and hurried back to the car.

Sergeant Awbrite glanced out of his office window.

'*Another* comically dressed midget,' he chuckled. The one he'd seen earlier had been with a clown on stilts, sticking flyers to car windscreens advertising the Bohemian Circus. He'd noticed the Big Top yesterday, as he drove past the park. He smiled as he realised *this* wee chap was wearing a big baggy chauffeur's uniform. 'I'll bet he drives one of those joke cars that explode and fall in bits. I really must get tickets this year.'

The telephone rang. Awbrite strode back to his desk – and just missed this particular midget climbing into a vintage Rolls Royce.

'Awbrite here,' he said, automatically reaching for his notebook. 'Calm down, Sir. Now, what's the registration? Echo November nineteen ...'

Justin swapped his trainers for the shoes with the coffee mugs stuck beneath them, then sat in the driver's seat on the pile of cushions. Perfect. He could see clearly, looked taller, yet the brake, clutch and accelerator were all easily within reach. All he had to do now was wait for Robyn and Grandpa Lyall. His sister was the first to spot him.

'You *can't* be serious,' she said, laughing like a drain.

'Shut up and get in.'

Robyn opened the Rolls' back door and allowed her grandfather to climb in first. She was still giggling uncontrollably. 'Some genius! That wouldn't fool a myopic pensioner.'

Justin glared at her. 'Do try and control yourself. People are starting to stare.'

'Hardly surprising,' sniggered Robyn. She spoke with the obligatory mocking tone of an older sister but, secretly, was rather impressed. The pencil-necked geek was tackling things head-on for a change, instead of analysing all seventeen volumes of the Encyclopaedia Pratannica first. This might be fun.

Justin adjusted the sun visor to partially conceal his face. 'Any suggestions?'

'How about auditioning for the Wizard of Oz? You'd make a marvellous munchkin.'

'I meant *helpful* suggestions,' Justin muttered. 'Anyway, no one ever looks inside a moving car – the reflections on the windows hide everything. We'll be fine ... as long as we don't have to stop at too many traffic lights.'

Robyn remained sceptical, but Grandpa regarded Justin thoughtfully.

'It might work,' he said. 'Except for one thing: *your eyes*. Eyes are always a dead give-away. Try these on.' He withdrew an old pair of sunglasses from his pocket. With an arthritic groan, he leaned forward and handed them to Justin.

'Thanks.' Justin slipped them on and looked at his reflection in the rear-view mirror. The mirrored lenses obscured his eyes completely. 'How do I look?'

'Better,' said Robyn, trying not to sound too impressed. The transformation *was* astonishing. 'What shall we call our new chauffeur, Grandpa?'

'Oh, I er ... I haven't a clue,' he murmured. Then brightening suddenly he announced. 'I know ... let's call him MacIver.'

Robyn giggled. 'Home at once, MacIver,' she ordered, 'and give it some welly.'

Justin turned the ignition key; Enigma's finely tuned engine purred as he pressed the accelerator. Minutes later they had crossed Rosen Bridge and were zooming along Glen Thyme Road. It ran along the west side of Loch Ness and had breathtaking views, but, as always in spring, progress was unbearably slow. The tourist season had started, and on Saturday that meant just one thing: Nessie hunters. Hundreds of cars and coaches crawled along, all hoping for a glimpse of the elusive Beastie. Eventually the traffic ground to a halt.

Justin glanced in the rear-view mirror. Grandpa gazed at the loch, looking happier than he had all day. Even Robyn, who classified the monster along with fairies, pixies and Little Green Men, stared dreamily across the water. It was impossible to resist.

Justin however, had his mind elsewhere: whilst making a mental note to ask his dad if Sir Lyall ever had a chauffeur called MacIver, he had the sudden and inescapable desire to sneeze. Forgetting that his own clothes were beneath the chauffeur's uniform, he fumbled through its pockets and found a starched cotton handkerchief. As he unfurled it, he saw something that stopped the sneeze in its tracks: embroidered on one corner was a crest badge of a boar's head, and the motto *Nunquam Obliviscar*. Justin gasped. There was no need to ask Willoughby anything; it was the crest of the Clan MacIver. Language wasn't his forte, but he knew enough Latin to translate this: *Nunquam Obliviscar* meant – I will never forget.

The drive home took a good two hours, but Justin was oblivious to the traffic jams. He kept casting surreptitious glances at Grandpa in the rear-view mirror. There seemed to be only two possibilities: either the old man really *was* Sir Lyall Austin Thyme with chronic amnesia, *or*, he was a professional confidence trickster who'd researched his role and acted the part to perfection. He might even have planted the handkerchief then manoeuvred him into finding it.

Justin shook his head. I'm getting as bad as Nanny, he thought.

It was nearly teatime when they arrived back at the castle. As Justin drove into the garage he caught a fleeting glimpse of Sir Willoughby marching out of the front door, wearing an anxious frown.

'Now you're for it,' hissed Robyn.

Justin had an unpleasant feeling she was right. He had hoped that once his dad learnt it was Grandpa who had asked to drive Enigma, all would be forgiven; now he wasn't so sure. He cudgelled his brains for an excuse, then a bony old finger prodded his shoulder.

'Get that uniform off ... *quick*,' Grandpa whispered, 'and swap seats.'

112

Justin felt almost too astonished to obey. Almost. He pulled the jacket over his head, dragging the wig and cap off with it. Then he climbed out, rolled them into an untidy bundle, and kicked them under the car. While he tried to remove the chauffeur's trousers, Grandpa Lyall settled himself in the driver's seat. Justin struggled to maintain his balance, but the coffee mugs glued to his shoes made it awkward. The ominous sound of Sir Willoughby's feet scrunching across the gravel courtyard drew closer.

Robyn groaned. Better rescue the little dweeb, she thought – well, at least he tried. She ran round the car and shoved Justin headlong onto the back seat. Then grasping the seat of his pants, she tugged with all her might, removing them in one swift yank, complete with the shoes *and* mugs. 'You owe me one,' she hissed, stuffing the whole lot into a handy carrier bag. Then, with immaculate timing, she turned to smile at her father striding through the garage door.

'Hello Daddy darling,' she said in an uncharacteristically sugary tone. 'We're back. Grandpa offered to take Nanny to the station in his *own* car.'

'Of *course*!' groaned Willoughby, slapping his forehead with the heel of his hand. 'I should've realised Pops could take you.' Then turning to Sir Lyall he added, 'What's it like – back behind the wheel of the old Rolls?'

Grandpa grinned. 'Great. Though I *am* rather rusty,' he said, giving Justin a conspiratorial wink. 'Old age I suppose. I'll need lots of practice before I can risk driving on my own.'

'Well naturally, you're ...' Sir Willoughby stopped, cocking his head on one side. Soon they all heard it; the distant sound of a police siren, growing steadily louder. 'M'afraid I've done something rather stupid,' Willoughby admitted, looking sheepish. 'I assumed you'd taken Nanny in a taxi ... so when I saw the Rolls missing I phoned the police.'

The siren was now quite deafening. Once they walked out of the garage they could see the squad car's flashing blue light through the archway. It roared into the courtyard and swerved to a halt,

113

spraying gravel chippings left and right. The door clunked; a solidly built man in uniform stepped out, and after a brisk salute, crunched towards them.

'Sergeant Awbrite, sir. Inverness Constabulary.'

'Good afternoon, Sergeant,' said Willoughby. 'I must apologise at once for wasting your time. My father, Sir Lyall, took the Rolls and forgot to tell me.'

A deep sigh reverberated from beneath the policeman's luxuriant moustache; it quivered like a mouse in a thunderstorm. Awbrite looked at Willoughby for five full seconds, analysing every nuance of his body language before responding:

'*Really?*' he said, glancing at each of the Thymes in turn. He had the penetrating gaze of an eagle, Justin decided, as the sergeant's eyes hovered over his flattened-down hair and unlaced trainers. 'I'll still be required to file a full report, sir. Regulation procedure.'

Sir Willoughby's heart sank to his boots; Justin's heart sank even lower – to roughly where his coffee mugs might have been, if he'd still been wearing them.

Willoughby tried desperately to think, but the only thought that came into his head was how much the big white squad car with its sleek stripe reminded him of a gigantic whisky marmalade sandwich. 'Perhaps you'd like to step inside, Sergeant,' he suggested. 'I'm sure cook will be able to rustle up some tea and cakes.'

'Thank you, sir,' replied Awbrite, brightening a little. 'Don't mind if I do.'

'This way,' sighed Willoughby.

The Thymes marched to the kitchen in silence, listening to the thump of their hearts and the squeak of the policeman's highly polished boots. As Sergeant Awbrite entered the kitchen, Mrs Kof dropped an enormous soup tureen – and it didn't bounce. With an almighty crash, it shattered into at least a googol pieces.

Everyone gasped. Sir Willoughby jumped, Grandpa Lyall nearly collapsed – but Justin and Robyn nudged each other, guessing at once what had alarmed the cook: she thought the sergeant had come to arrest her. Robyn propelled Mrs Kof into the pantry, reassuring her in her native tongue. Justin filled the kettle.

Sergeant Awbrite paid scant attention. Clumsy cooks were no concern of his; he had his duty to perform. He removed his peaked cap, revealing a bald head that looked as if he polished it as vigorously as his boots. The sergeant was one of those men who had thick, dark hair growing on each side of his head, but absolutely zip on top. Several pairs of eyebrows rose in astonishment. Unaware of the suppressed giggles behind him, Awbrite pulled a stool from under the kitchen table and balanced himself upon it. After finding the correct page in his notebook he cleared his throat:

'Fourteen-hundred hours: received notification of the afore-mentioned stolen vehicle. I proceeded to make inquiries. Reports of a circus midget acting suspiciously in the proximity of a vehicle matching my description, led me to deduce ...'

CRASH!!!! A priceless Spode teapot found itself effectively converted into subatomic particles. Justin deduced that the shine from the aforementioned domed skull had dazzled Mrs Kof, causing her to drop it in the proximity of her huge bare feet.

Undeterred, the policeman cleared his throat a second time: 'Led me to deduce ...'

'Is this *really* necessary, Sergeant?' asked Sir Willoughby. 'The car *is* safe in the garage. Why not forget all about it and have an éclair?'

Sergeant Awbrite looked tempted. Willoughby beckoned urgently to Robyn, emerging from the pantry with a tray of Mrs Kof's confectioneries. Apart from éclairs there were custard tarts, triple-chocolate brownies, toffee meringues and buttery triangles of strawberry shortcake. The sergeant hesitated for a moment then admitted defeat. He removed the offending page from his notebook, tore it to shreds and helped himself to a large sticky meringue.

115

⧗

'Imagine Nanny's face if she'd seen us scoffing like pigs,' sighed Justin, looking at the last custard tart. 'Seems a pity to waste it ...'

Robyn gave a strangled gasp. '*Manners* Poppet!' she said, in a perfect imitation of Nanny Verity's prim voice. 'Och, I remember the days when we served cucumber sandwiches so thin you could practically *see* through them.'

Sergeant Awbrite grinned. He swiped the remaining custard and wrapped it in a napkin. 'Can't resist,' he said. 'It's so custardy, I'm taking it ... er ... into custody!'

Mrs Kof grinned. 'You likes cuss-turds? You want ressi-pee off Missiz Kof?'

'*Cough*? What kind of name is that?' chuckled Awbrite. 'You'd better watch out,' he added, turning to Justin, 'or it won't be the Kof that carries you off, but the coffin she'll carry you off in!'

As jokes went, it had whiskers on it – yet somehow, they couldn't help laughing.

'And now, I really ought to be going,' said the sergeant. He brushed the crumbs out of his moustache and returned his cap to its polished perch.

Willoughby, Justin and Robyn accompanied him out to his squad car. He climbed in, wound down the window, and fixed Justin with a disconcerting stare.

'I'm still rather mystified about that circus midget,' he whispered. 'But whoever he is, I don't suppose he'll try driving again for another four years or so ... do you?'

Justin blushed. It was almost as if Awbrite's piercing gaze had read the truth in his eyes. 'No Sergeant,' he replied huskily, 'I'm certain he won't.'

'Splendid,' said the policeman, with the merest flicker of a wink. 'Well, goodbye Sir Willoughby, Master Thyme, Miss Thyme. Thank you for a most enjoyable tea.' He saluted in farewell, then flashed his headlights and hooted his horn as he drove out of the courtyard.

'Jolly nice chap,' remarked Willoughby, placing his hand firmly on Justin's shoulder. 'I sincerely hope he won't need to visit us again any time in the imminent future.'

'Er ... no,' Justin mumbled, never guessing that Sergeant Awbrite *would* be returning to the castle – and much sooner than *any* of them expected.

Sunday was one of those rare days when it felt warm enough to use the outdoor swimming pool. After a late breakfast Robyn floated on a Lilo, still bleary-eyed from her midnight internet chatting. Grandpa watched from the comfort of the Jacuzzi. Sir Willoughby lounged in a deckchair. He'd planned to read his newspaper – but someone had got to it first and cut a large hole in the front page. Huffing irritably, he closed his eyes and tried to imagine what Henny was doing at that precise moment; hacking through virgin rain forests or swinging across piranha-infested rapids probably. And having an absolute blast, if he knew her.

Lady Henny *was* having a blast – but not quite as her husband imagined. She was hopping round a smouldering campfire, yelling and looking uncommonly ruffled.

'BLAST! My left boot's vanished ... *again!* I know you two are responsible, and it's *not* funny. The pair of you oughta grow up!'

'It wasn't me,' said Hank, grinning broadly. 'Honest.'

'Me neither,' giggled Polly. 'And we didn't lose the compass, burn the map ... or collapse your tent last night either – so don't keep blaming us.'

Henny glared at them both, certain they were lying. She was about to point out that it was odd how nothing ever happened to any of *their* stuff, when Eliza ambled up, grunting excitedly.

'Eliza find gorillas today. Meet silverback gorillas.'

'Sorry Eliza. I told you yesterday, I need you to stay in camp and look after Alby.'

117

Eliza frowned over her laptop. 'Find gorillas tomorrow?'

'We'll see,' said Henny. 'Now Hank, you'd better fetch my darn boot or else ...'

The resounding thud of flabby feet on granite disturbed Sir Willoughby's daydreaming. He yawned squeakily and opened one eye. Mrs Kof was plodding towards the edge of the cliffs. She wore a voluminous black and white costume that made her look like a giant killer whale. Her arms and legs were as thick as tree trunks, slightly hairy, and with incredibly well-developed muscles. With a flourish, she removed her gypsy head scarf, and to Willoughby's astonishment he discovered she was even balder than Sergeant Awbrite. Without any exaggeration, her head was completely and utterly hairless. She seemed quite unabashed, and gave them all a cheery wave as she prepared to dive off the cliffs into the loch below.

'I swims across locket,' she yelled in her deep gruff voice. 'Maybe I catch fishy.'

Justin seriously doubted *that*. As Willoughby and every other Monster debunker delighted in pointing out, Loch Ness was hardly the most well stocked of waters. A sudden thought struck him: he hoped Mrs Kof wouldn't frighten poor Nessie.

Professor Gilbert had left the castle early with his binoculars and a packed lunch. Nobody had seen the Gilliechattans, though Tybalt the Octo-puss was busy spinning a huge web across the castle archway.

Justin decided to spend the morning drafting out some initial designs for his time machine. With his head now full of time-warps and wormholes he rarely gave a moment's thought to the mysterious origin of his watch – or its cryptic warning. 'I'll puzzle it out later,' he told himself. 'I need to complete my blueprints this week and scan them into my PC. Then I can generate some three-dimensional wire-frames and start building a scaled-down prototype model.'

He gazed at his tartan notebook, a glimmer of pride in his eyes. As theories went, it was years ahead of its time – but he still hadn't thought of a name for it. His brain clicked through its various hypotheses: the fusing of General and Special Relativity with String Theory, and his ideas about forks and loops weaving together like a tartan, to create the fabric of time. Then it came to him in a flash: *Tartan Theory*.

The time machine itself was another matter entirely. His initial preference was to design a device that avoided all contact with the earth's surface. He thought about how Foucault's pendulum moved in relation to the earth's rotational plane. The scale made it impracticable of course, but it was a starting point. Perhaps something like a huge gyroscope would work, *if* he could make it hover – though stability would doubtless become an issue. And he mustn't forget to give it adequate chronology insulation, something his father had overlooked with dire consequences. By lunchtime, he'd rejected all his early sketches and consigned them to the shredder. Never mind, he told himself, it's a work in progress. Alter your perspective; avoid needless complications; keep it simple. And above all ... *focus*.

There was *one* thing he *had* decided: although not essential, a degree of mobility would be useful. The logical solution was to adapt an existing vehicle. It would save considerable time and look much less conspicuous, but after yesterday's incident his father would never allow him to buy a car, much less tamper with those they owned. Anyway, a car was unnecessarily cumbersome; something smaller would be more convenient and simpler to convert.

It was Willoughby who unwittingly provided the solution. He'd been feeling sorry for Justin. After all, it was only natural for a boy of his age to want to drive, especially a boy with such precocious abilities. When *he'd* been Justin's age his obsession was motorbikes. Before he went to college, Sir Lyall had bought him a second-hand Norton and a sidecar. She was his pride and joy, and he was still driving her around when he married Henny.

In those days they'd lived in a cosy second floor flat in Edinburgh, but after they moved to the castle, he hardly used the bike at all. In time, Justin's income provided them with grander vehicles and the old Norton became superfluous. She'd languished at the back of Willoughby's workshop under a greasy tarpaulin. But he hadn't forgotten her.

After a picnic lunch – (Mrs Kof had packed a huge basket and left it on the kitchen table), Willoughby sneaked into his workshop on a mission. It took him at least twenty minutes to unearth the tarpaulin beneath umpteen years of junk. Eventually, perspiring and breathless, he reached his goal. Somewhat apprehensive, he peeled back the oily shroud, and saw to his relief that the old girl was in surprisingly good fettle. She had a patch of mildew on her saddle, and some specks of rust on her chrome handlebars, but nothing some rags and elbow grease couldn't fix in a jiffy. He spotted the registration plate attached to the fender and chuckled to himself: **BE 55Y** – *that* brought back memories.

He would never forget Henny's jealous fury on their third date. He'd tried to cut it short, saying he ought to get Bessy home before it started raining. Henny wrongly assumed that he was two-timing her, and demanded to meet Bessy in person. Later that night she discovered the truth, and during an unguarded moment as she muttered her apologies, Willoughby stole their first kiss. Yes, Bessy had certainly played a pivotal role in his life – and all because he never got around to fixing the sidecar's leaky roof.

Sir Willoughby opened its door and discovered a squat, coppery-eyed toad had taken up residence on the scarlet leather seat. It belched and blinked indignantly as he ushered it into a new home between a grubby oil can and his toolbox.

Willoughby stuck his head out of his workshop door and spotted Robyn wandering towards the castle, wrapped in a brightly coloured tartan towel.

'Do me a favour,' he yelled, beckoning her over. 'I'm going to polish this up as a surprise for your brother – problem is, it's too dingy in here, and I don't want him to see me wheeling it round the back. Nip up and distract him, would you.'

'Boys and their toys,' Robyn grumbled as she plodded off, leaving a trail of drips up the south tower staircase. 'Do they ever grow up?'

She diverted her brother's attention by "*accidentally*" knocking a bottle of ink across his latest design; not quite what Willoughby had in mind, but it did the trick.

'Hey! Watch out, clumsy,' yelled Justin, blotting the ink with a wad of paper tissues.

Robyn leaned out of the window and gave her dad the arranged thumbs-up sign. Suddenly, something caught her eye: a brilliant flash of light glinting enigmatically from the opposite shore of the loch. 'Quick, Dustbin,' she hissed. 'You know Morse code, don't you? I think someone's trying to signal by reflecting the sunlight off a mirror.'

'A heliograph?' asked Justin curiously. 'Wow ... let me take a look.' He wheeled his telescope over to the window and positioned himself in front of it.

'I saw it first,' said Robyn, giving him a big-sisterly shove. She peered through the telescope, and adjusted the powerful lens until the shore directly across from the castle came into crisp focus. 'It's only binoculars,' she sighed, disappointed that something so mysterious could turn out to be so mundane.

'It isn't code either,' said Justin, who had been trying to decipher the flashes. 'Not Morse code. I think it's just sunlight bouncing off the lenses as they scan to and fro.'

'*Wait* a *minute*!' gasped Robyn. 'It's Professor Gobbledygook.'

Justin elbowed her aside. He leaned forward and readjusted the focus. It was indeed Professor Gilbert – perched on a rock by the water's edge.

'He's spying on us,' said Robyn indignantly.

'Bird-watching.'

'People-watching more like. He's looking directly at the castle – and there isn't a single bird between us. Admit it Dustbin.'

She was absolutely right, but Justin had no intention of saying

121

so. 'Perhaps it's a *really* small bird,' he suggested. 'A goldcrest or something.'

Robyn snorted – a bad habit she appeared to have picked up off Nanny Verity. 'Let me take another look.'

Justin stepped back and braced himself for a fiery reaction. Professor Gilbert was no longer alone. Mrs Kof had emerged from the bushes, settled herself down beside him, and was sharing the contents of his haversack. The last thing he'd observed was the unsettling sight of her opening a beer bottle with her teeth.

Robyn leapt back from the telescope as if it had suddenly burnt her. 'WEIRDO!' she shouted, and flounced out of the room, slamming the door behind her.

Justin silently speculated whether she was referring to the cook or their tutor. It was a close call, though he strongly suspected the professor had mystified Robyn by his choice of feminine company – though feminine hardly seemed the most appropriate word.

With a sigh of resignation, Justin returned to his work, reminding himself that the best ideas often sprung to mind when you least expected them. He decided that the time machine, or chronopod as he called it, should be compact; suitable for one person travelling alone. It needed to be resilient enough to withstand dramatic changes of gravitational force, yet light enough to manoeuvre easily. He reviewed his sketches, but none of them looked right. The pods were too futuristic, and would look incongruous in the present, let alone the past. His design ought to be based on something retro, he thought, and chewed the end of his pencil as he waited for inspiration.

That evening, Sir Willoughby kept rubbing his hands together and hopping from one foot to the other, as if he could barely contain his excitement. Straight after supper, he took Justin out to his workshop.

'Meet Bessy,' he said, wheeling out his beloved old motorbike. 'She's all yours, but on one condition: you must promise to never drive her off Thyme property.'

For a moment Justin couldn't speak, and then, when he did, his words tumbled out in a burst of enthusiasm: 'Wow-*thanks*-Dad-it's-*FANTASTINCREDIBRILLIANT!*' he gasped, running his hands over the old Norton's gleaming chrome. Better than that, he thought to himself, it meets absolutely all my time machine design criteria. The sidecar makes the ideal chronopod; it's small and light, yet surprisingly strong – and having the motorbike attached solves all the mobility problems. I can run wires from the bike's battery to the subatomic wormhole-vortex accelerator, and there's easily enough room under the seat for the negative-energy generator and the anti-gravity unit. I'll need to line it with something that gives complete chronology insulation, but otherwise it's perfect.

He readily promised to remain within the boundaries of the Thyme estate, and fervently hoped that time travelling wouldn't break that promise. The castle had stood there almost seven centuries; so strictly speaking, he needn't ever *leave* their property – even on quite a lengthy journey into the past.

The following morning no mail was delivered. Justin assumed it was a postal strike, and made good use of the extra time before lessons checking the stocks of chemicals in his lab. He examined the contents of his store cupboard, jotting down the symbols of any elements that were missing. Three bottles were empty: chlorine – *Cl*, uranium – *U*, and einsteinium – *Es*; only one of which he anticipated needing.

There were seven specific elements Justin required: indium, sulphur, uranium, lanthanum, titanium, oxygen and nitrogen. He planned to combine these at ultra-high temperatures until they reached the correct thermal conductivity and dynamic viscosity. The resulting metallic compound – *pamangra-oxide* – would insulate the chronopod.

Later that evening, Willoughby helped Justin detach Bessy's

sidecar. Then, the two of them struggled across the courtyard with it, whilst no one was about. Once they were inside the castle, their problems really began. The staircase to the top of the south tower was narrow and twisty, which meant one person took the majority of the weight alone. Willoughby was hardly the fittest of men; his notion of a daily workout consisted of lifting alternate eyebrows and winking. By the ninth step his eyes were bulging, and if he could have summoned the breath he would have asked his son why the heck his laboratory couldn't have been on the ground floor. By an uncanny coincidence, Mrs Kof happened to turn up with a jug of lemonade, and came to their rescue. Looking oddly like Atlas, she hoisted the sidecar onto her beefy shoulders and marched up the staircase with no effort at all.

The rest of the week was uneventful, but without Nanny's strict eye on them both, Robyn spent longer online than ever, and Justin repeatedly worked until way after midnight, stripping out the old sidecar's interior. Then, on Friday morning, Professor Gilbert caught him off guard and bluntly asked what he was inventing. For once, the professor wasn't the one stuttering. Justin stammered, unable to think of an evasive yet truthful reply. Fortunately, Robyn, spying an opportunity to tease the professor, came to his rescue.

'Did you know you've got a secret admirer?' she asked, twirling a strand of hair around her forefinger. 'A ... er ... certain *someone* thinks you'd look funky without a beard.'

Professor Gilbert's ears turned a spectacular shade of magenta, and he was incapable of speech for several minutes. Despite his relief, Justin couldn't help feeling sorry for him and tried to put him at ease by turning the conversation to ornithology.

'Are you planning any bird-watching tomorrow, sir?' he asked.

'*"R-r-r-rising early in the morning,"*' sang Professor Gilbert. 'I'm p-pl-planning to record the dawn chorus tomorrow ... so I'll be leaving the c-castle while it's still dark.'

The professor was not the only person with plans for Saturday. During supper, Angus Gilliechattan stuck his head in through one of the dining room windows and informed the family he had an appointment in Edinburgh at nine o'clock the next morning.

'It's aboot ma wee bard,' he explained. 'I'll be teckin' 'im tae see a parrot chappie at tha zoo. He's bin coughin' all week and he soonds vairy hoarse.'

Burbage coughed solemnly right on cue. '*A horse, a horse, my kingdom for a horse!*' he remarked mournfully, and coughed again in case there had been any misunderstanding.

According to her postcard, Nanny Verity was due back at Inverness Station late that night. Half an hour after Willoughby left to pick her up, a surprising fax came through from Lady Henny:

> Expedition has been a total nightmare: lost maps, lost boots, lost film, lost passports – pretty near lost my mind! It's Hank and Polly, of course – but they deny it. Plan to fire them during return flight. Not that it'll make much difference; our careers are finished anyway. Catching flight shortly. Arriving Prestwick 9 a.m. Please collect me – can't face driving home with those two exasperating jokers!
> Henny.

Why on earth would Hank and Polly sabotage the expedition, Justin wondered. Surely they weren't silly enough to risk their own careers. Or were they? In the past, Henny had threatened them with the sack on numerous occasions, but they'd always charmed their way out of trouble. Maybe this time they'd gone too far.

Justin dialled his father's mobile number, frowning thoughtfully.

'Hi Dad. Mum's just sent a fax. She's wants picking up at nine tomorrow morning ... and I've decided to come with you if that's okay.'

'*Ohhh* ... do you *have* to?' sighed Sir Willoughby. 'I'll need to leave at five, and you're not exactly a morning person, are you? I don't want you making me late.'

'I've broken my plasma cutters, and I could do with another remote fusion-manipulator. We can get them at McFly's on the way back.'

'Can't you order them online?'

'Yes, but this'll be quicker. Don't worry, Dad ... I'll be up on time, I promise.'

'Hmm ... I'll believe *that* when I see it!'

Justin left the fax under the paperweight on the hall table then headed up to his lab to finish preparing the sidecar. But things didn't go according to plan. Shortly before one o'clock he realised there wouldn't be enough room for his anti-gravity unit and had to redraft the entire design. Engrossed in his work, the hours flew past, and by the time he collapsed into bed it was almost dawn.

'I *KNEW* you'd do *THIS*!' roared Sir Willoughby, bursting into his son's bedroom. He leaned over the bed and shook Justin by the shoulders. 'I've been waiting downstairs for the last *TWENTY* minutes.'

Justin opened one bleary eye, and tried to work out what his father was shouting about. 'Ahhhhh-mus've-slep-throo-larm,' he said, his words muffled by a chasmal yawn. 'Sorry, Dad. Get the car out; I'll be down in five minutes.'

'You'd *better* be – or I'm going without you!' Willoughby marched out of the room, slamming the door behind him.

Justin peered at his watch and groaned. 'Urghh ... barely two hours' sleep!' He leaned over the side of his bed, groping underneath for a stray sock – then rolled back, drew up one knee and tried to concentrate on his foot. His eyelids felt heavy; horribly heavy. He sank back against his pillow and let them close. 'Just for a few seconds ...' he murmured. 'Jusssssssst ...'

The next time Justin opened his eyes, the sun was streaming though his bedroom window. As the tower clock began striking, he lay still, counting the chimes under his breath, cringing as the numbers grew higher: '... six ... seven ... eight ... nine. *Ohhhh!* So that few seconds' nap lasted three and a half hours! I wonder how long Dad waited.' He rolled out of bed and trudged into the bathroom.

Once he was washed and dressed, Justin made his way down to the kitchen.

'Hello Nanny,' he yawned, giving her a welcome home hug. 'Where *is* everybody?'

'I assume your sister's still in bed; Sir Willoughby's gone to the airport – and he wasn't in the best of moods by the sound of it; your fake grandfather vanished in his Rolls Royce; and the cook left this,' said Nanny Verity, pointing to a note on the table. 'And yes, I *did* have a lovely time ... thanks for asking.'

'You're starting to sound like Robyn.'

'Heaven forbid,' Nanny snorted, and passed him Mrs Kof's note.

It was brief and to the point:

> ## Having Off – Day.
> ## Plenty foods in my Panties.

'I think she means pantries ... er pantry,' Justin explained. 'I hope she does anyway.'

She did. Mrs Kof had stocked the pantry with enough delicious

127

goodies to last them all day. Five minutes later, after Nanny had brewed a big pot of tea and Justin had almost summoned the energy to tackle a warm chocolate-filled brioche, the doorbell rang. As he plodded across the entrance hall, the telephone began ringing too.

'Get the phone for me, Nan,' he yelled. 'There's someone at the door.'

'*Please*,' said Nanny Verity, giving him a reproving glance.

As Justin opened the castle door, he heard Jock the postman chuckling.

'What Thyme is it?' he asked, handing Justin a wad of envelopes secured by a rubber band. 'Oh ... it's Justin Thyme.'

Justin cringed. He tossed Fergus his stick of Edinburgh rock and excused himself quickly, shutting the door with a firm click.

Nanny handed him the phone. 'It's Sir Willoughby,' she whispered, 'in a phone box.' She took the bundle of letters and started to flip through them.

Justin braced himself for the inevitable lecture. 'Hi Dad ... look, sorry about ...'

'Oh, so you've finally decided to get up, have you? Thanks to you I'm half an hour late and still miles from the airport. Your mum'll be frantic. The battery on my mobile's gone dead, and this is the last of my change ... so I need you to contact her for me.'

'No problem,' said Justin. 'Hang on a tick, Nanny's trying to say something. Oh ... oh ... all right Nanny. Dad, she says there's a letter for you marked EXTREMELY URGENT.'

'Bother,' groaned Willoughby. 'You'd better read it to me, quick before the pips go.'

Hearing his distant, muffled voice, Nanny tore the envelope open and withdrew a grubby sheet of paper. She handed it to Justin, a furrow on her normally placid brow. He unfolded the note and gasped. For a fraction of a second, he wondered if this was one of Hank and Polly's ridiculous practical jokes; then, with a stomach-churning jolt, he realised it was all horribly real.

'Listen *very* carefully Dad,' he said. But before he could utter another word he heard several loud pips, an ominous click, and then a continual buzzing noise. Sir Willoughby had been disconnected.

'What's to do Poppet?' Nanny asked anxiously.

'It's a ransom note,' replied Justin, shaking his head in disbelief. 'Mum's been kidnapped.'

Nanny Verity turned a ghostly white and gripped Justin's arm to steady herself. The entrance hall felt like it was spinning; her eyes glazed over and her knees buckled. 'I think ... I'm going to ... faint,' she murmured, thrusting the bundle of letters towards him. 'Here ... hold ... these ...'

Disaster is virtually inevitable once we open our minds to infinite possibilities. Why? Because we have to accept the infinite probability of taking the wrong fork, and heading for calamity. Even the most insignificant of decisions can result in a life-changing timefork. For the sake of our sanity, we are probably better off not thinking about what our future may hold.

For example: A lady bought her husband a new necktie. She found it difficult to decide between a striped tie and a spotted tie. Eventually she chose spots. That evening she gave the tie to her husband who pretended to like it even though he didn't. He decided that on his way to work the following morning, he would stop off at the store and exchange it for a striped tie.

As a result of that minor detour, he got caught in traffic and was late for work. Meanwhile, a fire broke out at his office killing all who were on time. He was only alive because his wife had poor taste in ties; had she bought him a present he liked - she would, in effect, have sentenced him to death. Try thinking about that next time you buy somebody a gift – it certainly won't make your choice any easier

Infinite parallel universes are suddenly a lot less appealing, but is the alternative any better?

CHAPTER NINE

Henny's Abduction

By the age of three, Justin had memorised pi to the ninety-ninth decimal place, and could mentally calculate the volume of a hypothetical dodecahedron, but none of that was any use to him right now. It wasn't that he couldn't think what to do; no, it was just that there were so many things that ought to be done immediately, his sleep-starved brain couldn't decide which to tackle first. Prioritise, he told himself, but *that* was easier said than done. A host of perplexing questions bombarded him like hailstones, thwarting his efforts to concentrate. Desperate to clear his mind, he shut his eyes and took several deep breaths. Gradually, his thoughts focused and things became clearer – but then Robyn appeared.

'Wake up, *dweeb*,' she said, giving him a hearty shove. 'What's up with Nanny?'

'Fainted, I think.'

'So you decide to have a power-nap. I fail to see the logic myself – but then *I'm* not the genius.'

Robyn knelt beside Nanny Verity and checked her pulse, then ensured her airways were clear and moved her into the recovery position. Finally, she gave her brother a look of pure disgust. With a sheepish grimace, Justin passed the ransom note to Robyn and waited silently as she read it through – twice.

'Envelope,' she demanded.

Justin handed it over.

'Hoax,' said Robyn authoritatively. 'Has to be – look at the postmark: local, first class. That means somebody posted it nearby, before teatime yesterday. Mum hadn't even left the Congo then ... so, she *can't* have been kidnapped.'

Justin could have kicked himself; it should have been obvious. Then a disturbing thought occurred to him: 'What if someone's planning to kidnap her when she lands?' he said. 'If they mailed the ransom note *after* abducting her, it wouldn't arrive until Monday. They'd want us to get it quickly; so perhaps they sent it yesterday – ahead of the actual kidnapping.'

Robyn admitted it was a remote possibility, but not one that especially worried her. 'She's got Hank, Polly and Eliza to protect her; and Dad ought to be there by now ... *he* won't let anything happen to her.'

Justin shuffled his feet. 'Dad's er ... running a bit late,' he mumbled, avoiding his sister's questioning gaze. 'And Mum decided to fire Hank and Polly during the flight home.'

'Typical!' Robyn glanced at her watch. 'Nine twenty-seven. We've probably just got time to warn her. Assuming the flight was on time, they'd taxi to the arrival gate by about ten past. At least another ten minutes through passport control ... even allowing for first class fast-tracking. Baggage claim next, then customs. She should be perfectly safe as long as we can stop her before she reaches the arrivals lounge.'

Justin was already dialling his mum's mobile, fervently hoping she had it switched on.

Lady Henny wouldn't have thought it possible, but the return journey was even more stressful than the flight out. Shortly after takeoff she informed her film crew that she no longer required their services. The news went down like a lead balloon. Hank glowered at her, ordered three double brandies and dispatched them one after the other; Polly shed a few silent tears and avoided all eye contact. Henny wasn't sure which was worse.

Eliza was firmly on Hank and Polly's side; or to be precise, she was on any side except Henny's. For virtually the entire expedition Henny had left her at base camp, baby-sitting, and as a result she hadn't met one single male gorilla. Eliza felt thoroughly disgruntled – and a gorilla rarely hides its feelings, gruntled or otherwise. She scowled at Henny continually, and whenever Henny spoke, replied by blowing big, wet raspberries.

Albion gazed happily at the miniature monitor attached to his armrest. The in-flight movie was a ridiculously complicated time-travel story way beyond his comprehension, but he seemed engrossed nonetheless. Henny tickled his bare toes and reached to pick him up.

Eliza grunted irritably, flicked open her laptop and rattled the keys. 'Baby watch TV,' she said, gesturing at Henny to leave Albion alone. 'No touch baby. Baby sleep soon.'

Being more familiar with Albion's moods, the gorilla knew the monotonous noise and flickering images would lull him to sleep, but Lady Henny ignored her, certain she knew best. Moments later, hysterical screaming filled the first class cabin. Eliza snatched Albion from his mother, and rocked him until he started to doze. After settling him back in his seat, she fixed Henny with an insolent stare.

'Baby not want human mother,' said an extremely strict voice. 'Baby only want gorilla. Baby love Eliza!'

Henny felt homesick; nobody seemed to like her any more. She picked up her cell phone, desperate to hear a friendly voice, but then she noticed the sign:

Mobile phones disrupt radio contact with Air Traffic Control
Do NOT use during flight ✕ Maximum penalty imposed

It was almost worth the risk, Henny thought – but not quite. She switched her mobile off, slipped it into the pocket of her safari jacket and gave a deep sigh.

Once the plane landed, things deteriorated rapidly. The official at Passport Control eyed them suspiciously and asked numerous pettifogging questions; clearly someone remembered Hank and Polly from the out-going trip. Henny fumed as they marched towards baggage claim, silently cursing officialdom and practical jokers. A large jostling crowd blocked their view of the luggage carousel, and, as Hank elbowed his way through, several people turned to stare at Eliza.

'Look, it's that talking gorilla off the telly,' said a boy, tugging his mother's sleeve.

'And *that*'s Lady Henny,' gasped his father. 'Remember what she always says: "*Thyme's running out now – so tune in next week.*"'

Henny cringed, and frowned at Polly who'd dreamt up the catchphrase during their first ever film-shoot. More people turned, craning their necks for a better view, and someone began whistling the *Thyme-Zone* theme tune. The boy hurried towards them, brandishing an autograph album. Polly groaned and scuttled off after Hank. With a sigh of resignation, Henny reached for her pen.

'No, I want Eliza's autograph,' the boy said.

'Gorillas can't write, Honey,' explained Henny, sounding slightly miffed.

Eliza opened her laptop. 'Gorilla draw picture,' she said, her computer replicating Marge Simpson's gravely voice. 'Eliza draw. Give Eliza pen.'

'Ooh, I want a picture,' shouted a little girl.

'Me too!'

In no time at all, Eliza was surrounded by a host of excited children all screaming and waving scraps of paper. Meanwhile, Hank and Polly wheeled their trolley out through customs, laughing at Henny's infuriated expression. Hank winked at Eliza and waved goodbye to baby Albion.

'Upstaged by an ape!' giggled Polly. 'That's show business!'

Gradually the crowd dispersed until only Henny, Albion and Eliza remained. Henny glared at the luggage carousel as the last lonely item, a luminous pink surfboard, passed for the umpteenth time. Her suitcase had gone astray. She glanced round, looking for someone to complain to, but the place seemed deserted. It was truly astonishing, she thought, how security guards vanished the second you needed one. Finally, an airport cleaner appeared to mop up a puddle of fizzy orange. Henny asked his advice about the missing case.

'Lost luggage department, that's what yer want,' he said lugubriously, leaning on the handle of his cart.

Henny was well aware of that. Trying *very* hard not to lose her patience, she asked for directions.

'Here ... let *me* try,' snapped Robyn, snatching the phone off her brother.

Justin sighed. 'I suppose she'll magically switch it on just because *you're* dialling.'

'What about voice-mail?'

'I've left two messages already ... both urgent.'

Robyn yelled at the telephone, shaking the receiver vigorously as if this would somehow help. '*Arghhh* ... SWITCH IT *ON woman!*'

'*Very* scientific,' said Justin, stifling a yawn as his sister glared at him.

'Switch what on, Poppet?' groaned a faint voice, between their ankles.

'NANNY,' they both cried, and knelt beside her dropping the phone.

'You fainted,' said Robyn, stating the obvious. 'Get her some water, Dustbin – *quick*!'

'Out through Customs, turn right, up the escalator, turn left, keep walking until yer see the sign for the restaurant,' the cleaner explained. 'But don't follow it, no – turn right, then take the lift down three floors, as yer exit the lift go left, then left again, then second right and it's the fifth door on the left. Or is it right? Anyway yer can't miss it.'

Henny felt like screaming. She rummaged through her pockets for a pencil and paper, but all she found was her cell phone. She pulled it out, pressed the *on* switch, and watched it light up. There were two messages.

'Do yer want *me* to teck yer?' said the cleaner.

Henny almost hugged him. The messages could wait; this was an opportunity too good to miss. 'If it's no trouble,' she sighed, slipping the mobile back into her pocket.

'None at all. I'm due for m'coffee break about now,' he said. 'I can take yer the short cut through the staff quarters.'

'Wait here you two,' said Henny, handing Albion to Eliza. 'I'll be right back.'

'Is that a feller in a gorilla suit?' asked the cleaner, peering short-sightedly at Eliza through his thick lenses. 'I'll bet he's blinkin' 'ot in there.'

Henny followed the man through a door marked private, trying to ignore his endless blether. He was an odd looking chap: he walked with a pronounced stoop, making it impossible to estimate his height. Owlish spectacles magnified his vivid blue eyes, and his mop of black hair made it hard to determine his age. Henny shrugged; he could be Chief of the BaAka pygmies for all she cared, as long as he helped locate her suitcase.

They turned down a narrow, empty corridor and stopped outside a door labelled *SUPPLIES*. The man removed a small glass bottle from his cart, unscrewed the lid, and poured some clear fluid onto a cloth.

'*THE PHONE!*' shrieked Robyn suddenly. 'We forgot all about it ... *quick*.'

Justin grabbed the receiver off the floor and began dialling his mother's number.

'Smell this new disinfectant,' said the man, suddenly straightening up. Then before Henny could decline he clamped the cloth firmly over her nose and mouth, locking her tightly in his grasp.

Henny held her breath and struggled valiantly, but it was useless; eventually she had no choice but to inhale the chloroform fumes, and slowly she started to lose consciousness. The man opened the supply-closet, pushed Henny roughly inside and slammed it shut. She slumped to the floor, collapsing beside an unconscious airport cleaner, stripped of his uniform and badge. The last thing she saw was the hazy outline of her suitcase; the last thing she *heard* was her cell phone.

'It's ringing,' Justin shouted, but when it was still ringing five minutes later, his relief turned to dismay. '*Still* no answer. Do you want to try yelling at it again?'

'No,' growled Robyn, grinding her heel into the hall rug. 'We're probably too late.'

The bogus airport cleaner removed his disguise. Beneath the ill-fitting cleaner's uniform he wore an immaculate suit and tie; around his neck hung a stethoscope. He stuffed the chunky spectacles in his pocket, replacing them with an old-fashioned monocle. Finally, he removed the black wig and attached a false moustache to his upper lip. The transformation was complete. He hurried along several corridors emerging in the arrivals lounge of the airport terminal. He marched to the information desk and introduced himself to a young woman busy glossing her lips.

'Professor Nation,' he said in an overly refined Edinburgh accent. 'I'm collecting a patient of mine, with severe mobility problems. I phoned ahead to request a wheelchair. I trust you have it ready.'

Without looking up, the woman smacked her lips a couple of times, examining them in a hand mirror to give herself time to think. No one had told *her* about having a wheelchair ready, but the doctor needn't know that. The airport had strict guidelines concerning the care of disabled travellers; they couldn't afford any bad publicity.

'I'll have one brought for you immediately,' she said, her radiant smile displaying her lustrous lips to perfection. 'Just sign here, sir.' She lifted the receiver of the internal phone system and dialled customer relations.

'What if she's unconscious?' asked Justin, finally putting the receiver down.

Robyn shuddered. 'I think it's time we phoned the police.'

A tear trickled down Nanny Verity's face, and her lower lip quivered.

'Mmm ... I guess so,' said Justin hesitantly, not entirely certain how his dad would react. He suspected the kidnap had something to do with the time machine, and Sir Willoughby wouldn't want anyone learning about *that* – even the police. A hot prickle of guilt flushed Justin's cheeks; *if only I hadn't made Dad late*, he thought.

'What about Sergeant Awbrite?' Robyn suggested. 'He seemed okay.'

'There must be *something* we can do,' sniffed Nanny.

Justin wasn't listening. He was pacing up and down, muttering to himself: 'It's *so* frustrating being thirteen. A few years older and I could drive there myself. *No* – I'd still be too late. Aarghh ... come *on*! I've got to do something *now* – and all I've got is brain-power and a telephone. Wait! A *TELEPHONE* ... that's *it*!'

He checked his watch. It might just work, he thought. As long as nothing else has delayed Dad, he should be arriving at the airport any time now.

'Listen, you two,' he said. 'I've got a plan.'

The bogus medical professor pushed his wheelchair along the narrow corridor to the supply-closet. Once again, he had slipped through a door marked private without being stopped; nobody ever questioned him in his doctor's disguise. *Yes* Doctor, *this way* Doctor, people said, terrified of litigation in the event of someone's death. Tricking that hapless cleaner had been simple, he grinned to himself; getting Lady Henrietta Thyme safely out of the airport shouldn't present any difficulties either.

Justin's plan had three distinct parts; one for each of them – and if it worked, gave them a reasonably good chance of rescuing Henny. Robyn ran to the west tower and hurtled up the thirty-nine steps to her room at the top; Justin hurried to his lab in the south tower. Meanwhile, Nanny Verity dialled the enquiry number of Prestwick airport.

'Customer infor*mat*ion ... how can I *help* you?' said the glossy-lipped woman, in the irritating sing-song voice all telephonists seem to adopt.

'I need to speak to Sir Willoughby Thyme,' said Nanny. 'Please page him at once.'

'Is it an e*mer*genceee?' sang the woman.

'Yes.'

'Please hold the *line* then.'

Nanny Verity listened to the muffled click of a microphone being switched on, and a loud static thud as the woman tapped it with a shiny fingernail. Nanny winced, and held the receiver away from her ear. After a discordant chime, she heard the woman's voice amplified – only this time she sounded as if she was holding her nose.

'Paging Sir Willoughby *Thy*me – please come to customer infor*mati*on – you have an emergency *phone* call.'

Five minutes passed.

'I'm afraid we're unable to lo*cate* him.'

'Keep trying,' Nanny insisted. 'It's extremely urgent.'

The queue into the airport car park had been horrendous. Then, when Willoughby reached the kiosk the attendant refused to accept his fifty pound note, saying it would use up all of his change. While a dozen irate drivers hammered on their horns, he dashed from car to car asking if anyone could break a fifty. After finding a parking space that seemed light-years from the terminal, it started spitting with rain. He turned up his collar, glanced at his watch, then trudged towards the distant building. Henny hated to be kept waiting. He imagined the look of exasperation on her face.

Lady Henrietta Thyme slept peacefully as Professor Nation dragged her out of the closet by her ankles. Clasping both hands around her waist, he hoisted her up and dumped her unceremoniously into the wheelchair, accidentally dislodging something from her pocket. A small metallic object fell to the floor with a clatter. Kneeling down, he fumbled beneath the chair and retrieved Henny's cell phone. He regarded it for a moment before tucking it into his own pocket. Yes, he thought, that might come in *very* handy indeed.

Henny snored noisily – and dribbled. The professor covered her with a big tartan blanket he'd just bought at the souvenir shop; it hid her distinctive clothes completely.

'Now to hide your famous face,' he sniggered. If anything, that was even simpler. From his pocket he pulled an oxygen mask, and slipped it over her nose and mouth snapping the elastic behind her head. Last of all, he placed the cleaner's thick spectacles over her eyes, and the straggly black wig on top of her short blonde hair. No one would ever guess this helpless invalid was really a jet-setting female explorer.

'Hey Presto!' he said, standing back to admire his handiwork. 'Another terminally sick patient for my exclusive sanatorium!'

In her room at the top of the west tower, Robyn switched her computer on. Her assignment was to contact Eliza. All Robyn had to do was compose a concise message that would grab the gorilla's attention, galvanising her to immediate action.

She typed a few short words, and then hesitated, examining the monitor to ensure they were perfectly clear and understandable. Yes, that should do the trick, she told herself. Using her mouse, she slid the cursor to the top of the screen and clicked SEND.

As Sir Willoughby stepped through the automatic sliding doors the first thing he heard was his name being broadcast over the Tannoy system; *that* didn't improve his mood at all.

'Celebrities!' he muttered under his breath. 'Not one *scrap* of patience. Justin must have contacted her by now. Couldn't she just have a cup of coffee and wait – or is that too much to ask? Clearly it *is*! I'll bet she's phoning from a taxi to say she's on her way home. I've come all this way for nothing.' He cast around for the customer information desk, and then strode over to it, his footsteps reverberating across the polished floor.

'Sir Willoughby Thyme,' he snapped at the perky-looking woman on duty. 'You have a call for me.'

A muted chime drew Eliza's attention to her laptop. She flipped it open and noticed the mailbox icon flashing in the top right-hand corner of the monitor. With remarkable sensitivity, she ran a huge forefinger over the mouse-pad, and clicked READ. She waited, listening to the gentle whirring of the hard drive as it converted Robyn's message into pictogram symbols. Seconds later they appeared on screen:

Eliza raised her eyebrows in mild surprise. It seemed urgent; and that bit about an alarm was perplexing. She read the message again to be certain she understood it:

> HENNY IN DANGER – HENNY LOST
>
> FIND HENNY – LISTEN ALARM
>
> FIND HENNY QUICKLY – SWITCH ON WEB-CAM

Eliza cocked her head. She could hear only two things: the crowd milling to and fro beyond the customs gate, and the occasional blast of wind from Albion's rear end – neither sounded remotely like an alarm bell.

'Och, Sir Willoughby, thank goodness,' gasped Nanny Verity, fighting back the tears. 'That letter ... the one young Master Justin was going to read to you ... it was a ransom note. Lady Henny's been kidnapped.'

For an instant Willoughby thought he was dreaming; soon his alarm clock would ring, waking him up in good time for Henny's flight. Any second now ...

'Are you still there?'

'Yes Nanny,' muttered Willoughby, almost too depressed to reply. It *wasn't* a dream. Inevitable really. He'd been expecting something like this ever since Justin first mentioned the time machine. His heart sank as he glanced round the crowded terminal. He knew better than anyone what a master of disguise their enemy was; he could be anywhere.

'Master Justin has a plan,' Nanny continued, her voice quavering a little. 'Now listen very carefully ...'

Professor Nation paused behind the door marked private that opened into the busy arrivals lounge. The last crucial stage, he thought, taking a deep breath. All too often this was the time when things went wrong. So far, everything had gone smoothly – almost too smoothly. He couldn't afford to get overconfident; you always had to expect the unexpected. He grasped the handles of the wheelchair and pushed the door with his back. It was the fourth time he'd opened the door that morning – and *this* time his exit did *not* go unnoticed. A security guard marched towards him.

Eliza slid the laptop into her rucksack, and clipped the web-cam to the front strap; then tucking Albion under one arm, she stalked out of Baggage Claim.

Two customs officials eyed her apprehensively. Both had seen her before, on numerous occasions – with that eccentric TV explorer and her film crew, though – never alone. Having no desire to search a gorilla, they decided she was unlikely to have anything to declare, and waved her through. Eliza sauntered past, gazing at them with ill-concealed contempt.

He'd found them – well, *almost* found them. Justin knew he'd kept a record of the code numbers; the problem was remembering how to access it. The document was encrypted, and there were two separate passwords for maximum security; one had seven letters, the other, six. But what were they? He'd been just eleven years old when he'd chosen them, and hadn't opened the document since. Horribly aware that precious minutes were ticking by, Justin frowned at the computer screen, his mind a complete blank.

'What's the *matter* with me this morning?' he groaned, pounding his forehead with a clenched fist. 'It can't be *that* much of a puzzle!'

That was it. Suddenly, his brain felt as if it fizzed with sparks of electricity and the passwords came to him in a flash: Two words, both meaning puzzle. He typed them swiftly and clicked CONFIRM. The computer bleeped, the screen flickered, and there they were: the PIN numbers to each of his family's cell phones. All he had to do was dial his mum's PIN number, and her mobile would emit a deafening alarm – and only *he* had the code to switch it off. It was the invention that had earned him his millions – but now, he hoped it would save his mother from being kidnapped.

He keyed the thirty digit number into his cell phone, careful not to make *any* mistakes: 815234152515212318920 5 ...

'Let me get that for you, sir,' called the security guard, reaching for the door and holding it wide-open.

'Thank you, my good man,' said Professor Nation, nearly forgetting his fake accent in the momentary panic. 'This really is a *most* efficient airport. I shall write to the management. What's your name? I'd like to bring your friendly service to the attention of your superiors.'

The security guard blushed, and pointed to the name Gideon Paramax on his ID badge. The professor feigned considerable interest, but his focus was somewhere else entirely …

… 11191919. He'd done it. After double checking, Justin placed his mobile, face up, on the desk beside him.

Seconds later, he was online to Eliza's laptop. Through her web-cam he could see virtually everything *she* saw – even if it was a little bumpy. He slipped a DVD into the disc drive and clicked RECORD.

As soon as the foolish guard stopped babbling, the professor moved on, pushing the wheelchair ahead of him. His eyes darted from side to side, scanning the terminal for signs of danger. A gigantic gorilla prowled towards him from the left; Sir Willoughby Thyme hovered about twenty metres to his right. Both looked alert and were scanning the crowd. So far, they'd overlooked him, but he wasn't safe yet. He was still some thirty or forty paces from the automatic sliding doors to the car park – and he daren't rush. Slowly, almost casually, he ambled forwards, counting each step under his breath.

Justin grabbed his mobile phone, then snatched a quick look at the scene through Eliza's web-cam. Several people backed away from the big gorilla clutching their children's hands. In the distance, he could see his father poised for action. It was now or never. Hoping he wasn't too late, he took a deep breath and pressed DIAL.

For a minute or so, everyone in the terminal froze in shock at the sudden ear-splitting sound of the alarm. A few peered outside, assuming the noise was a police car; others sniffed the air, trying to detect any hint of smoke. Only three people kept moving: Eliza and Willoughby ran towards the noise, and rushed round in circles, desperate to spot Henny's face amongst the crowd.

'Find the phone and we've found our kidnapper,' Willoughby kept muttering to himself. The noise grew louder as he drew closer. Finally, both he and Eliza pinpointed the source simultaneously, and hurtled towards a smartly dressed man. As they reached him, he removed the blaring cell phone from his pocket and stared at it in bewilderment. Well, that beats all, he thought – then suddenly he found himself pinned to the floor by a 267 pound gorilla, and everything went black.

Meanwhile, the kidnapper kept on walking – right out of the terminal and across the car park. There was no way he could have guessed about the alarm; no way at all. But all his instincts had warned him: *ditch the phone* – never keep anything incriminating. Planting it in that hapless security guard's pocket had been a stroke of genius, he thought, but the diversion it created was pure luck.

Justin gnawed his lip pensively as he viewed the ensuing pandemonium. It had all gone pear-shaped. Albion screamed and pounded his tiny fists on Eliza's chest. Willoughby stood with both hands in the air, surrounded by burly security guards. It didn't seem real; it was like watching a DVD. If this was a movie, Justin thought, any second now the police would appear.

8

Study the "necktie" scenario again, this time taking the alternate viewpoint: that the fabric of time is unalterable and our timelines fixed.

From this angle, we may claim that the man was meant to live – and therefore, his wife was predestined to buy the spotted tie he hated. But that doesn't make sense. If he was predestined to live, how could a mere tie alter anything? Even if he had adored the tie, and been on time for work, he would still have lived – perhaps escaping the inferno by slipping out of the office to buy his wife some flowers.

This scenario seems a whole lot more appealing than the previous one – but only if your predestined role is that of survivor. If the man had been doomed to die, being absent from his office wouldn't help him. He would die anyway – perhaps killed accidentally by the fire engine hurrying to extinguish the flames. This is a depressing thought. It would mean that every reasonable precaution taken for our safety is useless; we have absolutely no control over any aspect of our lives. Suddenly this option does not look so attractive either.

Should we believe in the existence of an infinite parallel multiverse - or do we accept that our destiny is irrevocably mapped out? Perhaps the most feasible option lies somewhere between the two ...

CHAPTER TEN

Lack of Thyme

Failure was not something that Justin was accustomed to. It had been two and a half years since his last failure – or, to be precise, his only failure. The teleportation incident had depressed him terribly, and although Nanny Verity had told him to look on the bright side, he hadn't been able to find one. He couldn't find one now either.

'Flux!' he shouted, slamming his fist on the desk. 'The kidnapper must've ditched Mum's phone. If only I'd dialled a minute or two earlier, Eliza would've caught him for certain.'

An uncomfortable feeling of guilt swept over him as he recalled Nanny's warning about keeping his eye on the time and not working too late. Was lack of sleep the reason he'd struggled to remember the phone-alarm passwords? And if Sir Willoughby had arrived at the airport on time, would they have been able to thwart the kidnapper?

'It's all my fault,' Justin groaned, glaring at the image from Eliza's web-cam. If anything, he decided, his interference had made things worse. Not only had he failed to save his mum, but his dad appeared to be pleading with the guards, and Eliza had a tranquilliser gun pointed at her. And here he sat, over 130 miles away – helpless. The frustration felt like a knot of razor wire tightening in his stomach.

Justin wished he could hear what they were saying, or at least lip-read, but Albion's blurred features kept looming towards the screen, distracting him. Poor Alby; judging from his scrunched expression he was concentrating on a spectacular bowel movement. Justin watched, unaware that his brother's whiffy pants were about to save the day.

The chief security guard frowned at the gathering onlookers. "Disperse this crowd,' he barked at a couple of his officers. 'Tell them there's no call for panic.' Then, glaring at the cell phone beside Eliza, added: 'And someone stop that infernal racket."

No one attempted to retrieve the mobile, but the officer wielding the tranquilliser gun, kept its sights trained on Eliza. During his nine years' service at the airport, such a situation had never arisen before. Furthermore, he wasn't familiar with his weapon. The dart gun was a legal requirement in case a ferocious dog escaped from its transportation crate, but so far, the odd runaway pooch had never required anything more drastic than a length of rope and a dog biscuit. Dogs were one thing; gorillas, however, were entirely another.

The tranquilliser gun held only one dart at a time, leaving no margin for error. It contained a powerful morphine-based sedative, and to calculate the correct dosage the guard needed to estimate Eliza's body weight. Unfortunately, guessing the size of gorillas had never been part of his job description, and even if it had, there was no guarantee it would help. What worried him most was that the metabolic rate of each species altered the speed at which the sedative took effect. If the dose was inadequate, the gorilla might become angry and violent, but too much morphine and there was a danger it would collapse instantaneously, crushing the baby as it fell. The guard reminded himself that the safety of the baby was paramount.

Eliza read the scenario with her customary depth of insight. She'd watched Henny use a tranquilliser gun on numerous occasions, and had no desire to be on the pointy end. She remained calm, thinking the whole situation through, and realised that Albion was the only thing between her and a swift route to oblivion. At that precise moment, it became abundantly clear to everyone within a 50 metre radius, (in possession of two fully operative nostrils), that Albion needed changing – *urgently.*

Moving slowly, so as not to alarm the security guard, Eliza opened her rucksack and pulled out a clean nappy, talcum powder and a tub of chamomile bottiwipes. She placed Albion on the floor in front of her, and leaned over to remove his soiled nappy, gambling that the guard wouldn't risk firing at her in that position. With the efficiency of a professional nanny, she cleaned Albion's rear end, powdered it, then carefully fastened the Velcro tabs on his fresh nappy; Albion chortled happily throughout the entire procedure, and the security guard started to relax; clearly the gorilla was *not* the hazard he'd anticipated. Eliza breathed a little easier – but she wasn't out of danger yet.

As Justin viewed the silent drama, it suddenly occurred to him that the alarm on Henny's cell phone must still be ringing, and unless someone keyed the correct code into it, it would continue blaring indefinitely. He decided to rectify the matter at once.

Eliza gathered the soiled nappy and dirty wipes, tidying them away into a scented biodegradable bag. From the guard's posture and body language she could see that his tension had decreased. Perhaps this was a good time to negotiate, she thought. Slowly, she slid the laptop out of her rucksack and flipped it open. The guard watched in genuine astonishment. He cast a quick sideways glance at his superior, still busy interrogating Sir Somebody-or-other, the tall, well-spoken gent with untidy hair. He decided not to interrupt.

A faint chime drew Eliza's attention to the mailbox icon. It was another e-mail – and a strange one: A row of thirty numbers followed by two pictogram symbols:

SWITCH-OFF ALARM

Despite the clarity of the message, Eliza's brow furrowed thoughtfully. She had no problems counting; her numerical skills were comparable to those of a teenage human. Her expression of rapt concentration was for another reason entirely: she was memorising the entire code. Why gorillas were born with such incredible memories had always been a mystery to Justin, but nature had its reasons – elephants were not the only creatures who never forgot.

With her head tilted slightly to one side, Eliza considered the guard, trying to assess which voice in her repertoire would be most suitable. She scrolled down the pictogram symbols in her vocal menu, dismissing each in turn until she came to the very last one:

XAVIER POLYDORUS

Xavier Polydorus, or The Xtraordinary Xavier as he called himself, was a famous conjuror and hypnotist. He always wore a voluminous black cloak lined in scarlet silk, had intensely piercing blue eyes and a rather fake looking moustache. Eliza first saw his performance on a late-night satellite TV broadcast. His calm, hypnotic voice had utterly mesmerised her, and she instantly decided to record a sample of his speech for her computer to replicate synthetically. He had the unique distinction of being the first male voice she'd ever chosen to adopt. She could see the huge potential: where one of her usual voices failed to get her her own way, the Xtraordinary Xavier might just succeed. But disinclined to use a male voice, she'd almost forgotten his symbol in the voice menu – until now. Eliza's dextrous fingers tickled the keyboard:

'I switch off alarm now,' said the Xtraordinary Xavier soothingly. 'I make bad noise go away. I stop loud noise for you now.'

The security guard looked even more astonished – but not especially concerned; the calm, hypnotic voice had worked. After a furtive glimpse at his superior, he smiled peacefully and nodded. Slowly, Eliza reached for the phone, and gradually drew it towards herself with one big, black digit. She lifted it gently, keyed in the entire code from memory, and instantly the alarm stopped ringing.

'Thank *goodness*,' said the chief security guard without turning round.

'No problem,' replied the Xtraordinary Eliza.

Hearing the unfamiliar yet strangely captivating voice, the chief glanced back and did a conspicuous double take. 'It can *TALK?*' he gasped.

'Yes,' snapped Willoughby. 'That's what I've been trying to tell you. She's a tame gorilla. You must've seen her on my wife's TV show. We were trying to prevent Henny from being abducted. The kidnapper can't have got far. You should be looking for *him*, not questioning me.'

'But ...'

'Listen, I know it sounds unlikely, but a ransom note arrived after I left home this morning. I can prove it; Eliza, get Justin online and ask him to e-mail a copy.'

Eliza stood up and prowled over towards them. The security guards edged back.

'No need, sir,' said the chief. 'We'll take your word for it. Now, in the interest of airport security, we must request that you and your travelling circus leave. If your wife really has been kidnapped, I strongly recommend you contact the police – at once.'

⌛

'I really think we ought to phone the police,' said Robyn, as soon as Justin had finished telling her and Nanny about the disappointing outcome of his plan.

Justin nodded gloomily. 'I guess so. I'll do it now.'

'Not until you've had some breakfast,' said Nanny firmly. 'Half the morning's gone already and neither of you have eaten a thing. Besides, I think you should leave the grown-ups to deal with the police; I expect Sir Willoughby's contacted them already.'

Justin and Robyn exchanged exasperated glances. Nanny Verity was probably the only person in the castle who still insisted on treating them both like children. Robyn opened her mouth to protest, but Justin nudged her. He could see that Nanny was trying to be brave for their sake.

'There's no point in upsetting her,' he whispered. 'And anyway, I want to check a few things out before the police get involved.'

Despite Nanny's protestations, Justin insisted a proper breakfast would have to wait. To placate her, Robyn grabbed a large plate of almond croissants and a jug of orange juice, then hurried to the south tower after her brother.

The first thing Justin wanted to do was to review the DVD recording of the scene through Eliza's web-cam. He hadn't noticed anything significant at the time, but perhaps there was something he'd overlooked. The initial viewing was unproductive – the computer monitor too small to show any real detail.

'What about the big plasma screen?' Robyn suggested.

Justin promptly removed the DVD from the disc drive, and they both slid down to his private sitting room two floors below.

'Watch the crowds,' said Justin, his face pale and tense. 'The kidnapper might've planted Mum's phone in the guard's pocket *after* it started ringing.'

'*Arghhh*, it's hopeless,' groaned Robyn. 'As soon as Eliza starts running, the camera shakes too much to see *anything*. Try it in slow-mo.'

Justin notched the speed down to one-sixteenth. Initially it looked as if everyone in the terminal froze when the alarm rang, and only Willoughby showed any sign of animation – but one other person was moving the *whole* time. 'Look! That smartly dressed chap pushing the wheelchair; he glances towards Dad and keeps on walking. Suspicious or what?'

'FREEZE IT,' Robyn ordered.

Justin pressed the pause button, and the image became motionless.

Robyn grabbed the remote. 'Where's the zoom function?'

'There.'

She pressed the button three times, gradually enlarging the wheelchair until it filled the entire 56 inch screen.

'Look,' she said, pointing to the tartan blanket covering the occupant of the chair.

Justin saw at once what she meant: a slender hand was just visible, protruding from under the blanket. Robyn highlighted it then pressed the zoom button again – and kept on pressing until the whole screen showed nothing but the hand. The image was blurred and grainy, but it looked as if she was correct.

'Can you clean it up a bit?'

'I guess so,' said Justin. 'Though I'll have to do it on my PC.'

They raced back upstairs, and five minutes later were both staring at a crisp, sharp image on the computer monitor. Robyn grinned triumphantly. On the hand was an engagement ring: a giant opal surrounded by thirteen diamonds. When Henny had chosen the ring, Willoughby tentatively suggested that it might be unlucky, but Henny scoffed at the idea. *I have a good feeling about it,* she insisted. Willoughby relented. Several years would pass before he realised Henny *always* had a good feeling about expensive jewellery.

'Well done, Bobs,' whispered Justin. 'Mum was right about that ring. We're one step closer to finding her.'

Sir Willoughby felt depressed; although he'd been annoyed with Justin for making him late, he felt entirely responsible for Henny's disappearance. After thirteen years of maintaining complete secrecy, he'd blurted the forbidden words *time machine* out loud. Evidently somebody had overheard him – and not just anybody – probably his old enemy from *TOT*.

Rain pounded on the windscreen. Willoughby flicked a lever, speeding up the wipers, and peered in the rear-view mirror, irritated by the continual bleep-bleep-bleep of a computer game. Eliza scowled back at him, looking cramped and uncomfortable; the Beetle's designer hadn't taken the vital statistics of a mountain gorilla into account. Even Albion, normally so sunny and placid, grizzled and grumped, weary of the endless travelling. Willoughby glanced at his watch; it would be at least another couple of hours before they got back to the castle.

'Cheer up, little chum,' he called over his left shoulder, giving Albion a reassuring grin. 'Perhaps he's thirsty Eliza – try giving him his bottle.'

Eliza paused *Ape-Invaders* and rummaged in her rucksack. Meanwhile, Sir Willoughby grabbed his mobile phone, and glared at the illuminated display. No signal – and the battery was still recharging. He needed to talk to his son. A pay phone was out of the question – much too public, and Henny's cell phone wouldn't work properly until Justin reset it. He *had* to find out what had happened. The conversation with Nanny Verity had been hopelessly vague. *Young Master Justin has everything under control,* she'd assured him. *You just listen out for that alarm on Lady Henny's phone.* There hadn't been time to ask her *anything*. Now his brain was positively bursting with questions, and there wasn't a single person around to answer them. Or was there? Glancing again at his rear-view mirror a sudden thought occurred to him.

'I wish we could see his face,' muttered Justin. 'The few seconds he's in shot, his head's turned the wrong way completely – and that navy suit gives nothing away.'

Robyn grabbed her brother's arm. 'Hey look – I think there's something on his sock.'

Justin highlighted the kidnapper's left ankle and zoomed right in. Sure enough, a miniature playing card pattern was barely discernible.

'*Cards!*' growled Robyn. She slouched back in her chair, her excitement snuffed out like a candle. 'I'd hoped it was a monogram. That's useless.'

'*Perhaps*,' said Justin, 'but it's all we've got ... apart from the ransom note.' He cleaned up the playing card image, and saved it. Then, while it was on his mind, he slid the ransom note into his scanner and copied it to his hard drive. 'The police are going to need this – though it's a bit late dusting it for fingerprints now we've all handled it. I should've thought of that.'

Before returning the note to its envelope, Justin took one last look:

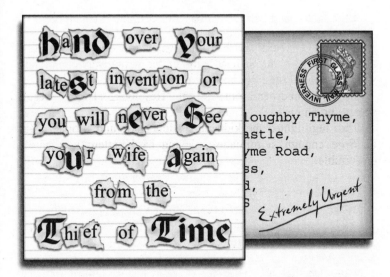

It was a stereotypical ransom note, made from scraps of torn newspaper, but the closer Justin looked, the more convinced he felt that the lettering was significant. Still blaming himself for what had happened, he exported the scanned note to an image file and magnified it, desperate to find *anything* that might help his mother.

'What happened to Hank and Polly?' asked Willoughby.

He waited patiently as Eliza's huge fingers clattered over her laptop.

'Gone,' the computerised voice replied simply. 'Henny not like jokes. Too many jokes.'

'Where did they go?'

'Gone away. Hank cross. Polly sad. Not like Henny now.' Then after a brief pause she asked: 'Where Henny?'

'I thought I was the one asking the questions,' Willoughby groaned. He took a deep breath. 'Henny's been kidnapped and ...'

Eliza interrupted. 'New word,' she said. 'Not understand.'

Willoughby sighed. How does one explain kidnapping to a gorilla, he thought. Oh dear – it's going to be a long drive home.

Justin stared intently at the magnified ransom note on his computer monitor; the clues were there, he was certain. Using his mouse he clicked COPY and PASTE then isolated all the elaborate gothic-style letters by dragging them to one side of the screen. Robyn watched, her irritation escalating by the second.

'What are you *playing* at dweeb?' she yelled. 'Mum's in danger and you're solving puzzles. Try rearranging this: *GRIP – DUSTBIN – A – GET!*'

Justin replied in measured tones, but his muscles were taut and a threadlike vein pulsed on his left temple. 'If you've got any better ideas, I'd love to hear them.'

'Fffhuhhh!'

'I'll take that as a no, then,' said Justin, returning to his painstaking task. 'There's a time for action – and when it comes, I'll gladly stand back and leave you to jump in with both feet. But right now, the only way we can help Mum is by analysing our one decent clue.'

'Explain!' snapped Robyn.

'It's a hunch. Actually, what you said about the envelope gave me the idea.'

Robyn snatched it off the desk and glowered at it. 'All I said was: the postmark means someone mailed it locally before six yesterday. Typewritten address. Other than that ... well, it's just crumpled and grubby ... as if it was hanging around a few days before it got mailed.'

'Five days I suspect. The ransom note confirms it. Look for yourself, applying the same methodology.'

Simmering with impatience, Robyn stomped over to the window and unfolded the note. To her astonishment, an image of the kidnapper formed in her mind as she read it.

'He's an amateur; a pro would demand cash and address the

note to you ... you're the one with the dosh. He hasn't given us a deadline or directions about paying the ransom. If he made the note days ago, then he's hopelessly inefficient; he probably planned this on a whim, not realising Mum was out of the country. He must be a stranger or he'd know Dad's inventions are worthless. And he's even spelt Thyme wrong; he calls himself the Thief of T-I-M-E.'

'Illogical logic,' said Justin, shaking his head. 'Watch this ...'

The rain eased off and a small patch of blue sky appeared between the dark clouds. Willoughby sighed with relief; only an hour or so to go now, he thought. Albion was sleeping soundly, Eliza had just dozed off, and the roads were quiet. But Willoughby's mind was racing, plagued by a perpetually nagging fear that his old enemy from the past had successfully infiltrated Thyme Castle. What other explanation could there possibly be? He hoped that despite the emergency, his son would still heed his solemn warning never to mention the time machine to anyone – *anyone* at all.

Using his mouse, Justin rearranged the ten torn paper shapes on his computer screen, lining them up until they fitted together like a jigsaw puzzle.

Robyn couldn't help being impressed, but she had no intention of showing it. 'So *that's* why you assume he made it last Sunday. *Big deal!* At least it explains his spelling of time.'

'Not entirely,' replied Justin, lowering his voice to a whisper. 'I think *this* thief really *is* planning to steal time – or to be more accurate, a time machine.'

Robyn rolled her eyes and groaned.

'Dad's inventions haven't always been worthless,' Justin continued. 'He built a time machine when you were just a baby.'

'As if!'

'It's true. Dad's kept it secret for years – but he told me everything last week, and now Mum's been kidnapped. It can't be a coincidence. Somebody must have overheard him talking, which means the kidnapper is someone we know.'

'You mean ... here at Thyme Castle?'

'Probably.'

Robyn shook her head, her pursed lips and derisive glance betraying her scepticism. 'You've been reading too many detective stories,' she muttered. '*And* science fiction. *Honestly* Dustbin, time travel isn't *real*.'

'The kidnapper thinks it is,' said Justin. '*That's* why he hasn't demanded cash; a time machine is worth *far* more. And the way he abducted Mum at a crowded airport proves he's pretty smart. But there's one thing that still baffles me: if he overheard Dad on Thursday, why wait until Sunday to make the ransom note?'

'And why not kidnap Mum on Friday before she left home?'

'Too much of a rush,' said Justin. 'He's a pro; it probably took him all week to plan things thoroughly. As for giving us no deadlines or instructions ... well, I'm certain we'll be hearing from him again in the very near future.'

Sir Willoughby's mobile phone emitted an elongated bleep and its battery icon turned green.

'Finally!' he sighed, steering the Beetle into a lay-by. 'Hardly seems worth phoning now, though – we're barely twenty minutes from home. But still ...'

He was about to press the speed dial for Thyme Castle when he spotted a miniature envelope-shaped icon at the top of the display:

it was a text message. Willoughby highlighted READ MESSAGE, and was astonished to see that it came from Henny's cell phone.

That doesn't make *any* sense, he thought. Hen's phone is still in Eliza's rucksack, and needs resetting. Eliza's one seriously smart gorilla, but I doubt she's *that* clever. Perhaps Henny sent the message while my battery was flat – or maybe the kidnapper used her phone before disposing of it. Yes – that makes perfect sense. My number would be stored in its memory, ready for him to use.

The phone bleeped again, and an oddly abbreviated message appeared on the tiny glowing screen. Willoughby gasped in horror as his worst fears became a reality. The stakes were impossibly high and the deadline far closer than he'd expected.

'Clever,' muttered Willoughby, through gritted teeth. 'He's planning to keep us *so* busy we won't have time to trace him. No point phoning Justin now; I need to get home – and fast.'

He threw his mobile onto the passenger seat, turned the ignition key and slammed the accelerator to the floor. The Beetle hurtled along the lochside like a chromium-plated rocket. Eliza checked her seat belt, Albion giggled in his sleep – and Willoughby fervently hoped that Justin had *not* contacted the police. The last thing he needed right now was some resolute, well-meaning plod prying into his past.

A mournful rumbling noise echoed from the depths of Robyn's stomach.

'Hungry?' enquired Justin, checking his watch. 'It's way past lunch-time. Might be sensible to grab a quick bite of something before Dad gets back.'

Robyn frowned. 'How can you think of food at a time like this?'

'Blame Mrs Kof. I don't know where she gets her recipes from, but her ...' He broke off, startled by a loud exclamation from his sister. 'What's wrong?'

'That's just reminded me,' Robyn spluttered, her face flushing with excitement. 'Last Sunday morning I saw Mrs Kof cutting something out of a newspaper. I thought it was just a recipe, so I kept quiet. I didn't want to get her into trouble; you know how Dad grumbles if anyone spoils his Sunday paper. I wonder if ...'

The noise of a car roaring into the courtyard below interrupted her. They both listened as it skidded to a halt, spewing plumes of gravel in its wake.

'That sounds like Dad now,' said Justin, heading for the fireman's pole. 'Come on.'

Robyn squinted through one of the clear panes of glass bordering the enormous tower clock face. 'No, it's Enigma,' she called. 'Grandpa must be back.' But Justin was already half way down the pole. Robyn slid after him and, together, they ran along the castle corridors towards the kitchen.

'Odd coincidence Mrs Kof vanishing like that,' panted Justin, as they dashed along the portrait gallery. 'Today of all days.'

'Cooks are entitled to a day off, Dustbin. Anyway, she's not the only one missing, is she? The Gilliechattans are out – *and* old Gobbledygook.' Robyn stopped suddenly, clutching her brother's arm. 'You know, you could be right; perhaps there *is* a traitor in Thyme Castle. But I bet the police wouldn't believe us. Our best chance of rescuing Mum is to try and work out who it is ourselves. With you for brains and me for ... for ...'

'Action?'

'Yeah! Brains and action – we're the dynamite duo.'

'Okay ... but *you've* got to keep everything I've told you a secret. Dad'd have a fit if he knew I'd said *anything* about the time ma ...'

The castle doorbell clanged, drowning Justin's words. For a moment, he watched his sister gallop through the dining room, then shot after her, determined to extract a solemn promise.

Robyn raced into the entrance hall and skidded to a halt behind the studded oak door. She lifted the blackened iron latch. 'Hi Grandpa,' she panted – then gasped with genuine surprise.

It wasn't Grandpa Lyall, Sir Willoughby, Mrs Kof, or anyone else she might have expected, but a tall, solidly built man, smelling strongly of carbolic soap and boot polish.

'Good Afternoon, Miss,' said a deep, friendly voice.

'Hello Sergeant,' Robyn gulped, almost too astonished to speak. 'I suppose Dad phoned you to report the kidnapping. You'd better come in.'

TARTAN THEORY suggests that each timeline is a combination of FREE WILL, RANDOM CHANCE & FIXED EVENTS.

Although we negotiate an infinite number of timeforks, most do not dramatically alter our lives. Many have little or no effect; others, that seem to go off at a tangent, loop around to rejoin our timeline at some later stage. Even when we make decisions that seem to radically change the course of our lives, we are gradually and inexplicably drawn back to our original timeline.

The majority of decisions we make are unlikely to alter our long-term goals in life. To illustrate: You are late for an appointment and find yourself stuck in traffic behind a particularly smelly bus. Spying a narrow lane forking off to one side you are eager to see if this alternate route will lead to your destination more efficiently. (Note how your destination remains unaltered despite your change of route). The lane allows you to move swiftly in a long, wide arc, and vaguely in the right direction. But what inevitably happens? Eventually it loops back to the road you left earlier, just a little further along, and behind that same old bus.

Likewise, many of the forks on our timeline make no appreciable difference to our ultimate destination in life.

CHAPTER ELEVEN

Henny's Ordeal

Lady Henny's temples throbbed painfully and the slightest movement made her dizzy and nauseous. Even before opening her eyes, she knew this was like no headache she'd ever experienced. She felt dazed and confused, and had no idea whether she had slept for several days or just a few minutes. The only thing she *did* remember was the nightmare; a surreal cocktail of images had waltzed through her subconscious: mops, suitcases, wheelchairs and cell phones – and she vaguely recalled a fleeting, blurry glimpse of Eliza and Willoughby running through a crowded building. It had all seemed so real; too real.

Cautiously, Henny tried opening her eyes, half expecting to find herself in the enormous bedroom she shared with Willoughby in Thyme Castle's west tower, but she could see nothing. Wherever she was, it was darker than the Crypt of Erebus. Then she realised: she was wearing a blindfold. She tried sitting up, but her arms and legs steadfastly refused to function, and the exertion left her reeling. Henny lay still, reminding herself not to panic; she'd been in many a situation worse than this.

Her first priority, she decided, was to work out where she was, and try to remember how she'd got there. That would require a clear head. She took a few deep breaths, hoping to banish the fuzziness within her skull, and although the air was stale, it helped. The chloroform had dulled her wits, but things were getting clearer; gradually, all five senses started to function. After a couple of gasps she noticed the faint taste of diesel fumes in the atmosphere, and the gentle thrum of an engine. She felt rope biting her ankles and wrists, rough carpet bristles grazing against her right cheek, and heard the roar of traffic, the splatter of rain.

'I'm in the trunk of a car,' Henny gasped. Most mothers would have panicked at such a notion – but Henny was not your average mother. She felt oddly exhilarated.

Wow, another kidnapping, she thought, instantly transported back to her first abduction in Thailand the month before she met Willoughby. Seven nights in a teak forest tied to the back of an elephant – now that *was* uncomfortable. 'Poor Willo,' she murmured. 'Marrying a foreign correspondent seemed so romantic – until those terrorists snatched me in Spain barely eight weeks after our wedding. I was only missing three days that time, but when I turned up in Luxemburg he was a total wreck. And as for Lesotho back in ninety-nine – well, I never dared tell him, but I sure taught those cannibals the meaning of fast food.'

In every instance, Lady Henny had escaped – thoroughly enjoying herself in the process. The worst bit had been having to play the whole thing down once she returned home. Willoughby could be rather an old woman at times, and would have tried persuading her to avoid anywhere dangerous in future; but where would the fun be in that? It was probably best if he only learned the truth when she published her memoirs.

As her brain became less befuddled, she started to suspect her bizarre nightmare had been a hazy memory. This came as a shock. She'd never seriously considered the risk of being kidnapped in Scotland. Being so near home, she assumed this wasn't a politically motivated abduction; a desire for cold, hard cash was the incentive here. That meant timing would be vital. While the kidnapper waited to receive the ransom, she would probably have at least three or four days to put an escape plan into action.

Henny knew her family would worry, especially Willoughby who fretted about practically anything. The money, of course, wouldn't be a problem. She speculated about possible ransom amounts, and hoped the kidnapper hadn't under-priced her. After all, she thought, the more he counts on getting, the more disappointed he'll be when he ends up with zilch.

She could hear less traffic now, and the occasional sharp bend sent her rolling from side to side. They must have left the main roads, she decided, which meant they were getting closer to their destination. There wouldn't be enough time to free herself from the ropes – so surprising her kidnapper was out of the question. Experience had taught Henny that you only got one chance to escape; if you blew it, you didn't get another. When the time was right, she would know. Meanwhile, she had to remain alert and gain every available advantage. First priority was to learn as much about her captor and place of imprisonment as possible. Then, when her opportunity came, she'd be ready.

Whilst lurching around the boot of the car, Henny's cheek had made painful contact with a sharp lump on a few occasions. Guessing it was probably a bolt, she squirmed awkwardly in the darkness, searching for it with her nose and lips. Once she found it, she turned her head to the left, trying to snag the bolt on the edge of her blindfold. After several frustrating failures she felt it catch, and gently eased it up a couple of millimetres before it slipped off the bolt. Rapidly, she turned her head to the right and snagged it a second time, raising it a fraction higher before it slid free again. With incredible patience, she repeated the process until the blindfold was loose enough to shake off.

Lady Henny sighed, feeling a mixture of relief and dismay. She was free of the blindfold, but still couldn't see anything in the darkness. She lay still, wondering what to do when her captor unlocked the car boot. There was an excellent chance she'd catch him completely off guard and get a good look at his face. If she was *really* lucky, she might catch a swift glimpse of the surrounding area too. Unfortunately, her present position restricted her view – and if the car backed on to a wall or garage, she'd see nothing and would have blown her cover.

Alternatively, she could pretend she hadn't regained consciousness. This would leave the kidnapper with no choice but to carry her. If she managed to play the part convincingly, he might not even bother with the blindfold – especially if he couldn't find it. While he struggled to lift her out of the car, there would be ample opportunity to peek at her prison. And this ploy had another advantage: her captor might leave her unattended or even untied – though she had to admit it was highly unlikely.

Henny settled on the second plan; while not guaranteeing a clear view of the kidnapper's face, its numerous advantages far outweighed this one minor problem. However, the measure of its success depended on the disappearance of the blindfold. As Henny considered the problem, the car turned sharply, and instead of gliding along another smooth lane, it bumped along what felt like a steep, rural cart track. Had they reached their destination?

In a frenzy, she grovelled around the filthy floor until she felt the blindfold brush against her cheek; from its silky texture she'd already guessed it was a man's necktie. The car came to an abrupt halt, reversed and stopped again. Henny knew she needed to act fast; grasping one end of the tie between her teeth she began drawing it through her lips with her tongue, trying not to gag. It tasted foul, but the sound of a car door slamming prompted her to gobble it faster. A lonely pair of footsteps plodded towards the rear of the car. Breathing through her nose, she crammed the final few centimetres of necktie into her mouth and flopped down, feigning lifelessness. Keys jangled, then, with a soft hydraulic *shhhlunk,* the boot lid flew open.

Henny heard the kidnapper gasp, and lay motionless as cold, clinical fingers examined her bruised forehead and gashed cheek. She could feel his hands trembling. Was it anger or concern, she wondered; after all, a dead hostage was a worthless bargaining tool. The icy fingers slithered down her neck, and paused to check her pulse. Hearing a sigh of relief, Henny fought the urge to smile; so far her plan was working perfectly. She listened to the sound of departing footsteps, and when it seemed safe, eased herself up and took a cautious peek.

The car backed on to a wooded hillside. Above her, at the end of a steep track, she saw an old caravan wedged beneath a craggy outcrop. The kidnapper stood with his back to her, fumbling with a bunch of keys outside its door. If Henny's mouth hadn't been stuffed full of necktie she would have laughed out loud. It was hardly a high-tech top security penitentiary. This was going to be a breeze.

The caravan's rusty door squeaked open – and in a burst of overconfidence, Henny decided to chance a second lightning-quick peep as her captor re-emerged. It was risky, but the thought of identifying him to the police appealed tremendously. However, when the kidnapper stepped outside he wore a black balaclava, obscuring everything but his eyes. Disappointed, she slumped back down before he could glance in her direction.

Lady Henny lay perfectly still as her captor groped inside the boot for the missing blindfold. Unable to locate it, he took a deep breath and heaved her over one shoulder in a feebly executed fireman's lift. This was exactly what she'd hoped for.

Henny suspected they were still somewhere north of the border, but the last thing she expected to see was Thyme Castle standing directly across the loch. She glanced hurriedly left and right, trying to absorb as much as possible. The caravan was on the eastern side of the loch somewhere between Whitefield and Inverfarigaig. It was several hundred yards back from the nearest lane – so screaming for help would be futile. Although Thyme Bay looked close, reaching it would take at least an hour by car, or an eternity trudging the thirty-odd miles on foot. But if she located a boat with a reliable outboard motor, she could be home in five minutes or less.

As the kidnapper climbed the caravan steps, Lady Henny took a final furtive glance and observed a huge padlock hanging from the bolt. Drat, she thought; a lock and a loch between me and Thyme Castle – and both considerably larger than I would've preferred.

Henny felt groggy and nauseous; the effects of the chloroform still hadn't worn off completely. She closed her eyes and resumed her inert performance, her confidence only slightly dented. Then, with a sudden jolt, she realised she'd forgotten to check the most important thing of all: the make and registration of the kidnapper's car. Her eyes flashed open again, but it was too late. They were inside now, and as she breathed the stale, musty atmosphere, she could tell that the caravan had been empty for years.

The kidnapper dumped Henny onto a bed. She peered warily from beneath half-closed lashes. The walls oozed with sweaty patches of mould, and spots of mildew dappled the faded pink upholstery like freckles on grubby cheeks. Her captor scowled down at her, massaging his back. Meanwhile, Henny blinked slowly, pretending to regain consciousness. Her mind raced. She'd have to start talking soon – and needed to hide the necktie in case she wanted it later.

After a swift glance at his hostage the kidnapper headed back out to his car. This would probably be her only chance. She peered frantically round in search of a hiding place for the tie. Beside the bed stood a cheap bedside cabinet with a dusty lamp on top. Henny wriggled forwards and pulled the middle drawer open with her teeth, spat the necktie inside, then nudged it shut again with her head. It was far from ideal.

Lady Henny flopped back on the bed, cursing the ropes, and wondering if she had time to cut herself free. Hanging from her key-ring was a miniature Swiss penknife; small, but razor sharp. She wriggled clumsily, desperate to reach the right pocket of her jungle fatigues, but with both hands tied together it was virtually impossible. Determined not to be beaten, she struggled on, until a resounding crash caused her to jump in alarm. She glanced up, and saw her captor looming in the doorway beside a heavy Gladstone bag brimful of chains.

'Looking for *this*?' drawled a harsh voice, oddly muffled by the woollen balaclava. The kidnapper strolled towards Henny, holding the penknife delicately between his thumb and forefinger as if reluctant to touch it. His vivid blue eyes blazed with an icy fury as he glared down at her. 'I'm not stupid, my dear. I confiscated it whilst you were sleeping ... along with these ...' He reached into his pockets and withdrew a motley assortment of objects, including keys, pens, a comb, a pair of tweezers, a toothpick and Henny's PDA. With a sinister snigger, he threw them all, including the penknife, into a utensil drawer behind him, and slammed it shut. He wriggled his fingers as if they felt contaminated, and wiped them down the front of his jacket. 'Your garbage will be returned to you when you leave,' he snarled. 'Or perhaps I *should* say, *if* you leave. Your ultimate fate lies in the hands of your witless husband ... so I wouldn't advise getting overly optimistic!'

Henny glowered back, furious with herself for her carelessness. 'Who *are* you?'

'Surely you don't expect me to answer such a ridiculous question. I expected a tad more intelligence from a woman of your calibre.'

'At least you can tell me *where* I am,' Henny persisted, hoping to dispel any suspicions he might have about what she'd already seen.

'A long, long way from home,' said the kidnapper. 'So don't expect anyone to find you.'

'What do you want?'

'That's none of your concern, my dear,' he whispered in Henny's ear. Then almost exploding with rage, he slapped her brutally across the face with the back of his hand, and roared 'NO MORE QUESTIONS.'

Henny fell silent and watched with mounting dismay as he pulled a chain out of the old leather bag. He yanked it taut along the length of one arm, and examined the links closely with one frosty blue eye. Things were a lot worse than she'd anticipated.

At least he doesn't realise I know where I am, she told herself; there's still a glimmer of hope. But five minutes later that glimmer had dwindled to the palest guttering flicker.

The kidnapper threaded the chain through the rope binding

Henny's feet. After padlocking it securely to the foot of the bed, he untied her wrists. Henny could lie flat on her back without too much discomfort and push herself up into a sitting position – but otherwise she was immobile. Finally, the kidnapper placed a dozen bottles of natural spring water and a plastic mug within reach on the bedside cabinet.

'Help yourself, your ladyship,' he murmured, with a malicious chuckle. 'Though I wouldn't recommend drinking too much; I plan to call just morning and evening to allow you to relieve yourself, and deliver a few scraps of food. Lucky you – all the comforts of home, plus a guaranteed peaceful night's sleep,' he concluded, withdrawing a hypodermic syringe and a narrow phial of colourless liquid from his pocket.

Henny struggled as he filled the syringe and flicked it with his forefinger to remove any bubbles.

'DON'T YOU DARE,' she screamed, knowing escape would be impossible if he kept her constantly sedated.

'Oh, but I *do* dare,' came the chilling reply. 'And I would strongly advise you *not* to thrash about like that. If the end of this needle breaks off, it could be *very* painful indeed. It might even turn septic ... and if it does, I certainly *won't* be summoning the doctor.'

Henny realised it was pointless to resist, and lay as still as a corpse as the needle pierced the side of her neck. Her eyes blazed with hatred as she stared into the depths of her captor's cold, cerulean eyes. One day, she would make him pay dearly for this.

'Sweet dreams, my dear,' he whispered. 'Sleep tight ... and by the look of this place I'm fairly certain the bedbugs *will* bite.'

While Henny drifted into a pleasant, dreamy trance, he tossed the syringe back in his bag and ambled out of the caravan, slamming the door behind him. He fastened the enormous padlock, dragged a few scrappy branches across the front of the caravan and then stood back to admire his handiwork.

The kidnapper opened the car door and climbed in. He removed his balaclava, tossed it onto the passenger seat, and gave himself a conceited smirk in the rear-view mirror. So far, the day had gone perfectly according to plan. Just one minor matter to attend to – or dispose of – then he could relax, put his feet up and open an ice-cold beer.

Inside the caravan, Henny breathed slowly and peacefully as the sedative flooded through her veins. She didn't feel angry any longer; just dazed, confused and very, very sleepy. Somewhere in the dim recesses of her mind, she had a vague recollection of being kidnapped – but it didn't worry her in the least. Where was she this time? Krakow? Fiji? Namibia? Well, wherever it was, it didn't matter – she was certain to escape sooner or later. She smiled, as if an amusing thought had just occurred to her:

'When I finally get around to writing my memoirs,' she yawned, 'this is going to make a really ... exciting ... chapter.'

ach timeline exerts a strong 'gravitational' force, constantly drawing the diverging strands of time together. Therefore, relatively few timeforks create a parallel universe, merely looping back to the original timeline. This phenomenon, known as the FORK & LOOP EFFECT, is a fundamental pattern, which, like fractals, repeats whatever the scale. Some forks may result in loops lasting several years, incorporating numerous smaller forks and loops of their own. We may believe this is no detour, but a new phase of our lives. However, the combination of free will and fixed events that govern time, inevitably draw us back to our original course.

To illustrate: imagine you decide to take a new direction for your afternoon stroll. Instead of a leisurely amble to the local pub, you head briskly in the opposite direction. You turn as the whim takes you – yet your apparently random choice of direction gradually draws you towards your usual goal. You emerge from a narrow lane you have never traversed before, and find yourself approaching the same pub - but from a different angle. Although initially surprised, you aren't entirely disappointed. Many theorists suggest that on some level of consciousness, your seemingly random choices were subliminal decisions. The journey might have been a product of chance - but the ultimate destination was not.

But, if our course remains largely unaltered, what is the purpose of these repeating forks and loops?

CHAPTER TWELVE

Understanding a Gorilla's Habits

'KIDNAPPING!' exclaimed Sergeant Awbrite, raising his left eyebrow. '*What* kidnapping?'

Robyn cast a guilty sideways glance at her brother, her heart sinking to the bottom of her iridescent designer boots. The clock in the entrance hall ticked slowly but relentlessly as silent seconds stretched into mute minutes.

'Well?'

Justin knew he'd have to say something; the problem was ... *what*? His brain fizzled. Judging from the expression on the sergeant's face, he guessed his father had *not* reported the abduction. Dad must want this kept hush-hush, he thought, but thanks to Robyn that's no longer an option. He decided to be truthful but circumspect. 'You'd better come in, Sergeant,' he said, with a deep sigh of resignation. 'I'll tell you all about it.'

Sergeant Awbrite removed his peaked cap and wiped his large black boots vigorously on the doormat.

'Mum was kidnapped this morning, shortly after landing in Prestwick,' explained Justin. 'We assumed Dad would phone you.'

'If this is your idea of a joke, young man – it isn't very funny.'

'It's the truth, *honestly*,' said Robyn. 'Show him the ransom note, Dustbin.'

Justin could have cheerfully kicked his sister – and might have done if a member of the local constabulary hadn't been present. It was obvious he needed to get rid of her before she blurted out that the invention referred to in the note was a time machine.

'I'll take the sergeant to the south tower and show him what we've discovered,' he said firmly. 'You find Nanny. Ask her to brew a fresh pot of tea and take it along to the library with one of Mrs Kof's Dundee cakes.'

Robyn scowled at her brother, then turned to the policeman flashing him one of her sunniest smiles. 'I'll catch up with you in a minute Sergeant. I want to show you how I spotted Mum's ring on the ...'

'Leave *that* to me,' Justin interrupted, fixing his sister with a meaningful glare. 'Just tell Nan about the tea, okay? And try calling Dad afterwards ... he's probably recharged his mobile by now. Let him know Sergeant Awbrite has arrived.'

Finally, the unspoken message came through loud and clear: Warn Dad – so he can decide how much he wants to reveal to the police. Robyn blushed. 'Okay Dustbin,' she mumbled, and headed off towards the kitchen.

As they marched to the south tower, Justin gave Sergeant Awbrite the full story – with a few significant omissions. Pausing at the door of his sitting room, he handed over the ransom note, then ushered the policeman inside.

'Take a seat, sergeant,' he said, pointing to a modern angular sofa. 'The disc I told you about is upstairs. I'll bring it down so you can view it on the big monitor.'

Justin shot up the south tower steps two at a time, leaving the policeman to open the envelope. Awbrite remained standing, and frowned at the ransom note – almost as if he suspected Justin of playing some childish prank. Then, with a shake of his head he tucked the paper into his notebook and contemplated the sofa's flawless white leather in trepidation; it looked too perfect to sit on.

Glancing around the large, simply decorated room, Awbrite realised the few items on display probably cost more than the entire contents of his cottage. The minimalist style contrasted sharply with the traditional highland décor throughout the rest of the castle. The walls were a dazzling white. A black concert-grand piano stood to his left, its highly polished surface reflecting a single white orchid on the windowsill; to his right he saw a strange-looking wooden instrument with two metal antennas. Above a huge stone fireplace hung what appeared to be a chrome-framed abstract painting. Bewildered by modern art, Sergeant Awbrite crept over for a closer look, uncomfortably aware of his size eleven-and-a-half boots clonking noisily across the birch-wood floor. As he leaned forward to examine the picture his heart almost stopped as the geometric monochrome shapes of the Picasso seemed to melt and trickle away. Frozen to the spot, he watched in fascination as the pattern swirled, transforming seamlessly into a Constable landscape.

'I see you're admiring *MAC*,' remarked an unexpected voice immediately behind him.

The sergeant jumped and turned sharply. The door remained closed and he had heard no footsteps, yet somehow, Justin had magically materialised in the centre of the room.

'Mac who?'

'*M*orphing *A*nalytical *C*anvas,' Justin explained. 'There's a hidden micro-camera – *here* – transmitting every detail of your physical appearance to a computer. An iridology programme scans your iris, automatically generating artwork to match your personality profile. It can even sense subtle mood fluctuations and adjust accordingly.'

The rural scene metamorphosed into a strange surrealist image. Meanwhile, Awbrite's gimlet eyes flickered across the ceiling, his alert expression morphing into a smile. 'And it's changed again because you've just slid down that pole?'

'No. It's designed to give guests priority, but it takes a while to analyse a stranger accurately. Constable was probably its first attempt based on your uniform.'

'A computer with a sense of humour. Whatever next?'

Justin shrugged, and pointed a remote beneath the plasma screen. A concealed panel slid back to reveal the very latest in audio-visual equipment. He inserted the disc containing the web-cam recording into a DVD player, strolled over to the sofa and flopped down. Awbrite looked aghast; he had an uncomfortable feeling the equipment cost more than his cottage, let alone its contents. Minute beads of perspiration glistened on his forehead.

'I hope Sir Willoughby won't mind us using his private study. Perhaps you ought to wait until he gets home before tampering with all this expensive equipment.'

Justin almost burst out laughing, and only just managed to restrain himself. If Awbrite had read the ransom note demanding Willoughby's latest invention, he'd naturally assume the Laird of Thyme was a successful inventor and this was, indeed, his study. Justin decided not to disillusion him; it was imperative to avoid ticklish questions.

'Relax,' he said, as a bustling airport terminal appeared on the monitor. 'Dad's pretty easygoing – for a genius.' The mysterious figure of the kidnapper appeared on the screen; Justin froze the image, zoomed in on the wheelchair and highlighted his mother's opal ring.

Sergeant Awbrite's eyebrows rose in astonishment – like two hairy caterpillars crawling over a rugby ball.

'What's wrong?' asked Justin.

'I ... I didn't realise ... er, I mean ... I thought this was just a silly prank. Her ladyship really *has* been kidnapped.'

Awbrite snapped into official mode, becoming brisk and efficient. He examined the recording again in slow motion, asked numerous questions and wrote copious notes. Meanwhile, Justin gazed out of the window, and watched Sir Willoughby's chrome VW hurtle through the castle gates and along the driveway.

'Dad's home,' he said, crossing to the opposite window. Willoughby swerved to a halt beside *Enigma* in the courtyard below. 'That reminds me, you never explained why you were driving Grandpa's Rolls.'

'A farmer found it abandoned on his land,' explained the sergeant. 'The keys were in it, so the farmer's wife phoned the police station. I recognised it at once, and thought I'd deliver it back home. A constable should be along with my squad car shortly.'

'I wonder what's happened to Grandpa. Nanny said he left early this morning. I hope he hasn't forgotten how to drive again.'

'Mmm ... and no circus midget to chauffer him home this time!' replied Awbrite, with a sly wink. 'Now, I'd like to ask your father a few questions, if you could escort me down to the library. Erm ... *no!*' he added, as Justin grasped the fireman's pole. 'The dignified route.'

Justin led the policeman downstairs and held the library door open. Sergeant Awbrite gazed round the cosy, traditional room approvingly. That's more like it, he thought. A prim middle-aged lady in a starched nanny's uniform presided over a teapot and an enormous golden cake encrusted with nuts and cherries. Awbrite rubbed his hands together expectantly, eased himself into a worn chesterfield armchair and half closed his eyes, inhaling the soothing aroma of antique leather, smouldering pinecones and Earl Grey tea.

'Sir Willoughby will be along soon,' whispered a timid voice.

Awbrite turned to find Nanny Verity Kiss offering him a steaming cup of tea and a slice of cake, whilst simultaneously attempting a rather wobbly curtsey. The effect was nothing short of hilarious.

'Erm ... thank you, Ma'am,' he said, suppressing a benign chuckle.

Nanny felt too flustered to notice. 'Oh dear ... Albion's milk is getting *quite* cold,' she muttered, lifting his bottle off the silver tray. 'I *do* hope Eliza will hurry.'

'Who's Eliza? I assumed *you* were the Nanny.'

Nanny Verity explained, and in no time at all they were chatting like old friends. The sergeant seemed fascinated – but this was no idle chitchat. He manoeuvred the conversation with practiced skill, imperceptibly steering Nanny on to the subject of Sir Lyall disturbing her at dawn. She described hearing the old Rolls rumble out of the courtyard and how, sitting up in bed, she'd watched it stop by the castle gates to pick someone up. Awbrite opened his notebook discreetly and jotted a few key words.

For a second or two, Justin felt anxious that Nanny might reveal too much. She was such a credulous soul, and would naively answer all Awbrite's queries, never once suspecting he was questioning her. Then he realised it didn't matter; she'd been on vacation when he'd started work on the time machine. And anyway, he thought, I could build a nuclear reactor, and she'd still prattle happily about knitting patterns and the regularity of Albion's bowels.

Justin overheard Nanny mention her grandchildren, and was just about to rescue the poor sergeant from the inevitable baby album when Sir Willoughby hurried through the library door. He looked harassed, and his hair stood up in untidy tufts. Justin glanced sheepishly at him, wondering if he was in any trouble, and felt a rush of relief when Willoughby placed a reassuring hand on his shoulder.

Meanwhile, Awbrite rose politely, brushing cake crumbs out of his moustache.

Sir Willoughby marched over and shook the policeman briskly by the hand. 'Sorry to keep you, Sergeant.' He perched on the arm of a chair and took a piping hot cup of tea from Nanny. 'Any leads yet?' he demanded.

'Hardly,' replied Awbrite. 'Until a few minutes ago I had no idea her Ladyship was missing. I'm astonished you didn't report your wife's abduction sooner.'

Willoughby hesitated.

'I expect it's all my fault,' said Nanny. 'Sir Willoughby would naturally assume I'd call the police.'

'Nonsense,' Willoughby insisted, gently patting Nanny Verity's hand. 'Now leave this to Sergeant and me, Nanny dear.' He drained his teacup in a single gulp and turned back to the policeman. 'Fact is,' he said, taking a deep breath, 'I panicked. I just wanted to hurry home and check the rest of my family were safe. It didn't seem real. It was ...'

As Willoughby spoke, the library door creaked open and Robyn ambled in, followed closely by Eliza. The gorilla marched majestically on all fours, with Albion perched precariously on her back, chortling. Despite Nanny's reassurance, the gorilla's powerful brooding presence still rattled Awbrite somewhat. He stared as Eliza sat down abruptly and the baby slid to the floor with a wallop. To his consternation, the Thyme family seemed oblivious. Even the Nanny bustling over with the bottle, was more concerned about the temperature of the milk. The baby rubbed his head and gave her a bemused grin.

'How's Nanny's brave little soldier?' she clucked – and before Albion could gurgle in response, she inserted the teat between his rosebud lips. 'Really Eliza, I wish you'd be a little more considerate. That drink's almost stone cold.'

'Baby happy,' replied Eliza, having selected QUEEN from her voice menu to avoid any arguments. Then, noticing the sergeant, she grunted with excitement and rushed over to shake his hand. 'Hello zoo-keeper man,' she said, her fingers rattling over the keyboard. 'You have gorillas in your zoo?'

The sight of a gorilla impersonating a Monarch of the Realm appeared to rob Awbrite of speech. Justin tried to distract Eliza, explaining that, despite the similar uniforms, this was a policeman *not* a zoo-keeper – but she wouldn't listen. First she tried the sergeant's cap on, then she grabbed his notebook and drew a picture of herself.

'Picture – me,' she explained, tapping the page eagerly. 'Show picture other nice gorillas.'

Awbrite gulped and nodded silently. Eliza hadn't met many zoo-keepers, but she thought they were friendlier than this. Disappointed, she returned his notebook and prowled off, her lips pursed in a thoughtful pout.

Still rather dazed, the sergeant returned to checking Sir Willoughby's account against the notes he'd scribbled earlier. Unfortunately, Willoughby hadn't noticed the man pushing the wheelchair, and was terribly disappointed his face wasn't visible on the DVD.

'Not to worry, sir,' Awbrite reassured him. 'I'll contact Airport Security and see if they spotted anything.'

Willoughby cringed. No doubt he and Eliza would still be uppermost in their minds. He gestured towards the telephone on the library desk, and watched as Sergeant Awbrite picked up the receiver. After dialling, he handed Sir Willoughby the ransom note. The laird unfolded it gingerly with the tips of his fingernails.

'Too late for that, sir,' sighed the sergeant, keeping his ear pinned to the receiver. 'I suspect it's covered in fingerpr ... 'scuse me.' He pointed to the mouthpiece, and then spoke in the official tone of a life-long policeman. 'Sergeant Awbrite – Inverness Constabulary. I need details of any passengers requesting the loan of a wheelchair this morning. Yes ... yes, I'll hold.'

There was a full minute of expectant hush, interrupted only by the sound of Eliza slurping her tea – and a bizarre disembodied cough. Then the instant Awbrite spoke again, Justin and Robyn whispered frenziedly to their father, bringing him up to date. Once the policeman started to write, Willoughby tossed Justin his mobile phone. Nanny Verity rattled the tea-things to disguise his murmured explanation about the kidnapper's text message. But before Justin could read it, Sergeant Awbrite cleared his throat:

'May I give them your fax number, Sir Willoughby? There's something I'd like them to send over right away.'

Willoughby leapt up and scrawled 117739-399 on the blotter. Awbrite read it out in his stentorian voice, then after replacing the receiver turned to face the Thymes.

'According to Customer Information, only two wheelchairs were borrowed today. One by a Mr and Mrs Smith – Mr Smith had broken his leg, skiing; the other by a doctor with an Edinburgh accent and a moustache. The woman I spoke to remembered *him* particularly because he failed to return the chair; a security guard found it abandoned in the car park. The good news is that Professor Nation, as he called himself, signed for the wheelchair.'

The fax machine bleeped and spewed a sheet of copy paper into its plastic tray.

'And this,' said Awbrite, removing the fax, 'is his signature. I'd like you all to examine it and see if you recognise his handwriting.'

Sir Willoughby looked at it first. Then, with a deep sigh, shook his head and passed the paper to Nanny Verity.

'No,' Nanny declared firmly. 'Sorry.'

'Me neither,' said Justin, giving the signature a cursory glance before handing it to his sister.

Robyn studied the paper assiduously, hoping to impress the sergeant. She was just about to give up when something caught her eye: 'Look at this,' she gasped, thrusting the paper under Awbrite's nose and jabbing the first three letters with a glittery fingernail.

Pro Christian Nation

'Pro is short for professional; the correct abbreviation for professor is Prof. Why would he make such a silly mistake?'

'That's my question too,' said Sergeant Awbrite. He folded the paper in half and tucked it carefully in the back of his notebook.

'Fancy *you* missing that, Dustbin,' Robyn gloated. 'Some genius.'

Justin remained silent, gnawing his lower lip. He hadn't missed it. The signature had troubled him instantly, though for quite a different reason. He whispered the words softly, slurring the sounds together: 'Pro-Christian-Nation.' It sounded oddly familiar, yet he was convinced it wasn't the name of *anyone* he had ever met.

He glanced at Robyn, basking in the sergeant's admiration. Her account of the morning's deductive exploits held his full attention, so it seemed reasonably safe to risk a covert peep at Willoughby's mobile phone. Justin held it, partially concealed between his leg and the arm of the chair. He highlighted READ MESSAGE and peered down, trying to decipher the code-like abbreviations.

Like most text messages, it was easier to understand out loud. Justin murmured the words under his breath: 'I have your wife. Leave time machine outside castle gates next Saturday after midnight. Don't phone police or else! You have been warned ... *Pro-Christian-Nation.*'

As he whispered the kidnapper's puzzling pseudonym a second time, Justin stared at the fireplace with a glazed expression on his face. For the last few days he'd tried to avoid looking at the old Thyme Clock. He knew it was illogical but, since his nightmare, the sinister jester with his cards and dice unsettled him in ways he couldn't express. One glimpse of its cold ivory face and those terrifying dream images flooded back, making him shudder.

High above, the tower clock struck four, its deafening chimes echoing down through three floors. Then, as the last note died away, the library clock emitted a faint whirring noise and the mechanical figure of Old Father Time swung his scythe forward, simultaneously striking its golden bell and a chord in the depths of Justin's brain. His spine turned to an icicle, and suddenly the meaning of the signature became horribly clear.

Although too small to be visible from his chair, a vivid mental image of the two words engraved on the bell flashed into Justin's mind: *Beware Procrastination. That* was why the kidnapper's name sounded so familiar. But *why* would he sign himself

Procrastination?

Justin glanced down at his watch, frowning at the circle of minuscule letters spelling the same ominous phrase. Had the person who'd left it been trying to warn him of his mother's impending abduction? Surely not ... but, then again, it seemed unlikely to be a coincidence.

A hollow cough interrupted his silent speculations. Justin blinked and glanced round, uncomfortably aware that everyone was staring at him.

'What's to do, Poppet?' asked Nanny.

Before he could think of a suitably evasive reply, Robyn butted in. 'Senility,' she sniggered. 'Your mouth was hanging wide open, Dustbin.'

It was rapidly becoming one of those days when Justin felt the urge to banish his sister to a Swiss finishing school – preferably one that would finish her off permanently.

Nanny Verity bustled round with the teapot and milk jug, asking if anyone wanted a refill. Only the sergeant did. He might have fancied a second slice of cake too, if Eliza hadn't been picking the glacé cherries off and sucking them noisily. Nanny gave her a reproving glare and was about to criticise her shocking lapse of manners, when a movement outside distracted her attention. With a muffled cry, she dropped the empty jug and pointed through the window.

'Gracious! That's who Sir Lyall picked up this morning.'

Everyone clustered behind her and peered out. A clean-shaven man wearing mousy tweeds and a deerstalker was heading up the driveway. The closer he got, the more puzzled they all felt – especially when he waved; clearly *he* recognised *them*.

'It's the lodger,' said Robyn, shrieking with laughter. 'Professor Gobbledygook – without his whiskers. Doesn't he look *frightful*?'

'*Really* Robyn!' said Nanny Verity. She fumbled in her apron pocket for her spectacles. 'I think he looks rather handsome.'

Robyn snorted explosively. Sergeant Awbrite spluttered into his teacup to disguise a chuckle, and then leaned out of the open window to hail the professor:

'Come round to the library at once. I'd like some information, if you don't mind.'

Wearing an expression of pure terror, Professor Gilbert rushed through the archway and across the courtyard. Without even pausing to remove his haversack he hurried through the dining room and along the portrait gallery.

'Are you going to ask him about Grandpa?' enquired Justin, as they waited.

'Perhaps,' Awbrite replied. 'I'm curious to see if he can account for his whereabouts since nine a.m. The kidnapper knew what time your mother was due to land, so I have to consider the possibility he had inside information.'

'Ridiculous,' sniffed Nanny, sounding scandalised at the very thought. 'I'm certain no one in the castle would dream of such disloyalty.'

'Has he been with you long, Sir?' asked Awbrite, ignoring Nanny's protestations.

'Er ... about two and a half years,' said Willoughby, doing a quick mental calculation. 'He's a damn good chap ... just frightfully nervous.'

'He stutters,' explained Justin.

'*And* sings,' Robyn added, not entirely helpfully.

'*Sings?*'

Before anyone could explain, the library door burst open and Professor Gilbert stumbled in, his newly shaven cheeks looking decidedly flushed. He closed the door behind him and leaned against it, trembling.

'I believe you're the private tutor here at Thyme Castle' said the sergeant, finding a blank page in his notebook. 'Correct?'

'Y-y-y,' stuttered the professor. Then abandoning speech he nodded dumbly.

'Name?'

'P-p-prrrr ...'

'Professor Wilfred Stanley Gilbert,' Justin whispered over the

186

sergeant's shoulder. The professor cast him a look of gratitude.

'And what have you been doing today?'

'C-c-c-c ...'

'Kidnapping?' suggested Awbrite. 'Don't stammer and yammer at me again, man. I'm losing all patience with you.'

Willoughby and Justin gasped audibly, Nanny snorted in disgust, Robyn smothered a giggle – and somebody coughed. Even Eliza seemed agitated. Poor Professor Gilbert looked utterly mortified, and realising he had no alternative cleared his throat and took a deep breath. '"C-cl-*climbing over rocky mountain, skipping rivulet and fountain,*"' he sang. Then, as usual, once he'd got started, the words started to flow a little easier. 'I w-went climbing, down by the loch.'

'He's an ornithologist,' Justin explained. 'He's been recor–'

'No interruptions please,' said Awbrite. 'Otherwise we'll all be talking at once and won't know *where* we are.' Turning back to the professor he asked: 'Now – can anyone verify your movements?'

'S-S-Sir Lyall gave me a lift as far as Brackla. I w-walked the rest.'

'Did anyone else see you?'

Professor Gilbert shook his head. Sergeant Awbrite wrote *NO ALIBI* at the top of the page. 'Did Sir Lyall mention where *he* was going?'

'A p-p-picnic,' stammered the professor. 'He had a hamper on the back seat.'

'Open your haversack.'

Professor Gilbert slid it from his shoulders and fumbled nervously with the buckle. Sergeant Awbrite peered inside, examining the contents methodically. 'Climber eh?' he said. 'Don't climbers normally carry ropes?'

'I'm not th-that sort of climber. Just an or-or-ordinary bird-watcher really.'

'And why would an ordinary bird-watcher need a Global Positioning System?' inquired the policeman, lifting an expensive

GPS unit out of the haversack.

'It w-was a gift from Justin,' replied the professor proudly.

'I am informed that you normally sport a *beard*,' said Sergeant Awbrite, pronouncing the word beard as if it was a distasteful toxic fungus. 'Why did you shave it off? Some sort of feeble disguise?'

'N-n-no,' replied Professor Gilbert, looking more uncomfortable than ever. 'I've had it since my uni-ver-versity days, but Miss Robyn kept saying it made me look an old fuddy-duddy; so this morning I decided to find out whether I looked any better without it. S-s-sadly, I don't.'

There was an uneasy silence, until Nanny, determined to come to his rescue, said that it made him look much younger. Professor Gilbert's ears turned a deep shade of crimson; he glanced round, hoping for further signs of approval. Sir Willoughby and Justin shuffled awkwardly, unable to agree, but not liking to disagree; Robyn, who thought his chin looked like a badly peeled potato, made no attempt to disguise her giggling; Sergeant Awbrite wore an expression of contempt; but Eliza seemed most upset of all. She made breathy grunting noises gradually working up to a crescendo, then she hurled the Dundee cake against the wall, sending almonds and brazils rolling across the floor in all directions. Albion gurgled with glee. He picked up a handful of cake and squeezed it through his fingers like modelling clay.

'What's up with her?' asked the sergeant, nodding towards the gorilla.

'Er ... jet-lag probably,' said Justin in a wary voice.

Eliza scowled at him, bounded across to the hearth rug and slammed both fists down angrily. Then, turning her back on everyone, she sat, hunched over, sulking.

'C-c-can I go now?' begged the professor, looking ready to faint.

'Very well,' replied Awbrite. 'But I'll be advising Sir Willoughby to keep an eye on you.'

Professor Gilbert scuttled out of the library, tripping over his feet in the process.

'*Americans!*' sighed Awbrite. 'I wonder if they're all like that.'

'My wife happens to be an American,' remarked Willoughby frostily.

The big policeman lifted one eyebrow, and scribbled in his notebook as if this latest revelation was of particular significance.

'Will that be *all,* Sergeant?' said Willoughby, in a tone that implied he hoped it was.

'One final question, sir.'

'*Well*?'

'That invention mentioned in the ransom note,' said Awbrite, looking suddenly self-conscious. 'I just wondered what it was. Most kidnappers demand cash, and – if you'll pardon the cheek – you're not exactly short of the wee bawbees.'

Willoughby's mind went blank. Justin and Robyn stared at him – then panic struck, and, in discordant unison, all three Thymes blurted out the first bogus inventions they could think of.

Eliza roared, beating her chest with rage, and then hurtled out of the library, almost blasting the door clean off its hinges. The sergeant gasped and stepped back.

'*Arrghhhh,*' groaned Willoughby, burying his head in his hands. 'My wife's missing; I've been awake since dawn; the traffic's been a *blithering* nightmare. And now the family gorilla's on the rampage.' He stared at the policeman pointedly. 'If that *IS* all ... may I, er ...'

'Certainly, sir,' replied Awbrite, collecting his peaked cap. 'It sounds as if that young constable of mine has turned up with the squad car. I'll be in touch if there's any news.'

He saluted and marched out of the room. Sir Willoughby, ruffling his hair and muttering about the Thyme curse, trotted after him, anxious to escort the policeman to the castle door.

Meanwhile, Albion, whose bottom lip had been quivering dangerously since Eliza's tantrum, burst into tears.

'There, there, Poppet,' said Nanny. 'That nice policeman'll find yer mammy, so don't fret.' She bundled him up to the nursery, leaving Justin and Robyn together.

Robyn had a steely glint of determination in her eyes. 'Come on Dustbin,' she said. 'We've got some investigating to do.'

'You go ahead,' murmured Justin, his brow puckering. 'I need to do some research first.'

'Research?' gasped Robyn. '*RESEARCH!* Mum's in danger and you want to read a *book*!'

'Two books, as a matter of fact,' said Justin, returning her glare. 'Anyway, *you're* the action; *I'm* the brains – remember?'

Once he was alone, Justin strode over to the library's reference section, tugged out a couple of books and carried them over to the desk. The first one was written by Lady Henny, and had a picture of her and Eliza on the front cover. Justin opened it, ran his forefinger down the table of contents, and then flipped to chapter thirteen: *Primate Behavioural Patterns*.

My Fair Gorilla   267

Gorillas are uncomplicated creatures, and whether they communicate verbally or otherwise, lying is completely alien to them. They have no reason to lie, and appear to have no grasp of the concept. In the wild they live in peaceful family groups, and, if angered, usually resort to displacement behaviour, like slapping the ground or beating their chests. This settles most disagreements.

From an early age, it became clear that lies distressed Eliza, prompting similar behaviour. She would throw things, venting her feelings by figuratively casting the source of her anger away. She is not a living lie-detector. She cannot identify a specific lie, or even pinpoint an individual liar in a group. It is something far more nebulous, like sensing an aura of dishonesty. But the more lies she hears, the more unsettled she gets.

'Hmmm ... I *thought* so,' Justin sighed, half wishing he hadn't made this *particular* connection. 'It looks as though the professor hasn't been entirely truthful.'

The second book was an enormous Oxford Dictionary. Ever since he'd realised the kidnapper's pseudonym was a play on the word *procrastination* a nagging thought had been tickling Justin's cerebrum – and now, at last, he could scratch his mental itch. He already knew the definition, of course, but there was something else – a proverb or a saying. He ran his forefinger down the page – proclaim, proclivity, proconsul, procrastinate ... and there it was:

> **Procrastination**
> Putting off an action until later. Often referred to as the "Thief of Time!"

The THIEF OF TIME – it *couldn't* be a coincidence. Justin tried to remember the precise wording of the ransom note, certain the same three words ran along the bottom. The kidnapper certainly had a warped sense of humour, but what was he trying to tell them?

Then, as Justin hauled the dictionary back across the room, everything fell into place.

'*TOT!*' he gasped, carefully sliding the dictionary between a huge thesaurus and *Newton's Principia*. 'Another connection! Dad was right. His past has finally caught up with him.'

Justin bordered on the obsessive about his books, arranging them all alphabetically by authors' names. He stood back for a moment, admiring the orderly rows of volumes and, to his dismay, spotted an unauthorised absence from the fiction section. Taking pride of place amongst the 'W's, stood the complete works of H G

Wells bound in matching ivory leather – and one was missing. The gap unnerved him; conspicuous as a missing tooth in a familiar smile. Who would borrow such a valuable book without his permission?

Worse still, he had an uncomfortable inkling the missing book would be his priceless autographed copy of "The Time Machine," but he had to be absolutely sure. He leaned forward, running his fingers over the row of gold-embossed spines – peering anxiously at each of the titles ...

Little threads of cotton seem weak and insignificant; but weave and loop enough of them together and the fabric they create is strong. Likewise, each timeline is an inconsequential thread of time; but by weaving constantly amongst numerous other threads it strengthens the fabric of time.

Usually, our individual threads run alongside those of our family and close friends, and mostly in the same direction. Even when a timeline terminates in death, an equivalent birth will introduce a replacement thread, instantly anchored by adjacent loops. Each fork and loop we create naturally alters the course of surrounding timelines, requiring others to make decisions that prompt forks and loops of their own. All of these mingle continually and STRENGTHEN THE FABRIC OF TIME. Ironically, it is our complete freedom of choice that perpetuates the stability of time itself.

If all timelines ran roughly in the same direction the fabric would still have a fundamental weakness. Therefore, it is essential that many timelines cross our own, intersecting briefly and at regular intervals. These are perhaps work colleagues or acquaintances with whom we interact daily, but whose lives follow a different direction. Other timelines cross our own infrequently, but whenever two timelines intersect, decisions create further stabilising loops. This crossing of timelines constitutes the warp and weft of the fabric of time and forms discernible patterns resembling TARTAN.

CHAPTER THIRTEEN

Alibis or Lies?

'"*The War of the Worlds*" ... "*Kipps*" ... "*The Island of Doctor Moreau*,"' Justin whispered to himself, checking each novel in turn. '"*The Invisible Man*" ... "*The* ...'

An eerie, sepulchral cough interrupted his search, causing the hairs on the nape of his neck to bristle. He spun round and surveyed the empty room uneasily, as if a *real* invisible man lurked close behind him.

It was at least the fourth cough he'd heard that afternoon, and seemed to come from the direction of the window which was ever so slightly ajar. Justin pushed it wide open and leaned out, but all he could see was Sergeant Awbrite's squad car parked outside the castle gates; a young constable lounged in the driver's seat counting his pimples in the rear view mirror. The disembodied cough continued to baffle Justin, until a single, snowy feather floated down and landed on his shoulder.

'Burbage!' he exclaimed. 'Come down this instant.'

A pair of beady, black eyes peeped over the pelmet. Then, after a sullen squawk, the cockatoo descended the curtain, grasping alternately with his beak and claws. He hopped onto the windowsill and raised his sulphur-yellow crest in a show of defiance.

'*How long a time LIES in one little word!*' he remarked balefully, in a perfect imitation of Willoughby's well-educated voice.

'What's *that* s'pposed to mean?' snapped Justin, forgetting for a moment he was talking to a bird. Burbage cackled with laughter and, after a quick ruffle of his feathers, swooped out of the window towards a rusty old Morris Minor chugging through the castle gates, clouds of black smoke exploding out of its exhaust pipe.

Justin could hardly believe his eyes; it was Mr Gilliechattan. The gardener had supposedly taken Burbage to see a parrot specialist in Edinburgh. Quoting Shakespeare himself for once, Justin felt that the whole situation had "*a very ancient and fish-like smell.*" He rushed out of the library and pelted along the corridors, determined to catch Sergeant Awbrite before he left. This was a matter for the police to investigate.

The last thing Robyn wanted was to bump into Professor Gilbert. She could tie him up in verbal knots if necessary, but his footling questions would waste too much time. She hovered on the north tower landing, ears akimbo, until a soft tenor voice drifted down from his bathroom:

> *... I'm very well acquainted too*
> *with matters mathematical,*
> *I understand equations,*
> *both the simple and quadratical ...*

All clear, Robyn thought. She pushed the schoolroom door open and crept across to her desk. Seconds later, she hurtled down the servants' staircase and out into the kitchen garden, clutching a notebook and pencil. After finding a shady corner in the apple orchard, she wrote the words: *Robyn Thyme – Private Investigator* on the front cover.

It was time to prove who had the *real* talent in the family.

When Justin arrived in the entrance hall he was almost too out of breath to speak. Sir Willoughby was shaking Awbrite by the hand, and held the front door open, impatient for him to leave.

'Mr ... huh ... Gilliechattan ... huh ... is back,' Justin panted. 'He lied ... huh ... he never ... huh ... took ...'

Before he could finish, the spotty constable, who had just sprinted through the archway and across the courtyard, interrupted in an equally breathless voice. He saluted clumsily and informed the sergeant he'd received a radio message about an old man answering Sir Lyall's description, last seen wandering towards Inverfarigaig.

'Good work, Knox,' said Sergeant Awbrite, returning his salute. Then, noticing Justin's anxious expression added, 'I'm not through yet; take the squad car and collect Sir Lyall. And radio HQ. Inform them of a possible kidnapping. Prestwick Airport; mis-per IC1 female.'

Once Constable Knox had departed, Awbrite turned to Justin and raised his eyebrows. 'Well, now you've got your breath back, what have you got to report?'

'Last night, our gardener, Mr Gilliechattan, told us he had a nine o'clock appointment in Edinburgh,' said Justin. 'Burbage – that's his parrot – had a cough, so he was taking him to see a psittacine zoologist.'

'Sitta-what?'

'Parrot expert. Mr G returned a couple of minutes ago ... but Burbage has been in the library for at least an hour. I heard him coughing while we were having afternoon tea.'

'Aha!' said Awbrite. 'I'd better ask this gardener of yours a few questions.'

'I knew it,' groaned Sir Willoughby. 'I always thought there was something dodgy about that chap. Follow me, Sergeant. He'll be back at his cottage by now. We can put a call through to him from the east tower.'

After marching into the kitchen, Willoughby paused by a window and pointed out the Gilliechattans' cottage at the bottom of the vegetable garden. He lifted the receiver of the internal telephone system and dialled seven, drumming his fingers on the table top as he waited for an answer.

'Ah – Angus. There's a policeman here wanting a word with you,' he said. 'Would you nip over to the kitchen?' Then after listening to Mr Gilliechattan's terse reply, added, 'Right-ho. Might as well bring Mrs G along too, eh?'

Justin stayed by the window and watched the Gilliechattans bustle out of their front door and up the garden path, their Chattan kilts rippling in the breeze. The gardener's face looked almost as red as his beard, and he appeared to be arguing with his wife. Justin wished he could hear them – then he noticed a slight movement in the orchard. Hiding amongst the blossom-laden trees was Robyn, and judging from her rapt expression, the Gilliechattans were well within earshot.

'A policeman!' Mrs Gilliechattan grumbled. 'What if he asks about ...?'

'Stick to our story,' her husband interrupted. 'I'm sure it's nothin' to do with us. He's probably tryin' to catch a thief. A burglar must've tried robbin' Thyme Cas ...'

'But ...'

'But nothin' woman. I told you to keep that bird locked in his cage. Now we might have to face some awkward questions.'

'Don't worry,' said Morag Gilliechattan, her sharp eyes glittering like hatpins. 'I've got an idea. Listen carefully ...' She lowered her voice, and although Robyn crept behind them as close as she dared, their whispered scheme was inaudible.

The housekeeper rapped on the kitchen door and let herself in. Mr Gilliechattan followed, but only after he'd removed his boots and left them on the doorstep. His wife had him well housetrained, and forbade him from wearing them inside the castle, muddy or not.

As soon as the back door clicked closed, Robyn sat on the kitchen step and made the first official entry in her notebook. As she wrote, she kept one ear pinned to the door, and one hand

197

clamped firmly over her nose and mouth to avoid inhaling the sour odour emanating from the depths of Mr Gilliechattan's footwear.

'Are you Angus Glengarry Gilliechattan?' asked Sergeant Awbrite, eyeing the gardener's highland regalia and incongruous parrot with disapproval.

'Aye, that'll be raight, Jimmy.'

'That'll be right, *Sergeant*,' Awbrite corrected him. 'Now listen carefully: her Ladyship was kidnapped between nine-thirty and ten this morning. As part of my routine investigation, I need to establish everyone's whereabouts at that time.'

'Aye?'

'Perhaps I'm not making myself clear. Where exactly have you been today?'

'Seein' a parrot chappie at Edinburgh zoo,' replied Gilliechattan, still omitting any mention of the policeman's rank. 'Ma poor wee bard's got a nasty cough ... *Jimmy*!'

Sergeant Awbrite glared at him. 'Then how do you account for your *poor wee bird's* appearance at the castle – at least an hour before your return?'

The big gardener tugged his bristly red beard and regarded Awbrite with insolent green eyes; his wife stepped forward to speak.

'If you'll pairdon me sair, aye'm the lassie tae blame.'

'And you are?'

'Morag McGinty Gilliechattan, Sair ... castle hoosekeeper,' she said in her exaggerated highland accent. 'On the way bairk we storped orf at Whitefield fer a bait ta eat. I let the wee baird escape and he flew home – raight across the loch. Soo, that'll be how he got home a good 'oower b'forr we did.'

Poor Awbrite looked crestfallen – no easy feat considering he was bald.

'Hang on a tick,' said Justin. 'When I saw your old Morris drive through the gates, Mr Gilliechattan was the only person inside.'

'Noo laddie. I'd drawped ma fainest cairngorm brooch and

werra bendin' doon ta faind it,' said Mrs Gilliechattan. 'I didna want ma poor wee kitty prickin' wunna his *numerous* paws on it,' she added, with a simpering smirk.

As always, Mrs Gilliechattan had trumped them with her ace card. Although both Justin and Willoughby felt certain she was lying, they preferred not to risk any mention of her eight-legged cat in front of Awbrite.

'Will that be all, Sairgeant?' she asked, with a sneering sideways peek at Justin.

'Just one final question: what was the name of the er ... parrot expert you visited?'

There was an uncomfortable pause, during which the Gilliechattans exchanged sly glances and Burbage gave one of his hollow, hacking coughs.

'Erm ... Mr Shakespeare,' said the gardener eventually.

Sergeant Awbrite wrote dutifully in his notebook while Justin and Willoughby fumed silently.

'Well, that's all for the present,' said Awbrite, tucking his notebook into his breast pocket. 'Though if you'll pardon me for saying so – I've never met a gardener *quite* like you before.'

'*Comparisons are odorous*,' cackled Burbage.

'So are his boots,' muttered Robyn, and fled through the arched garden gate before the Gilliechattans could open the door and find her on the step. She waited on the other side of the wall until they'd scrunched back down the gravel path to their cottage. Neither of them spoke, but Burbage squawked something that sounded like '*Dogberry*' which made them both snigger. Robyn jotted it down in case it turned out to be important later.

Sergeant Awbrite checked his watch and planted himself on a kitchen chair; it would be another twenty minutes or so before Constable Knox returned with his squad car. Sir Willoughby dithered by the door looking moody and exasperated. He felt torn between the desire to avoid any ticklish questions and the obligation to be hospitable. At length, he thought of a solution:

'Hope you'll excuse me Sergeant. Things to do, and all that. I'll send Nanny along to brew more tea.'

Awbrite thanked him, and smiled to himself at the prospect of seeing the sprightly wee nanny again. The combination of her prim manners and fussy chatter felt homely and reassuring, taking him back more years than he generally liked to remember. However, his nostalgic trip down memory lane came to an abrupt end when Justin volunteered to make the sergeant's tea himself. Willoughby breathed a sigh of relief and bolted.

Justin felt equally relieved, but for quite a different reason. He wanted a few moments alone with the sergeant to broach an awkward subject. Grandpa Lyall, (if that was indeed his real name), had been living with them barely nine days, and Justin was uncomfortably aware that only he and Nanny Verity still harboured any doubts about his authenticity. Turning up at Thyme Castle on the very day the time machine was first mentioned seemed an amazing coincidence. His long white hair could easily be a wig, and the beard a fake attached with spirit gum.

The amnesia could be bogus too, Justin thought; after all, Dad's enemy sounds like a remarkable actor. But if Grandpa Lyall turns out to be genuine, Dad'll never forgive me for betraying the head of the Thyme Clan.

As Justin filled the kettle, he wondered how to avoid arousing the sergeant's suspicions yet prompt him to check out the old man's alibi. Realising he'd have to choose his words with the utmost care, Justin turned nonchalantly to Awbrite and spoke in what he hoped was a casual voice:

'So Grandpa left his Rolls on the other side of the loch then?'

'That's right.'

'Anywhere near Whitefield?'

'Somewhere between there and Inverfarigaig. Why?'

'Nothing ... I just wondered.'

'Wondered what?'

'Well ... er,' Justin faltered, doing a passably good acting job himself. 'I thought you might ask if he ... er, noticed the Gilliechattans. Maybe he could verify their ... er, Ali Baba ... or whatever it's called.'

Sergeant Awbrite looked downright offended. He frowned, rubbed his shiny bald pate and stared at Justin in silent contemplation. Time plodded. The kettle clicked off and the back door creaked open a few millimetres – and still, the policeman's gaze never wavered. A few days ago he'd seemed jovial and friendly; now, in an instant, his manner became incisive and detached, his voice crisp.

'Do you seriously expect me to believe that a boy, whose vocabulary includes pretentious terminology for a parrot specialist, can't recall an elementary word like alibi?'

Justin blushed. He tried to explain, but before he could utter a single word Awbrite raised his hand to silence him. 'I realise that your average Enid Blyton copper is nothing but an inept, bumbling buffoon – but reality is a little different. After forty years in the force, you can rest assured I'm perfectly capable of solving a crime without the assistance of schoolchildren.'

A muted snort from outside made Justin blush deeper still. He'd graduated from Enid Blyton when he was three.

'I'm sorry,' he mumbled, 'It's just that, well ... I'm *really* worried about Mum and ...'

'Forget it,' said Awbrite. He gave Justin a regretful smile, his chocolate-drop eyes suddenly crinkling at the corners. 'I'm sorry too. I shouldn't have been so hard on you; naturally you're anxious and don't want me overlooking any important leads. But you can rely on the professionals. Knox will have chatted to your grandpa all the way home, and found out absolutely everything we need to know – I promise.'

Justin reached for the kettle, but the distinctive sound of tyres on gravel arrested him.

'That sounds like my squad car arriving,' said the sergeant, pushing his chair back. 'You make that cup of tea for your grandpa instead ... I expect he'll be ready for it.' He gave Justin a firm pat on the shoulder then marched briskly out of the kitchen.

Instantly, Robyn sloped in looking superior; if the sergeant didn't need the assistance of children, then he wouldn't get it.

'I realise that your average child is nothing but a dim-witted kiddiwinkie,' she said, mimicking the policeman's brisk tones. 'But reality is *very* different. After only forty *minutes* as a private investigator, you can rest assured I'm already closer to finding Mum than he'll ever be.'

Five minutes later, Grandpa Lyall sipped hot tea and gazed around the enormous kitchen with an expression of pure bewilderment. His hands trembled, and every so often, a single tear would trickle down a furrowed cheek and melt into the depths of his snowy beard.

Robyn fussed over him, tenderly wrapping a tartan blanket round his shoulders and tempting him with buttery fingers of shortbread, but Justin felt so guilty he could hardly bear to look at him, especially his beard. He had to admit it couldn't be false, unless it was the work of a highly skilled makeup artist – and that didn't seem very likely.

The little confidence Grandpa had gained during the past week had completely evaporated, leaving him feeble and confused. In many ways he'd regressed to the same hazy mental condition they'd witnessed when he arrived. Once again, he appeared to be under the impression that Thyme Castle was a hospital, and kept asking for someone called Olivia. When Robyn shrugged, baffled and helpless, he broke down and sobbed.

If that's acting, Justin thought, it's an Oscar winning performance. He suspected they would never truly understand why the old man had driven off at dawn, taking nothing but a picnic hamper.

Sergeant Awbrite came to a less charitable conclusion:

'Rich and strange,' he remarked to the constable. 'That's the gentry for you! Years of inbreeding – half of them doolally, the rest as mad as hatters.'

Knox nodded his vacant pimply head, and thought about fish, chips and mushy peas wrapped in newspaper for his supper.

Awbrite had never considered Sir Lyall as a potential kidnapper – not for an instant. Now, ashamed of his recent misgivings, Justin too, mentally crossed the old Laird off his list of suspects.

Up in his laboratory, Justin stared at the scan of the ransom note on his computer screen, wondering whether he should have told Sergeant Awbrite how the words *"Thief of Time"* matched the kidnapper's signature – or if it would have prompted too many awkward questions. Shaking his head, he reached for the off-switch, but a soft chime announced the arrival of an e-mail.

To:	justin@thymecastle.co.uk
From:	napkinsdomestix.com
Subject:	Your New Butler

Napkin's Domestix are pleased to report that we have found you a butler with impeccable references. Mr Peregrine Knightly has worked at several royal residences, but your generous salary has tempted him to join you at Thyme Castle. He has now completed his week's notice, and should be with you on Monday May 12th. He will inform you of his estimated time of arrival in writing.

Yours faithfully,
Hubris Napkin – Napkin's Domestix.

PS. We hope the cook we sent has proved satisfactory.

Justin sighed deeply. With everything that had happened lately, the long-awaited arrival of a new butler had completely slipped his mind.

At about six-thirty the Thymes drifted down to the kitchen, even though none of them felt the least bit hungry. There was still no sign of Mrs Kof, but Nanny Verity checked the pantry and found a cold haunch of roasted venison and a large jug of neep and tattie soup. Ignoring the loud protests, she made a big plate of venison sandwiches and heated the soup in the microwave, insisting they all at least *tried* to eat *something*.

'Och, starving your wee selves won't help her ladyship,' she told them firmly.

Sir Willoughby, who looked too preoccupied to argue, carried Albion to the dining room and settled him in his highchair; Justin laid the table, then ran back to the kitchen to help Nanny carry the dishes; and Robyn volunteered to fetch Grandpa, knowing he would dodder along the portrait gallery at a snail's pace, giving her a valid excuse to do nothing else at all.

A disconsolate silence hung over the dining table. After a meaningful look from Nanny Verity, Sir Willoughby picked up his soup spoon with an air of resignation, and the others gradually followed suit. Despite her admonitions, Nanny ate less than anyone, and behaved almost as if Lady Henny had died, persistently referring to her in the past tense. Tears welled up in her eyes as she watched Albion dribble soup down his bib.

'She was such a good mother,' she sniffled.

No one commented, which made Justin feel guiltier than ever. It wasn't that Henny was a bad mum, he thought – no, of course not. But since Albion's birth, her filming commitments had kept her away from home with increasing frequency. At the castle, Nanny always took care of Albion, but out on location he spent more time with Eliza than he did with his mother. Justin suspected he was only whimpering now because the gorilla had refused to leave her room. Eliza was sulking again; the east tower sounded like Notre Dame Cathedral as she swung from the rafters, clanging her empty banana bucket against the walls. Albion listened, his bottom lip wobbling.

'Langa-baggle,' he shouted, and banged both fists on a slice of buttered bread.

'Lively little chap, isn't he?' remarked Grandpa Lyall, mopping out his soup bowl with the remains of a venison sandwich. He hadn't seen Lady Henny since the day he arrived, and appeared to have no recollection of her whatsoever. His hearty appetite and benign smile were starting to irritate Nanny Verity.

'Humbug,' she muttered, fighting back the tears, 'When poor Sir Willoughby's putting on *such* a brave face for the sake of the wee ones.'

Robyn flicked breadcrumbs and twiddled with her napkin, reminding herself for the tenth time in five minutes that her mother thrived on adventure. It didn't help. Desperate to get her mind off Henny, she slid a piece of paper out of her pocket and squinted at it under the table, her insides churning like an egg-whisk.

To:	rob@thymecastle.co.uk
From:	blueeyedboy@nine.com
Subject:	Dead-Brainz 2

Hi Rob!

Since meeting U in the Dead-Brainz chatroom I've got up 2 level 17. Therz a secret oubliette from the Corpus Callosum Crypt in level 16.

U asked about my age and hobbies – well, I'm nearly 15 and I'm in2 orienteering, wildlife conservation and designing websites. ☺
What about U?

This one sounds too good to be true, she thought. Okay, so he still thinks I'm a boy – but my last e-mail should rectify *that* little

misunderstanding; or at least the photo I've attached will. Surely –
surely, he'll reply tonight.

Grandpa Lyall yawned. Spying an opportunity to escape, Robyn
offered to escort him up to his bedroom.

Justin hardly noticed their departure. Apart from muttering 'no
thanks, Nanny,' a couple of times, (when she'd offered him a
sandwich), he'd barely spoken throughout the entire meal. He
stared into the depths of his soup, lost in thought.

While drawing his blueprints and stripping out the old sidecar,
the prospect of eventually *building* the time machine had seemed
strangely unreal – but now, with his mother's life in the balance
and a deadline looming, the reality of it made his stomach lurch.
He pushed his soup bowl away, wondering how he would ever
concentrate on the task ahead when endless questions kept
buzzing round his head like flies: Could the kidnapper have
infiltrated Thyme Castle? Had someone left the watch as a cryptic
warning? Was its similarity to the library clock a coincidence?
And did the words *Beware Procrastination* actually mean *Beware
the Thief of Time*?

Justin glanced uneasily at his father, realising he'd put off
talking to him about the watch for long enough. But before he
could speak, Sir Willoughby rose unsteadily, letting his napkin
slide to the floor. He stood, rubbing his furrowed forehead, as if
unsure what to do next.

Meanwhile, Nanny Verity, eying the untidy table with dismay,
lapsed into one of her periodic bouts of nostalgia.

'Och, I remember when the castle had a permanent staff of
thirteen,' she said, lifting Albion out of his highchair. 'There was
Tredwell the butler, dear old Fluff the housekeeper, Mrs Wight the
cook, a footman, a valet, a chauffeur, a gardener, an errand-boy, a
kitchen maid, two housemaids, Rebecca the tweeny and ... er ...
oh, me of course.'

Justin guessed this was her roundabout way of reminding them
that looking after a baby was a full time job, and that her duties
shouldn't include cooking or clearing up. Taking the hint, he

started gathering spoons and stacking the dirty plates and bowls.

'Don't worry, Nan ... the replacement butler should arrive on Monday.'

Nanny Verity gave a satisfied nod and bustled off to the nursery with Albion.

Justin peered at his father, still frozen like a statue; staring at nothing, oblivious to everything. 'Dad ... er ... did you hear me, Dad? ... *DAD*!'

Sir Willoughby turned towards him with a befuddled frown. 'Hmm ... what?'

'I said the new butler's coming on Monday. Weren't you listening?'

'Not really,' said Willoughby, his voice dead and flat. 'More to worry about than ...'

Justin groaned as he lifted a heavy silver tray loaded with dishes and cutlery. 'I got an e-mail from the agency who sent Mrs Kof,' he explained, struggling towards the kitchen.

Sir Willoughby trotted a few paces behind, frowning and ruffling his hair. 'Never mind about that *now*,' he muttered irritably. He held the kitchen door open for his son, and spoke again, his voice growing steadily louder. 'We need to have a serious talk about the week ahead. You'll need to get busy building a *certain something* – and, in the meantime, I'll try to locate your mother.'

'But ...'

'I'm convinced she *can't* be too far away,' continued Willoughby, now almost shouting. 'When I mentioned the *you-know-what* last week, somebody must've overheard me. That means there's a spy right here in the castle. And I still think my old enemy from *TOT* is behind this. 'Spect you spotted the "Procrastination" and "Thief of Time" clues?'

Justin nodded; this was his chance. He put the tray on the kitchen table and took a deep breath. 'Listen, Dad. You know the old library clock? Well, have you ever noticed the engrav–'

'OH, not *CLOCKS* now!' roared Sir Willoughby. 'What's

wrong with you? First it's butlers, then it's that Victorian monstrosity in the library. What next? The weather? Have I read any good books lately? *Aaarghh*, get your priorities sorted out; your mother's in grave danger.'

'But my wristwat–' Justin stopped abruptly, alarmed by the sudden fire in his father's eyes. Maybe this wasn't the right time after all. 'Sorry Dad, it's just that ...'

Sir Willoughby swept on with mounting agitation. 'Have you forgotten the Thyme Curse? One of us is *certain* to die this year. What ... what if it's Henny? *Aaarrghhhhhh!* That's *it* isn't it? The same hideous pattern; you'll lose your mother just like I lost mine.'

'I thought your imaginary curse was meant to be broken,' snapped Justin, gripping his father by the shoulders and shaking him. 'If Grandpa's alive and well, we haven't had a death in the clan for twenty-six years. Most families would consider that a blessing.'

There was a moment of uncomfortable silence. Justin could feel his father trembling.

'Yes ... yes, of ... of course,' faltered Willoughby. He gave a prolonged sigh, and seemed to deflate like a pricked balloon. 'You ... er ... you're right. Nothing's going to happen.'

'We won't *let* anything happen,' said Justin, wishing he felt as confident as he sounded. 'Don't worry, Dad. I've got a plan ... but I'd rather not talk about it down here. It'll be safer up in my lab where we can't be overheard.'

Sir Willoughby shivered as they crept along the portrait gallery. Moonlight filtered through the stained glass windows casting eerie distorted patterns across their faces. Their footsteps echoed, and the painted eyes of their ancestors appeared to follow them.

'I suppose it's only my imagination,' he whispered, 'but now I know there's a spy in the castle everything seems so sinister.'

'So – who's your prime suspect?'

'That blasted gardener,' hissed Willoughby, 'with his "*och aye the noo*" and "*see you Jimmy*" ... who does he think he's kidding? What I'd give for a good, hard tug at that ginger beard. I'd bet anything I could rip it clean off.'

'I wouldn't recommend it,' Justin warned. 'If he's the wrong man and his beard's real, he'd probably rip your entire head off ... *and* make you swallow it.'

The psychedelic style of Robyn's room contrasted sharply with the minimalist decor her brother preferred. The walls were multicoloured and most of her furniture was either inflatable or glittery. Lava lamps bubbled; mirrored disco-balls twirled and sparkled. Mrs Gilliechattan complained that just dusting in there made her feel dizzy, and for once Robyn felt inclined to agree. Her stomach turned somersaults and her heart pounded. Holding her breath, she pressed the power button on her PC, bathing the room in a soft bluish-white glow. And there it was: the tiny envelope-shaped icon she'd been longing for.

'So, what's your plan?' asked Sir Willoughby.

They were safe and secluded at the top of the south tower. Justin had activated the motion sensor alarms on each of the three floors below, and in the lab, the faint flicker of a Bunsen burner was their only illumination.

'Well,' said Justin, in a hushed voice, 'firstly, I've got to build the time machine – in barely a week – without arousing any suspicion whatsoever. That'll probably mean spending most mornings in the schoolroom, and eating meals with the family as usual. I'll be working until late each night, so we'll need to black out the lab windows – and the clock face – or my welding torch might attract unwelcome attention. During the day I want you to make plenty of noise in your workshop to distract our resident spy. If he believes *you're* busy out *there*, he won't come prying up here.'

209

'Got it,' said Willoughby. 'Plenty of flash-bang-wallop! The old misdirection trick.' He spoke with a kind of forced enthusiasm, but his eyes had a glazed, distant look.

'That's why openly searching for Mum might be a big mistake,' Justin continued. 'If you're right – and I'm pretty sure you are – he's probably watching your every move. He addressed the ransom note to you, so he obviously thinks *you're* the one building the time machine. If we're ever going to catch him, we need to fool him into thinking his plans are working.'

'Go on.'

'To begin with, he mustn't guess I'm the one building it. He knows an awful lot, but that's one thing he *doesn't* know.'

'Absolutely!' gasped Sir Willoughby. 'I don't want *you* in any danger; I know only too well what a ruthless swine he can be.'

'More important than that – it gives us a tremendous advantage.'

'How?'

'He'll be watching *you* ... not me.'

Willoughby's face blanched suddenly and he shuddered, as if the memory of some past horror had just resurfaced. 'Don't worry, son ... I'll distract him alright. But are you sure you can complete your er ... *contraption* by the seventeenth? It took me ages.'

'Technology has advanced a bit in the last decade, Dad. I'm not saying it'll be easy, but I'm fairly confident I can finish it by next Saturday. And if all goes according to plan – we'll rescue Mum *and* catch our spy by the weekend too.'

'I *suppose* so,' said Willoughby, not sounding entirely convinced. 'There aren't *many* suspects – once you've ruled out the family. But if I'm busy clattering in my workshop all day, and you're doing all the real work up here in the lab, who's going to be trailing our suspects?'

'The only other person we can trust,' explained Justin. 'Our amateur detective – Robyn!'

Robyn had read the e-mail a dozen times already – but once
more couldn't hurt:

To:	rob@thymecastle.co.uk
From:	blueeyedboy@nine.com
Subject:	📎 Fab Photo

Hi Gorgeous!

Wow! So U R a girl! Hey ... thatz gr8. Any girl who
plays Dead-Brainz is OK by me. Whatz Rob short
4? Roberta? No, U look way 2 cool 2 be called
Roberta!
Just got home. Been out canoeing all day. I'm wet
and exhausted. ☹
Recent photo of me attached. Hope U fancy me as
much as I fancy U. I'll B in touch soon. ☺

Chris.

She clicked the paperclip icon and downloaded a photo of him,
looking every bit as handsome as she'd imagined; practically a
fashion model.

Robyn stored the image in her personal folder, then switched on
her X-Box and spent the next few hours blasting cranio-zombies.

Eliza sat on the roof of the east tower, staring at the stars. She
grunted softly and shook her head; humans were beyond her
comprehension. No matter how many times the word 'kidnap' had
been explained to her, she couldn't grasp why anyone would do
such a terrible thing. With a deep sigh, she swung down to the
battlements and climbed the ladder to her room. Half way up, she
paused, peering towards the gates.

211

A dark, hooded figure had stepped onto the drive and was walking slowly towards the castle.

At a quarter to twelve Robyn got ready for bed. From the darkness of her room she peered out across the courtyard, and noticed an ethereal glow illuminating the window beside the pantry.

'*Weird!*' she whispered to herself. Then after collecting her notebook and a torch, she crept down the west tower staircase and along the portrait gallery, full of curiosity. She had a sneaky suspicion *who* was in the kitchen – but the thing that really baffled her was *what* they were up to.

Looking at the pattern created by previous threads of time, we might believe it possible to statistically predict the future – but speculating what lies ahead is pointless, because there are countless potential futures, depending on the decisions made at each timefork.

Apart from free will, two other factors determine the Tartan of Time's pattern. These are: fixed events and random chance. Only events have a relatively fixed place in time, and by their very nature alter the course of individual timelines. FIXED EVENTS are usually unavoidable and historically significant – like earthquakes or floods. Whilst they are unalterable, they alter many lives, and no single decision on any timeline can prevent them.

A major fixed event will precipitate numerous minor forks, collectively creating a major loop as many lives alter direction simultaneously. Along this diversion, individual threads continue to fork and loop, strengthening the tartan and gradually returning each timeline to its original course. A true alternate timeline forking into a parallel universe would only occur when time travel creates an otherwise unsolvable paradox.

If we cannot change history, do we ever alter our own present whilst visiting the past, or do we simply create a parallel present we never see?

CHAPTER FOURTEEN

Investigation & Adventure

The kitchen door was slightly ajar, and the faint luminescence Robyn had observed from her bedroom, now slanted across the entrance hall floor in a long, narrow shaft. She tiptoed along it, her footsteps deadened by the rubber soles of her slippers. Robyn stood outside the door and put her ear to the crack. Apart from her own heartbeat, all she could hear was a gentle, sporadic clicking. It was barely audible, yet sounded oddly familiar.

Holding her breath, Robyn peered cautiously round the door – and there, basking in the cold, eerie light of the kitchen computer monitor, sat Mrs Kof, clicking the mouse periodically. She hadn't even bothered to remove her hideous grey duffel coat, or pull down the hood. She leaned back, slurping from a can, her bare feet propped on top of a large suitcase. Robyn stared at it, wondering what was inside.

After a final click the room went black. Robyn heard the scrape of a chair, and flabby footsteps pounding across the kitchen towards her. She glanced around for somewhere to hide – but it was too late.

The kitchen door swung open and Mrs Kof marched into the entrance hall, bumping right into her. The cook gave a startled yell, and dropped the case on Robyn's foot.

'*Ow!*'

'Ahoy Miss Robbing. I backs now – finished nice off-day.'

'That's jolly heavy,' Robyn groaned, rubbing her toes. 'What's in it – the Crown Jewels?'

'Waiters,' boomed the cook, 'for making big muzzles. You 'ungry?'

'No,' said Robyn, with a puzzled frown at the suitcase. 'I thought somebody'd left the kitchen monitor on, so I came down to check.'

'I goings on-the-line like you showings me,' explained Mrs Kof. 'Order many foods from big soupy-market ... clicketty-click-click.'

'Oh,' said Robyn, suddenly feeling rather silly. 'Of course.'

'You wants I make you special midnight feasting?'

'No thanks. I'll just get myself a drink and go back to bed. Goodnight, Mrs Kof.'

The cook climbed the east tower stairs to the servants' quarters; Robyn ambled into the kitchen and poured herself some milk. As she sipped it, she gazed out of the rear window at the gardener's cottage.

A light still shone on the ground floor and, immediately, Robyn's curiosity got the better of her. Leaving her glass behind on the table, she unlocked the back door and crept along the garden path. There was a narrow gap in the torn curtain, just wide enough for someone to peep through.

Robyn had expected the housekeeper's home to be meticulously spruce, but was surprised to find it looking untidy and disorderly. The decor was every bit as overtly Scottish as the Gilliechattans' clothes, cluttered with ceramic highland cattle, tartan cushions and baskets of dried heather. Two faded prints hung over the fireplace – both utterly predictable: *Monarch of the Glen* and *The Mountain Eagle*.

Morag Gilliechattan was thumbing through a sheaf of type-written papers, whilst her husband worked at a stylish laptop, tapping its keyboard at warp-speed. An old grandfather clock in the corner struck mournfully, waking Burbage who was roosting on top of it.

'*The iron tongue of midnight hath told twelve,*' he screeched.

Angus Gilliechattan spoke to his wife. His voice sounded muffled through the glass, and Robyn could only pick up tantalising, intermittent scraps between deafening squawks.

'Our pseudonyms .... secret agents ... . we can't risk ... . our true identities .... finished.'

Robyn could hardly believe her ears. She opened her notebook, leaned it on the windowsill and wrote furiously – leaving gaps for the bits she couldn't hear.

'The trouble with Harry Hawkins .. ... got no .... If ... kidnapping ..... doesn't get .... time m. .... Willoughby terminated!'

Suddenly, something warm brushed against Robyn's leg, making her jump. It was Tybalt the Octo-puss, crouched with his tailed curled over his back, looking like a gigantic black scorpion. He catapulted himself onto the windowsill.

'Miaow.'

'Shhh,' whispered Robyn. 'Go away; you'll ruin everything.'

Tybalt took no notice. He mewed louder and scratched the windowpane with several of his paws. Burbage cocked his head on one side and announced his arrival:

'*Tybalt, you rat-catcher,*' he cackled. '*Good King of Cats.*'

Robyn barely had time to dive down behind a cucumber frame before Mrs Gilliechattan bustled over and opened the window. She rubbed Tybalt's head affectionately and he started to purr. His purring was just as ghastly as his appearance: a guttural clicking combined with a noise like fingernails scraping down a blackboard. Robyn hated it; it was the sound he made when he discovered some helpless bird entangled in one of his enormous sticky webs.

Mrs Gilliechattan leaned out of the window and gazed up at the castle, silhouetted against the moonlit sky. 'Do you think they suspect anything?' she asked, without the slightest trace of a Scottish accent.

Angus Gilliechattan laughed. 'What? *That* lot? Too trusting by

216

half ... except for the girl. We'd better keep a close eye on her. If she gets too inquisitive you know how to silence her!'

The laboratory windows were small, narrow slits, and a thick piece of card was sufficient to cover each of them completely. However, the glass face of the tower clock needed two enormous tartan blankets, one draped either side of the central mechanism. Justin held the final blanket taut while Sir Willoughby worked his way round the wooden frame, firing with a staple gun. He shouted in staccato bursts between each report.

'When – *BANG* – are you – *BANG* – going to – *BANG* – tell Robyn – *BANG* – our plan?'

Justin peeped under a loose flap towards the west tower, expecting to see the usual flashes of light from his sister's X-Box.

'Odd. Perhaps she's having an early night. I'll send her an e-mail.'

'An e – *BANG* – mail?' said Willoughby, firing the last few staples. 'You both – *BANG* – live in – *BANG* – the same building. *BANG* – finished!'

Justin grinned. His dad still hadn't fully embraced the latest technology. Why hike all the way to the west tower, when he could contact his sister instantly? He imagined that Victorian parents had felt equally baffled by the convenience of the telephone.

'She always checks her computer first thing in the morning,' he said. 'I'll ask her to pop over here for a pre-breakfast chat.'

Sir Willoughby leaned against the wall. 'Look – do we have to get Robyn involved in this,' he whispered. 'It's just that ... I ... I ...' He shook his head, unable to continue. His cheeks looked hollow, and there were dark shadows under his eyes.

'Go on, Dad.'

'Had another damned flashback last night. Worst yet,' he said, his voice scarcely audible. 'I could almost feel the electrodes fastened to my temples and the biting chill of the electro-conductive gel. Dashed maniac! He told me how my brains would melt like ice-cream in a microwave, relishing every moment of my terror. Then, he set the voltage to the highest level, and laughed as I watched his finger hovering over the master switch.'

Justin shuddered.

'Finally, he grew tired of his teasing, and injected me with a powerful anaesthetic. As I drifted into unconsciousness I tried with all my might to focus on one thought.'

'What?'

'*You!* You'd only just been born. I visualised my new son nestled in his mother's arms. If I remembered only one thing, I wanted it to be that. If not, at least my last thought would be a happy one.'

Suddenly, Justin felt sick.

As soon as Mrs Gilliechattan drew the ragged curtains, Robyn sped back to the kitchen. She locked the door, then ran through the entrance hall and along the portrait gallery without pausing for breath.

Climbing the west tower staircase she felt tempted to tell Justin about her adventure immediately, but a swift glance out of the landing window changed her mind. She'd expected to see signs of him at work in his lab – but to her amazement there were no lights flickering behind the face of the old tower clock. The south tower was in total darkness.

'Odd,' Robyn whispered to herself, 'perhaps he's having an early night.'

Sir Willoughby threw his jacket on the bed and kicked his shoes off. He padded to the window and gazed across the moonlit loch, wondering how his wife was coping with her first night in captivity.

Then, loosening his tie, he glanced up at Justin's lab and shook his head. The boy's plan was dazzling in its brilliance – naturally. But he *was* just a boy after all; he didn't know everything. Far from it.

Perhaps in time ...

An ear-splitting scream jolted him out of his silent contemplation. Willoughby hurtled up the stairs three at a time, overtaking Nanny Verity on the way. He burst into Robyn's room to find her standing on the bed, clutching a pair of slippers against a rather skimpy nightie.

'Oh Daddy,' she gasped. 'It was a mouse ... an enormous one. It ran right across my bare feet just after I'd taken my slippers off.'

'Where is it now?' asked Willoughby nervously, not particularly fond of small, scurrying rodents himself.

'It's gone. It ran out through the door when I screamed.'

'Hardly surprising. You probably terrified it.'

'What's to do?' Nanny Verity panted from the doorway, her face as pink as her flannelette dressing gown.

Robyn explained, whilst Willoughby clattered furniture and stamped his feet.

'Do you want to come and sleep in the nursery, Poppet?'

'No, I'm fine now,' Robyn assured them both. 'It was just the shock ... that's all.'

Nanny wasn't convinced, and insisted on making her some cocoa.

Robyn agreed reluctantly. I'd best play along for now, she thought – I don't want them getting suspicious. She jumped off the bed and wriggled her feet back inside her slippers. Then, when she was certain no one was looking, slid something into her bedside drawer – something small and hairy.

The whole mouse story had been pure invention ... but there *was* a *thread* of truth to it; the scream had been genuine. When she'd first clapped eyes on it in the dimly lit room, it really *had* looked like a mouse – not a moustache.

Robyn slept fitfully, unable to get the evening's strange events out of her mind. She woke much earlier than usual and, tired of tossing and turning, got up to check her mailbox. Her brother's request for a pre-breakfast chat intrigued her – and she could hardly wait to relate her own nocturnal adventures.

Justin's bedroom door was open, and he was still sound asleep when Robyn crept across the snowy-white carpet towards his bed. She glanced at his alarm clock blinking 07:15 and considered the various methods of waking him. She was hardly in the mood for jokes, but couldn't resist the subtle approach, placing the false moustache on the white cotton pillowcase beside him, then blowing softly on his face.

The result was spectacular. Justin opened one bleary eye, and the first thing he saw was something resembling a giant hairy caterpillar crawling across his pillow.

He vaulted out of bed, grabbed one of his slippers and walloped it with every ounce of strength he could muster. At this stage he noticed his sister.

'It had the same effect on me too,' remarked Robyn. 'You should have heard me scream.'

Justin's initial reaction was the overwhelming urge to find out whether she could swallow an entire duvet, but then he decided it was too much effort and flopped back on the bed.

'You'll regret that,' he yawned.

'Oooh I'm quaking already,' said Robyn, pretending to shiver. 'Anyway, you'll have to wait your turn. I'm expecting Mrs Gilliechattan to assassinate me first.'

Justin sat up, looking bewildered. It was too early to cope with his sister's warped sense of humour, especially after working in the lab until three. He yawned again and rubbed the sleep out of his eyes.

'She's a secret agent,' Robyn continued. 'So's Mr Gilliechattan. I was spying on them late last night.'

She told Justin how she'd investigated the light in the kitchen, bumped into Mrs Kof after she'd been using the computer, and then listened outside the gardener's cottage window.

'When I got back to my room I found *this* stuck to the bottom of my slipper,' she added, retrieving the dead caterpillar from the floor and handing it to her brother.

Now he could see it properly, it was obviously a false moustache – dark, luxuriant, and curled up at the ends.

'I probably stood on it outside the Gilliechattans' cottage,' Robyn concluded.

'I don't think so,' said Justin, taking it to the window. He held it in the sunlight, examining the spirit gum residue closely. 'Look how clean it is. It must've stuck on your slipper after you came back indoors. What *exactly* did Mr G say?' he added, wondering if his sister could have misunderstood.

Robyn showed him her hastily scrawled notes, and they tried to work out what the gardener had probably said. The gaps made it difficult, but they did manage to agree on the final sentence:

> *If kidnapping Henny doesn't get me the time machine, I'll have Willoughby terminated.*

Justin looked visibly shocked. He gazed across the loch with unfocussed eyes, applying every available brain cell. The kidnapper's face hadn't been visible on the DVD – but when Sergeant Awbrite phoned the airport, someone mentioned that the man who borrowed the wheelchair had a moustache. It *could* be a coincidence, but ...

A sudden movement by the water's edge distracted him. Justin glanced down, half expecting another glimpse of the elusive Nessie – but it was Mrs Kof. She dived into the loch and struck out vigorously, carrying a large haversack strapped to her beefy shoulders.

'I wonder ...' he mused. 'Listen Bobs: did you see what Mrs Kof was wearing under her duffel coat last night?'

'No.'

'When she bumped into you, could she have dropped her case *and* the moustache?'

'Perhaps.'

'Could you have stood on the moustache when you ran back through the hall later?'

Robyn nodded.

'Last Sunday, when you saw her cutting something out of Dad's newspaper, did you notice where she put it?'

'In her recipe book,' said Robyn. 'That's why I assumed it was a recipe.'

'I wonder if it's still there.'

Robyn gasped. 'Are you suggesting *she* made the ransom note and then kidnapped mum ... disguised as a man?'

'Not exactly,' said Justin. 'But we need to find her recipe book before she gets back. If there's *no* cutting inside – then it looks pretty suspicious.'

Robyn was out of the door in a flash, furious with herself for overlooking something so obvious.

Justin tied a dressing gown over his pyjamas, tucked the moustache in his pocket and hurried after her. By the time he reached the kitchen, Robyn had already located the recipe book and extracted a scrap of newspaper.

'Dead end,' she said, wearing her gloomiest scowl.

'A recipe?'

'No ... just an advert.'

Justin read it carefully:

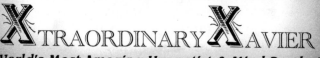

THE

BOHEMIAN
CIRCUS

VISITING INVERNESS FROM
SUNDAY 4TH TO SATURDAY 17TH OF MAY

Featuring

The Flying Fiorellos — *on the trapeze*

Balthazar *the Elephant from East of Shanghai*

Musetta — *a Woman Alone on the High wire*

Lipizzaner Horses *dancing to Waltzes from Vienna*

Maxara Pidgeon — *& her Performing Parrots*

Beppe, Tonio & Canio — *the Clowns*

Juno *& the* Paycock

Plus

EXCLUSIVE APPEARANCE ON SATURDAYS ONLY

XTRAORDINARY XAVIER

World's Most Amazing Hypnotist & Mind-Reader!

'The date's correct, but this cutting won't be from the *Sunday Times*,' said Justin, shaking his head. 'It's a national paper; it wouldn't advertise a circus in Inverness.'

'But I saw Mrs Kof cut it out of the front page,' said Robyn, 'and we know the kidnapper used the *Sunday Times* to make the ransom note.'

'So Dad's newspaper *can't* have been the *Times*.'

'Doesn't Dad usually get *Scotland on Sunday*?' asked Robyn, baffled.

Justin turned the cutting over and smiled. 'You're right,' he said, 'look.' He showed his sister the reverse side. It was mostly incomprehensible: the right half of one column, the left half of another, a fragment of headline and part of the newspaper's title.

nd on Su

HIEVES DIAL M

for murder of a very lderly man who was calling out for help eral minutes before bund under the skin, been seen carrying a case said to contain ffering a reward for eturning the case of b the Police Station.

Dozens of his neighbours all describing Mr Elstree who worked as a waiter a often seen walking in the game of darts with friend local pub - The Paradine He was a member of the Society. Local solicitors Jonathan drew up his pre will, which has since disa

R VISIT SKYE
visits the Isle of Skye next
day. Campers try singing

'*Scotland on Sunday,*' said Robyn, sounding dejected. 'That rules Mrs Kof out.'

'I suppose so ... but why did she want the advert?'

'Perhaps she just likes circuses. I'll bet that's where she went yesterday on her day off.'

Justin shrugged. 'Unless ...'

Suddenly, the back gate to the vegetable garden creaked open, and a pair of flabby, bare feet plodded towards the kitchen door. Robyn hurriedly slid the recipe book back in its drawer.

Justin pulled the moustache out of his dressing gown pocket and threw it on the floor behind them, outside the pantry door. Robyn glared at him, and was about to retrieve it when Justin grabbed her arm.

'Leave it,' he hissed, passing her a cereal spoon. 'Watch in this.'

At first, Robyn stared at it in bewilderment – then she realised its shiny convex surface reflected the entire kitchen in miniature. The door flew open. Mrs Kof marched in, swathed in a massive robe, her bald head wrapped in a towel.

'Ahoy Master Justink, Miss Robbing,' she called cheerfully. 'You not lying in beds?'

'No,' said Justin casually, 'but my sister can lie quite convincingly sitting in a chair.'

Robyn looked infuriated and kicked him under the table.

'I bin swims in locket.'

'We saw you,' said Robyn. 'Was it cold?'

'Frizzy,' Mrs Kof replied firmly. 'I sees Professor Gimlet out paddling his little butt.'

'Did he see you?'

'Yes. He ask what I doin' carryin' heavy hoversuck. I tells him for buildin' big muzzles.' She rolled up the arms of her towelling robe and displayed a pair of biceps that looked as if she'd built them up quite enough already. 'You wants I make you fast-break?'

'Yes please,' said Justin, winking at his sister.

They both asked for cranberry crumpets, and then peered avidly at the backs of their spoons as Mrs Kof headed for the pantry. She hesitated by the door, glancing furtively over her shoulder; when she was certain they weren't looking, she bent down, swept the moustache off the floor and tucked it into her robe pocket.

Robyn nudged her brother. 'Doesn't it get boring?' she whispered.

'What?'

'Always being right.'

Half an hour later, Sir Willoughby marched in, looking even more stressed than usual. He wore a crumpled linen suit and a battered Panama hat, and carried a couple of newspapers folded under one arm.

'Been out already, Dad?' asked Justin.

'No choice,' Willoughby grumbled. 'Gilliechattan normally fetches the Sunday papers, but he's in a frightful mood. Kept ranting on about somebody trampling over his cucumber seedlings during the night. Thought I'd better get the papers myself, and check whether there's any mention of your mum.'

'Is there?' asked Robyn.

'No – the sergeant promised to try and keep it out of the media. Safest, he said. But I was worried someone at the airport might've talked. After all, she *is* quite famous. Last thing we need right now is a swarm of blasted reporters hammering on the door.'

'I doubt there'd be anything yet,' said Justin. 'It's not even twenty-four hours since she was kidnapped.' He craned his neck to peer at the newspaper titles. 'Is that the *Sunday Times*?'

'No. I always get *Scotland on Sunday*.'

'Told you,' said Robyn. 'Mr G usually borrows it when you've finished, doesn't he Dad? He gets the *Sunday Post* for Mrs G. She reads the Doctor's page then passes it on to Nanny.'

'Doesn't anybody get the *Times*?' asked Justin.

'*NO!*' snapped Sir Willoughby, looking decidedly irritated by their sudden newspaper fixation. 'If it's *that* urgent, cycle into the village – but I've told you, your mum isn't in any of them. I've checked.'

Justin and Robyn exchanged furtive glances. Meanwhile, their father threw his hat on top of the fridge, and left the *Sunday Post* by the back door for the housekeeper.

'Any coffee?' he muttered, striding over to the table.

'Yes, Sore Will-berry,' said Mrs Kof, giving him a gappy grin as she fetched the pot.

Willoughby settled back in a chair and opened his own newspaper – but not for long. As the cook came towards him, she stubbed her toe on the table leg, lurched forward and spilt hot coffee in his lap. Willoughby bellowed like a stag and jumped up, his chair crashing to the floor. He held the newspaper at arm's-length, the bottom half stained and dripping.

'Just look at my sodden paper,' he roared, (or something like that). 'It's a pulpy mess.'

Mrs Kof began apologising profusely – or so they assumed – reverting to her native tongue whenever her grasp of English seemed inadequate. She threw the ruined newspaper in the tidy bin, then blotted Sir Willoughby's groin vigorously with a tea towel.

'Leave me alone, woman,' he shouted, overcome with embarrassment. 'I'll take the other damn paper and read it upstairs, after I've changed.'

But at that exact moment the back door opened and Mrs Gilliechattan stepped in.

'Och, a see yer managed tae get ma *Poost* this week,' she said, whisking the paper from under Sir Willoughby's nose.

'But ... but ...' he spluttered.

'They'd ran oot lairst week. Angus had tae get the *Taimes* instead.'

Even as Henny fought to stay awake, she knew sleep was inevitable. She had a plan, of course – but constant sedation wasn't part of it. Desperately, she struggled to arrange her confused ramble of thoughts before succumbing to oblivion. When her captor had arrived, she remembered feeling conscious though groggy; whether three minutes or three hours had elapsed since then, it was impossible to tell. The sedative trapped her in a bizarre time warp, and to make matters worse, her watch had been confiscated. All she knew for certain was that her head ached and her mouth tasted like a jogger's sock.

The kidnapper had thrown two soggy pieces of toast at her, and poured lukewarm coffee out of an old thermos flask. Henny felt tempted to spit it in his face, but knew it was wiser to reserve her strength. Before leaving, he administered the sedative again – this time in her arm.

'Stay awake ... you *must* stay awake,' she repeated to herself – and the warning echoed endlessly in her dreams as she slept.

At 9:24 precisely, Sir Willoughby and Justin stood side by side in the blacked-out lab, synchronising their watches.

'Okay Dad – I need three hours of bangs and flashes, starting six minutes from ... NOW!'

Willoughby slid down the fireman's pole, then hurried through the castle and out to his workshop.

Justin waited patiently for the diversion to begin, mentally reviewing his timetable for the week ahead: if he could complete the preliminary adaptation of the sidecar by lunchtime, he could start building the anti-gravity unit later that afternoon. That would keep him busy until Monday night at least; the negative-energy generator should be ready by Wednesday morning, leaving him three full days to build the subatomic wormhole-vortex accelerator – that would be the biggest challenge. If everything went according to plan, that still left him most of Saturday to fit it all together and wire it to the computerised Minkowski space-time coordinates display module. It was a tight schedule, but there was no alternative.

Robyn wandered through the entrance hall, sipping her hot coffee thoughtfully. She hated to admit it but, so far, her investigations had left her feeling confused. The kitchen door opened, and she watched Mrs Kof tramp up the east tower staircase to get dressed. The sight of her huge, bare feet triggered another interesting speculation: had the cook's stumble been genuine? Robyn had her doubts – and with good reason. She'd lost count of the times she'd "accidentally" spilt something over the boy genius when he became too insufferable. (*Whoops ... soooo sorry, Dustbin; I hope that wasn't an important equation!*) She didn't fool him for an instant of course, but Henny never guessed. *You'll have to make allowances for your sister*, she'd say, *she's going through that awkward stage.*

Robyn grinned to herself. She'd been going through an awkward stage for as long as anyone could remember, and what's more, she'd no intention of growing out of it ... even when she had grandchildren.

The more Robyn thought about Mrs Kof's clumsiness, the more it bothered her. She raced back to the empty kitchen and spied a pair of scissors on the draining board and a trail of coffee drips leading towards the tidy bin.

Barely able to contain her excitement, she groped inside for the partially sodden newspaper and hauled it out. Her hunch was correct: something had been snipped out of the dry, top half of the front page.

Several loud clangs confirmed that Willoughby had arrived at his workshop. Justin scrolled down his computer's music menu and clicked on Shostakovich Recital activating a chip inside the concert grand two floors below. A piano arrangement of Symphony Number 3 in E-flat echoed throughout the south tower, establishing his alibi. He ignited an oxyacetylene torch, lowered

229

his protective goggles and squeezed beneath the chronopod.

Back in her psychedelic bedroom, Robyn switched on her computer, and checked the inbox. Still no e-mail from Chris. A few days ago, he'd been contacting her at least a dozen times by breakfast. Now he knew she was a girl he seemed to be cooling off – despite swapping photos. Robyn decided to give him one last chance before dumping him. She typed a brief e-mail then jabbed SEND.

To:	blueeyedboy@nine.com
From:	rob@thymecastle.co.uk
Subject:	Want 2 Chat?

Hi Chris! R U online yet & feeling up 4 a chat? ☺
Robyn.

There was a gentle tap at the door and Nanny Verity bustled in looking flustered.

'Oh Poppet, I wondered if ...' She stopped mid-sentence and frowned at the computer disapprovingly through her spectacles. 'I do wish you'd spend a bit less time staring at that screen, dear. You'll ruin your eyesight. When I was your age ...'

'When you were my age pigeon-post was newfangled,' groaned Robyn. 'Honestly Nanny, you're so old-fashioned. If you had your own PC and got online I bet you'd love it. You can have my old laptop if you want.'

'Och, I don't think so. I don't trust computers.'

A melodic chime drew Robyn's attention back to the screen; he'd replied.

'Did you want something, Nanny?' asked Robyn, her forefinger hovering over the mouse.

'Never mind,' Nanny sighed, and trudged out, closing the door behind her.

Robyn clicked the envelope icon:

To:	rob@thymecastle.co.uk
From:	blueeyedboy@nine.com
Subject:	Re: Want 2 Chat?

Hi Robyn.

Sorry I was so busy yesterday. Having a lazy day 2day. How about U? Anything happening @ your place?

Chris.
PS. Robyn is a wicked name!!! ☺

A deafening explosion rattled Willoughby's workshop and wisps of blue smoke seeped from beneath the doors. Robyn giggled. Yes, there's plenty happening, she thought. The question is: how much should I reveal?

Actions taken whilst visiting the past rarely alter our present. The majority of forks initiate loops; minor actions in the past will create minor loops. Most of these rejoin our timeline well before the present, which usually remains as we left it. Travel back far enough and even major diversions have sufficient time to loop back to their original course.

Imagine visiting your home twenty years in the past and accidentally breaking a window. Would you expect to find it broken when you returned to the present? No. Analysing the situation logically, somebody would have repaired the window in the intervening years.

Such minor actions are too insignificant to create new timelines; we need not imagine two different worlds where the window is both fixed and broken. However, if the broken window triggers a major disruption – such as a fatal accident to the person fixing it – then looping back may be impossible. To avoid a paradox, the timeline must branch off into an alternate parallel universe – but our own present-day world remains unchanged.

This suggests that meddling with history is pointless. Trying to prevent a past death, for example, wouldn't restore that person to life in the time traveller's present, but merely create a parallel world in which they didn't die at that point in time.

CHAPTER FIFTEEN

Red Herrings or Evidence?

'I just can't get my head around it,' groaned Robyn for at least the tenth time. 'Time travel doesn't make any sense.'

Justin felt tempted to reply that *she* was the one not making any sense, but he bit his tongue, too busy to argue. Only yesterday, his sister had dismissed time travel as the comic-book fantasy of teenage boys. Yet shortly after lunch, she'd burst into his lab and bombarded him with numerous complex questions.

'Shouldn't you be out trailing suspects or something?' he asked, wishing his sister would leave him to concentrate on his anti-gravity unit. He glanced at his watch, uncomfortably aware that hours were passing like minutes. He'd assured his father the time machine would be ready in a week, but with one day gone already, Justin felt a burgeoning knot of panic in the pit of his stomach.

Robyn shook her head. Her investigations were at a temporary standstill; she could see or hear everyone from right where she was, peering round the edge of the blackout curtain. Professor Gilbert drifted in his rowing boat, scanning the loch through a pair of binoculars. The Gilliechattans lounged in deck chairs on the cliff top, (Mrs G reading a newspaper whilst her husband appeared to be knitting). Eliza leaned over the castle ramparts, dropping grapes on Nanny Verity as she pushed Albion's pram round the courtyard below; Alby chortled gleefully, having no intention of taking his afternoon nap. Clattering noises came from

Willoughby's workshop, and the deep voice of Mrs Kof rang out from the kitchen. Grandpa Lyall was snoring in the library – the din reverberating through three floors and almost drowning the computerised concert grand in Justin's sitting room.

'Delightful!' he groaned. 'A piano rendition of Haydn's Symphony Number 101 in D major, complete with nasal accompaniment!'

Robyn abandoned her vigil and walked over to her brother's workbench.

'Using words of one syllable – and assuming this pile of nuts and bolts will actually work,' she added, kicking the chronopod. 'Why, *precisely,* can't you travel back in time and stop Mum from being kidnapped?'

'If you'd read my notebook properly you'd understand,' grumbled Justin. He turned to frown at his sister, and a minuscule titanium flange-coupling toppled into a Medusan vortex of wires. 'Oh – *flux!* Pass me my pneumatic-sprocket nippers, quick – no, not those ... *those.*'

Robyn picked up a few random tools and slammed them down again, until Justin lunged out and grabbed one. After several seconds he spoke again, trying to keep his voice impassive: 'I'm fairly certain you can't *undo* the past, Bobs. If you travelled back and tried to change things, all you'd get is an alternate version of the same events. Mum has *already* been kidnapped; interfering might make it happen differently, but it wouldn't stop it. At least, that's the theory. To be honest, nobody knows for sure.'

'But if Mum had *never* been kidnapped, then ...'

'Then there'd be no need to finish the time machine by next weekend ... and if I didn't finish it, I couldn't travel back and stop her from being kidnapped. My theory suggests that her abduction is a fixed event in the Tartan of Time.'

'The *what?*'

Justin took a deep breath. 'It's ...'

'Oh, never mind,' snapped Robyn. 'What about travelling forwards in time, asking Mum where she was imprisoned, then coming back to the present to rescue her? *That* wouldn't alter the past.'

'You're confusing science fiction with science fact,' sighed Justin, starting to lose his patience. 'The pod isn't designed to travel into the future, because there isn't just *one*. There might be billions of futures – all of them different – and there's no way of telling which one is ours. In some futures Mum might not survive. Didn't you read *any* of my notebook? Time travel is incredibly risky.'

Robyn looked mutinous. 'Well ... *I'd* take a few risks to rescue Mum.'

'Me too – but it wouldn't prevent the kidnapper trying again.'

'Are you saying that the only way to get Mum back safely is to hand over this ... this *thing,* at midnight on Saturday?'

'No. I'm saying that we've got to discover who's spying on us. There's a leak at Thyme Castle and it makes us vulnerable. That's why *your* job's so important.'

'Well, I've narrowed things down considerably,' said Robyn. 'Assuming the kidnapper's in disguise, there can only be three possible suspects. He'd have to check on Mum at least once a day, so all I need to do is watch their daily routines.'

'I make it four suspects – if Dad's old enemy *is* one of the household,' said Justin, narrowing his eyes. 'But he probably wouldn't infiltrate the castle unless it was unavoidable. My guess is he's got a spy here who reports back to him; so you can't rule anyone out. If he's as clever as Dad says, *even* the spy might not realise they're being used as a spy.'

Robyn gave one of her explosive snorts. 'How can someone be a spy without realising it?'

'Simply divulging information to someone they don't suspect; like last year, when those two TV executives talked about Mum in front of Eliza. They didn't realise she understood every word, and would tell Mum what they'd said.'

'Surely you're not suggesting Eliza is a spy?'

'You're missing the point.'

'Which is?'

'Don't trust *anybody*.' He was about to explain when the phone in the library started ringing. 'You get it,' said Justin, 'I'm meant to be doing my piano practice, remember?'

Robyn slid down the fireman's pole, landing in the library with a gentle thump. Grandpa Lyall was shuffling towards the desk, but Robyn raced across the room and snatched up the phone before he could reach it.

'Hello. Thyme 802701.'

'Ah, good afternoon, Miss. Sergeant Awbrite here. May I speak to Sir Willoughby?'

'I'm afraid he's er ... busy working,' said Robyn. 'Can I take a message?'

Awbrite hesitated. 'Arhhh, well ...' he said. 'I would prefer to speak to your father personally, but under the circumstances I'll make an exception. This is something all of you need to be aware of. I got through to Edinburgh Zoo; it turns out they *do* have a veterinarian called Shakespeare.'

'Oh,' said Robyn, pulling a face.

'Yesterday morning he examined a sulphur crested cockatoo with a cough. He said it's been a patient of his for three years, and his description of the woman *with* the parrot matched your housekeeper perfectly. Furthermore, the vet claimed her husband usually brought it, but he had a prior appointment. I think we can guess what *that* was ... so, I thought I'd better warn you.'

'Are you going to arrest Mr Gilliechattan?'

'There isn't enough evidence – yet. I'll call round tomorrow morning and invite him to assist the police with their inquiries ... if you know what I mean.'

'Interrogation,' gasped Robyn.

'He'll be as sick as a parrot!' said Awbrite, chuckling at his own joke.

'But if Mr G *is* the kidnapper, wouldn't it be best to watch and see if he leads us to Mum.'

'You're a smart young lass and no mistake,' said the sergeant.

Red Herrings or Evidence?

'That's why I wanted to talk to your father. I need Sir Willoughby to keep a close eye on the Gilliechattans this evening and early tomorrow morning. Can you explain all that to your father for me?'

Robyn paused a moment, choosing her words carefully. 'You can rely on me.'

If the sergeant had known her better, he would have realised that *that* meant Robyn had other plans entirely.

At five past four Justin decided to reward himself with a well-earned drink. He hadn't heard the tea gong – but he assumed it had been drowned out by the phoney piano practice. With a few swift clicks of his mouse he stopped the music, and then dashed along to the west tower.

He was surprised to find the Great Hall empty, so headed for the kitchen instead, where he found Robyn, Nanny and Mrs Kof arguing over a tray of anatomically correct gingerbread men decorated with cashews and hazelnuts.

'*Eurghh*, gross,' said Robyn, prodding one with a teaspoon. 'I'm *not* eating *those*.'

For once, Nanny and Robyn were in full agreement, though Mrs Kof was baffled.

'You not likings nuts?' she asked.

'What's happened to afternoon tea?' enquired Justin.

'We're not having any 'til it's suitably dressed in some nice little icing-sugar underpants,' replied Nanny primly. 'And anyway, Alby's still having his nap; Eliza says your grandpa's asleep in the butler's bedroom; and when I went to fetch Sir Willoughby, I couldn't get him to hear over all that terrible din he's making, no matter how hard I hammered on the door.'

Meanwhile, Mrs Kof was slamming cups on saucers, wearing a scowl that would curdle milk.

'Did Nanny tell you the good news?' asked Justin, hoping to diffuse the tension. 'No more struggling with all those heavy dishes, Mrs Kof. You can stay in the kitchen whilst our new butler ferries them to and fro.'

Nanny nodded approvingly, but to Justin's surprise the cook's face turned raspberry-red.

'I not struggles with dish,' she said huffily. 'I strong enuff to lift whole flippin' tables.'

A shrill whimpering echoed from Nanny's midriff. 'Och, *botheration!*' she exclaimed, withdrawing a baby monitor from her apron pocket. 'The wee imp's woken up.' She bustled out of the kitchen almost colliding with Professor Gilbert hovering in the doorway.

The professor cleared his throat and sang softly, trying to relax his vocal cords. '"N-n-*now for the tea of our host, now for the rollicking bun.*" D-d-do excuse the interruption,' he added, with a timid glance at Robyn. 'M-might I have a p-p-private word with you, Justin?'

'Certainly, sir,' said Justin, hurrying into the entrance hall. 'What's the problem?'

'I w-w-wondered if I might take a week off?' whispered the professor, his ears turning a vivid pink. 'I'd like to re-grow my b-b-beard without being the butt of Miss Robyn's perpetual teasing.'

'I'm so sorry. What ...'

'P-p-please don't ap-p-pologise,' stammered Professor Gilbert. 'She keeps making em-ba-barrassing remarks about designer stubble. Normally I can tolerate it ... b-b-but as I'm due some time off I wondered ...'

'Of course,' said Justin, realising this meant he could work on his time machine all day without arousing anyone's suspicion. 'Take as long as you like.'

'Oh, thanks. Just a few days ... until Saturday perhaps. The b-beard should be well under way by then. I should never have shaved it off in the f-f-first place.'

That night, Robyn collected her notebook and a torch – planning to keep the Gilliechattans under close surveillance. She crept along the upper corridors and down the servants' staircase, but as she tiptoed down the final flight she heard a hushed voice echoing across the entrance hall. Robyn peered over the banister, holding her breath. Mrs Kof was using the telephone.

'No ... they suspects nuffin',' whispered the cook, glancing furtively over her shoulder as she listened to the reply. 'Yes ... be readies for Saturday,' she said, then after a brief pause added: 'Yes ... for twelve.'

Robyn's investigations were a total disaster. At around ten o'clock, Angus Gilliechattan trudged out of the castle gates carrying a sack. Robyn trailed him conscientiously, but he merely checked a succession of traps round the castle perimeter, set to catch the rabbits plundering his vegetable garden. When the sack was full, she followed him back home, chilled and weary, only to discover his wife had gone out in their rusty old Morris Minor.

Determined not to be out-foxed a second time, Robyn set her alarm for six o'clock the following morning.

When she awoke, she dressed swiftly, then crept out of the castle and along the path to where the Gilliechattans parked their car. After prising its back door open, she hid behind the front seats under a moth-eaten tartan blanket that stank of cats. By eight-thirty, Robyn felt cold, stiff and bored – then, the back door to the Gilliechattans' cottage creaked open. She heard the sound of footsteps coming towards the car, and the jangle of keys. The car door squeaked, and Robyn almost screamed when something heavy landed on top of her. For an instant she thought it was a dead body – which was startlingly near the truth. It was a sack containing the skinned corpses of about two dozen rabbits.

Moments later they were bumping along the road to Drumnadrochit. Robyn lay still, inhaling the nauseating concoction of petrol fumes, rabbit carcass and cat pee. Being a private detective was *not* as glamorous as she'd hoped.

Justin fastened his jeans and pulled a baggy tee-shirt over his head. He reached for his comb, then, after a sleepy glance in the mirror, decided the trendily dishevelled look rather suited him; the shadows under his eyes, however, did not. He'd worked until dawn again, but, realising there were no lessons this week had allowed himself the luxury of an extra half-hour in bed. It didn't feel like anywhere near enough.

Hearing the Gilliechattans' old Morris chug back into the courtyard, he opened his bedroom window and watched it drive past the east tower towards the gardener's cottage. As it came to a halt, it backfired and a plume of acrid smoke belched out of its exhaust pipe.

This time Robyn *did* scream – but fortunately the highland tattoo blaring out of the car radio muffled it completely. To her immense chagrin, Morag Gilliechattan had done nothing more sinister than drive to the local butchers, and exchange the dead rabbits for a large frozen haggis.

Still under the blanket, Robyn peered between the front seats at the clock on the dashboard; it was nine o'clock. The housekeeper slammed the car door and disappeared into her cottage, then, five minutes later, she bustled off to the castle with Tybalt the octo-puss trotting behind her.

Robyn scrambled out of the car and ran across the cliff top, peering over the kitchen garden wall in search of Mr Gilliechattan. She couldn't see him anywhere – and to make matters worse, Henny's boat, (usually moored beside the jetty at the foot of the cliffs), had vanished too.

Robyn trudged through the kitchen feeling thoroughly discouraged. Even the scent of freshly made banoffee pancakes couldn't brighten her mood. Desperate for a long, hot shower, she shot across the entrance hall, and narrowly missed bumping into her brother.

Red Herrings or Evidence?

'Don't ask!' she snarled, seeing his nose wrinkle-up in disgust.

Justin didn't. Having eaten next to nothing since his mother's abduction, he felt decidedly hungry this morning, and headed for the kitchen, drawn by the sizzle of hot bananas and toffee.

Still damp from her morning swim, Mrs Kof presided over a huge frying pan, while Eliza sat close by, peeling bananas with her feet.

'Ahoy Master Justink!' bellowed the cook. 'You wantings baniffy pankicks?'

With Professor Gilbert away, Mrs Gilliechattan decided to blitz the schoolroom. After clearing out the professor's desk, she turned her attention to an ancient bookshelf that looked as if it hadn't been moved in centuries. Anticipating Tudor grime and baroque cobwebs, she grasped the shelf with both hands and gave an experimental tug, sending an avalanche of dusty encyclopaedias over Tybalt. With a yowl of rage he scuttled downstairs like an over-wound clockwork spider.

Meanwhile, Justin, feeling like he'd eaten one baniffy pancake too many, was standing on the castle doorstep chatting to the postman.

'Grand weather' remarked Jock, handing over the usual bundle of mail.

Fergus, his Scottie dog, sprang out of the van and sat up, begging for his daily stick of rock – but before Justin could fish it out of his pocket, Tybalt streaked across the entrance hall behind him. Unable to resist chasing a cat with twice the standard quota of legs, Fergus darted past Justin, barking with excitement. Tybalt skidded into the kitchen, zipping between Mrs Kof's huge bare feet ... with Fergus panting in his wake, claws clattering across the tiled floor.

'Fergus – COME HERE!' yelled Justin, dropping the envelopes and racing towards the kitchen. But like all Scotties, Fergus had a selective hearing impediment and feigned deafness.

Jock hung back, not liking to enter the castle uninvited. 'His bark's worse than his bite,' he called, taking a tentative step over the threshold – but the sound of smashing crockery and the cook's booming voice sent him scurrying back to his van.

Meanwhile, Tybalt hurtled out of the open kitchen door and across the vegetable plot with Fergus in hot pursuit. Justin shot after them, hardly daring to look at the rows of trampled herbs and seedlings. At the Gilliechattans' cottage, Tybalt catapulted himself through the cat-flap, and then, to Justin's horror, Fergus dogapulted himself through it a split-second later.

'*FLUX!*' roared Justin, thumping the cottage door in exasperation. He hesitated, listening to the clatter of toppling chairs, Fergus snarling, and Tybalt hissing and spitting like a firework. Justin glanced over his shoulder at the schoolroom windows, expecting Mrs Gilliechattan's head to appear at any moment. Finally, after a thunderous growl and the crash of what sounded like a grandfather clock, he took a deep breath, grasped the doorknob and ran indoors.

The room looked like a tacky highland gift shop ... after an explosion. Tybalt clung to the pelmet, his tail lashing, with Fergus tugging the curtains beneath. Justin removed his belt, fastened it to the little dog's collar, and then tidied the room with one hand whilst struggling to restrain Fergus with the other. He straightened the grandfather clock and set the pendulum going, returned various tartan cushions to their respective armchairs, reloaded the coal-scuttle, picked up umpteen pots of dried heather, and resurrected a grisly-looking hat-stand made from antlers. Finally, he stooped to gather the snowdrifts of typing paper littering the floor. He placed them on the desk ... and there, beneath a pair of scissors and a pot of paste, he saw a stack of old newspapers.

Justin gasped, and reached for the top paper – but before he could confirm his suspicions, Mrs Gilliechattan burst in. Too breathless to speak, her dagger-like eyes demanded an explanation.

'I er ... I had to rescue Tybs,' mumbled Justin, dragging the

Scottie towards the door. 'Sorry about the mess.' He slid past the housekeeper before she could recover her breath, and hurried back up the garden path to the castle. Fergus trotted beside him looking remarkably pleased with himself, his tail wagging like a metronome.

⧖

After returning Fergus to his master, Justin examined the morning mail. One envelope stood out from all the others. For a moment it filled him with alarm, then he realised that quality parchment and elegant calligraphy were hardly the trademarks of a kidnapper. It was from the new butler, confirming his arrival.

Dear Sir,

I plan to arrive at 5 pm. After inspecting the household staff I would appreciate a comprehensive tour of the castle. My intention is to formulate an efficient management plan. As an ex-royal butler, you can be assured of my discretion and confidentiality. Please have the staff lined up in the entrance hall no later than 4:55. I trust this will not inconvenience you.

Yours faithfully,
Peregrine Knightly.

Confidential or not, Justin thought the new butler sounded rather intimidating. He seemed to expect a whole regiment of servants. A whimsical nanny, a kilt-wearing gardener and his parrot, a gigantic bare-footed cook, and a meddlesome housekeeper with an eight-legged cat were probably going to come as something of a shock.

By the time Robyn came down for breakfast it was almost half past ten. As she crossed the entrance hall she heard the sound of tyres on gravel and peered through a window. It was a police car; Constable Knox remained in the driver's seat whilst Sergeant Awbrite marched towards the Laird's workshop. He rapped smartly on the door, wondering if Sir Willoughby would hear him over the hammering and banging from within.

Robyn dashed outside in a flurry. 'Dad doesn't want to be disturbed,' she shouted – truthful so far. 'He says I can tell you all about him keeping an eye on, er ... *thingamabob*.'

'Thank you, Miss,' said the sergeant. 'Quietly does it, though. We don't want everyone listening in.'

They walked along the cliff top together, Robyn giving a highly romanticised account of "her father's" misadventures trailing the Gilliechattans.

'Bad luck,' said Awbrite. 'Still, a couple of hours in a police cell should loosen the gardener's tongue.' He regarded Robyn for a moment through shrewd narrowed eyes, then smiled. 'Meanwhile, *you* might have more success with only the housekeeper to watch.'

After lunch, Mrs Gilliechattan stormed into the castle, furious about her husband's arrest. Burbage clung to her shoulder, and Tybalt lurked beneath her voluminous kilt, hissing and spitting. She collected an army of mops and dusters, and announced she was going to spring clean Professor Gilbert's rooms. Everyone knew it was just an excuse to pry – and Robyn felt rather peeved she hadn't thought of it herself.

At four o'clock, Nanny Verity carried a tray of tea up the north tower, and caught Mrs Gilliechattan rummaging through the professor's wardrobe.

'Somebody's going to pay dearly for this,' she snarled, glaring at Verity Kiss as if she held her personally responsible. Tybalt leapt onto the bed, his tail whipping furiously, and as Nanny stepped back, she heard Angus Gilliechattan's gruff voice immediately behind her.

'*O, a KISS long as my exile, sweet as my revenge!*'

Nanny spun round, terrified – only to find Burbage perched on the dressing table, mimicking his master with uncanny accuracy. She ran out of the room and down the north stairs, covering her ears to block out the echo of his sinister laughter.

At four-thirty, the squad car returned with Angus Gilliechattan. He tramped past the kitchen windows and down towards his cottage, wearing an expression of surly resentment. Realising the workshop was now silent, Sergeant Awbrite knocked on the castle door.

'Ah, Sir Willoughby – glad to catch you,' he said. 'Your gardener has provided us with a satisfactory alibi that we've been able to verify.'

'Oh?' said Willoughby, unaware that Mr Gilliechattan had ever been missing.

'What was he up to?' Robyn asked, squeezing passed her father.

'I'm not at liberty to say, Miss,' replied Awbrite. 'Confidential. But we've ruled both him and his wife out of our investigations completely. Disappointing – but we're pursuing several other promising leads; we'll trace her ladyship soon, don't you worry. '

Robyn was not convinced.

At 4:59 precisely, Mr Knightly's shiny black BMW turned in through the castle gates. He drove slowly along the drive, through

the archway and round the courtyard, timing his arrival at the castle door to coincide perfectly with the tower clock striking five. Everybody had gathered in the entrance hall to greet him – including Justin, who, at the last minute, had hurtled down from his lab and stepped in place beside Sir Willoughby, glancing surreptitiously at his watch.

As Mr Knightly climbed out of the car, the Laird of Thyme stepped towards him with his hand held out. 'Welcome to Thyme Castle,' he said. 'Allow me to introduce everyone. This is my son, Justin.'

The butler was tall and bony. He stooped down and grasped Justin's hand in a grip as cold and clammy as a dead fish. 'Good afternoon, sir, I'm Peregrine Knightly,' he announced in a dramatic stage whisper. A dewdrop dangling from the end of his large nose quivered dangerously, and Justin hoped it wouldn't pick that particular moment to drip off.

While he shook Robyn's hand, she surveyed his outfit with ill-concealed contempt. He looked as if he'd stepped out of a period costume drama – complete with tail coat, wing collar, cravat and white gloves. Albion rubbed his nose; the smell of eucalyptus oil and stale socks made him want to sneeze. Next in line was Grandpa Lyall, looking befuddled.

'Would you like me to get undressed *now*, Doctor?' he asked.

Mr Knightly assured him that he most certainly did *not,* thank you very much. Eliza stepped forwards next, holding her huge fist out politely.

'Me Eliza. Me nice gorilla,' she said in her most royal voice – then ruined the civilised effect by sniffing his clothes and asking, 'Why you smell bad?'

The butler looked at her as though she was a stuffed specimen from a museum, and then turned to inspect the staff. Robyn fought desperately to subdue a fit of hysterical giggles.

Mrs Gilliechattan curtsied, introducing herself and her husband in the proper manner; but the cook gave him a bone-crushing bear hug and kissed him on both sallow cheeks.

'Ahoy Periscope Nightie,' she boomed. 'I Mrs Kof. I cooky the measles here.'

'The *family* may call me Knightly,' he sniffed, disentangling himself with some difficulty. 'However, the staff will address me as *Mr* Knightly.'

Finally, the butler turned to Nanny Verity – dithering by now and, as a result, hopelessly muddled. 'I'm Nanny Knightly,' she spluttered. 'Pleased to meet you, Mr Kiss.'

Knightly smirked and peered closely at Nanny with pale, watery eyes. 'You seem vaguely familiar,' he said in a condescending tone. 'Have we met before?'

'Och, no Sir,' gasped Nanny, looking horrified at the very thought. 'Certainly not.'

'*Good!*'

Knightly dismissed the staff, telling them to await further instructions in the kitchen, then turned back to Sir Willoughby with a sycophantic smile. 'What a charming rag-tag bunch – and with a little discipline probably quite tolerable. Now, could I impose upon you to give me a tour of your delightful home?'

Willoughby nodded. 'Spect you'd like to see your room first,' he said. 'This way.'

Eliza scowled at the departing butler and rattled the keys on her laptop. 'Old man smell like dead mouse,' she said.

Robyn almost exploded. '*Charming!* I wonder which morgue *he* escaped from.'

Justin didn't reply. He was staring in the direction of the east tower, listening attentively as the butler traipsed upstairs.

'What's wrong?' asked Robyn.

'His shoes,' replied Justin, sounding puzzled. 'They squeak!'

At about ten past eleven, Justin decided to take a break. The lab felt stuffy and his head ached – but to keep on schedule, he still had at least three hours work before going to sleep. He slid down to his bedroom and opened the French windows, hoping the fresh air would revive him. It was a fine night, so he stepped out onto the battlements between the south and west towers, gazing at the stars and half listening to the noises from Willoughby's workshop. Suddenly, another much softer noise made him jump.

'Psst.'

He peered over the crenellated walls, wondering if someone was lurking in the courtyard.

'No ... over here ... quickly.'

Justin turned and saw Nanny Verity beckoning urgently through a window.

'What's up Nanny V?' he asked, running along the battlements towards her. Ancient rust-covered bars stopped the nursery windows from opening properly, but Nanny reached through and grabbed hold of his hands. She seemed frightened, and her face was as pale as the moon.

'Master Justin,' she whispered, almost inaudibly, 'there's something I must tell you.'

'Go on.'

'Och, I'm terribly afraid that ... er, well ... I'm not *absolutely* certain, but ... er ... I think ...'

Nanny stopped abruptly, glancing over her shoulder. The nursery door creaked opened and a narrow shaft of light fell across her abandoned needlework.

'Who's there?' Nanny called softly.

'It's only me,' said Robyn, peeping through the gap. 'I couldn't sleep. Any chance of a cup of cocoa?'

'Of course,' replied Nanny. 'Though I'm not sure if I've got quite enough milk up here for the three of us. Would you ... er ...'

'I'll get some from the kitchen,' yawned Robyn.

Five minutes later, they were all sitting on Nanny's bed, sipping cocoa and munching custard creams.

'So, what's troubling you, Nan?' Justin asked.

Nanny Verity swept some thread, scissors and a pair of well-darned stockings into her sewing box. 'Never mind now, Poppet, she said. 'It's probably just my imagination. It'd best be my little secret until I'm sure.'

Justin looked dubious, but before he could object they heard the sound of footsteps climbing the west staircase – squeaky footsteps. All three of them crept out onto the landing and waited silently. Moments later, Knightly descended from Robyn's room.

'Ah, there you are, Miss,' he droned. 'You rang. Is there something you require?'

'No,' said Robyn, 'and I *didn't* ring.'

'Ah well, the bell system *is* rather old-fashioned,' remarked the butler. 'Perhaps it was somebody else and the wires got crossed. Goodnight Miss – Goodnight Sir.'

'That man gives me the collywobbles,' whispered Nanny Verity, as they watched him squeak out of sight.

'Me too,' said Robyn, with a shudder.

On Tuesday morning Justin overslept. He'd worked half the night to complete his negative energy generator, and would have dozed all day if Robyn hadn't burst into his bedroom and woken him up.

'*IT'S SABOTAGE!*' she shouted, shaking him vigorously by the shoulders.

'What is?' Justin yawned.

'Somebody's cut the plug off my computer. I'll bet it's that creepy butler.'

Justin hoped he was still dreaming, but when his sister shook him a second time he realised he wasn't. Robyn explained:

'Every morning, after I've opened my e-mails, I type up the latest evidence from my notebook. Today the computer wouldn't switch on. When I bent down to check if the plug had come out ... there was *no* plug!'

'Calm down ... I'm sure we can afford another one.'

'That's not the point, Dustbin. I'm going to ask Knightly why he was snooping round my bedroom last night.'

Justin groaned. He had visions of the butler handing in his

notice. Diplomacy wasn't Robyn's strong point – especially when she was feeling stroppy.

'Hang on a tick; I'll come with you.'

Ten minutes later they hurried along the portrait gallery.

'Let me do the talking, Bobs' Justin begged.

'Okay,' said Robyn sullenly. 'You go ahead. I forgot my pen. I'll catch up with you.'

Justin heard the tower clock striking 9:45 and wondered if he had time to confront Knightly before his sister returned. The dining room was empty and the table cleared apart from his solitary place setting. He marched through the entrance hall to the kitchen – but that was deserted too.

Then, as he turned to leave, Justin heard a sudden, piercing scream and a dull thump from the direction of the vegetable garden. He rushed to the door and opened it, stumbling out over Gilliechattan's boots on the step. He could hardly believe his eyes. A clothesline hung between the east tower and an ancient pear tree – and beneath it, sprawled in the centre of a neatly trimmed lawn, was Nanny Verity.

Trampling neat rows of herbs, Justin ran towards her crumpled, inert form. Nanny lay near a laundry basket, clutching a clothespeg in one hand. There was a deep gash on her skull, and beside her, a hefty glass paperweight glistened in the sunlight.

'HELP!' he shouted. 'QUICK – *HELLLLP!!!*'

Mrs Kof's bald head poked out of her bedroom window immediately above, then hastily withdrew. Seconds later, Robyn sprinted through the kitchen.

'What's wrong?' she gasped. 'Nanny fainted again?'

'I think she's dead,' replied Justin, a single tear trickling down his ashen cheek.

'But ...'

'She was going to tell me something last night. I think she'd noticed something suspicious ... *so* suspicious, that someone at Thyme Castle has killed her to keep it a secret.'

trangely enough, some minor actions whilst visiting the past CAN visibly alter our present. How? Imagine you examine the unblemished trunk of an ancient tree, then travel back in time and carve your initials on the same younger tree. Would they be visible when you returned to the present? Probably – although they would appear to have been there many years.

What makes this case different? Nobody could 'uncarve' the initials in the intervening years. A past event that naturally leaves an after-effect, despite the passage of time, would be visible in the present. Again, we need not imagine two worlds, for trees with and without carved initials, unless they trigger some major incident. Even then, we cannot assume that events will never loop back to their original course. Once time travel is in the equation, the time period in which a paradox can be resolved is almost limitless.

So, in theory, interfering with past events should either ... have no discernable effect on the present; resolve within a loop of time; or, fork into an alternate world. The problem for the time traveller is that it is virtually impossible to tell the difference between an inconsequential action and one with the potential to create a parallel universe.

CHAPTER SIXTEEN

Re-enacting Nanny's Attack

'Perhaps she's still alive,' said Robyn, kneeling beside Nanny Verity.

Justin watched helplessly, paralysed by overwhelming sorrow and deep anger. How could anyone harm his loveable, trusting nanny?

'There's a faint pulse,' said Robyn. 'We've got to get her to a hospital at once.'

Justin almost sobbed with relief. 'I'll phone for an ambulance,' he whispered huskily, stumbling towards the castle.

His cries for help had brought everyone rushing through the kitchen – almost everyone. The banging from Willoughby's workshop continued unabated.

'No – go and fetch Dad,' said Robyn, taking charge. 'Leave everything to me.'

Justin hurried through the arched garden gate and ran round the east tower. He could hear his sister giving orders with cool efficiency:

'Knightly: phone for an ambulance – *no*, a helicopter; tell them it's an emergency. Mrs Gilliechattan: fetch some blankets – Nanny's cold, but I don't want her moved until help arrives. Mr Gilliechattan: find a first aid kit – I'll see if I can stem this bleeding. Eliza: go to the nursery and take care of Albion. Mrs Kof: we might need some brandy.'

'What's happened?' asked old Sir Lyall in a bewildered voice.

'Did she fall?'

Robyn glanced up, expecting Grandpa to be the only person left, but to her amazement, Henny's ex-film crew were beside him. Hank leaned forwards, eager to help. Polly dithered in the background looking queasy.

Justin hammered on the workshop door and shouted, but his father seemed unable to hear above the deafening clatter. In desperation, he opened the adjoining garage and squeezed past the cars to the internal connecting door. He ran his fingers along the lintel where Willoughby kept the spare key hidden. Finally, he unlocked the door, rushed through, and had his second shock of the day.

All the noise came from a bizarre Heath Robinson-style invention, constructed from a peculiar array of tools and oddments: a pneumatic drill, an old rowing machine, a welding torch, an upturned lawnmower, a spinning wheel, several hammers and a dustbin lid – all connected to a timer, set to activate them in a random sequence.

Sir Willoughby was missing.

'The paramedics are on the way, Miss,' droned Knightly. 'Is there anything else?'

'Find out what's taking the Gilliechattans so long,' groaned Robyn.

'There's a first aid kit in the Land Rover,' said Hank, 'will *that* do?'

Robyn nodded gratefully.

Grandpa Lyall removed his jacket and draped it over Nanny Verity.

'Poor Mrs Kiss,' he said, reaching into his trouser pocket. 'Would a clean handkerchief be any use?'

Before Robyn could reply, Hank returned with a small white

box in his huge black fist. He handed it to her.

'Thanks.' Robyn unwrapped a wad of cotton wool and pressed it on Nanny's head.

'Lucky we called in,' said Hank. 'Actually, we were worried about Henny.'

'Then you must be psychic,' snapped Robyn. 'The police kept all news of her kidnap out of the media.'

'KIDNAP!' gasped Polly. 'We had no idea ... did we Hank?'

'*No way*! Henny's never fired us for longer than a couple of days before. We thought she must be ill or something.'

They both looked so genuinely astonished that Robyn would have burst out laughing if the situation hadn't been so serious.

Mrs Gilliechattan appeared with a pile of blankets, and after Grandpa retrieved his jacket, laid them over Nanny Verity one at a time. Robyn applied a clean dressing and gently bound Nanny's head in a length of bandage. As she finished, Angus Gilliechattan returned. Robyn was about to make some scathing remark when her brother rushed through the garden gate.

'Where's Dad?' she asked.

'He ... er ... can't come right now,' said Justin. Baffled by his father's mysterious absence, he needed time to consider the possible significance before telling his sister.

Robyn looked exasperated, but the noisy arrival of the air-rescue helicopter saved Justin from further questions. Knightly hurried across the cliff top and escorted the paramedics to the kitchen garden. Carefully, they manoeuvred Nanny on to a stretcher and carried her back to the chopper. Justin and Robyn ran alongside, clutching Nanny's hands. Everyone else jostled anxiously behind them.

'Glad to see somebody's bandaged her up properly,' said one of the paramedics.

'Thanks,' said Robyn. 'It's a good job Nanny taught me first aid. Can I go with her to hospital?'

'Okay ... but we'll need a grown-up too,' said the other medic. 'There'll be forms to sign if she's still unconscious.'

254

'I'll go,' offered Knightly, 'it's my responsibility as head of domestic staff.'

'No-no-*no!*' growled the cook. 'Man not goings. Missiz Kof go horse-piddle with her.'

Robyn scowled and nudged Justin. She didn't want either of them anywhere near Nanny. They were both suspects after all.

'Do something,' she hissed. 'If one of them attacked Nanny, they might want to finish her off properly.'

'Shall I go?' asked Polly gently, before Justin could reply. 'Hank can follow in the Land Rover and bring us back later.'

'Oh, thanks Polly,' sighed Robyn. 'You can't imagine how grateful I am. Hank, could you take Nanny's dressing gown and slippers in case they keep her in overnight?'

Hank nodded. He and Polly were hardly the most reliable pair – but they were harmless enough when they weren't playing jokes, and neither was on Robyn's list of suspects.

Robyn dashed back inside the castle and up to the west tower. The paramedics opened the helicopter door and adjusted the ramp. Justin stood alone beside the stretcher, trying to shelter Nanny from the rotor blade's pulverising downdraft. Suddenly, her eyelids flickered open and she grasped hold of his arm. She whispered so weakly he could scarcely hear:

'Keep ... a close eye ... on Robyn.'

'Don't worry, Nanny V,' shouted Justin. 'I won't let anything happen to her.'

'No Poppet ...' Nanny murmured, 'I ... I mean ... she might ...' Then after a feeble shake of her head, she lapsed back into unconsciousness.

The paramedics lifted the stretcher into the chopper, waited for Polly to climb in, then slammed the doors and took off.

Robyn heard the helicopter leave as she packed Nanny's overnight bag, and almost wept with frustration. Thank goodness Nanny's safe with Polly, she thought, I'll ride with Hank – we'll be at the hospital in no time.

But once Robyn got downstairs she had a dramatic change of

heart. As everyone wandered back indoors she stared at each of their familiar faces in turn. If her brother was right, one of these people had just tried to kill Nanny Verity – and that couldn't be ignored.

Hank was waiting in the Land Rover with the engine ticking over. Seeing Robyn dash across the courtyard, he leaned over and opened the passenger door.

'I'm staying here,' Robyn panted, placing Nanny's bag on the seat. 'There's something I need to do. Promise you'll phone as soon as there's any news.'

Justin and Robyn stood side by side, watching Hank's Land Rover roar through the archway.

'Dad should be with her,' sniffed Robyn, hearing the whine of a drill from his workshop.

'Nanny'll be fine,' said Justin, giving his sister a reassuring squeeze.

For a split second, she hugged him back – until she realised what she was doing and shoved him firmly aside.

'Cut the mush, Dustbin ... we've got work to do.'

Robyn didn't fool Justin for an instant. He knew that a tender heart lurked beneath her tough exterior; it was just extremely well hidden. And she was right: they had work to do.

Back indoors, Justin marched over to the hall table. Knightly had left the morning mail in its customary place, but the old millefiori paperweight was missing.

Robyn huffed impatiently, as Justin picked up the pile of envelopes. The top one felt hard and lumpy – and, to his consternation, was addressed to the Thyme Family in what looked like his own hand-writing. Stifling a gasp, he tore it open quickly before his sister turned round, and tipped out a fabulous diamond-encrusted watch, its face smashed, its hands frozen at 9:40.

'Look!'

'The time Mum was kidnapped,' cried Robyn. 'What if she's ...'

'There's a note with it,' said Justin, extracting it with his fingertips. He shook it carefully open and they read it together:

256

no Police
or She dies
This is your
last warning

Thyme Family,
me Castle
hyme Road,
erness,
and.

Robyn gulped.

'Perhaps we *should* phone Sergeant Awbrite,' suggested Justin.

'*No way!* We daren't put Mum in any more danger.'

Justin looked relieved. He didn't want the police involved either; not with his handwriting on the envelope. And it was too risky until he knew what his dad was up to. Their resident spy might realise Willoughby wasn't building the time machine.

'We can handle it,' he said.

'This confirms your theory, Dustbin; now we're doubly sure our suspect is in the castle.'

Triply sure, thought Justin. He glanced hurriedly at the envelope before concealing it in his pocket. There was no postmark on the stamp – just a strange pale brown stain, which meant it hadn't been delivered with the rest of the mail. 'While *we* looked after Nanny, somebody must've slipped it amongst the other envelopes. Knightly, Mrs Kof and the Gilliechattans all had opportunity. Even Grandpa had chance. I suppose the only person who seems to be in the clear is Professor Gilbert. He's away until Saturday.'

Robyn frowned. 'Mmm ... I wouldn't be so sure about that,' she said mysteriously. 'Though I think we can rule Grandpa out; he doesn't have a motive.'

'Well, Hank and Polly do,' said Justin. 'Mum fired them! Hank could have planted it when he fetched the first aid kit.'

'Mum's always firing them,' said Robyn. '*This* time she did it on the flight home. They wouldn't have had time to plan a kidnap, unless one of them's a mind-reader. And don't forget ... the first ransom note was posted locally while they were still abroad.'

'True,' Justin agreed, 'but a good detective never rules *anybody* out.'

Ten minutes later they were examining the scene of the crime.

'*Yuck!*' said Robyn, prodding the paperweight. 'There's blood and hair on it.'

'And now your fingerprints are all over it as well,' grumbled Justin, pulling on a pair of latex gloves. He placed the paperweight in a clear plastic bag.

Several of Albion's bibs swung on the clothesline, the rest lay in the abandoned laundry basket. While gathering the scattered pegs Justin noticed three deep circular indentations in the lawn.

'Heel prints?' Robyn suggested. 'Somebody crept up behind her, cracked her on the cranium and legged it.'

'Not enough time.' Justin squinted for a moment, trying to recall the scene. 'I shot out of the door the second I heard Nanny scream. No – I suspect somebody dropped the paperweight from up there.' He pointed to the east tower. Five small windows faced the garden: two belonged to the empty guestrooms directly above the kitchen; on the next floor Knightly and Mrs Kof had a window apiece; Eliza's room was right at the top.

Hardly aware of what he was doing, Justin pegged the rest of the laundry on the clothesline. Meanwhile, Robyn scurried through the kitchen and ran to the library, where a second millefiori paperweight was kept on the desk. She grabbed it, sprinted back to the entrance hall, and shot up the east tower stairs two at a time. As Justin pegged out the final bib something whistled passed his head missing him by millimetres. It struck the lawn with a dull thud, embedding itself beside the laundry basket.

'What the *helium* are you *doing*?' he roared, glaring at his sister.

'Re-enacting Nanny's attack,' Robyn hissed, leaning out of Knightly's window. 'It looks as if you're right – *as usual*. Come on up.'

'Hang on a tick.' Justin crouched to retrieve the paperweight. Lifting it carefully, he found that the indentation it left matched the other three almost perfectly.

A couple of minutes later, he crept into Knightly's room to find his sister rummaging under the butler's bed. 'What are you up to *now*,' he whispered, glancing nervously over his shoulder.

'Looking for clues,' said Robyn. 'I've got a theory about our so-called butler. Check the dressing table. Don't open that little drawer though,' she warned, holding her nose. '*Socks*!'

Robyn appeared to be enjoying herself, but Justin felt uncomfortable rifling through someone else's private belongings. However, his feelings changed radically when Robyn found her missing computer plug at the bottom of Knightly's wardrobe.

'I *knew* he took it,' she hissed. 'I'll bet Nanny spotted him with it – so he tried to bump her off.'

'It doesn't make sense,' said Justin, frowning. 'Why would he want to disable your computer? And last night, Nanny seemed frightened and was about to tell me something ... yet that was *before* Knightly went up to your bedroom.'

Still puzzled, they crept into Mrs Kof's room.

'Look ... it's her false moustache,' whispered Justin, opening a little velvet-lined tin lying on the dressing table.

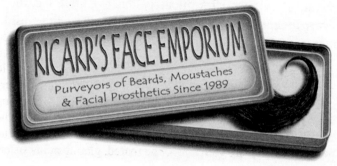

RICARR'S FACE EMPORIUM
Purveyors of Beards, Moustaches
& Facial Prosthetics Since 1989

Robyn was busy peering under the cook's bed.

'Here's the suitcase I told you about,' she called. 'The one she dropped on my foot last Saturday night. Aaarghhh ... it weighs an absolute ton; help me drag it out, Dustbin.'

The case wouldn't budge – even with both of them pulling together. Justin was about to suggest moving the bed instead when Robyn made another fascinating discovery: a second newspaper clipping tucked inside a well-thumbed Czech bible. She flopped down on the bed to read it out loud:

otland on Sun

X-RATED HYPNOTIST AT CIRCUS

By Miranda Oxpage

The Bohemian Circus announced last night that it has cancelled next Saturday's special appearence by the Xtraordinary Xavier.

The surprise announcement came after yesterday's embarrassing fiasco. Xavier Polydorus missed the afternoon performance. Later, during his evening act, he hypnotised an elderly lady, telling her to act like a Nautical Skipper. Unfortunately, due to a slight hearing impediment, Beatrice Haver, (aged 93), thought he told her to act like a Naughty Old Stripper! Her impromptu performance offended several audience members and severely traumatised Balthazar the Elephant.

When asked if she planned to take legal action, Miss Bea Haver replied: "No, I've never had so much fun in my entire life; I'd like to take it up professionally!"

Rumour has it that the famous TV hypnotist, conjuror and mind-reader has been suffering attacks of stage fright.

"He hasn't performed in front of a live audience for years," explained Tonio the Clown. "This will finish him."

Mr Polydorus, (aged 57) started as a chimpanzee trainer originally, discovering his latent hypnotic skills by accident. Last night he declined to comment, however, Ringmaster, Armando Pixage, admitted that the hypnotist was so distressed he had decided to retire immediately, and hoped to spend some time travelling around the Scottish Highlands with his son.

The Circus has already booked a replacement act for next Saturday: The Dark Falcon - World's Stronge

'So *that's* what she cut out of Dad's Sunday paper,' sighed Robyn, looking perplexed. 'But why didn't she want us to see it?'

'There's always a reason,' said Justin. He photographed the cutting with his mobile's built-in digital camera then slipped it back in the bible. 'I'll download it later, and give it some thought.'

Lady Henny slept soundly, but her dreams were far from sweet. A persistent anxiety gnawed deep inside her brain. She knew she was asleep, but she also knew that she'd never escape whilst sedated.

Morning and evening, her captor slapped her awake when he arrived, then pumped her veins full of sedative before he left. During her brief spell of consciousness, Henny ate, drank and relieved herself; she also plotted furiously, determined to use those few minutes each day to her advantage. But putting her plan

into action depended on waking up before her captor arrived – and
that seemed almost impossible.

After a late start, work on the subatomic wormhole-vortex
accelerator progressed slowly. Justin's head ached, and he
struggled to concentrate, distracted by the conglomeration of
clues: the computer plug in Knightly's wardrobe, the newspapers
and paste in the Gilliechattans' cottage, Mrs Kof's ten ton suitcase
and false moustache ... and now, most perplexing of all, his
father's mysterious absence.

He knew that, somehow, *everything had to connect to
everything else*, but it felt like doing an enormous jigsaw puzzle,
and whenever a picture started to emerge there were always a few
pieces missing... or a couple of clues that stubbornly refused to fit.

With a sigh of frustration, Justin downed tools fifteen minutes
ahead of schedule and wheeled his telescope to the window
overlooking the loch. He peeled back a corner of the black-out
screen and inserted it through the gap.

At twelve-thirty the clanging from the workshop stopped
abruptly. Moments later, Sir Willoughby strode across the
courtyard towards the castle. Anyone seeing him would naturally
assume that he'd just emerged from his workshop – but he hadn't.
Justin had watched him sail Henny's boat across the loch, moor
her beside the jetty, then scurry up the cliff steps checking his
watch. His father had some serious explaining to do after lunch.

'Accidents *will* happen,' Sir Willoughby mumbled through a
large mouthful of roast beef sandwich. 'Nanny's a tough old bird
... I expect she'll pull through.'

The fresh air had clearly given the Laird of Thyme an appetite;
Justin, however, felt sick.

'You should have gone to the hospital with her,' said Robyn,
frowning. 'Surely you could have sacrificed a couple of hours.
She's practically family.'

'Don't take that tone with me, young lady. Your brother needs me to make diversionary noises. I can't be in two places at once – can I?'

Willoughby glanced at his son for support, but Justin could hardly bear to look at him. Not only could his father appear to be in two places at once, he was being decidedly two-faced about it.

'It wasn't an accident, Dad. Someone tried to murder her; they left this.' He handed his father the envelope containing the second ransom note and the smashed watch. 'Mum's in serious danger.'

Willoughby blanched as he read the note. He pushed his plate aside and sat with his elbows on the table and his head in his hands, mumbling about Henny and the Thyme curse.

After lunch, Robyn disappeared with her notebook, determined to find out where everybody had been at the time of Nanny's attack. Justin begged her to be diplomatic – but Robyn merely rolled her eyes and groaned.

Sir Willoughby plodded out of the dining room, still mumbling and shaking his head. Justin crept after him, through the entrance hall and across the courtyard.

'Shouldn't you get back to your lab?' asked Willoughby, clearly eager to shake off his son. 'I'll be ready to start hammering ... bang on two o'clock.'

'Really? Or are you planning another cruise?'

Sir Willoughby scowled and his cheeks flushed. 'So that's why you've both been treating me like a criminal all through lunch.'

'I haven't told Robyn anything ... but I think *I* deserve an explanation.'

'Okay, okay. Perhaps I should've told you,' Willoughby muttered. 'But it was so dashed boring clattering about, that by the end of the first morning I decided to build something to make the noises for me.' He unlocked his workshop door and stepped in, gesturing at the contraption. 'Just a few odds and ends connected to a random timer. Had it finished by Sunday night.'

'So what have you been up to since then?'

'*UP TO?*' snapped Sir Willoughby, his eyes widening. 'Looking for your mother, of course. If the kidnapper or one of his spies really *is* here at the castle, then Henny can't be too far away.'

'But ...'

'Mark my words,' Willoughby shouted. 'If Hen's conscious, she'll be signalling for help. I spent all yesterday scanning the north-western shore of the loch through my binoculars – then this morning I searched from Scaniport to Dores. No luck so far, but this afternoon I'll sail past Whitefield and Inverfarigaig, then tomorrow ...'

'Forget it Dad – it's too dangerous,' said Justin. 'If *I* spotted Mum's boat, then the kidnapper might too. The "*Zeitgeist*" is too distinctive; I doubt there's another converted lifeboat on the entire loch. You could ruin everything.'

'DON'T TELL *ME* WHAT I *CAN'T DO*!' roared Willoughby. He swung round to face his son and banged one fist on his workbench. 'Has it ever occurred to you that I'm sick and tired of being treated like some senile old buffer? I'm perfectly capable of thinking for myself, you know. Perhaps my memory isn't quite as bad as you think. Perhaps I've ... er ... I've ...' His voice trailed off.

After an awkward pause, Sir Willoughby forced a sad lop-sided smile. His anger had subsided as quickly as it flared up, but in that brief unguarded moment there had been a flash of resentment in his eyes that Justin had seen only once before: in his nightmare, when his father had pointed a gun at him and pulled the trigger.

Justin took a deep breath and tried to keep the panic out of his voice. 'Go on, Dad. Perhaps ... *what*?'

'Nothing,' murmured Willoughby. He glanced away, running his fingertips over a row of dusty spanners. 'I'm ... I'm just anxious about Henny – that's all.'

'No that's *NOT all*,' said Justin, grasping his father's sleeve. 'You've been losing your temper all month – ever since I made

264

those silly wishes. And when I told you I wanted to build a time machine ...' (Willoughby winced at the forbidden words, but Justin quelled him with a narrow stare). '... I felt sure you were hiding something. I blamed your memory problems at first; trauma from the flashbacks. But ... but I'm starting to have doubts. Come on, Dad. What *really* happened the night your memory got wiped? You *must* remember *something*.'

'*Ohhhh* I do – but you won't like it.'

The haggard expression on his father's face turned Justin's blood to ice.

Sir Willoughby slumped back against the wall and closed his eyes. For a full minute he remained silent. When he finally spoke his voice sounded cold and detached:

'When I woke from the sedative I felt damp and shivery. I realised I'd been dumped in some woodland. I didn't recognise where ... but having just had my memory wiped, I didn't expect to. Then it hit me: I remembered the memory-wipe! Impossible, I thought – yet I remembered my name, how old I was, where I lived – absolutely everything. There seemed only one explanation: my ex-assistant had bodged the whole thing. He was an astonishing actor, but he wasn't the sharpest tool in the shed. Anything more complicated than a pocket calculator and he ...'

'Just hang *on* a tick,' yelled Justin. 'Are you telling me that all these years there's never been *anything* ... *ANYTHING* wrong with your memory?'

'I had *no* choice,' retorted Willoughby, bristling defensively. 'I lay there for hours that night, thinking the whole thing through. If I went straight back to Henny, it'd be obvious my memory was fine. He'd abduct me and do the job properly ... or kill me. I guessed he'd be watching the newspapers, so I decided the safest course was to act like a total amnesiac and get myself picked up by the local police.'

'Okay,' said Justin 'But *surely* he wouldn't keep watching for *THIRTEEN YEARS* – not if he thought the memory-wipe had worked.'

'I planned to drop the act after a month or two,' said Sir Willoughby. 'But I got cold feet – and the longer I waited, the more paranoid I got. What if he'd *wanted* me to think the memory-wipe had failed, but he'd never actually done it? Maybe giving me the anaesthetic then dumping me before I regained consciousness was all part of some elaborate con-trick. It made perfect sense. His time machine altered time and age concurrently, confining his travels to within his past life. He was obviously afraid to use it ... but suspected *I* knew how to fix it. Why would he erase that knowledge? No, all he had to do was keep me under surveillance until I built another time machine, then swoop in and steal it. So ...'

'You kept pretending,' said Justin, shaking his head in disbelief.

'As it turned out, your grandfather had disappeared barely a month before, so I inherited the castle and we all moved in,' Willoughby continued. 'It was like one long holiday, pottering about reading my newspaper, sitting in the sun – and it suited Henny too. You know what she's like; always jetting off somewhere. She was glad to know you and Robyn were safe with me.'

'Mum'll go *ballistic* when she finds out about this.'

'She's known for years,' said Willoughby. 'She guessed early on, and played along for the sake of the family. It was a strain at first, but once you were old enough to take over the financial side of things, well ...'

'You could relax in your deckchair and leave me to do the work!' Justin growled. The emotional right side of his brain baulked at the truth, whilst the logical left side calmly pointed out that the clues had been there. 'No wonder you didn't want me surfing the net for the latest about amnesia. I should've guessed. Now I come to think of it, your so-called flashbacks did seem incredibly detailed. You humbug – you've missed a career on the stage.'

'Look ...'

266

Justin shouted over him, his fury increasing by the second. 'I suppose *that's* why you didn't want the police involved; putting Mum's life at risk to hide your guilty secret.'

'That's not fair.'

'Isn't it? Ever since Mum disappeared, I've been groping in the dark for *anything* that might help identify her kidnapper. I didn't press you – because I assumed you'd told me everything you could remember. Whereas you *could* have told me plenty.'

'Such as?'

'His name, for a start,' snarled Justin. 'You've never mentioned what you called him.'

'I never knew it,' murmured Sir Willoughby, his face downcast. 'We always used code names. Mine was formed out of my initials ... but I never guessed *his* real name. I don't even know any names beginning with the letter X.'

'That was his code name? Just ... X?'

'Agent X,' said Willoughby, shuddering.

'What about his age? His appearance?'

'I guess he'd be in his mid to late fifties by now; but he's such an incredible master of disguise he might look older or younger.'

'Go on.'

'He had blue eyes ... not deep blue like ours ... but a really vivid sky blue. I suppose that's why he sometimes wore mirrored sunglasses. Oh – I've just thought of something else: he always wore the same tie – frightfully tasteless – had a sort of playing card pattern on it. Probably isn't important.'

Justin gasped. 'Robyn spotted a playing card pattern on the kidnapper's socks,' he shouted. 'You should've told me all this days ago, Dad. If anything's happened to Mum ...' He paused for a moment, unable to speak. 'And as for Nanny,' he added, his voice choked. 'If she dies it'll be on your conscience.'

Willoughby gave a sad apologetic little shrug. 'Did you save the playing card image?'

'There's a copy on my hard drive,' said Justin, already opening the workshop door. 'I'd better check it out at once – it *can't* be a coincidence. Switch that noise-contraption on, then keep out of sight. And no more sailing – except after dark.'

Sir Willoughby nodded – but his son had already rushed out of the workshop and across the courtyard.

Justin hurried along the castle corridors, trying to make sense of the shocking revelations, but it was impossible.

Thirteen years of lying, he thought. *Now* I understand that nightmare. On some level I must have sensed Dad's duplicity, and the dream was simply my subconscious trying to decipher the confusing signals. But why has Dad hidden the truth from me for so long? Perhaps it's my fault – maybe I take on too much responsibility and Dad resents it. But that doesn't add up either; I only stepped in because he tricked me into believing he couldn't handle things himself.

Justin shook his head. 'This isn't the time for analysis,' he whispered. 'It's time for action.' He switched focus, and mentally shuffled the pack of bewildering clues, adding this latest card to the deck. 'I'll have to double-check of course, but apart from Grandpa Lyall, I think the only other blue-eyed person in the castle is Mrs Kof.'

Up in his laboratory, Justin turned his computer on, opened his clue file and accessed the playing card bitmap image:

The sequence of cards appeared to be random – but Justin doubted that was the case. The kidnapper clearly had a warped sense of humour and delighted in leaving a tantalising trail of enigmatic clues; the *procrastination* and *thief of time* hints certainly proved *that*. Perhaps the cards contained some concealed coded message.

The top two cards were both the same suit; the two and four of diamonds. Side by side they looked like the number 24, and it took Justin less than three seconds to calculate that X was the 24th letter of the alphabet. It could be a fluke, he thought – but then he realised that the cards themselves held the key to cracking the code. With playing cards, the letter *A* stands for an *ace*, instead of the number 1. It was the simplest code imaginable: where 1 = A and so-on.

Justin could have kicked himself for overlooking something so obvious. He grabbed a sheet of paper and scribbled the alphabet down the margin, adding the numbers one to twenty-six next to the letters. Then, assuming each suit represented a different letter, he jotted down the four code numbers: 9 – 1 – 13 – 24. Seconds later he had the equivalent letters of the alphabet: I – A – M – X, or, to be precise: *I am X.*

Justin gasped with grudging admiration, his scientific brain seeing at once what an appropriate name Agent X was for his dad's old enemy. The letter X was generally used to denote the unknown quantity in an equation, standing in for something you knew existed but couldn't identify.

Agent X was definitely a major part of the mysterious equation at Thyme Castle – but the problem was, Justin still had no idea of his identity.

vents are fixed in the fabric of time, while freedom of choice governs the direction of our individual timelines. But TARTAN THEORY suggests that a third factor is very much part of the equation. It is such an unknown quantity, that during calculations to plot conceptual timelines, it is traditionally represented by the letter X.

This third factor is RANDOM CHANCE – often referred to as coincidence. Prodigious amounts of chance sway our apparent freedom of choice. The entire course of our timeline can be altered by something as unpredictable as the toss of a coin, the roll of a dice, or the turn of a card.

Occasionally, coincidences are enjoyable or beneficial; we might find ourselves in the right place at the right time, or make a fortunate discovery by accident. This is known as serendipity. All too often the opposite is true; we find ourselves in the wrong place at the wrong time, and it frequently appears that if something can go wrong, it will. This is referred to as serendumpity.

The methodical passing of time seems to be the embodiment of precision and orderliness. Random chance is often so unpredictable that we might consider it to be the antithesis of time.

But is chance really as random as it appears?

CHAPTER SEVENTEEN

More E-mails - More Envelopes

Robyn slouched at the kitchen table, frowning over the latest entries in her Private Investigator's notebook. She chewed on the end of her cherry-scented glitter-pen, her teeth leaving row upon row of minute dents in the transparent plastic.

Following Sergeants Awbrite's example, she'd engaged each suspect in casual conversation, imperceptibly luring them into relating their own version of events. Her initial investigation was almost complete, but there was still one person she needed to interview: Knightly ...if, indeed, that *was* his real name.

She'd left him until last, because discovering where he was during Nanny's attack was only part of the puzzle. Robyn wanted to tackle him about the computer plug, but more importantly, she wanted to test her latest theory: Peregrine Knightly had arrived at Thyme Castle *after* Professor Gilbert had left. The two had never met. Could the professor have returned in disguise, she wondered – and had Nanny guessed his true identity? As much as she hated to admit it, her brother was right; she couldn't just accuse the butler bluntly. The sound of squeaky footsteps crossing the entrance hall heralded his approach. Robyn's mind raced. With seconds to spare she decided to surprise him and observe his reactions closely.

'Oh, Professor,' she called, as Knightly marched to the pantry.

The butler ignored Robyn completely. Undeterred, she waited for him to emerge.

'Ah, Knightly, I wonder if you could do something for me?'

'Yes, Miss.'

'I'd like you to fix ... *THIS!*'

With a dramatic flourish, Robyn withdrew the plug from beneath the table. Staring into the depths of Knightly's pale, watery eyes, she searched for any veiled glints of surprise, but there wasn't a glimmer. He merely inhaled his dewdrop – though whether this betrayed a guilty secret Robyn was unable to tell, having no experience of chronic nasal problems.

'Certainly, Miss,' he droned, glancing round the kitchen. 'What does it belong to?' He walked towards her, but his nose ran; gradually the glistening globule reconstituted at the end of his hawk-like beak.

Robyn glared at him with reluctant respect; clearly he was either an accomplished actor or the genuine article. There seemed little point in toying with him any longer. 'My computer.'

'Very well, Miss. I'll fetch the tool box and fix it directly.'

As they walked through the entrance hall, Robyn nonchalantly mentioned the morning mail, asking Knightly when it arrived.

'Twenty past nine, Miss. I remember particularly, because the postman asked what time it was as I opened the door. Funny little man; he seemed utterly lost for words when he saw me. Scuttled back to his van and drove off without another word.'

'What did you do then?'

'I left the envelopes on the hall table, under the paperweight. I would have sorted them into several piles, one for each family member – but they were all for young Master Justin.'

Robyn found *that* especially interesting. Justin had told her the ransom note had been addressed to *the Thyme Family*, so it *must* have been placed on the pile later – or, of course, Knightly could have added it himself before taking the paperweight upstairs. She peered at him out of the corner of one eye as they marched along the portrait gallery. With every squeaky step he took, his dewdrop trembled, only surface tension holding it tenuously in place.

'Did you hear Nanny scream?' Robyn asked.

'I'm afraid not,' the butler replied gloomily. 'Head full of catarrh ... I could hardly hear anything. I went up to my room to fetch a nasal spray, but I'd left it in the servants' bathroom, so I had to wait until Mrs Kof had finished her shower. After a couple of squirts I could hear fine. She knocked on the bathroom door and shouted that there'd been an accident and I'd better hurry downstairs at once.'

Robyn nodded. Knightly's story appeared to verify Mrs Kof's account, yet either of them could have dropped the paperweight on Nanny whilst the other was in the bathroom. It was very confusing.

Five minutes later, the butler had fitted the plug and left Robyn typing feverishly at her computer keyboard. Once her investigation notes were up to date, she checked her e-mails. There were two; the first had been sent last night. Tingling with anticipation, she clicked the mailbox icon:

To:	rob@thymecastle.co.uk
From:	blueeyedboy@nine.com
Subject:	R U Ok?

Hi Robyn!

Anything U want 2 chat about? Is your mum back from her xpedition yet? Is your dad working on any interesting new inventions?

Chris ☺

Robyn scowled. She wished she'd never told him about her father. A week ago she'd been chatting to Chris about their ambitions, and he'd casually mentioned that *his* was to become a world-famous inventor. What a coincidence, she'd typed, and promptly revealed that her dad invented stuff too. Almost immediately, she'd realised her mistake: from then on he seemed absolutely fascinated – though not always with her. Indifferent now, she opened the second e-mail:

To:	rob@thymecastle.co.uk
From:	blueeyedboy@nine.com
Subject:	Worrying

R U OK? Worried I didn't hear from U last night. ☹ Please get in touch A.S.A.P. Chris.

Serves him right, Robyn thought with a callous grin. She flicked the computer off without sending a reply. Let him stew a bit longer – that ought to teach him a lesson.

Work on the subatomic wormhole-vortex accelerator had come to a complete standstill. After deciphering the words *I am X* on the kidnapper's socks, Justin found himself unable to concentrate on anything else. He stared intently at the baffling array of clues on his computer screen, oblivious of the time. He arranged them methodically in pairs: two newspaper clippings – both mentioning the Xtraordinary Xavier; two ransom notes made from two different newspapers; and two envelopes – each unique. The first: neatly typed, addressed to Sir Willoughby and bearing a postmarked stamp. The second: hand-delivered and addressed to the Thyme Family in what looked like his own handwriting.

It was a forgery, of course – though quite a skilful one. But the thing that intrigued Justin most was the stained stamp. A pale brown stain curved from the top right-hand corner of the stamp down towards the bottom left-hand corner. There was something strangely familiar about it. He racked his brains, certain he'd seen another stained stamp quite recently, remarkably similar to this one. But with fifty or sixty envelopes arriving daily, remembering who'd sent it seemed an impossible task.

A knock at the door jolted him out of his silent deliberation.

'Who is it?'

'Me – Robyn. I've brought you a cup of tea.'

Justin glanced down at his watch; he'd missed afternoon tea by almost an hour. He squinted through the peephole, wondering what had prompted such an uncharacteristic outburst of sisterly concern. Obviously Robyn wanted something. Curious, Justin unlocked the door.

'So, what d'you want?'

'*Nothing*!' said Robyn, her eyes wide and innocent-looking. She slammed a teacup down on his desk, spilling tea in the saucer. 'I just thought you might be thirsty. Can't think why I bothered, really.'

'Neither can I,' replied Justin, impervious to her tactics.

Robyn turned to leave – then paused in the doorway as if a sudden thought had just occurred to her. 'Unless you'd like a quick look at my notebook.'

'So, action-girl finally admits that logical thought has its uses too, eh?'

'As *if*! I just wanted to see if you'd noticed ... er ... the same things I noticed.'

Justin opened the notebook to the latest entry and put it on his desk – but as he reached for his drink, the pages fluttered over, losing his place. After a quick sip of tea, he stood the cup on the edge of the notebook to hold the pages open. Robyn scowled.

Whereabouts of Suspects when Nanny was Attacked (approx 9:45)

Mrs Kof - Didn't hear Nanny scream. Claims she was taking a shower. Saw Hank through upper corridor windows when she left the bathroom. He was sat in his Land Rover. Heard Justin shout for help as she dressed. Told Knightly.

Mr Gilliechattan – *Claims he was weeding the rose beds outside the west tower. He didn't hear Nanny scream, but heard Justin shout. Tapped on the window and told his wife.*

Mrs Gilliechattan – *Claims she was dusting in the great hall. Didn't hear Nanny scream or Justin shout. Could see her husband working outside the west tower at the front of the castle. Both of them noticed Hank's Land Rover turn in through the castle gates and drive through the archway.*

Grandpa Lyall – *Claims he was in his room when Nanny screamed. Saw Polly enter castle through front door.*

Knightly – *Claims to have been in the bathroom – but didn't hear Nanny scream. Mrs Kof told him there had been an accident. Left the mail on the hall table under the paperweight – (note probably added later in the confusion after Nanny's attack).*

Could Knightly be Professor Gilbert in disguise?

'Wow! Radical theory,' gasped Justin, pointing to the last line on the page. 'Let me think: if we have to hand over the *you-know-what* on Saturday night, Knightly could disappear while Professor Gilbert returns safely to the castle. The prof could bide his time here, knowing the police would be searching for a butler. As Knightly, he'd need to change his accent and drop the stammer ...

276

but I suppose a really talented actor might pull it off.'

'Or maybe the stuttering American tutor was the act all along,' suggested Robyn.

Justin was about to say: '*What? For three years?*' when he stopped dead. Why not, he thought – Dad's been acting for thirteen. 'There is *one* slight flaw,' he said, after a moment's reflection. 'Latex prosthetics are pretty sophisticated these days ... but I doubt anyone's devised a false nose that actually drips!'

Robyn shrugged. She wasn't about to abandon her theory so swiftly. Justin returned to the notes and considered the other suspects.

'I'm surprised Mrs Kof could see inside the Land Rover from directly above,' he remarked. 'Unless she has X-ray eyes.'

'I'd wondered about that too.'

Justin knew that she hadn't – and Robyn knew that *he* knew – and they both knew that if he said anything he'd never get a glimpse of her notebook ever again.

'The Gilliechattans are lying,' continued Justin.

'Of *course*,' Robyn agreed, nodding vigorously, 'er ... what gave them away?'

'When Nanny screamed I fell over Mr G's boots on the back doorstep as I ran out. Either he was inside the castle or gardening barefoot. And another thing: Grandpa saw Polly enter the castle – but *we* walked from the library to the kitchen without meeting anybody.'

'Well spotted, Dustbin,' said Robyn in a patronising voice, replacing her brother's teacup in its saucer. 'Now if you'll excuse me, I've got some investigating to do.' She reached over to retrieve her notebook, assuming his moonstruck expression was due to her sheer audacity.

Justin hardly noticed Robyn leave. All he could think of was the circular tea stain he'd just seen on her notebook. He yanked his desk drawer open and scrabbled frantically beneath the envelopes. 'There's one in here somewhere,' he muttered. 'Aha! Got it!'

He withdrew a small, shiny rectangle: a Royal Mail stamp-book.

Justin placed his teacup on top of the six self-adhesive postage stamps, then removed it and blew the stain dry. Finally, he peeled off the stamp at the bottom right-hand corner and placed it beside the one on the second ransom note. They were almost identical.

'Eureka,' he whispered to himself. 'And I'm certain whoever made *this* ransom note has written to Thyme Castle before, using one of the other stamps. I can visualise it ... but unfortunately I can't visualise the envelope it was stuck to. I've opened hundreds and ...'

The library telephone rang out, disturbing his train of thought. Justin ran to the fireman's pole, slid swiftly to the ground floor and scooped up the receiver.

'Thyme Castle – Justin speaking.'

'Hi, Polly here,' said a familiar gentle voice. 'I promised I'd call as soon as we had news about your *darling* nanny.'

'Oh, thanks Polly. How is she?'

'Still very groggy and confused ... but she's going to be okay.'

Justin breathed a huge sigh of relief and flopped into one of the library chairs. His legs felt like jelly.

'The doctor thinks she's incredibly lucky,' Polly continued. 'I scribbled down everything he said, so I wouldn't forget. There's no sign of epidural or subdural haematoma. I don't know *what* that means, but it sounds hopeful. The skull X-rays didn't indicate any fractures and the CT-scan confirmed there's no brain damage.'

'That's great news,' said Justin. 'When can she come home?'

'They want to keep her under observation for the next twenty-four hours – but if there are no complications she'll be back first thing Thursday morning. She looks frightful, poor dear ... bandaged up like a mummy. *Oh fiddlesticks!* Speaking of mummies ... I should've visited my daddy this morning; he's rented the house across the bay from Thyme Castle. I must phone him at once and explain why I forgot.'

'Hang on a tick, Polly. I want to ask you something first: Why exactly did you visit the castle this morning?'

'I've been naughty. I borrowed a book from your library without asking, and was hoping to slip it back without bumping into anybody.'

'Well, you succeeded,' replied Justin sharply. 'I walked from the library to the entrance hall ... and *I* certainly didn't bump into you.'

'I know,' admitted Polly, sounding rather embarrassed. 'I was walking along the portrait gallery when I heard voices. I panicked and hid behind a suit of armour until you'd passed. Utterly pathetic! Hank says I behave like a silly schoolgirl. I had to do the same thing later on or your housekeeper and gardener would've spotted me.'

'Did you hear Nanny scream?'

'No. Too far away I suppose. It was only when I got back to the entrance hall that I realised something was wrong. Everyone was rushing towards the kitchen ... so I followed.'

'Where was Hank?'

'Is this an interrogation?' Polly giggled nervously. 'I assume Hank waited in the Land Rover until he heard all the commotion. You do believe me, don't you? The book proves I'm telling the truth; I left it on the library desk with a note – and I couldn't be in two places at once, could I?'

Justin glanced at the desk. 'I've got the book,' he said, reaching for a small brown-paper package with his name on. Then skilfully evading Polly's question added: 'Thanks for taking care of Nanny. I'd better let you phone your father now.'

'Ooh yes,' gasped Polly. 'Now, call if you need us for anything. Hank and I are staying with Daddikins until Saturday. Bye.'

'Bye Polly,' said Justin, staring at the parcel. 'The missing volume from my H.G. Wells collection,' he whispered as he replaced the receiver. 'I never *did* find out if it was "*The Time Machine*."' He was about to tear off the paper when Polly's handwriting caught his eye; it was elaborate and flowery, and Justin knew he'd seen it recently on a letter to his mother. 'Perhaps *that* was the envelope with the stained stamp!' he gasped. Then dropping the unopened parcel on the desk, he rushed out of the library and along the corridor.

Henny was easygoing about most things, but when it came to recycling she was an absolute stickler. She insisted that everyone in the castle divided their refuse into various categories and deposited it in one of several recycling bins hidden behind the Gilliechattans' cottage. The whole family supported her, even if they did grumble occasionally. Now, the contents of one of those recycling bins might unmask her kidnapper. Carrying a pair of stepladders and a couple of bin bags, Justin marched past the first five bins, (clear glass, brown glass, green glass, plastic packaging and aluminium cans), finally stopping at the sixth: paper. He hauled open the lid, climbed the stepladders and leaned inside.

An hour later, Justin had retrieved every envelope stamped with either an April or May postmark – all 2,319 of them. Hot and tired, he struggled back to the castle, hauling the bin bags behind him. Mrs Kof grinned at him as he stumbled through the kitchen door.

'Where you beans?' she asked, spooning out two enormous portions of sticky-toffee pudding. 'You missin' dinners.'

'Sorry, Mrs Kof,' said Justin, glancing at his watch. 'That took longer than I expected.'

The cook shrugged, ignoring the bin bags completely. Master Justin was young, Scottish and ridiculously wealthy – eccentric behaviour was only natural. Knightly appeared, carrying a silver tray. He collected the puddings and a steaming jug of custard, then after a resounding sniff, squeaked off to the dining room. Eliza was sitting at the kitchen table feeding Albion, who wasn't in a cooperative mood. Chortling mischievously, he pushed a garden pea up one nostril and blew a big gravy bubble out of the other.

'Binga-bagga-boo,' he squealed, flinging a handful of mashed carrots at his brother.

Eliza scowled darkly, and tapped at her laptop: 'Eliza not

nanny,' said an imperious royal voice. 'When human nanny come back?'

'Thursday ... maybe,' replied Justin, 'if she's well enough. I'll ask the doctor when we visit her tonight.'

'You better quicky up,' said Mrs Kof. 'Sore Will-berry and Miss Robbing leafs in five mints. I keeps dinner worm until you gets back.'

Justin hurried out of the kitchen and across the entrance hall, dragging the bin bags after him. In the dining room, Willoughby and Robyn were finishing their puddings.

'I always knew Dustbin was the perfect nickname,' remarked Robyn, eyeing the bags of envelopes curiously. 'So, is garbage collection your latest passion?'

'What time are you leaving, Dad?' Justin asked. Still furious with his father, he kept his voice devoid of emotion, his eyes hard. 'Is there time for me to wash and change?'

'If we don't go in a couple of ticks, we'll never make it,' said Sir Willoughby. 'Visiting time's seven 'til eight, and you know how long it takes driving to Inverness in the season.'

Justin looked disappointed. He was desperate to see how Nanny Verity was – but knew he'd never be ready in time. Worse still, he'd already lost half a day's work on his time machine, mulling over the clues – and *now* he had all these envelopes to sort through.

'I'd better stay here,' he mumbled. 'I'm running behind on my er ... project. Give Nanny a big hug from me and tell her to get well soon.'

'You could always send her a card,' suggested Robyn, peering into the bin bags. 'Grandpa's bought her a box of chocolates, the Gilliechattans are sending a bottle of home-made wine, Mrs Kof's made some shortbread, and Knightly's got her some grapes.'

'Well, I hope you're not planning to give her any of them,' Justin whispered, looking perfectly horrified. 'Somebody tried to kill her this morning, remember?'

'Gracious!' gasped Willoughby. 'Thought never occurred to me.

281

Suppose we'd better leave them all in the car and buy a big bunch of flowers from everybody instead.' He fidgeted awkwardly, avoiding eye contact with his son, then excused himself, muttering something about car keys. Robyn rushed upstairs to fetch her jacket. Up in her room, she noticed the mailbox icon flashing on her computer monitor – and even though her father was backing the VW into the courtyard, couldn't resist a hurried peek at the latest e-mail:

To:	rob@thymecastle.co.uk
From:	blueeyedboy@nine.com
Subject:	Letz Meet!

Hi Babe!
Have U fallen out with me? ☹ Haven't heard from U 4 ages. Long-distance friendships R tuf. I've got plans 4 Saturday – but if they don't work out maybe we should meet up. R U up 4 it? ☺
Chris.

WOW, thought Robyn, whistling through her teeth. *Finally, we're getting somewhere!*

Once the VW zoomed down the drive, Justin dumped the bin bags in the library and cleaned himself up. Knowing he'd work more efficiently on a full stomach, he returned to the kitchen and collected a tray of Mrs Kof's leftovers.

'I gives you extra big bowels of ticky-tocky pudding,' she boomed.

'Thanks,' said Justin, desperately trying to banish the mental image. Her malapropisms are getting worse, he thought. She sounds like a hammy actor in an old movie. He returned to the library with the tray, and placed it on the desk.

'Absolutely not,' Willoughby insisted. 'Don't even think about it. Meeting a total stranger is out of the question. *Never!* I can't believe you even asked ...'

Robyn folded her arms and stared out of the car window. She tapped her purple fingernails on the seatbelt buckle, waiting for her father to run out of steam. His blustering protestations didn't concern her in the slightest; she was used to getting her own way with him. Her mother was an entirely different matter; she was quiet but firm, whereas Willoughby blew his top for ten minutes, spouting a lot of hot air. She knew he'd crack in the end – he always did.

The trick was getting him on his own, which was why she'd brought the subject up the moment they turned onto Glen Thyme road. If Justin or Nanny were around to back him up, it was much more of a struggle. She glanced at her watch: five minutes to go, she thought, then I'll counter attack with a barrage of well-aimed flattery. By the time we reach Inverness, I'll have him wrapped around my little finger.

Justin wiped his mouth on his napkin and gave a deep sigh of satisfaction. Without any doubt, he thought, that's the best "bowel of ticky-tocky pudding" I've ever tasted. As he leaned back in his chair the library clock struck seven. He listened to the chime of its small gold bell and shuddered as he thought about its mysterious inscription:

'Beware the Thief of Time,' Justin whispered to himself, staring at the two carved figures representing Time and Chance; dependable Old Father Time and the mischievous jester. 'Odd that the jester's side of the clock should have a border of playing cards ... quite a coincidence.'

But was it really a random chance, he wondered, or something much more sinister?

283

Justin brushed the thought from his mind. With more than two thousand envelopes to sift through and a long night of catching up on his subatomic wormhole-vortex accelerator, he couldn't afford distractions. He was, however, determined to satisfy his curiosity on one matter: which book had Polly borrowed? He drew the parcel towards him and tore back the brown paper, expecting to reveal "*The Time Machine*" embossed in gold on the cream leather spine. But he was wrong.

'"*The History of Mr Polly*,"' he gasped. 'I didn't expect *that* – though, on reflection, I suppose it should've been obvious.'

'... And I don't want to hear another word on the subject,' concluded Sir Willoughby.

'Okay Dad,' said Robyn, in her meekest voice. 'What a shame. He'll be *so* disappointed; he was *really* desperate to meet you. But if you insist ...'

'Meet *me*?'

'Forget it. I promise never to contact him again.'

'Why would he want to meet *me*?'

Robyn picked an imaginary piece of fluff off her kilt and yawned, as if the whole conversation bored her to tears.

'Well?' Willoughby insisted.

Robyn concealed a triumphant smirk. It worked every time – it was almost too simple. So much for not wanting to hear another word on the subject.

'Chris wants to be an inventor when he leaves school,' she explained. 'I told him you were the greatest inventor in Scotland ... probably the world.'

'You told him *WHAT*?' roared Willoughby, almost swerving into a tree. 'How many times have your mum and I warned you? Never divulge personal information to strangers. What else have you told him?'

'Nothing,' said Robyn. This wasn't turning out as well as she'd planned.

Justin strolled across the library and returned the missing book to its rightful place. As he slid it onto the shelf beside its matching companions he noticed something sticking up between the pages. Curious, he pulled it out. It was a sheet of pastel notepaper with his own name at the top in Polly's flamboyant handwriting:

> *Dear Justin,*
>
> *I must apologise for borrowing this book without permission and taking so long to return it. My only excuse is that the title was so intriguing I simply couldn't resist reading it!*
>
> *With Best Wishes,*
>
> *Xavier Polydorus II*

'*Polydorus!*' gasped Justin. 'I always thought Polly was an odd nickname for a man.' I should've guessed ... but I kept focusing

---

♥ Did you assume that Polly was female? If you look back at where Polly appears in the story, you will see that the words he/she/him/her are never used, allowing you to jump to the wrong conclusion. Honest yet misleading descriptions of him may have misdirected you further – but they are all perfectly fair; men can have long blonde pony tails too!

on people *here* at Thyme Castle, and none of them have a name starting with X. Yet surely he's too young to be Dad's old enemy. Even though he's a makeup artist I doubt he could disguise himself to look less than thirty.

'*Of course!*' he groaned. 'Polly is Xavier Polydorus the *second.* The hypnotist mentioned in the news clippings must be his father; h*e'd* be about the right age. I suppose *he* mailed the first ransom note while Polly was still in the Congo. Meanwhile, Polly made sure he and Hank got fired so Mum would be alone at the airport. Mr Polydorus was late for his performance the day Mum was kidnapped, and the circus closes this Saturday ... the very night Agent X wants us to hand over the time machine.

'I'll bet Nanny Verity spotted Polly leaving the second ransom note as she came through the entrance hall with the laundry. Realising Nanny had to be silenced immediately, Polly must have grabbed the paperweight and ran up the east tower staircase to drop it on her. He knows the guestroom windows overlook the clothesline, because he slept there the night before Mum's expedition ... the same night Dad told me about building his own time machine.'

It sounded entirely plausible – but who, he wondered, was responsible for leaking inside information to Polly or his father?

Robyn talked about Chris all the way to Inverness, hardly pausing for a moment's breath. He was well-educated, adventurous, intelligent, cool, looked fantastic, had a great sense of humour and was the same age as her. The perfect boyfriend or what? Despite his reservations, Sir Willoughby felt himself start to buckle under the pressure.

'How do you know he's telling you the truth?' he asked, somewhat half-heartedly, reversing the VW into a hospital car parking space.

'Credit me with some intelligence, Dad. He sent me his photo. He's not some homicidal maniac preying on young girls. The first time we chatted online, he thought I was a boy; my user name's Rob. Even after we swapped e-mail addresses, he still thought I was a boy ... until I sent him *my* photo.'

'Didn't that teach you *anything*?' chuckled Willoughby, with an indulgent shake of his head. 'Perhaps *he* isn't a boy either.'

Robyn laughed too, sensing she'd almost clinched it.

'I *did* wonder at first,' she confessed. 'His chatroom ID was a bit ambiguous; it's just X.'

The phone on the library desk rang suddenly, startling Justin out of his silent speculation.

'Hello – Thyme Castle, Justin spea–'

'It's me,' whispered Sir Willoughby. 'Listen carefully: I've just discovered our security leak ... and it's somebody we never thought of.'

Chance and time are the yin and yang of our universe. One cannot exist without the other. For the Tartan of Time to retain its richness and colour, a certain amount of unpredictability is a vital part of the pattern. This doesn't mean that bizarre coincidences are predestined. No, it simply means that both contrasting elements are an integral part of life.

To illustrate: imagine that our timelines are woven together by two opposing forces, each seeking to influence their direction. One half of this syzygy is orderly and precise, like Old Father Time methodically measuring our lifeline with his hourglass. The other is like a mischievous jester, whose random pranks may alter our lives unexpectedly.

If our lives were without order, chaos would prevail; however, we could also argue that without coincidence our lives would become dull and monotonous. Random chance equals the odds between weak and strong, wise and foolish, putting them all on an equal footing – a fact recognised since biblical times:

"I returned, and saw under the sun,
that the race is not to the swift, nor the battle to the strong,
neither yet bread to the wise, nor yet riches to men of
understanding, nor yet favour to men of skill;
BUT TIME AND CHANCE HAPPENETH TO THEM ALL."
Ecclesiastes IX - XI

CHAPTER EIGHTEEN

A Number of Surprises

'It *can't* be!' gasped Justin. 'Robyn wouldn't help somebody kidnap Mum.'

'I'm not saying she's betrayed us on purpose,' Sir Willoughby explained. 'I'm certain she hasn't a clue. She was simply telling me about this boy, Chris, she's met on the internet; when she said his ID was X, you could have knocked me down with a feather. It's a good job I'd parked the car by then or I dread to think what would've happened.'

For a moment, the anxiety in his father's voice almost made Justin forget his anger, then it rushed back like air into a vacuum. He kept his tone icily formal. 'What did you say to her?'

'*Nothing!* How I kept my cool I'll never know. Shock I suppose. I should've guessed he'd try something like this; I told you what a charmer he is. I'm furious with myself.'

So you should be, thought Justin. 'Where's Robyn now?'

'I suggested she saw Nanny alone at first, in case having two visitors was a bit overwhelming. It was all I could think of; I just had to phone you immediately or I'd have exploded. She's going to get a piece of my mind on the way home, I can tell you!'

'No! Don't say anything,' warned Justin. As he spoke, he imagined his father's resentment at being told what to do again, but he brushed it aside. 'We might be able to turn this to our advantage. I'll hack into Robyn's computer and learn all I can.

There's always a chance this is some bizarre coincidence; Robyn might be innocent.'

'There's no such thing as coincidence where X is concerned,' said Willoughby bitterly.

Justin knotted both bin bags and stowed them under the library desk. There was no time to sort through the envelopes now, and the way things were going, it probably wouldn't be necessary. He glanced at the clock; it was twenty-five minutes past seven – an hour and a half before Robyn would be home. He hurried over to the reference section and located a copy of "*Names & Their Meanings*" by Madox Peagrain. He suspected Chris might be short for Christian Nation – the name the kidnapper had used at the airport. X appeared to have a warped sense of humour, and Justin suspected that his choice of pseudonyms was no fluke. He found it:

CHRISTIAN: A follower of Christ. Sometimes symbolised by the letter X, an equivalent of the Greek letter *khi*, the first letter of Khristos.

'It looks like Dad's right,' he murmured. 'Robyn was the leak all the time.'

At the top of the west tower, Justin crept into his sister's room and switched her PC on. A dialogue box appeared requesting her password – precisely as he'd expected. He slid the disc he'd brought into the disc drive and waited. The modem whirred and squeaked for about fifteen seconds then a window opened. Justin highlighted ENGLISH, selected the number of letters, and then clicked DECODE PASSWORD. He'd designed the program at the age of nine, and it worked by using the computer's own dictionary. As long as the password was a single word in Standard

English, he should have it in minutes. He leaned back in the chair and waited patiently.

After fourteen minutes and seven seconds, ACCESS DENIED flashed onto the screen. Undeterred, Justin instructed the computer to search for a combination of shorter words totalling the same number of letters. Twenty minutes and fifteen seconds later, ACCESS DENIED appeared again. Trust Robyn, he thought gloomily, the password's probably in another language. He had no desire to search the computer code line by line; finding an eight-letter password could take hours, and he'd wasted almost half his time already.

Justin hunched over the computer, his fingers rattling furiously across the keyboard. Time flew by as he peered at the rapidly scrolling lines of data, oblivious to everything else. For the next fifteen minutes or so, he instructed the computer to scan its code for any foreign words of the right length: it found nineteen, but none of them worked. Robyn had chosen something sneaky – either spelling the password backwards or randomly mixing upper and lower case letters. That would normally complicate things, but fortunately he'd designed the program with such difficulties in mind. He highlighted SEARCH FOR OFFBEAT OR REVERSE SPELLING, JUMBLES, ANAGRAMS OR MIXED CASING, then sat back and waited. Sixteen minutes later, the computer hiccupped discreetly and displayed interminable rows of nonsense on its screen. Justin groaned silently and glanced down at his watch. Time was running out; Willoughby and Robyn were due back in less than a quarter of an hour. With a sigh, he started to examine the words methodically. The majority were just typos or coincidental anagrams, but eventually he spotted the odd word out. With a few swift clicks he returned the monitor to Robyn's welcome screen and typed *fo*RTun*E*s in the box; at last, he had access to his sister's computer.

Justin hesitated, uncomfortable about invading her privacy. He stared at the screen, wondering whether to open her inbox or the sent items folder first. Before he could make his mind up, he heard the scrunch of tyres on gravel. He peered through the window and saw Robyn climb out of the VW, slamming the door behind her. Her lower lip protruded, and she kicked at the gravel, scuffing her turquoise suede boots. She glanced up at the west tower, and Justin dodged back, even though he knew the darkened room obscured him. There was no time to examine Robyn's e-mails now; yet he couldn't risk her contacting X – if, indeed, it was him. He would have to think of something – fast.

Justin typed chris in the address box, hoping it was programmed to auto-complete. It was. He dashed off a rapid e-mail and clicked SEND.

Robyn stomped across the gravel looking sullen and petulant. It was the first argument she'd lost in years. Sir Willoughby marched after her.

'Nanny agreed with me wholeheartedly,' he said. 'Meeting boys on the internet is too damn dangerous.'

'She also thinks you can catch germs off a computer virus,' Robyn snorted, still furious with herself for allowing Nanny to wheedle everything out of her. 'She thinks Google is a pop group, and JPEGs are for hanging out the laundry.'

'That's beside the point. Finding your mother is our main priority right now – and I'm pretty sure what *she'd* say.'

Robyn flounced into the castle.

'How's Nanny?' panted Justin. He was flushed and breathless from galloping downstairs and sprinting along the portrait gallery, but Robyn was too intent on glowering at her father to notice.

'Scatty as ever,' she replied tersely. 'The doctor said there's no brain damage, but if there is, I doubt we'd notice *much* difference.'

'ROBYN!' roared Willoughby. 'That's the last straw; go to your room.'

'DON'T WORRY – *I'M GOING!*'

'Typical Bobs,' said Justin, breaking the awkward silence after her dramatic exit. 'Hiding her true feelings under a crust of contempt. She didn't mean it, you know.'

Willoughby looked sceptical. 'She never does. That's probably why we're in this mess. So – did you hack into her computer? Is she the leak?'

'I didn't get chance to find out. It's taken me all this time to crack her password. However, Chris's e-mail address ends with a nine – and in Roman numerals that's IX. It might mean *I am X* or it could be another coincidence.'

'I doubt it,' groaned Willoughby, running his hands through his hair. 'She's probably contacting him right now.'

'She can't,' said Justin. 'I've changed her password – and she'll never discover it without this,' he added, withdrawing the disc from his pocket.

'But ...'

'She'll think her computer's malfunctioning; when she asks for my help, I'll agree to fix it whilst she's visiting Nanny again. Before logging off, I e-mailed her so-called boyfriend suggesting an online chat tomorrow evening. I'll use the Honestimator Trojan to discover whether he's genuine. If he really *is* Agent X, I'll retrieve the last twenty or so deleted e-mails and we'll know exactly what Robyn's told him. Then if we want, we can turn the tables and start feeding him with bogus information.'

'The honesty-estimator?' gasped Willoughby. 'I thought you'd destroyed it.'

'You're not the only one with a secret,' Justin remarked coolly. 'There's no time to explain now – I'm way behind with my work. I know it's late, but I need some diversionary noises from your workshop until about twelve o'clock. Then meet me in the kitchen and I'll tell you everything.'

The following morning, Justin's alarm clock woke him at precisely twenty minutes to eight. Still desperately sleepy, he dragged himself out of bed yawning and complaining. After indulging in a midnight feast of cold sticky toffee pudding and cream with his father, he'd worked until dawn. As a result, he felt utterly exhausted – but at least he was back on schedule with his subatomic wormhole-vortex accelerator.

'My PC's playing up,' grumbled Robyn, between sips of coffee. 'Can you take a quick squiz at it later, Dustbin?' The door opened and Knightly glided in with a toast rack. 'It might be a *virus*,' she added, with a pointed sideways glance at the sniffing butler.

'You'll have to be patient,' said Justin, half smiling behind an oatcake. 'I'm snowed under; I probably won't be able to visit Nanny again.'

Robyn scowled. 'She'll be terribly disappointed. But Hank's visiting her tonight. Professor Gilbert told us; he came just before we left. Mrs Kof had sent him a message about Nanny. And before you gloat ... yes, I realise now that my theory about the prof was ...'

Knightly gave a loud sniff; Justin shot his sister a warning glance and kicked her under the table. What Robyn didn't know was that the butler had gone out in his car last night, barely five minutes after she and Sir Willoughby left the castle. Justin debated whether to tell her or not – then decided there was no point. He was almost certain that Polly's father was Agent X – and Polly ...

'Will Polly be visiting Nanny, too?' he asked, suddenly anxious.

'No, he's busy. But he and Hank are coming over tomorrow morning to welcome Nanny home. Polly's bringing his dad; he's renting old Dr Brown's place for the summer and is dying to meet us all apparently.'

Robyn never found patience an easy virtue. Halfway through the morning she knocked on the lab door, with a mug of coffee and a plate of shortbread, and casually reminded her brother about the computer. At lunchtime she mentioned it again, a little *less* casually. By mid-afternoon she was haunting the south tower, driving Justin to distraction. Finally, she extracted a solemn promise that he'd fix her computer later, while she was visiting the hospital.

'It'll be the ideal time,' Justin explained. 'Right now I need plenty of distraction from Dad's workshop to disguise the din up here. When he's out, I daren't risk anything noisy – and I did most of the silent work between midnight and dawn. So ...'

'But Dad isn't taking me,' said Robyn, looking surprised. 'He said he had to stay behind and help you with something. The Gilliechattans insisted on going tonight – so they're giving me a lift. But don't worry – I'll watch them like a hawk.'

Justin wasn't especially concerned. With the case practically solved, the gardener and his wife weren't under suspicion – though Robyn thought otherwise. He listened to her brag about the investigative questions she planned to ask during the drive. Her naivety astonished him; she evidently hadn't a clue that *she'd* been the security leak all along.

After waving Robyn and the Gilliechattans off, Justin hurried to the top of the west tower. He typed in the replacement password: TrEmbLeS – (the first word he'd thought of last night as he stared at his hands hovering tensely over the keyboard), and gained instant access to his sister's PC. He took the discs containing the Honestimator Program out of his pocket and inserted them into the disc drive.

He'd devised Honestimator a year ago, and initially had high hopes of it multiplying the Thyme fortune beyond his wildest dreams. The idea came to him after watching a news report about the dangers of internet chat rooms. It warned that unscrupulous adults posing as juveniles were attempting to lure children into meeting them. Most kids failed to take the problem seriously, and parents complained it was impossible to protect them without banning chat rooms altogether. Immediately, Justin saw huge potential for a product that gave children the freedom they wanted, whilst giving anxious parents peace of mind.

He decided to invent a program that could sense whether an e-mail correspondent was being truthful; a seemingly impossible task. Usually, lie-detectors depended on minute fluctuations in speech patterns, tone of voice, body language and heart-rate – but with e-mail these didn't exist.

Eventually he discovered the answer: faced with a question, the brain automatically thinks of a truthful response *before* it can formulate a lie. While typing lies, minuscule pauses between the keystrokes are barely discernible. To put it simply: lies are typed at a different speed to the truth. The difference is infinitesimal – but computers can easily calibrate it. Within a month, he'd designed a program capable of estimating the honesty of a statement typed on his own keyboard. That was the easy part: the real problem was working out how to bypass the service provider and access a stranger's keyboard.

The only viable solution was a Trojan; harmless, yet a virus of sorts nonetheless. It would invade the recipient's computer, analyse data from the keystrokes, then all e-mail replies would automatically include a hidden attachment containing an honesty estimate. Designing the Trojan was a mammoth job, but his problems were far from over. When he applied for a patent, he was advised that the legal complications would make it impractical. Infecting another person's computer without permission – no matter how well-intentioned – was an invasion of privacy. Misuse was inevitable. Vetting potential business deals with Honestimator might rock Wall Street and undermine global finance; divorce could skyrocket, and the resulting litigation from both could bankrupt the Thymes. It seemed that world stability depended on lies. He'd been urged to destroy the Honestimator without delay.

⧗

It took Justin the best part of an hour to install the program and run various system checks. He worked swiftly and silently, listening out for his father. As the only person familiar with Agent X, Sir Willoughby felt it wise to be on hand. Justin glanced at the digital clock in the bottom right-hand corner of the screen; it showed 19:16. He drummed his fingers on the desk; he'd asked his dad to be no later than quarter past. By the time he arrived, looking flustered and breathless, Justin was already chatting online to Robyn's "boyfriend."

'Sorry,' said Willoughby, smoothing his hair. 'Dozed off. How's it going?'

'Disappointing,' replied Justin, his manner still cool. 'I haven't learned anything at all yet. His replies are too short for the program to use. Watch ...'

He typed:

> U seem so mature. R we really the same age?

He clicked SEND; seconds later the answer appeared:

> Yes.
>
> HONESTY ESTIMATE: Insufficient Data to Analyse

'Not exactly co-operative,' said Willoughby. 'You don't think he's on to us do you? What if he knows Robyn's out tonight?'

Justin looked aghast; the thought hadn't occurred to him. He'd been convinced that Agent X was Polly's father. Perhaps he was wrong.

Sir Willoughby pinched the bridge of his nose. 'At least we can rule Gilliechattan out.'

'I'm afraid not,' replied Justin, shaking his head. 'Most modern hospitals have public computers in the dayrooms now; he could access his e-mail account there.'

'Well, he's about the right age,' said Willoughby. 'When we made our time machine, X was in his mid-forties, though he didn't

look a day over twenty-five. I haven't seen him for twelve years –
no, longer – not since the day after you were born, so by now ...'

'He'd be in his late fifties,' finished Justin, hurriedly typing a
new question:

> ## When exactly R U fifteen?

The surprising reply did nothing to brighten their mood:

> ### My fifteenth birthday is at the end of next February.
>
> HONESTY ESTIMATE: Absolute Truth

'Is there any way he could fool the Honestimator program?'
asked Willoughby.

'Definitely not,' said Justin. 'We've been barking up the wrong
tree I'm afraid; he really is a teenage boy after all. He's even
younger than Robyn.'

Sir Willoughby could hardly believe it; they'd both felt so
certain. He wandered off wearing a puzzled frown, leaving Justin
to conclude the e-mail chat politely. Halfway down the west tower
staircase he came to an abrupt halt, fumbled in his pocket for his
diary, then raced back to Robyn's room. He burst through the
door, babbling excitedly:

'It *is* X. He didn't say he'd *be* fifteen in February ... he only said
his fifteenth *birthday* was at the *end* of February.'

'Isn't that the same thing?' asked Justin.

'Not *next* year,' said Willoughby, waving the diary. 'It's a leap
year. People born on the 29th of February have a quarter the
number of birthdays we have.'

'Which makes him fifty-nine,' gasped Justin, after a swift
calculation.

'I should've remembered before,' said Willoughby, grimacing.

'It's only just come back to me. I used to tease him about how young he looked for his age, but he said he looked old considering how many birthdays he'd had. When I asked what he meant, his reply was *so* peculiar I can *still* recall the exact words: *"I am the victim of a clumsy arrangement, having been born in leap year on the 29th of February. And so, by a simple arithmetical process, you'll easily discover, that though I've lived forty-five years, yet, if we go by birthdays, I'm only eleven and a little bit over!"* '

'It *must* be him,' said Justin, reaching for a sheaf of paper. With a few clicks he instructed the computer to print every e-mail either sent or received during the last month, even those that had been deleted. He and Willoughby pored over them as fast as the printer could churn them out – but they were in for another surprise. Although X had asked an abundance of leading questions, Robyn had remained astonishingly loyal. Apart from accidentally mentioning that her father was an inventor, she hadn't revealed a single piece of information he could have used to kidnap Henny.

'I feel terrible,' said Justin. 'We should've known she was innocent.' With a deep sigh, he methodically obliterated all traces of their intrusion from his sister's computer and reinstalled her original password.

'But if he's not using Robyn to spy on us, how did he know the police were involved?' Willoughby grumbled, as they clattered down the west tower. 'Sergeant Awbrite phoned earlier; his investigation seems to be at a dead end too. And I still can't get that dashed curse out of my mind – I'm convinced X is going to kill your mother.'

'We're not beaten yet,' said Justin, and told his father about the mysterious tea-stained stamp he hoped to find. 'We've got a couple of thousand envelopes to sort through – but with both of us searching, we'll find it in half the time.'

Minutes later, the library floor was awash with paper. However, their perplexing discoveries only dismayed them further. They found nineteen padded envelopes of various sizes from a company called Kilmarnock Fusion Nucleonics; all were addressed to

Professor Gilbert, but had been sent to a post office box number rather than the castle itself. Otherwise, there was the note from Polly, warning Henny he'd heard rumours their TV show was about to be axed; and introductory letters from Knightly and Mrs Kof. Unfortunately, none of them had a stained stamp.

'Another dead end,' muttered Willoughby, refilling the bin bags.

'Maybe,' Justin replied thoughtfully.

Sir Willoughby frowned at the last padded envelope, then gave a forced laugh. 'You know ... if Professor Gilbert hadn't given you that watch, I'd be worrying it might have some kind of bugging device inside it.'

Justin gasped as if someone had punched him. He stared down at the watch, eyes wide with horror. 'But ... it ... it wasn't from the professor,' he whispered, scrabbling frantically at the scythe-shaped catch. 'He ... he gave me a ...'

'*WHAT?*' roared Willoughby. '*WHY* didn't you *TELL ME?*'

'Shhhhhhhh.' Justin yanked a desk drawer open, stuffed the watch under a pile of notepaper and slammed it shut again. 'Robyn convinced me it was from you and Mum.'

'*Arghhh*! For the last time: I did NOT give you that *blasted* wristwatch.'

'I realised *that* once Mum was kidnapped,' said Justin, grabbing his father's arm and dragging him towards the mantelpiece. 'I think whoever sent it was trying to warn us.' He positioned Sir Willoughby in front of the old Thyme Clock and pointed up at the bell. '*Beware Procrastination* – the exact same words are on my watch, encircling the X.'

Willoughby groaned. 'It's from Agent X alright. He's toying with you; his idea of a joke. You should've told me ...'

'I *tried* to,' snapped Justin, 'after Mum was kidnapped ... but you wouldn't listen.' He glared at his father, wondering how he had the nerve to accuse him of secrecy – but felt far angrier with himself for not realising the watch could be bugged.

'Haven't you asked round?' growled Willoughby. 'Tried to find out who left it?'

'Of *course* I have! But if the watch *is* from X, nobody's going to admit to it, are they?'

The library clock struck nine. Both father and son stared silently at the mechanical figures of Old Father Time and the jester, then, with a shake of his head, Willoughby plodded over to the courtyard window. The Gilliechattans' ramshackle old Morris had just trundled through the archway. Sir Willoughby sighed as he watched his fourteen year old daughter clamber out.

'How on earth am I going to tell her?' he asked.

'Tell her what?'

'That her boyfriend isn't fourteen going on fifteen ... but a man in his late fifties.'

'Don't say anything yet,' said Justin. 'No point. She hasn't leaked anything – and if we need to chat with X again, we can't risk her arousing his suspicions.'

They met Robyn in the hall. Her eyes were red, and her cheeks streaked with tears.

'What's happened to Nanny?' asked Justin, almost shouting.

'Nanny's fine,' Robyn mumbled. 'The doctor's arranged for her to be driven home tomorrow morning.'

'What's wrong then?' asked Sir Willoughby. He held his arms out, and Robyn threw herself into them.

'I've b-b-been an idiot,' she sobbed. 'Mrs G took Nanny some magazines. I was flipping through them and I found this.' She held out a torn page; it was a fashion advert showing a smiling teenage boy. 'That's the photo he sent me – the creep. You were absolutely right, Dad; he's probably an old man.'

Henny's captor arrived later than usual that evening, which finally gave her long enough to wake up and put the first phase of her plan into action. The second phase was hazy as yet, but she knew escape would be impossible if she remained constantly sedated. She needed to trick the kidnapper into giving her a smaller dose. Usually, she slept soundly until slapped awake – and by then, it was too late for pretence. Ironically, she needed to be fully conscious in order to feign unconsciousness convincingly.

Listening carefully for the sound of approaching footsteps, Henny searched for anything that might help her escape. She fumbled between the mattress and the bed head, then in the top drawer of the bedside cabinet where she found three useless looking items: a paperclip, a rubber band and a felt pen.

'A grappling hook, a crowbar and a bush knife would've been more to my taste,' she muttered, and hid them under her pillow, just in case.

Moments later the caravan door creaked open. Agent X stepped inside, his blue eyes glinting frostily through his balaclava. He strode over to his prisoner and shook her roughly. Henny flopped about like a rag doll, mentally bracing herself for the forthcoming slap; it was vital she didn't flinch. The first blow was bearable, but the second and third became increasingly brutal. Henny had to summon every ounce of self-control to keep from screaming. With a sudden roar of anger, he threw her down onto the bed.

Henny peered at the kidnapper warily from beneath her eyelashes. For the next five minutes he stamped around, glancing at his watch and muttering impatiently about the time. It would be almost fourteen hours before he could return – far too long to leave a prisoner without sedation; yet she was in no fit state for the customary dose. Finally, he did exactly as Henny had predicted, filling the syringe with half the usual amount.

After retrieving his wristwatch from the library, Justin trudged up the south tower stairs to his lab. Despite his habit of cannibalising watches, he felt strangely reluctant to dismantle it. In fact, to his astonishment, he'd found himself relying on the watch more each day, and the thought of accidentally damaging it horrified him. But it *had* to be checked; if it *was* bugged, then he was even more to blame for his mum's kidnap than he'd thought.

302

With the utmost care, he prised off the back and peered at the movement through his horologist's eyepiece.

Apart from the letters 𝒦𝒥𝒜 engraved on the wheel bridge – probably the maker's initials, Justin thought – little was visible. He lifted a tiny Perspex box out of a drawer, then, using a pair of tweezers, extracted a minuscule ant-sized microbot and placed it on the rim of the watch. After a few typed instructions on his computer keyboard, the robot blinked a solitary eye and scuttled inside. The watch's interior flickered onto Justin's screen; greatly enlarged, it looked just like the enormous movement of the tower clock whirring and clunking above him. Watching the image closely, he guided the ant through the labyrinth of cogs and wheels.

An hour later, Justin felt satisfied the watch was *not* bugged. He wondered whether to go and tell his father, but Sir Willoughby had disappeared after Robyn returned, saying he didn't want to be disturbed. A faint light shone through the curtains of his parents' room; Robyn's curtains were drawn too, and judging from the pulsating flashes, she was venting her feelings by blasting cranio-zombies.

Rubbing his eyes, Justin glanced over at his time machine, knowing he ought to be working on the subatomic wormhole-vortex accelerator – but he couldn't concentrate while the identity of their resident spy remained a mystery. Wondering if a relaxing bath might help him unravel the tangle of clues, he slid down to his bedroom.

Before undressing, he paused by the window and stared sleepily across the darkened loch. He felt suddenly drained of energy and almost too weary to move. 'You won't find any answers out there,' he muttered to himself. 'No, you'll find them in here,' he added, tapping his forehead. Then, after yawning widely, he closed the curtains and plodded into the bathroom.

As soon as she was alone, Henny opened her eyes and squirmed into a sitting position. A stale, sticky-looking sandwich lay on the bedside table, but she ignored it – her appetite replaced by a terrible sickening nausea.

Once she was sure the kidnapper was far enough away, Henny put the next phase of her plan into action. The lower dose of sedative seemed to be working slower than usual, but time was short and she felt dreadful. Her head throbbed painfully and she had started to shiver. Struggling to remain conscious a little while longer, Henny grasped the bedside lamp. She pointed it towards the window and started to signal, fervently hoping that someone at Thyme Castle would notice before she collapsed.

Justin rose early the following morning, determined to get a few hours work done before Nanny Verity came home. His long, hot soak the previous night hadn't helped at all. Despite reviewing all the clues in an orderly fashion he still couldn't make *Everything Connect to Everything Else*; clearly, a crucial piece of evidence was missing.

Agent X sensed something was amiss the instant he woke up. His nose felt twitchy, and that was always an infallible sign of trouble. After bolting an early breakfast he hurried to the caravan, half expecting to find the entire Inverness Police Force lurking in the undergrowth, but everything was exactly as he'd left it. He chastised himself severely as he fumbled with the padlock:

'Stop letting your imagination run riot,' he muttered under his breath. 'This isn't the time for an attack of the jitters; nothing's going to go wrong.' But as the caravan door swung open and a shaft of sunlight slanted across the bed, Agent X saw that his prisoner was seriously ill.

Henny seemed unaware of his sudden appearance. Her eyes were glazed and unfocussed, her cheeks flushed. Dewy beads of perspiration trickled down her forehead, seeping into dampened hair. She shivered uncontrollably and dark patches of sweat stained her khaki shirt.

Detached and calculating, Agent X strode to the bed and assessed her condition. As he peered at Henny, she shifted her position slightly, revealing a blotchy scarlet rash down the side of her neck. X staggered backwards, wondering what foul disease she'd contracted in the Congo. The thought of catching something contagious filled him with a morbid dread. He daren't risk it; a rash like that was a clue even the most bumbling of policemen would spot.

On reflection, he decided it would be safest to give her a massive overdose of sedative, then lock up the caravan and never return. Her death needn't jeopardise his plans; after all, nobody would know until it was too late. Once he'd got the time machine, he'd inform the Thymes where they could locate her body. Calmly, he withdrew a small glass phial from his pocket and filled a hypodermic syringe with a triple-sized dose of lethal colourless fluid. But as he grasped Henny's arm in his gloved hand, she gave a sudden convulsive shudder and leaned over the side of the bed, vomiting blood and mucus onto his shoes.

Agent X staggered to the door and leaned out, taking several deep gulps of highland air. Regaining his composure, he returned, retrieving the syringe from the bedside cabinet where he'd dropped it. When he grabbed Henny's arm a second time, she was too weak to put up any resistance. He injected the sedative and watched his victim plummet into terminal oblivion, his cold cerulean eyes frozen with contemptuous indifference.

After locking the caravan, X wiped his shoes on a clump of bracken and gazed dispassionately across the loch. By the time he reached the castle, Lady Henrietta Thyme would have lapsed into a fatal coma, and the Thyme family would have lost its intrepid celebrity matriarch forever.

'Any regrets?' he asked himself. Then staring at his blood-stained feet, sniggered: 'Only that she's ruined a perfectly good pair of shoes.'

Justin Thyme

When Hank's old Land Rover rumbled into the courtyard, Justin glanced at his watch; Nanny was due in twenty minutes. He switched off his oxyacetylene torch, slid down to his bedroom and changed into a clean white tee-shirt. From his window he saw Knightly open the castle door and usher in Hank, Polly and a tall, dark stranger. Justin guessed this was Polly's dad, and stared with intense curiosity until a movement on the loch distracted him. It was Professor Gilbert rowing his boat.

'Aha ... so Knightly and the prof *aren't* the same person after all,' Justin murmured, wondering why he'd ever allowed his sister to persuade him otherwise.

Mrs Kof had noticed the professor too, and stood on the cliff top waving an enormous red and white spotted handkerchief. She seemed very pleased to see him.

As Justin walked along the corridor to the west tower he heard a whimpering from the direction of the nursery. He rushed in and found Albion stood in his cot, looking irritable.

'You're wet,' he said, feeling Albion's bottom. Then, noticing the immense brooding gorilla hunched behind the door, asked: 'Why haven't you changed his nappy, Eliza?'

'Eliza not want human baby,' she replied, scowling. 'Baby make smelly mess. Nanny come home today. Nanny change baby.'

'Nanny would be very upset to find Alby like this,' said Justin, fetching the chamomile bottiwipes, talcum powder and a clean nappy.

Eliza watched him scornfully, her eyebrows arched in surprise. 'You change baby?' she asked.

'Really Eliza – it's not rocket science.' Justin fastened the Velcro tabs. 'There we *are*! All clean for Nanny.'

'Po-car,' chortled Albion, pointing to a seaside picture on the nursery notice board. He hugged his favourite teddy bear and smacked his lips together making loud kissing noises.

'Yes. Clever boy, Alby – that's Nanny's postcard. She sent us lots of special hugs and kisses, didn't she?'

Justin reached for the card. He'd glanced at it briefly when it arrived last week, but once Robyn had taken it up to the nursery he'd forgotten it completely. He vaguely remembered Nanny writing about a mysterious secret she'd learned. He'd dismissed it as trivial gossip at the time, but maybe *this* was what she'd tried to tell him the night before her attack. Justin turned the card over and read it again:

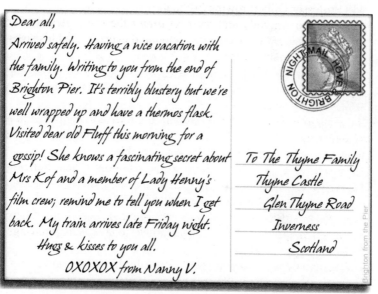

Dear all,

Arrived safely. Having a nice vacation with the family. Writing to you from the end of Brighton Pier. It's terribly blustery but we're well wrapped up and have a thermos flask. Visited dear old Fluff this morning for a gossip! She knows a fascinating secret about Mrs Kof and a member of Lady Henny's film crew; remind me to tell you when I get back. My train arrives late Friday night.
    Hugs & kisses to you all.
        OXOXOX from Nanny V.

To The Thyme Family
Thyme Castle
Glen Thyme Road
Inverness
Scotland

'Well done, Alby,' said Justin, patting his head. 'I think this is the missing clue I needed. But it still doesn't make any sense. Ah well ... I suppose Nanny will explain everything. I'll talk to her as soon as she gets home.'

'Nanny here now,' said Eliza, pointing through the barred window.

Justin glanced outside; sure enough, the ambulance had arrived.

He handed his brother over and hurried downstairs. Eliza prowled nobly in his wake, with Albion clinging to her back while still clutching his teddy. Justin pushed all anxious thoughts out of his mind as he opened the kitchen door. It was so crowded inside he could scarcely see Nanny Verity sat at the table, opening her get-well cards.

'Welcome home, Nan,' he said, giving her a huge hug. 'Sorry I didn't visit you in hospital; I've been rather busy.'

'I understand,' said Nanny, with a sad little smile. Her head was still bandaged, and she looked overwhelmed by the hive of activity surrounding her. Willoughby tempted her with a box of champagne truffles; Mr Polydorus magically plucked the ace of hearts from behind Nanny's left ear and presented it to her with an elegant bow; Knightly poured coffee from a gleaming silver pot; Mrs Kof removed a tray of hot croissants from the oven while Robyn fetched the plates; the Gilliechattans burst through the back door carrying a bunch of tulips, and a gust of wind scattered Nanny's get-well cards across the table; Professor Gilbert wedged them safely under his cup; Polly found a vase for the flowers and filled it with water; Eliza tickled Albion making him squeal with laughter; and Hank leaned against the pantry door, tossing strawberries in the air and catching them in his mouth – until Grandpa Lyall sneezed unexpectedly and he missed. A large juicy berry fell beside Hank's feet, leaving a sticky mark on the tiles. Tybalt patted it playfully with several paws, then Burbage swooped down and carried it off.

Nanny Verity Kiss took hold of Justin's arm and whispered softly:

'Before I forget: the ambulance driver told me that when he came on duty last night, he saw a flashing light way across the loch, and ...' She stopped mid-sentence, worried by the preoccupied expression on Justin's face. 'What's to do, Poppet?'

'Nothing Nanny ... I er ... I just ... *saw* ... something.'

In a trance, Justin turned and staggered towards the window, needing a moment to think. He stared at the little square of turf beneath the washing-line, concentrating every single brain cell on what he'd just seen in the kitchen. It was another *eureka* moment – like the time he watched Grandpa Lyall tossing a coin and instantly understood time travel. By a bizarre coincidence, something he'd just witnessed had ignited a train of thought that fizzled and sparked like the fuse to a stick of dynamite. Suddenly, a devastating idea exploded in his brain. Piece by piece, the bewildering jigsaw of clues fell perfectly into place and, at last, *Everything Connected to Everything Else*. No matter how unimaginable it seemed, he finally knew the truth.

Slowly, Justin crossed the kitchen and murmured discreetly in the impostor's ear: 'I think we should have a private talk upstairs,' he said. 'You see ... I know that *you* are our spy.'

Random chance is responsible for many unforeseen occurrences influencing our lives, but occasionally, a bizarre coincidence is part of TIME'S GRAND DESIGN. However, judging which force is accountable is something of an enigma. Try analysing this well-documented historical coincidence for yourself:

After being elected to congress exactly a century apart, Abraham Lincoln and John F. Kennedy both became Presidents of the United States; one in November 1860, the other in November 1960. Mr Lincoln had a secretary called John, while Mr Kennedy's secretary was called Lincoln. Both Presidents were assassinated on a Friday – one in Ford's Theatre, the other in a Ford car. John Wilkes Booth shot Lincoln in the theatre and then ran to a warehouse; Lee Harvey Oswald allegedly shot Kennedy from a warehouse window then ran to a theatre. The killers, born 100 years apart, were both shot before coming to trial. Both Presidents were succeeded by Southerners called Johnson – one born in 1808, the other in 1908.

We might describe this as HISTORY REPEATING ITSELF, but the correct term for a coincidence in time, of two or more causally unrelated yet identical events is SYNCHRONICITY. Such correlations of time and circumstances appear to prove that not all coincidences are coincidental.

But what purpose does synchronicity serve?

CHAPTER NINETEEN

Truth Revealed

Lady Henrietta Thyme had never felt so alive. True, she was battered and bruised, and her head ached – but none of that seemed to matter. Adrenaline coursed through her veins, and every muscle and sinew pulsated with an invigorating tingle of excitement.

Her plan had gone like clockwork. Thanks to the lower dose of sedative, she'd woken early, and by the time her captor arrived the scene was set. First, she'd opened one of the bottles on the bedside cabinet, filled the plastic mug with water, then used the rest to dampen her hair and clothes until they appeared to be soaked with a feverish sweat. Next, she'd taken the red felt pen from beneath her pillow and decorated the side of her neck with a blotchy rash – after which she chewed the pen's fibrous refill like a stick of gum. Finally, she'd crumbled the stale sandwich into small pieces.

The instant she'd heard the jangle of keys in the padlock, Henny had acted like lightning. She'd swept the pile of crumbs into her mouth and had taken a swig of water. Then, after spattering her forehead with fake beads of perspiration, she'd flopped back and started to shiver violently.

Henny knew she'd need to remain fully conscious to have any real chance of escape. Therefore, her plan was to replace the sedative with something harmless, but first she'd needed to misdirect her captor's attention before he'd tried to inject her. After tucking the refill under her tongue, she'd made loud vomiting noises and spat a mouthful of red dye and soggy breadcrumbs over his feet. Just as she had anticipated, the kidnapper was horrified. The instant he'd rushed to the caravan door, she'd squirted the contents of the syringe behind the bed, refilled it with water from the mug then replaced it on the bedside cabinet. All that remained was for her to feign unconsciousness after he'd injected her.

Once the kidnapper left, Henny wasted no time. The next phase of her plan was to retrieve her penknife and cut through the ropes binding her feet. Her captor had tossed it into a drawer on the other side of the caravan, along with all her other personal possessions. It was barely three or four feet away, but while she'd been tethered and unconscious, it might as well have been several miles.

First, Henny needed the necktie she'd hidden in the middle drawer of the bedside cabinet. She poked the paperclip through one end of the tie and twisted it into a makeshift grappling hook. By stretching the elastic band between her thumb and forefinger, she could catapult the miniature hook at the drawer handle. As soon as the drawer was open, she planned to repeat the process until she snagged the tiny Swiss penknife fastened to her key-ring. Simple; or so she'd thought. Henny soon realised that attaining the optimum speed and trajectory was tougher than darting a stampeding rhinoceros whilst steering a jeep. After an hour of sheer frustration she was almost ready to give up.

Justin paused outside the south tower sitting room, holding the door open. The spy scuttled in, perched primly on the white leather sofa, and cast him a look of tearful mortification. Justin remained silent for a moment, then sighed deeply. When he finally spoke, it was in a voice that betrayed his distress.

'I *still* can't believe it. You – of all people.'

'Och, I'm so sorry, Poppet' murmured Nanny Verity. 'But ...'

'Don't *Poppet* me. You're a traitor.'

'I confess,' sobbed Nanny. 'I knew I'd never fool *you*. What gave me away?'

'The clues[1] pointed to you all along, but I kept dismissing them,' said Justin. 'My trusty old nanny was always above suspicion – until finally, the evidence became too overwhelming to ignore. I suppose it all started the afternoon Dad first told me about his time machine. He was terrified somebody had overheard him. Mr Gilliechattan and Burbage were nearby – Professor Gilbert too. You were up in the nursery – but Eliza had left Albion's pram beside the workshop.[2] I suspect his baby monitor was inside, allowing you to eavesdrop.[3] During afternoon tea when Dad introduced Grandpa Lyall to us all, you seemed oddly preoccupied[4] – as though you thought he was an impostor. Actually, you were planning how to contact your husband – Agent X – very much alive despite your insistence on being a widow.'

'I'm truly sorry. But I promise you – I had no choice. You see, I ... I ...' Unable to continue, Nanny Verity broke down and wept. Tears coursed down her cheeks in torrents, as if she had held them in for far too long and finally let go. 'That man's bullied me for years,' she gulped at last. 'No wonder I'm a dithering wreck.'

Justin rummaged through his pockets. 'Tell me everything,' he said, handing her the cleanest tissue he could find.

'He once worked for a top secret organization,' sniffed Nanny. 'At least that's what he told me. By a rummy coincidence, your father was his lab assistant. Valentine – that's Mr Kiss – invented a time machine ... and Sir Willoughby stole the only blueprint.'

'Hang on a tick,' said Justin indignantly. 'You've got it back to front; it was Dad who invented the time machine.'

'I always suspected as much. But Valentine insisted otherwise. As you know, I'd been a maid here before I got married, so when

---

[1] If you want to check the clues later, footnotes will direct you to the right pages.

[2] Page 39, 43.

[3] Page 238.

[4] Page 57.

you were born, he persuaded me to apply for the job of Nanny. He said all I had to do was keep my ears open, and tell him if Sir Willoughby ever mentioned time machines. I agreed, but as the years passed Val started to doubt my loyalty. Eventually, I divorced him, but he threatened to harm our grandchildren if I didn't continue as his spy. Like I said – I had no choice.'

'I thought you'd looked worried lately,'[5] said Justin. 'But ...'

'Och, it gets much worse,' Nanny sobbed. 'About a year ago, Val told me he'd know if I ever tried to double-cross him. I wondered if he was going to plant another spy in the castle. Can you imagine how I felt when old Sir Lyall turned up the very day your father mentioned the time machine? When he insisted on driving me to the station, I was terrified. His enquiries about whether there was a Mr Kiss seemed like a veiled threat, especially when he mentioned my grand-children too.[6] As soon as I arrived in Brighton I phoned Val at once. He asked lots of questions, but I *never* guessed he was going to kidnap Lady Henny.'

'No wonder you fainted when the ransom note arrived.'[7]

'I was petrified the police would discover I was partly to blame.'

'So that's why you were so reluctant when Robyn suggested phoning Sergeant Awbrite,' said Justin. 'I thought it strange when you said: *there must be something we can do* instead of calling the police.[8] But you seemed so eager to help *prevent* Mum's kidnap, I never doubted you for an instant.'

'Saving Lady Henny would've got me off the hook,' Nanny explained. 'If we'd caught Valentine Kiss in the bargain ... so much the better. But your plan failed and Sergeant Awbrite turned up asking too many awkward questions.'

---

[5] Pages 86, 87, 101.

[6] Page 103.

[7] Page 129.

[8] Pages 138, 153.

'That was when Eliza got angry. I assumed Professor Gilbert was lying, but it was you,' said Justin. 'First you pretended not to recognize your husband's handwriting.[9] Then, when Sergeant Awbrite suggested that somebody in the castle had helped the kidnapper, you insisted that nobody would be so disloyal.'[10]

'*And* I fibbed about the professor looking younger without his beard,' said Nanny.[11]

'Then at supper that evening you behaved almost as if Mum had died.'[12]

'Guilt mostly,' Nanny admitted, her eyes filling with tears again. 'I'd got myself in a terrible pickle. It seemed the only way I could throw the police off my trail was by appearing to be the victim of an attack. The new butler hadn't arrived, so I dropped some hints to remind you to chase up the agency so you wouldn't be short-staffed,[13] then I started to make plans in earnest. I decided to use Mrs Gilliechattan's *Sunday Post* to make another ransom note.'[14]

'Sneaky,' said Justin. 'But enclosing Mum's dress watch was your first big mistake. Its hands were frozen at 9:40 – probably about the time Mum was kidnapped. At first I assumed it had got damaged in some kind of scuffle, but then I remembered she was wearing her digital travel watch when she left[15] – so I knew the second note *wasn't* from the kidnapper but from someone *here* at Thyme Castle. Otherwise, you had me baffled. I suppose hinting you had some mysterious secret to tell me the night before the paperweight incident was another of your red herrings.'[16]

---

[9] Page 183.

[10] Page 186.

[11] Pages 185, 188.

[12] Page 204.

[13] Page 206, 207.

[14] Page 226.

[15] Pages 85, 256.

[16] Pages 248, 249.

Justin Thyme

'I'm afraid so,' said Nanny uneasily, 'and I have to confess that I ... er ...'

'Cut the plug off Robyn's computer?' Justin enquired. 'You sent her down to the kitchen for some milk, giving you just enough time to race up to her room before I arrived from the south tower. I saw you put the scissors back in your sewing box.'[17]

'I'd been worried about Robyn,' Nanny explained. 'I kept remembering Val's warning that he'd know if I tried to double-cross him. I suspected he was e-mailing her.'[18]

'Impressive! I've been underrating you, Nanny. I suppose you rang for Knightly from Robyn's room to throw suspicion on him. Did you suspect he was another spy?'

'Och no,' said Nanny, in a firm voice. 'I know for certain he isn't.'

Justin was about to ask what made her so sure, when the sound of tyres on gravel distracted him. He moved to the window and watched Sergeant Awbrite clamber out of his squad car and knock on the castle door.

'After planting the plug in Knightly's wardrobe, you left your note on the hall table. You'd stuck a stamp on the envelope, hoping we'd assume it came with the rest of the mail. Thinking it might seem more threatening if the watch was smashed, you hit the envelope with the paperweight before you hid it in your laundry basket. That's why the broken hands pointed to 9:40, roughly five minutes before I heard you scream; I remembered the time, because the tower clock had just struck 9:45.[19] The dents on the lawn baffled me. They implied premeditation, as if your attacker had done some target practice beforehand – which ruled practically everybody out, until I realised you'd staged your own attack.'[20]

---

[17] Page 248.

[18] Page 230.

[19] Page 250.

[20] Page 258, 259.

'When did you guess?'

'Only a few minutes ago,' said Justin, glancing at his watch. 'I saw Hank tossing strawberries in the air and catching them in his mouth. He missed one, and it left a mark when it fell on the floor.[21] I suddenly realised the dints outside hadn't been caused by *dropping* the paperweight out of a window – but by somebody *throwing* it up like a ball, then losing their nerve and dodging back. Then, as I stared at the lawn I remembered hearing you scream *before* I heard the paperweight hit you.[22] A minor detail, but *very* significant. If you'd been unaware of it falling, you wouldn't have uttered a sound. You'd only scream if you *saw* it – but then why hadn't you dodged back? Only one scenario fitted all the clues: you threw the paperweight as high as you could. After chickening out a few times you finally steeled yourself to stay put, but couldn't help screaming as it hurtled towards you. Have you any idea how dangerous that was? It could have *killed* you!'

Justin wore his sternest frown of disapproval, but it was hopeless; one glimpse of Nanny's sheepish smile and he relented. 'I half suspected my sister. Before you were lifted into the helicopter you said: *keep a close eye on Robyn*, as if she'd attack *me* next.'

'I was trying to hint that she might have been in contact with my husband,' sniffed Nanny. 'Which reminds me: how did you guess I'd been married to Agent X?'

'Your postcard from Brighton[23] was absolutely bursting with clues,' said Justin. 'It was addressed to the Thyme family – just like the second ransom note – whereas the first ransom note was sent to Dad. Also, the stamp on the second note had a distinctive tea-stain across it. I *knew* I'd seen one just like it before, but I wrongly assumed it was on another envelope. I remembered you putting some postage stamps in your handbag the morning we

---

[21] Page 308.

[22] Page 250.

[23] Page 307.

took you to the station,[24] but I completely forgot about the postcard you sent us[25] until Albion reminded me. The matching stamp was in the corner – and your card even explained how they'd got stained. You said you were writing from the end of the pier; it was very windy and you had a thermos flask. My guess is that you wedged the stamp-book under your cup to prevent it blowing away. Finally, you concluded the card with a row of hugs and kisses. Like most people, you used an X to represent a kiss. All this time I'd been looking for somebody whose name *started* with an X, whereas Agent X simply stood for Agent Kiss! I thought your husband must be here in disguise – and *he'd* attacked you. Then Hank dropped that strawberry and everything clicked into place.'

'I'm dreadfully sorry,' gulped Nanny, her eyes reddening, 'I'd never do anything to harm the Thymes; you're my family.' She gave a choking sob. '*Ohhhh*, can you ever forgive me?'

Justin hesitated; he was still struggling to forgive his father's deception. He glanced at the chrome-framed monitor above the fireplace. *MAC* had metamorphosed through several works of art, finally displaying *The Scapegoat* by Hunt. That was all the reassurance Justin needed.

'Of *course* I can,' he said, giving Nanny's hand a squeeze. 'No harm done – well, apart from your dented cranium.'

'And you're *not* going to hand me over to the police?'

Before Justin could reply, the door crashed open and Sergeant Awbrite marched in followed by Sir Willoughby.

'Verity Kiss, you are under arrest,' barked Awbrite. 'You have the right to remain silent. Anything you say ...'

'*Really* Nanny,' Willoughby interrupted. 'Frightfully disappointing. We overheard your confession ... so don't deny it.' Then turning to Justin he added: 'The sergeant was on his way here when the station radioed with news of a possible lead. They've

---

[24] Page 101.

[25] Page 104, 125.

318

had a report of someone signalling across the loch late last night. I suggested he takes a quick look through your telescope before checking it out.'

'Gracious!' gasped Nanny. 'The ambulance driver told me that when he came on duty he saw a flashing light under Capricorn Crag. He assumed it was just kids messing about, but I advised him to phone the police at once in case it was an SOS. I tried to tell Master Justin about it in the kitchen earlier.'

'A likely story,' said Awbrite, unlocking a pair of handcuffs.

'Are those really necessary?' Justin asked, seeing Nanny's startled expression.

'It won't be for long,' replied the sergeant, trying to maintain a stern facade but having the good grace to look a little shamefaced. 'Can't take any risks. I need the squad car to go and search for your mother. Meanwhile, my young constable can guard Mrs Kiss. Once I get back we'll take her straight to the police station, then perhaps we can encourage her to reveal the whereabouts of her husband.'

Justin watched in disgust as Awbrite settled Nanny Verity on the piano stool and shackled her right wrist to the piano leg. She stared resolutely out of the window.

'Don't worry, Nan,' said Justin. 'Mum'll understand; she won't let anything happen to you.'

'I expect she'll be too late,' replied Nanny without turning round. 'Capricorn Crag is directly *across the loch*. I'll be locked in a police cell long *before the sergeant* can drive all the way round *and find Lady Henny*.'

Justin raised his eyebrows in astonishment. By placing a subtle yet distinct emphasis on certain words Nanny had told him something: *Cross the loch before the sergeant and find Lady Henny*. It was a trick he and Robyn had invented years ago, never guessing that the one person they'd tried to fool had understood their secret code all along. With a new respect for his dithery nanny, Justin formulated his reply: *'I'll get Mum* to come and bail you out before she does *anything else*.'

319

'Thank you, Master Justin,' Nanny continued. '*Tell Robyn to keep Albion quiet; she mustn't let him distract the constable.*'

'Okay Nanny.'

'Hurry up,' muttered Sir Willoughby. 'Bring your telescope down for the sergeant.'

'No, never mind. I'd rather get going,' said Awbrite, walking to the door. 'How do you lock this?'

Justin hurried past him onto the landing, and took one last anxious glance at Nanny Verity before placing his left thumb on the fingerprint recognition sensor. The door locked with a muffled thunk.

They found Constable Knox in the kitchen along with everybody else. They were all sipping coffee and watching Mr Polydorus perform some of his conjuring tricks. To Albion's delight, he made an egg vanish and reappear in Mrs Kof's apron pocket. Everybody clapped – except Robyn, who leaned against the pantry door looking scornful and unimpressed.

'He isn't much good,' she whispered to her brother as he beckoned her into the entrance hall. 'Come and watch.'

'Never mind about that now,' Justin hissed. 'Listen: you've got to keep the constable in the kitchen until I get back.' Then before Robyn could ask why, he added: 'No time to explain,' and rushed out of the castle door.

Meanwhile, Sergeant Awbrite gave Knox his orders and entrusted him with the handcuff key. After shaking hands with Sir Willoughby he marched out to his squad car.

Once Lady Henny opened the drawer, she felt certain it wouldn't take long to fish out the penknife fastened to her key-ring. However, her patience soon began to evaporate. Henny thought patience was all very well for people who did jigsaws of yarn-entangled kittens, or constructed models of the Eiffel Tower out of matchsticks – but jet-setting celebrity explorers prefer action. In the last hour she'd hooked a comb, a pair of tweezers, a handkerchief and umpteen dust-bunnies – none of which helped a single scrap.

Then, just as she started to get thoroughly irritated, she felt the paperclip catch on something heavy. Slowly, she drew the necktie towards herself, holding her breath as the keys gradually appeared, peeping over the rim of the drawer.

'Come on,' Henny whispered. 'Just a few more millimetres.' But when success looked almost certain, the key-ring snagged on something and firmly refused to budge. Henny pulled the tie harder; she tugged it, jiggling it to and fro; she jerked it a bit more forcefully – then, losing all patience, gave an almighty wrench. The tie twanged free, the keys clattered back into the drawer, and the paperclip flew across the caravan, landing way out of reach.

For a moment Lady Henny was speechless, then, hoping to quell an unfamiliar flutter of panic, she bellowed an ancient tribal curse taught to her by the chief of the BaAka pygmies: '*Nǫi Ťäŋit S'aŕ-Ĉǫ́ŗp!*'

She pressed her forehead against a dirty Perspex window and peered down the steep hillside to the road far below. 'What am I gonna do now?' she groaned. 'I could scream 'til I'm blue in the face, but nobody'll ever hear me from way up here.'

Frustrated beyond belief, Henny threw herself backwards on the bed ... and the caravan wobbled.

Bored by second rate sleight-of-hand, the castle residents drifted back to their usual routines. Professor Gilbert made his excuses and hurried up to his room to unpack; Knightly went to polish silver in the dining room; Grandpa Lyall pottered along the portrait gallery with a newspaper, and Mrs Gilliechattan bustled off to the utility room. Mr Gilliechattan announced he was going to trim the ivy on the west tower. He donned his Wellington boots on the back step, then fetched his ladder and a pair of clippers from the garden shed. Eliza, looking thoroughly disgruntled with her lot in life, headed back to the nursery with Albion. Even Mrs

Kof abandoned her clearing up and disappeared.

Sir Willoughby paced back and forth along the castle battlements, stopping periodically to run his hands through his hair and stare anxiously across the loch. Then, to his astonishment, he heard his workshop door slam shut, and saw Justin run down the cliff steps carrying a sack.

Robyn stood in the entrance hall, pondering over her brother's furtively whispered instructions. The mysterious mission intrigued her. Where was he dashing off to all of a sudden, she wondered; quite the little action hero.

'Penny for your thoughts,' said a deep chocolaty voice behind her, making Robyn jump. It was Mr Polydorus. He withdrew the knave of hearts from her empty pocket, and then snapped his fingers, making it turn into a joker. 'You will commit a crime, embark on a hazardous journey and fall in love with a handsome stranger,' he murmured enigmatically, fixing her with his piercing blue eyes.

'Honestly Dad,' groaned Polly. 'Leave Robyn alone; she's too old for your bogus mind-reading tricks. Hank, fetch the car quick ... he's embarrassing me.'

Robyn smiled politely; it seemed all parents had that effect on their children. She headed towards the kitchen and found the spotty constable slurping the last few drops from his mug.

'More coffee, Chief Inspector?' she asked, flashing him a winning smile.

Knox blushed. 'It's just plain old constable,' he mumbled. 'PC Gavin Knox to be precise.'

'More coffee, *Gavin*?'

'I shouldn't really ... but ...'

Henny knew her options were running out; she could either wait for her captor to return or try something incredibly risky.

'I'd bet there's nothing but a few old rocks wedged beneath the caravan wheels,' she murmured to herself. 'If I can just dislodge them, what's to stop it rolling right down to the road? Hmm ... nothing whatsoever, I guess – and *that's* the problem!'

Taking a deep breath, Henny threw her full weight against the wall. The caravan lurched dangerously, and before it had chance to come to a complete standstill, she slammed herself sideways a second time ... then a third time, and a fourth ... gritting her teeth as the rope tethering her to the bed bit into her ankles.

By the time PC Knox was munching his third piece of shortbread, Justin had crossed Loch Ness. He moored Henny's boat beside a rickety wooden jetty, grabbed the sack of tools and checked his GPS; Capricorn Crag was barely a few hundred metres southeast, though the terrain looked steep and uneven. Justin ran along the roadside searching for an easy route through the gorse and heather, but just as he reached the foot of a narrow muddy lane, he heard a piercing scream and looked up to find a dilapidated old caravan hurtling down towards him, bouncing dangerously over deeply rutted tyre tracks. He scarcely had time to dive out of the way, before it skidded across the road, toppled down a rocky embankment and plunged into the loch with a resounding splash. For a moment or two, the caravan floated on one side, looking like a gigantic Chinese lantern, then a narrow stream of bubbles rose to the surface of the water and it started to sink.

Justin stared at it, rooted to the spot – then the sound of more frantic screaming jolted him into action. He withdrew a hefty crowbar from the sack and waded into the loch. The bank shelved steeply, and within a few metres he was out of his depth. He swam towards the caravan and hauled himself on top of it. It was now almost two-thirds below the water and his added weight made it sink even faster – but he knew he'd need a firm footing to smash the window. He peered through the dirty Perspex, water dripping off his face and hair.

'MUM ... it's me! Don't panic, I'll have you out in no time.'

Henny stared back at him, her eyes wide with terror. 'Justin ... thank goodness ...'

Justin planted his legs either side of the window and lifted the crowbar above his head. 'Close your eyes, Mum,' he shouted, and then walloped the reinforced Perspex with every atom of strength he could muster. But instead of shattering the window, the crowbar bounced off, flying out of his hands. It sailed in a long, wide arc and plummeted into the loch.

'FLUX!'

'Hurry up,' yelled Henny.

Justin looked down and saw water lapping around her neck. 'Don't worry,' he yelled. 'I ... I'll think of something ...' But for once in his life, nothing sprang to mind. He glared at the tool sack on the bank, knowing the caravan would have sunk before he could swim and fetch it ... and there wasn't anything in it that would shatter the window anyway. Almost screaming with frustration, he pounded his skull with tightly clenched fists, willing his brain to find the answer. If only I was back in my lab, he thought. There must be a dozen corrosive acids in my chemical cupboard; I'd soon concoct something that could burn right through this Perspex in seconds. But stuck here ...

'We're almost outa time,' Henny called, her voice quavering.

'TIME!' gasped Justin. 'That's IT! Once I've built my time machine, I'll have all the time in the world.'

But you can't alter the past, echoed a quiet voice from the darkest recesses of his brain. *Once someone dies, nothing can bring them back to life. Not ever.*

Justin screwed his eyes tight shut, focussing every molecule of mental energy on the problem. 'There *HAS* to be a way,' he told himself. 'Perhaps I *can't* alter the *past* ... but the future hasn't happened yet. Mum's alive *now*. What if I plan a future trip back to this precise moment in time? Maybe I can shape what happens in the next few seconds. Maybe I ...'

A sudden dull clatter interrupted him. Justin opened his eyes to find a small metallic tube lying beside his feet, as if someone had thrown it onto the caravan. He snatched it up, unscrewed the lid and took a cautious sniff. The sulphurous fumes made his eyes run; it was definitely a caustic acid. It seemed impossible, yet his idea had worked. Glancing hurriedly at the bank, he saw a shadowy figure disappearing behind a gorse bush; his brain reeled, but there was no time to analyse the situation. He squeezed a thin line of acid around the edge of the Perspex then stamped on the window. It buckled inwards and, as it sank beneath the water, Justin slithered inside, sending a cold wave splashing over his mother's face.

Henny spluttered. 'PENKNIFE ... on my key-ring ... was in that drawer ... *SANK*!'

Several drawers were floating upside-down. Justin guessed they must have been thrown out as the caravan had toppled into the loch. The water was rising faster; Henny's nostrils were scarcely a millimetre above the surface. Unable to speak now, her eyes pleaded with Justin. Realising the penknife had to be somewhere under water, he took a deep breath and dived down. It was too dark and murky to see much, but he ran his fingers along the bottom of the caravan, clutching and discarding item after item. At last, when his lungs were ready to burst, he felt a bunch of keys, grabbed them and pushed up to the surface, gasping.

Henny was now completely submerged. Justin grabbed a swift lungful of air and dived again, swimming down to her feet. Using the penknife, he sliced through the rope and pulled it apart – then swam upwards, dragging his mother with him. They broke the surface together, coughing and spluttering, then hauled themselves out of the caravan.

'You okay, Mum?' panted Justin, as they scrambled ashore.

'Fine – thanks to you,' said Henny, between chattering teeth. 'Wow, I thought for a minute I'd ... I'd ...' Her voice seemed to crumple. She grabbed her son and gave him a huge, soggy hug, and when she finally let go, her eyes were shining with tears. They stood, huddled together, shivering, and watched the caravan sink out of sight with a final ominous gurgle.

Lady Henny turned to Justin and gave him a wry smile. 'Just in time,' she whispered.

Sailing back across the loch, Justin brought his mother up to date with all that had happened since her abduction. He explained how the kidnapper had been an old colleague of Willoughby's, known as Agent X; that he'd demanded the time machine as a ransom; how he might be Polly's dad; and that he'd once been married to poor Nanny Verity and had coerced her into acting as his spy.

'... and Sergeant Awbrite's just arrested her,' he concluded breathlessly.

'Ridiculous!' Henny snorted, still massaging her ankles to restore the circulation. 'I've known Xavier for years – and darling Nanny wouldn't harm a fly.' She straightened up and stood, silent for a moment, her lips pursed broodingly. 'Who else knows?'

'Just Dad. Why?'

'Because Nanny's in danger. Whoever this X guy is, if he learns the police are questioning her, I dread to think what he'll do to prevent her talking. Once he discovers his hostage is missing, he might blame Nanny. And remember: she's the only person who can identify him to the police. We've got to get her well out of harm's way – *quickly* – until he's been caught.'

'There's one problem,' said Justin. 'After handcuffing Nanny, Sergeant Awbrite gave the key to his constable in front of everyone in the kitchen. I don't know whether he mentioned her by name – I was talking to Robyn in the entrance hall – but even if he didn't, Nanny was the only person unaccounted for, so ...'

'If X was there, he knows already,' concluded Henny, taking the wheel and steering her boat alongside the Thyme Bay landing stage. 'We'll have to hope the constable is guarding Nanny vigilantly.'

Justin shuffled uncomfortably, certain his sister would have scotched any chance of *that* happening. 'Nanny said I had to get Robyn to distract him until I came back with you.'

'*Aaaarrghh* ... how long is it since you left her?'

Justin glanced down at his wristwatch. 'Hey – it's stopped!' he gasped. He tapped the watch face and then held it up to his ear. 'It must've got waterlogged when I jumped in the loch.'

'Never mind, darling,' said Henny, clambering out of the boat. 'I'll buy you a dozen watches if you want.'

Justin said nothing. He didn't want another watch; this one was special. He smiled, trying to hide his disappointment, but his mother was already running up the cliff steps.

'Let's hope we're not too late,' she shouted.

Justin hurried after her, wondering whether the constable would still be in the kitchen ... but when they dashed indoors and found him handcuffed to the table, he had to admit that Robyn had surpassed herself.

If Lady Henny had hoped to make a dramatic entrance on her return to Thyme Castle she was in for a disappointment. Apart from Mrs Kof dropping and smashing her customary piece of tableware, the reaction was low-key. Constable Knox looked too embarrassed to care, and Robyn was busy poking under the refrigerator with a spatula, muttering under her breath. When she glanced up and saw her mother, Robyn's response was typical:

'Oh, hello Mum ... you look wet.'

Henny laughed. 'Which roughly translated means *I'm thrilled to see you; you can't imagine how worried I've been,*' she said, giving her daughter a swift hug. 'What's going on?' She grabbed a kitchen towel and rubbed Justin's hair briskly, ignoring his indignant shouts.

'Gavin er ... PC Knox was showing me how his handcuffs work,' Robyn explained. Then with a sly wink at her brother added: 'But we seem to have er ... *lost* the key.'

Henny asked Mrs Kof to help. The big cook grinned good-naturedly, wrapped her huge, muscular arms around the fridge and hefted it up. Robyn scrabbled beneath, and with a mischievous giggle tossed the tiny chrome key to Knox – but Henny caught it in mid-air and dangled it just out of his reach.

'How about exchanging *this* handcuff key for the one in your pocket?' she said.

'Sorry, Ma'am,' replied Knox huskily. 'Sergeant'd have m'guts for garters.'

'Perhaps you'd prefer him to find you manacled to the table,' reasoned Henny. 'I'm sure he'll be impressed.'

Knox reluctantly admitted defeat and fumbled in his pocket with his free hand, muttering something that sounded like '*Now I know where the daughter gets it from.*' Utterly impervious, Henny waited with her hand outstretched – but apart from a rather snotty handkerchief, the constable's pockets were empty. Justin and his mother exchanged a worried glance before rushing out of the kitchen together.

'Hey – what about releasing me?' shouted Knox.

'Sorry, no deal,' Henny called back, as she raced through the entrance hall. 'Keep an eye on him, Robyn.'

'I'm an officer of the law,' Knox grumbled. 'Don't I deserve a *little* respect?'

'Of course,' laughed Robyn. 'And I promise to give you as little as possible.'

⧗

Henny reached the south tower first. She shouted to Nanny that help was on the way – but there was no reply. Justin arrived seconds later. Gasping for breath, he pressed his right thumb on the fingerprint sensor, unlocking the door. Slowly, it swung open to reveal an unsettling sight. *MAC* – the digital canvas above the fireplace – displayed a romantic eighteenth century painting by Fragonard.

'"*The Stolen Kiss!*"' exclaimed Justin.

In all other respects the sitting room was exactly as he'd left it – though with one very notable exception.

Nanny Verity was *not* inside.

Everyone has heard the expression TIME HEALS. Synchronicity is time's way of healing rents in its fabric. On rare occasions, when Father Time's grand plan falls foul of his mischievous opponent, the Tartan of Time may become temporarily and temporally disrupted.

When a crucial EVENT fails to occur precisely as it should, it must be relocated at a later point in time where many of the same threads can be rewoven in an identical pattern. Each disrupted timeline will need to generate new forks and follow significant loops, until eventually converging again – perhaps many years later. As the Tartan of Time repairs itself, it draws the surrounding threads closer together; inevitably resulting in minor disruptions to the fabric in another time or place that may not seem causally related.

Consisting of countless threadlike timelines, the Tartan of Time is an immense thread itself – the timeline of global history, frequently referred to as THE STREAM OF TIME. It forks and loops on a global scale in a similar way to its minor counterparts. Who knows, perhaps our entire timestream is merely an inconsequential global thread in a galactic fabric, too immense for us to contemplate. As time ticks by, its incredible tartan weaves indefinitely on, like a multiversal Möbius strip without beginning or end.

– CHAPTER TWENTY –

Unbelievable!

'I *don't* believe it!' groaned Sergeant Awbrite, removing his cap and scratching his shiny bald head vigorously. In the last quarter of an hour he'd repeated the same phrase at least a dozen times, looking more flabbergasted with each repetition.

Awbrite had turned up at Thyme Castle shortly after lunch, never anticipating the surprises that lay ahead. It had taken him the best part of an hour to reach Capricorn Crag, and though he'd found no sign of Lady Henny, evidence suggested that some vehicle, possibly a caravan, had recently skidded into the loch. He'd returned at once, wearing a sombre expression and professing a serious concern for her ladyship's safety.

His first shock had been when Lady Henrietta Thyme opened the castle door, now looking every bit as glamorous as she did on her television programmes; his second surprise had been finding his spotty young constable manacled to the kitchen table; and the third, to discover his prime suspect had performed an escapology act, breaking out of handcuffs and vanishing from within a locked room.

'Unbelievable,' he sighed. 'It's almost like magic.'

'I'm sure there's a perfectly rational explanation,' said Justin. 'Though I haven't the foggiest idea what it is yet.'

He had already scoured the room for clues and considered several theories, but one thing was certain: despite his newfound admiration for Nanny Verity, he seriously doubted she could have escaped single-handed. The tiny key Awbrite had entrusted to Constable Knox now lay on the floor beside the discarded handcuffs. And as resourceful as Nanny clearly was, she couldn't have fetched it herself – especially through a locked door.

'Somebody must've slid down that pole,' remarked Awbrite.

'Impossible I'm afraid,' replied Justin gloomily. 'My bedroom and ... er ... *playroom* have the same fingerprint sensitive security system. Both doors were locked – and my right thumb is the only key.'

'What about climbing *up* it then?'

'Equally impossible,' said Justin. 'Try for yourself.'

The sergeant did – but despite his best efforts the highly polished chrome was far too slippery. Unable to get a firm grip with either his hands or knees, he slid to the bottom of the pole, landing on the library floor with an ungainly wallop.

'Ouch,' he groaned, rubbing his posterior. 'You'd have to be an acrobat to rescue Mrs Kiss that way.'

'What makes you so sure she was rescued?' asked Justin, sliding down beside him. 'What if she's been eliminated? Her ex-husband sounds pretty ruthless according to Mum.'

Sergeant Awbrite raised his eyebrows. 'I hadn't thought of that. But don't you fret ... I radioed headquarters on my way back and asked them to send divers and a forensic team; they probably won't get much evidence from the submerged caravan, but they'll scour every inch of Capricorn Crag with a fine toothcomb. If the kidnapper's left any clues, you can be certain they'll find them. Never fear ... I'll catch the blighter, or my name isn't A–'

The door flew open and Knox burst into the library looking hot under the collar. Awbrite frowned; he'd banished the constable to the car in disgrace, to ponder over his shortcomings.

'This had better be important,' he growled.

''Fraid so, Sir,' said Knox. 'Forensics just radioed. They've reached the crime scene ... but it's been compromised.' He pointed towards the window. 'Look!'

Awbrite peered across the loch, his jaw dropping open in dismay. Justin turned to follow his gaze and gasped. A thick plume of black smoke rose from Capricorn Crag like a malevolent genie escaping its lamp.

'A forest fire!' whispered Justin.

Sergeant Awbrite slammed his fist down on the windowsill, roaring in frustration.

'*UNBELIEVABLE!*'

The instant Eliza realised Lady Henny was safely home, she'd rushed down from the nursery and pushed Albion into her arms.

'Your baby – your human baby,' Eliza said, over and over again. Then she'd stalked off to her room and spent the rest of the day hurling her banana bucket against the walls.

Justin knocked tentatively on her oak-panelled door, and then jumped back as something hit the other side with a resounding metallic *CLANG*.

'It's me, Eliza,' he called. 'May I come in?'

Taking the silence to mean *yes*, Justin took a deep breath and stepped inside the gorilla's room. A trapeze of ropes and tyres hung from the rafters between a maze of planks and climbing frames; it looked like a cross between a gymnasium and an oversized game of snakes and ladders. The walls were covered with brightly splodged canvasses – all Eliza's own handiwork. There was a custom-made four-poster bed, a mound of cuddly toys, and her very own gorilla-sized fridge. Everything a civilised primate could want – plus Sky TV.

But Eliza wasn't happy. She sat hunched in a corner with her back to Justin, rocking silently to and fro. Her laptop lay beside the bed, recharging.

Justin walked over and placed a pale hand on her massive black shoulder. 'All those things that went wrong on Mum's expedition ... the lost boots, the missing maps ... they weren't Hank and Polly's fault, were they?'

332

He felt Eliza's muscles tense beneath his hand. 'I know why you did it,' he whispered. 'You wanted to meet some boy gorillas, didn't you? When Mum kept leaving you behind at base camp, baby-sitting Alby, I think you decided to play a few tricks on her.'

Eliza shuddered.

'Well, I don't blame you,' said Justin, slapping her back. 'I know Mum's had a lot on her mind ... but I wouldn't have hidden her boots – I'd have *burnt* them.'

Eliza turned round, a look of relief in her eyes – and Justin realised she'd been cradling a toy gorilla wrapped in a baby-blanket. He felt a lump form in his throat and, for a second or two, he couldn't speak.

'Don't worry, Eliza,' he murmured eventually. 'I'll talk to Mum ... I'll tell her she's got to help you find a boyfriend.'

Eliza grunted with excitement and rushed over to her laptop. 'Tell Henny go quickly. Henny find cute gorilla for Eliza.'

Justin laughed. 'A big hunky silverback, right?'

Grabbing Justin in her huge hairy arms, Eliza hugged him as only a gorilla could.

Up in his lab, Justin stared gloomily at the waterlogged watch, wishing he'd taken it off before jumping into the loch. Then, as he replayed the morning's strange events in his mind, his despondent expression changed to one of profound relief.

He'd already guessed that the shadowy figure he'd glimpsed on the bank was his future self – and that by vowing to return to that point in time with an acid gel, (after finishing the chronopod, of course), he'd somehow *made* it happen. But in all the excitement he'd forgotten to memorize exactly *when* his mother had been rescued – and, as sure as tick followed tock, this was *one* appointment he *couldn't* be late for. Fortunately, the instant his watch got wet its hands had stopped at the precise coordinates he was going to need.

Realising the watch would have to be stripped down, cleaned

and oiled immediately, Justin opened his tool drawer, then hearing the sound of footsteps echoing up the south tower staircase, he hesitated, glancing expectantly at the laboratory door. Seconds later it swung open and Sir Willoughby stepped inside carrying a cup of tea and a plate of cherry gingerbread.

'Thought you might be feeling peckish,' he said. His eyes flicked towards the chronopod then back to Justin, hunched at his desk. 'Aren't you er ... getting on with the erm ...'

Justin shook his head. 'I *want* to ... but if I don't do something about this watch *now* it'll never work again.' He rummaged through the drawer, trying to look busy. If his father had come to apologise, it would take more than a slice of cake to wipe out thirteen years of deceit.

Sir Willoughby placed the cup and plate beside his son and then leaned over his shoulder, frowning at the inanimate timepiece. 'Does it matter? You can always buy anoth–'

'Yes it *DOES* matter,' snapped Justin. He glared at his father then took a huge mouthful of gingerbread, chewing it slowly to discourage further conversation.

Nobody seemed to understand what the watch meant to him, he thought; to be perfectly honest, he wasn't sure he *really* understood it himself. He knew his attitude to time was changing, but there was far more to it than that. Although unable to explain why, Justin sensed that the watch still had a key role to play in his time-travelling adventures. He wondered whether to tell his father how, by getting waterlogged, it *would* be – or, already *had* been – pivotal to Henny's rescue, but decided to wait until after he'd proved that for certain.

'I have a good feeling about this watch,' he whispered eventually. 'I know you think it's from your old pal Agent X, but I checked it for bugs and it's clean.'

Sir Willoughby shrugged. 'Well, they wouldn't work after a soaking anyway,' he said, the forced heartiness of his voice at odds with the hurt in his eyes. 'Look – why don't you let me fix it for you while you crack on with the er ... you-know-what?'

'No thanks, Dad.'

'I insist,' said Willoughby. 'I won't wreck it ... *honestly*.'

Justin, who had just taken another large mouthful of cake, shook his head vigorously. He'd been reluctant to dismantle the watch himself, but the thought of someone else doing it horrified him. He struggled to swallow his gingerbread in one big gulp and almost choked.

Sir Willoughby thumped his back with one hand whilst reaching across the desk with the other. Still coughing, Justin clutched at his father's arm.

'*Please*, son,' Willoughby begged. 'It's the least I can do to thank you for rescuing Henny.' He fixed Justin with an imploring gaze, but when no reply came, sighed: 'Oh well, if you don't trust me ...'

With a sickening jolt, Justin realised he had no alternative. 'Of *course* I trust you,' he spluttered, picking up a pencil and casting around his desk for something to write on. 'Hang on a tick, Dad.' He grabbed the sheet of paper he'd used to decode the playing card message and scribbled down the exact time the watch had stopped at, followed by the date. Then, satisfied the rescue coordinates had been safely recorded, he took a deep breath and handed the watch to his father.

That evening, in honour of Lady Henny's safe return, Mrs Kof prepared a banquet: starfruit-tangerine medley with ginger sorbet, Venison paté, grilled rainbow trout, butter-basted grouse stuffed with cranberries; all followed by raspberry pavlova and ice-cream. Everyone was invited, including Professor Gilbert and the Gilliechattans. As it was such a special occasion, even Knightly and Mrs Kof joined them around the huge rosewood dining table. Hank and Polly were included too, and, once Justin explained they hadn't been responsible for the recent pranks, Henny offered them their jobs back.

'Though how long it'll be before the show's axed is anybody's guess,' remarked Henny. 'But let's not dwell on that now; we're here to celebrate!'

At the end of the meal Mrs Kof stood up looking rather squiffy and excited – and broke her plate to attract everyone's attention.

'I having special good treats for everybodkin,' she announced. 'Before Lady Any go on exposition, I tells her about I borns in circus family. My papa was strongman; mama was bearded lady. Papa die very sudden when I fourteen. He choke on mint bumhug. I big strong girl, so ringmaster say: your papa star of whole flippin' show – and show mustard go on. He making me shave heads and wear false pistachio on lip, and say I perform papa's act every night. Many years go pass, and hair stop grow. Eventuality, I become big star and marry nice fire-eater ... but I tigress ...

'Last week I sees advert in newspooper. It say Bohemian Circus visit town – so on off-day I go visit many, many old friends. But they have catastrous disastrophe and scrap Mr Polythene's magic act. Ringmaster ask me to make special guest-star apparition on next off-day. I says: maybe I will – but only if you give me plenty ticket for my new friends as jolly-good soup-rise!' With a wide gappy grin, she withdrew twelve circus tickets from her apron pocket and fanned them out. Everybody gazed at them in stunned silence – except Henny, who had heard the cook's history the night she arrived.

'Thank you, Mrs Kof,' she said, looking genuinely pleased. 'How wonderful!'

Everyone nodded in agreement and murmured their appreciation.

'Last Sunday mornings, Sore Will-berry almost spoilin' souprise – but I throws coffee on newspooper so nobodies look on front page,' explained the cook proudly. 'That night I phone ringmaster. I tell him you suspects nuffin' and promise I be readies for Saturday. He ask do I still want free ticket and for how manys. I says: yes, for twelve.'

'Oh, so *that's* what you meant,' laughed Robyn. 'And I suppose that heavy suitcase you brought home really *was* full of weights for body-building?'

'I swims every day with waiters in hoversuck,' said Mrs Kof, nodding vigorously. 'Build big muzzles for circus act.'

'Unbelievable,' Robyn sighed to her brother. 'The newspaper clippings, the false moustache, the bald head, the swimming across the loch ... all perfectly innocent.'

'So it would appear,' he replied, looking thoughtful.

'I'll bet there's a rational explanation for *your* behaviour too,' Robyn continued, turning to the Gilliechattans. And before Justin could stop her, she asked: 'So, what are you guys *really* up to? Why the phoney accents?'

For a split second Morag Gilliechattan looked furious, then a sickly smile spread across her face. 'Clever girl,' she replied in cultured English tones. 'We always thought you'd be the one to catch us out, didn't we Oliver?'

'Indeed we did,' boomed Mr Gilliechattan, his voice dramatic and resonant. 'Naturally, Oliver and Ariadne Marsh could hardly remain incognito forever.' He gave a deep theatrical bow and paused expectantly; when no one applauded he continued, sounding a little hurt: 'Our last tour with the Giggleswick Shakespearean Players was a failure. Ariadne's *"Peaseblossom"* got booed off stage, and my *"Bottom"* was ridiculed by the critics. It looked as if we'd never work again.'

'So we changed our identities,' explained Mrs Gilliechattan. 'And Oliver decided to write a whodunit play, casting ourselves in the lead roles.

'Sounds f-f-fascinating,' Professor Gilbert remarked, his eyes twinkling. 'I *love* a good murder mystery! W-what's it called?'

'*"Evil Under the Sunflowers,"*' replied Oliver Marsh. 'It's about a gardener framed for murder and a nosey old housekeeper who solves the crime. When Sir Willoughby advertised for staff, it seemed the perfect opportunity to practice being our characters. I could concentrate on my writing while Ariadne could finally paste all our old reviews in a scrapbook.'

Justin nodded. '*Ahhh* ... so *that* explains the newspapers and paste I saw on your desk.'

'But I heard you talking about secret agents,' cried Robyn, turning to face the gardener. 'You even said Dad would be terminated!'

'Nonsense!' Mr Marsh insisted. 'I had an appointment with Hawkins, our theatrical agent, the day Lady Henny was kidnapped. You must've misunderstood. I said: "Our pseudonyms must remain a *secret. Agents* are notorious gossips; we can't risk him revealing our true identities until the play's finished. The trouble with Harry Hawkins is he's got no patience. If the kidnapping scene doesn't get rewritten in time my contract *will be terminated!*"'

'I thought you said you'd have *Willoughby* terminated,' groaned Robyn. 'But what did you mean about Mrs Gilli ... er, I mean Mrs Marsh silencing me if I got too inquisitive?'

'Private acting lessons,' laughed Ariadne Marsh. 'And a small part in our play if you promised to keep our secret. Which reminds me: we don't want anyone finding out who we really are, so please keep calling us Mr and Mrs Gilliechattan. And we'd like to continue working here until the play's finished ... if you don't object.'

Willoughby raised his wineglass. 'You're most welcome. Here's wishing you every success,' he said – then added rather untruthfully: 'I never doubted you for an instant.'

'*Doubt truth to be a liar*,' squawked Burbage, with his beak full of raspberries.

'That's enough of you taking centre stage,' said the gardener, and tapped the parrot's beak.

Justin gazed at his father in disbelief. Barely a few hours had passed since Henny's return – and already he was acting as if nothing had happened. He appeared to have forgotten that Agent X had probably masterminded Nanny's escape, and that he or a second spy might have infiltrated the castle. They could be right here at this table, Justin thought. Surely Dad can't be that gullible? Or is he *still* playing the role of damaged absentminded boffin? Beneath the table, Justin twisted his napkin in clenched fists, and was just thinking how implausible the Gilliechattans' story sounded, when Grandpa Lyall clutched his arm and whispered in his ear.

'Who's that?' he asked, gesturing to Henny. 'I don't remember seeing *her* before.'

By the time Justin explained, Knightly had fetched a huge gleaming coffee pot from the kitchen. His eternal dewdrop quivered precariously as he filled each of the cups in turn. Meanwhile, Mrs Kof distributed the circus tickets. She slammed them down in front of each lucky recipient, bellowing their names in her deep voice:

'Sore Will-berry, Lady Any, Master Justink, Miss Robbing, Baby Album, Grandpa Liar, Professor Gimlet, Mr and Mrs Grill-a-kitten, Mr Nightie, Elizamonkey, and er ... I forgets to ask you; where Mrs Nanny gone?' she said, waving the last ticket.

Henny and Willoughby exchanged a discreet glance. They'd discussed the situation at length and, despite his reservations, Sir Willoughby had reluctantly promised not to tell anyone the truth about Nanny Verity. Henny had insisted that as soon as Agent X was caught, Nanny must be found and returned safely to Thyme Castle – so the less everyone knew about her, the better. Justin had agreed, but deep within him, a gentle, persistent voice he hated, kept whispering the word *traitor* over and over again.

'I suggested another vacation,' said Willoughby, as

nonchalantly as possible. 'Rest and recuperation abroad after that nasty bump on the noggin.'

Despite Sir Willoughby's explanation, the abruptness of Nanny's departure puzzled everyone. Well, *almost* everyone. One particular individual – who knew the *exact* details of her disappearance – concealed a sly smile behind a large spoonful of raspberry pavlova and fought the overwhelming urge to chuckle hysterically.

Not everyone felt in the party mood. Eliza scowled sullenly and rejected all attempts to include her in the conversation with a dismissive flick of her huge hand. Justin gazed at her in astonishment and wondered what was bothering her now. Henny had promised to take her back to the Congo as soon as she had time – and had even phoned her father at the Bronx Zoo to see if he knew of any eligible bachelor-gorillas. Yet Eliza looked decidedly out of sorts. It didn't make any sense, unless ...

'Unless, perhaps, someone's been lying,' Justin murmured to himself. He looked around the table at each of the familiar faces in turn, and then pushed his meringue away, unable to stomach another mouthful.

'Odd of Mrs Kiss to leave without saying goodbye,' sighed Grandpa Lyall, who appeared to have grown rather fond of Nanny Verity.

'It *was* rather a surprise,' Henny admitted. Then desperate to change the subject she asked Hank and Polly whether either of them fancied using the spare circus ticket.

'We've got a couple already,' replied Hank, rummaging in his trouser pocket.

'Daddy got them for us,' Polly explained. 'Tomorrow night was going to be his farewell performance, but he er ... retired suddenly last week.'

Mrs Kof grinned. 'I knows who I giving ticket,' she said, tucking it in her apron pocket.

Unbelievable!

Justin retired to bed early that night, and for the first time in a week was asleep before midnight. The following morning he awoke feeling refreshed, and after snatching a quick breakfast with the family hurried up to his lab, determined to spend the entire day working on his time machine. His mother's safe return had removed the pressure of a deadline, but completing it seemed more important than ever now he knew it played such an important part in her rescue.

As Justin tinkered with the subatomic wormhole-vortex accelerator, he felt a tremendous surge of confidence, certain that glimpse of his future self proved his time machine would be a success. Then, with a pang of disappointment he saw the flaw in his reasoning: he might not get the chronopod to actually work for months ... years even!

Justin pushed the thought aside and tried to focus on something more positive. Now that he had chance to think about it properly, he was determined to find a way to save his mum's TV show. He remembered his own words: "*Computer animation ... it's out of the question given the timescale.*" Was it just another coincidence that time, or lack of it, was at the root of this problem too, he wondered. Gradually, the seeds of an idea started to germinate.

Sergeant Awbrite turned up shortly after lunch with Constable Knox in tow. He informed Lady Henny that her accommodation for the previous week had been dragged from the loch, but his forensic squad had salvaged little viable evidence. As for Capricorn Crag, it was now a wasteland of blackened earth and smouldering tree stumps.

'But don't you worry, Ma'am,' said Awbrite grimly. 'We'll track the bounder down eventually. We're hoping he left a fingerprint or two behind when he released Mrs Kiss.'

From the top of the south tower Justin heard Awbrite's size eleven-and-a-half boots clonk across the sitting room floor, closely followed by Knox's nines. For the next hour or so he worked quietly, and listened as the sergeant bossed his gormless constable about with mounting irritation. Poor Knox spent the afternoon scurrying back to the squad car on errands for Awbrite – and always managed to return with entirely the wrong thing. Finally the sergeant exploded with rage:

'Unbelievable!' he roared. 'There's something peculiar going on here.'

Unable to contain his curiosity any longer, Justin slid down a couple of floors to see what all the fuss was about. Sergeant Awbrite stood in front of the fireplace – seventy-three inches of barely bottled-up frustration. Behind him, MAC displayed Munch's *"The Scream"* mirroring the depths of his inner turmoil with uncanny accuracy.

'Has that housekeeper been cleaning in here since yesterday?'

'I don't *think* so,' said Justin uncertainly. 'Why?'

'Because there isn't one flaming fingerprint – not even the nanny's – that's *why*!'

Awbrite paused briefly in the entrance hall to don his sergeant's cap. He glowered after Knox plodding out to the squad car, and then turned to shake Justin by the hand.

'Goodbye, young man.'

'Sorry I can't find Dad anywhere,' said Justin. 'I'm sure he'd want to thank you.'

'Can't imagine why,' sighed Awbrite. 'This case is a nightmare. Not that I'm giving up, of course – but there's precious little to go on. And now with Mrs Kiss vanishing ... well ...'

Justin nodded sympathetically, half tempted to reveal his qualms about Mr Polydorus – but he knew that just some flimsy circumstantial evidence and a name starting with X would never convince a detective.

'She didn't tell you anything that might help us identify this husband of hers?' Awbrite enquired, looking rather desperate.

'Sorry. You and Dad burst in when I was right on the verge of asking her about him.'

'Typical! If only I'd ...'

A guttural chuckle interrupted the sergeant's deliberations. He and Justin turned to see Mrs Kof leaning nonchalantly in the doorway to the kitchen. 'I helps Cheer-upping Sergeant Orbit,' she said with a broad grin. Then plunging her huge hand into her apron pocket she withdrew the spare circus ticket. 'You wants come circus tomorrow night, Mr Policy-man?'

On Saturday, the sun shone brightly, but Justin spent the entire morning closeted in his lab making a corrosive acid. By lunchtime he'd concocted a gel that could burn through reinforced Perspex in less than five seconds. As he locked it in his chemical cupboard the tower clock struck twelve. Out of habit, Justin glanced at his right wrist, then cringed inwardly as he tried *not* to imagine how many pieces his watch might be in at that moment.

After sliding down the fireman's pole, he plodded along to the kitchen. Robyn had spent *her* morning tying up the last loose ends of her investigation, and as they munched their roast ham sandwiches together, she brought Justin up-to-date: 'I've discovered why the Gilliechattans were in the great hall the morning of Nanny's attack. Mrs G had been over-watering that hideous aspidistra behind the chesterfield. She asked Mr G to examine it; apparently, he's really quite green-fingered.'

'So why lie about it?'

'She thought there'd be trouble if it died,' grinned Robyn. 'And as for your precious professor – it looks as if he really *was* bird-watching through those binoculars of his. The only thing I *don't* understand is how Mrs Kof saw Hank inside his car from two floors up.'

'Oh, she told me,' Justin confessed. 'The Land Rover window was wound down and Hank had his arm dangling out. Should've been obvious I suppose.'

Robyn nodded and helped herself to a large slice of pecan pie. Justin stared at her out of the corner of one eye, staggered by her credulity. Like Willoughby, she seemed convinced that now

Henny was home all danger had passed, and believed that Nanny Verity had been sent on vacation to keep her out of harm's way. All thoughts of Agent X appeared to have been dismissed, yet Justin felt convinced he was still very much at large. His first dastardly plan had failed – but he was sure to bounce back more ruthless than ever.

By the end of the afternoon Justin had completed the last major component of his time machine. All that remained was for him to fit the subatomic wormhole-vortex accelerator, the negative-energy generator and the anti-gravity unit inside the chronopod and then wire them to the computerised Minkowski space-time coordinates display module – but that would have to wait until later.

The Thymes gathered for an early tea. Henny foraged in the pantry, which, of course, Mrs Kof had left stocked with plenty of delicious goodies before leaving for the circus. Then everyone hurried upstairs to get ready for their evening out.

Justin hated to leave his time machine unattended when it was so close to completion. As he changed into his favourite jeans, he kept reminding himself that his security system was second to none, and nobody could access his lab without amputating his right thumb. Furthermore, he knew that everyone from Thyme Castle would be with him at the circus – and they couldn't be in two places at once. But then he remembered Nanny Verity's inexplicable disappearance and started to have uncomfortable, nagging doubts. Locks hadn't prevented Nanny from escaping, and if she chose to return ... she might not be alone.

After locking the door to the south tower, Justin hurried along the upper corridor. As he walked past his parents' room on the west tower landing, their door swung open and Lady Henny appeared. She had abandoned Khaki for once, and was dressed entirely in white.

'Wow, Mum – you look fantastic,' gasped Justin.

344

'Thanks,' replied Henny. She stood, smiling and relaxed in the doorway, waiting for her husband.

'Listen Mum, I've erm ... had an idea about saving *Thyme-Zone*.'

'Doesn't that incredible brain of yours *ever* take a day off?' laughed Henny. 'What's the plan? Travelling back to this time last year and setting up that animation studio?'

Henny was joking, but Justin's reply was perfectly serious. 'No, I'm planning to travel a bit farther than that ... well, a *lot* farther actually. Tell me, Mum – if you could make a film about an extinct creature ... any creature at all ... which would it be?'

Lady Henny gasped, and then looked over her shoulder at Sir Willoughby fastening his tie in front of a mirror. She stepped softly onto the landing and, after closing the door behind her, leaned forward and whispered something in her son's ear.

'Mmm ... I *thought* that's what you'd say,' said Justin.

'Do you seriously think it's possible?' asked Henny, her eyes sparkling.

Justin grinned. 'Wait and see!'

They wandered downstairs together, discussing Justin's amazing plans and how best to keep Sir Willoughby from discovering them.

At the mention of her husband, Henny's face became serious. After hesitating a moment, she glanced back up the stairs and then drew Justin into the portrait gallery. 'Before your dad comes down, I want to ask a favour. Willo and I have been talking and he's pretty darn hurt you're being so cold with him.'

'*HE'S* hurt?' retorted Justin. 'Are you *sure*? Maybe he's just acting.'

Henny placed her hand on Justin's arm, but he shook it off, scowling. She lowered her voice. 'I know learning the truth about him has been a shock to you, but ...'

'He's lied to me my *ENTIRE LIFE*,' said Justin. 'Thirteen years of deception; it's unbelievable! It's ... it's ...' Unable to continue, he turned away. After a minute of silence, he spoke again, his

345

voice almost inaudible: 'Why?'

'It was done with the best of motives,' explained Henny. 'He never knew for certain whether the bodged memory-wipe was accidental or not. When you and Robyn were little, he feared you might be kidnapped if X discovered his memory was fine – so he kept on pretending. Poor Willo, he could've been the Einstein of our generation, but he sacrificed everything to protect his family. You especially; he wanted you to have the chances he lost.'

Justin's cheeks burned a fiery red. Hearing Sir Willoughby's footsteps on the staircase, Henny leaned forward and wrapped her arms around her son. 'Ask yourself what you'd have done in his place,' she whispered. 'Then try to forgive him.'

The Circus started at seven-fifteen, so Henny had suggested they all gathered in the courtyard at six o'clock sharp. Justin arrived first – and, for once, it was Sir Willoughby who kept everyone waiting. Finally, he hurried out of his workshop brandishing Justin's watch, his face glowing with boyish enthusiasm.

'It's working! I got it all back together before tea, but I wanted to check it was keeping good time.' He held out the watch to his son. Their eyes met; Willoughby's smile wavered for a moment and then faded. 'I ... I did the best I could,' he whispered gravely.

Justin nodded, wondering whether his dad meant the watch or the last thirteen years ... then, as he fastened the bracelet around his wrist, he decided it didn't matter.

'Thanks, Dad,' he said. 'No one could've done better.'

They needed three cars to ferry them all to the circus. Sir Willoughby drove the Bentley. Henny sat beside him with Albion on her knee, while Grandpa Lyall squeezed between Justin and Robyn in the back. Eliza joined Hank and Polly in their Land Rover, much to Alby's dismay, and Knightly followed in his

BMW with the Gilliechattans and Professor Gilbert.

From the moment they entered the Big Top they were all treated like VIPs. A red-nosed clown showed them to their ringside seats and handed out extra-large buckets of popcorn. Word soon got round that Mrs Kof's friends had arrived, and before long, a boy on a unicycle brought Eliza some bananas, a man in sparkly tights gave Albion a lollipop, and a short, chubby lady with seven vividly plumed parrots perched on her shoulders came and chatted to the Gilliechattans.

Sergeant Awbrite was the last to turn up. At first nobody recognised him dressed in a loud Hawaiian shirt instead of his sober uniform. When the equally bald Mrs Kof appeared wearing her false moustache, chest-wig and leopard-skin leotard, they looked like twins – and the sergeant laughed so hard that tears streamed down his cheeks.

The cook's performance was nothing short of astonishing. She lifted heavy weights, bent iron bars, smashed concrete blocks with her bare fists, and dragged Balthazar the elephant across the ring using nothing but her teeth.

'That explains the gap in her smile,' Justin remarked to his sister. But Robyn was too enthralled by the tattoo of a falcon adorning Mrs Kof's muscular back to reply.

Albion, who had never visited a circus before, enjoyed everything except the clowns. He hid behind Eliza for most of their act, whimpering. His favourites were the beautiful Lipizzaner horses dancing to Strauss's great waltz – *"The Blue Danube."*

After the performance, Sergeant Awbrite treated everyone to ice-creams, and then they all crowded into Mrs Kof's dressing room to congratulate her. The tiny caravan pulsated with the noise of their happy chatter – but Justin stood quietly in one corner chewing his lower lip. Now the circus was over, his thoughts returned to the time machine, and a sudden pang of anxiety twisted itself into a knot deep inside his stomach. Alarming scenes kept playing themselves out in his mind's eye: Nanny Verity unlocking the castle door; a tall, mysterious stranger creeping up

347

the south tower staircase; a pale hand opening the chronopod door.

The drive home seemed interminable, and with every second that ticked by his fears multiplied by a googolplex.

Back at Thyme Castle, Justin hurtled to the top of the south tower. He hesitated outside his lab door, panting; the logical left side of his brain calming his irrational fears whilst the imaginative right hemisphere tormented him with visions of catastrophe. Peace of mind was impossible until he'd checked the time machine was safe. He pressed his right thumb on the fingerprint recognition sensor, and waited for the soft metallic thunk of the deadbolts retracting. Hardly daring to breathe, he pushed the door open and switched on the light.

At first glance, everything appeared to be exactly as he'd left it. But as Justin gave vent to a deep sigh of relief, he spotted one thing that looked minutely different: the chronopod door was slightly ajar. As he lurched forward and wrenched it fully open, the knot in his stomach contorted into a double-helix.

A small rectangle of ivory parchment lay on the time machine's scarlet leather seat. Justin's heart punched against his ribs as he reached for the envelope, scarcely able to believe what was written on it:

This concludes the first section of my time thesis, in which I have outlined the fundamental basics of TARTAN THEORY, and examined some of the causal loop paradoxes associated with temporal journeys into the past.

The next section will examine the concept of travelling to the future, explaining why the infinite possibilities that lie ahead make it impractical. I will discuss the limitations that such a journey would impose, and state the PRINCIPAL RULES OF TIME TRAVEL – a must for all potential chrononauts.

Other topics will include: more about the effects of motion and gravity on time; the components required to construct a time machine and how they function; further paradoxes including the Twins Effect and Schrödinger's Cat; spacewarps, wormholes and singularities; Minkowski space-time; and the Chronology Protection Conjecture.

CHAPTER TWENTY-ONE

Truth or Hoax?

The handwriting on the envelope certainly *looked* like his own – if it *was* another forgery then it was a truly remarkable one. But what bothered Justin most was that somebody had managed to successfully bypass his lab's security and leave it inside the chronopod. However, when he tore the envelope open and read the letter, everything became clear.

Dear Justin,

Knowledge is a valuable thing – but foreknowledge of the future is priceless.

Of course, talking to one's self is often considered the first sign of madness – but writing to yourself, (from Thyme to Thyme), can have its uses!

The letter you are holding is the strangest you will ever ~~read~~ write. Are these words a paradox? Writing them feels most peculiar, especially as I can still recall the panic I felt when I found this self-same letter inside the chronopod.

Truth or Hoax?

Cinema special effects cannot compare with the wonders you will experience travelling through the wormholes of time. I planned this experimental first trip to coincide with your visit to the circus – although I see no reason why meeting one's self should be hazardous.

Can time travel disrupt the fabric of time? Reality may differ from theory – so every precaution <u>must</u> be taken. When the time comes, remember to write this letter yourself, to ensure the perpetuation of this self-consistent causal loop. After all, "Everything is Connected to Everything Else!"

Help! I'm getting carried away. I mustn't forget why I'm writing to ~~you~~ myself. At midnight you will get an e-mail from Robyn's old laptop; (Nanny stole it before fleeing the castle). Send the Honestimator Trojan to this computer before she uses the keyboard, to help determine the truthfulness of her words.

Interpret Nanny's e-mail using the full power of your brain. Analyse it later, taking nothing at face value – but right now it's time to get down to some serious work ...

Hidden away in this laboratory, ~~I completed~~ you will complete your time machine by dawn – and as the earliest rays of sunlight glide across the loch, you will embark on your first voyage through the fourth dimension.

Clues to the success of your invention are in your hand – so don't be afraid. Reading this note proves that time travel is possible, although you guessed that when you saw ~~me~~ yourself delivering the acid. That will be my next journey ...

Yours Paradoxically,   Justin Thyme.

By the time Justin finished reading, his hands were shaking and he realised he'd been holding his breath. The south tower security system hadn't been compromised after all. A surge of relief flooded through every cell in his body, rapidly followed by the electric tingle of excitement.

'Now I know for *certain* my time machine's going to work,' he whispered. 'Wow! I can't *wait* to get it finished. But what's all this about Nanny Verity e-mailing me first?' With a puzzled frown, he re-read the letter, wondering why the scenario seemed strangely familiar. Then he realised: 'Cooooool! I remember reading about this.'

Justin reached to the shelf above his desk and pulled down an old book he'd found in the library some weeks ago. He flipped to the right page and read the relevant section:

The Paradox Enigma – by Jim Huttensy   1997

Perhaps the most baffling of all paradoxes is that of a young man who discovers a dusty old manuscript about time travel which inspires him to build his own time machine. Many years later he decides to write about his time-travelling adventures, but accidentally loses the manuscript whilst visiting the past. It lies forgotten on a library shelf until, one day, his younger self finds and reads it.

The causal loop seems self-consistent and free of contradictions, but where did the knowledge of time travel originate? The young man wouldn't have built the time machine without reading the manuscript first, yet his older self couldn't have written it unless he'd travelled through time. Often referred to as the Knowledge from Nowhere paradox, it is a classic "chicken and egg" situation!

'Wow! This chap really knows his stuff,' Justin murmured, returning the book to its shelf. He'd read it scores of times – though experiencing it firsthand gave him a totally different perspective. 'I know I've got to use the Honestimator, but where did *that* knowledge originate? My future self has informed me by letter, but my future self only *knows*, because he's already received the same letter in his past from *his* future self!'

Justin sighed. This wasn't the right moment to ponder the mysteries of time-travel; with midnight ticking closer he couldn't waste a nanosecond. He hurriedly unlocked his concealed safe and extracted the Honestimator discs.

By 23:19, Justin had completed the installation and ran a few swift system checks. He composed a brief e-mail, supposedly to his sister, and typed Worried about VK in the subject box to arouse Nanny Verity's curiosity. He clicked SEND and leaned back in his chair; there was nothing more he could do. The Trojan would lurk at the ISP's server until Nanny went online, hopefully she would open his e-mail before typing one of her own.

At last, the tower clock struck twelve, sending musical shivers along the rows of chemical bottles. As the final note faded, Justin's computer added a thirteenth chime of its own, and a new envelope icon appeared. With a swift click of his mouse he opened the e-mail:

To:	justin@thymecastle.co.uk

☺ Dear Justin,

Clearly, I had to escape Thyme Castle. I was terribly afraid that if I stayed, the police would take me to jail. It's crazy; I feel exactly like a fugitive – but of course, I have just myself to blame. It's quite impossible for me to accept your help ... yet.

Once Agent X has been caught and imprisoned, I'll quite free to return. Meanwhile, I'm afraid to leave this place of hiding, and intend to keep well *hidden*! Don't attempt to find me, Justin. I left no clues – it would be far too hazardous.

Until quite recently you thought I was just your dizzy old Nanny. Events will have changed your mind I expect. However, I did need help to escape – though I've no idea who rescued me. To my utter astonishment, a mystery saviour turned up shortly after you locked me in.

Naturally, it was quite unexpected. I'd simply decided I'd give up and accept whatever disaster awaited me. It served me right. All the brazen lies I'd been telling the Thymes were finally getting their just reward. I knew I deserved whatever punishment lay immediately ahead.

Then, amazingly, I sensed that somebody was behind me. When I asked who it was, a deep voice said: "You must heed this *message*: Do not look back. You need to escape quickly, so I've fetched you the key to those handcuffs." A key was tossed onto my lap. "Find a safe place to hide in," the voice said. "The job you have done will be continued by the next agent."

There was no chance to ask questions. The person had vanished just seconds before I could turn around to say thank you. It was very puzzling. I'd better vanish too, I thought. *In* a taxi!

Even now, I find it quite impossible to identify the person who rescued me. I didn't get enough time to scrutinize the evidence. *First*, I hurried to my room to collect some money for the journey. Then I "borrowed" Robyn's computer; it's the only thing I could think of. She'll be utterly furious I expect – but writing *letters* is much too risky – so will you tell her I'm sorry.

Now Poppet, you must be very careful. My husband's a wonderfully talented actor, perfectly able to masquerade as anyone at Thyme Castle. You'll want to amaze everyone and unmask Agent X, but Nanny can't help – that would be just too dangerous. Don't try to locate me. Remember that Nanny has always loved you from the "heart of her bottom!" Look after Robyn and Alby.

☹ Missing you already! Love, hugs and kisses to all the Thyme Family,   Mrs Verity Kiss, (Nanny).

HONESTY ESTIMATE: Not Entirely Truthful

Truth or Hoax?

Justin shook his head in bewilderment. For such a long-winded e-mail it gave remarkably little away. Naturally, Nanny had needed to exercise caution in case it fell into enemy hands, but then why bother to contact him at all?

Even Nanny's vocabulary seemed oddly uncharacteristic; only the ending sounded like her. Some years ago, whilst telling the family she loved them *from the bottom of her heart*, she'd got into a typical Nanny Verity muddle. It swiftly became a longstanding joke – one that everyone at Thyme Castle was familiar with.

Because of the e-mail's length, even the honesty estimate didn't help. Justin knew *part* of Nanny's story was untrue – but the question was: *which* part?

And finally, where had Nanny suddenly learnt how to operate a computer? She'd always been a technophobe, wary of anything more complicated than a kettle. The more Justin thought about it, the more perturbed he felt. He wished he'd spent more time with Nanny before she'd vanished. He'd never found out how she'd managed to forge his handwriting on the second envelope, or asked about the secret she'd mentioned in her postcard ... something connecting their cook with one of Henny's film crew.

'I suppose it's only about the Circus,' Justin sighed to himself. 'She's probably discovered that Polly's dad and Mrs Kof are both performers.'

Perfectly true, of course, but that *wasn't* what Verity Kiss had meant *at all*.

After four solid hours of work, Justin stepped back from the chronopod and gazed at it with a confusing mixture of pride and foreboding. Without the motorbike, it looked like an immense chromium-plated egg – practical, yet oddly pleasing. Robyn would approve of the design, he thought. With her instinctive flair, she'd probably say that the ovoid style of the pod successfully combined quirky old-fashioned craftsmanship with high-tech futuristic pizzazz.

Justin grinned. He had absolutely no intention of letting his sister anywhere near the chronopod. 'Impulsive, headstrong Robyn and a machine that might disrupt the fabric of time,' he murmured. 'Now *there's* a recipe for disaster!'

A sudden, loud splash interrupted his thoughts. Curious, Justin peered under one of the blackout screens at the motionless world outside. The entire loch was as still as glass – but directly below the promontory at the entrance to Thyme Bay, an enormous ripple undulated slowly outwards, its concentric circles glistening in the first rays of the rising sun. Beneath the surface, he saw a monstrous shadowy shape plummeting out of sight.

The eerie scene made Justin shiver. It was the second time he'd seen Nessie – and something told him it would *not* be the last.

In the past, he'd dismissed the various hypotheses explaining its existence, but now Justin realised why they had never stood up under close scrutiny: he'd never factored time travel into the equation.

He smiled to himself as he considered the possibilities. If his plans worked, then his mum's show certainly wouldn't be axed – *Thyme-Zone* would be the envy of every TV company imaginable. Royalties from DVD rights alone would make a small fortune – and all without the hassle of an animation studio. Of course, the time machine would have to be kept a secret, he thought. But if the films were marketed as the ultimate in computer generated wizardry, nobody would ever guess the truth.

'But I daren't let Dad find out,' Justin reminded himself.

Now that he thought about it, Justin couldn't help wondering if there was more to his father's brusque dismissal of the Monster than simple disbelief. He had the oddest feeling that the fate of the Thyme Clan was somehow linked to the Beast of the Loch; be it past, present or future – or all three inexplicably entwined.

An icy chill prickled Justin's spine and a gaggle of goose pimples migrated across his arms and legs. Nanny Verity would have said someone had stepped on his grave. Normally, Justin brushed such nonsensical superstition aside – yet for a brief irrational moment he had the overwhelming urge to smash the chronopod to atoms.

He didn't, of course. The logical left side of his brain would never permit such unscientific behaviour. '*This* proves there's nothing to fear,' he whispered, patting the pocket that held the letter from his future self. 'And anyway ... I've got to make sure Mum gets rescued, haven't I?'

As soon as the thought flickered through his brain, Justin remembered that he'd need to fetch the corrosive acid compound for his second trip. Knowing its importance, he'd locked it safely away before going to the circus – but when he opened his chemical cupboard his heart sank; the little metallic tube was missing.

'Someone must've taken it while we were out, but ... but ...' He stood for a moment, his face screwed up in thought, then as the truth dawned on him he grinned broadly. 'Idiot! *I* took it, of course ... or at least, I *will* take it once I've travelled back in time; that's why I must've mentioned it in the letter.'

Remembering he'd need to write the self-same letter himself, Justin crossed to his desk and took a pencil and some notepaper out of the top drawer – then, as he tucked them into his pocket, he shook his head at the absurdity of his actions; the pencil and paper would be waiting for him in the past whether he took them or not.

'I guess time travel's going to take some adjusting to,' he murmured.

Justin hunted around for the scrap of paper he'd used to record the coordinates of his mum's rescue. He knew this would be in the past too, but it seemed safer to memorise it; after all, this time, his punctuality would be a matter of life or death.

Since cracking the playing card code, he'd found himself converting rows of numbers into letters as a sort of memory aid. Now, as he stared at the time and date he'd scribbled down so hurriedly, his eyes widened and his face turned pale.

10:11:18 – 15/05.

Using the same code, the hours, minutes and seconds became three consonants, whilst the day and month both converted into vowels. When all five letters were rearranged, they spelled out the word ...

JOKER!

It had to be a coincidence, he thought – but what were the odds of something like that happening by chance? At least a billion to one. Justin shivered again. He'd wanted to believe the watch was from some anonymous friend; now he suddenly started to wonder if his father had been right all along.

Slowly, he returned to the chronopod, opened its door and lowered himself onto its scarlet leather seat. Feeling stunned beyond belief, Justin sat for a moment, wondering if time travel would ever provide answers to the questions still tumbling around in his head: What was the significance of the two carved figures flanking the library clock? Was the sinister jester somehow linked to the Thief of Time? Was Sir Lyall Austin Thyme *really* his long-lost grandfather, or could his uncanny resemblance to Old Father Time be a fluke? Had Agent X managed to infiltrate Thyme Castle in person? Did he rescue Nanny, or was her e-mail a cruel hoax? Was the Thyme curse a product of Sir Willoughby's paranoia, or would a member of the family *really* die this year? And finally, who had left the mysterious wristwatch ... and why?

Once again, the engraved words on the back of his watch flew into Justin's mind. "*Everything is Connected to Everything Else.*" Would the answers to *these* questions be connected too? Were they all interlocking pieces of some paradoxical multi-dimensional puzzle?

Only time would tell.

With mounting trepidation, Justin keyed in the Minkowski space-time coordinates of his chosen destination in the past – then waited. Factoring in the earth's rotation, the computer completed its calculation and displayed an image of the pod's ultimate location: a metre to the left of its present position, to avoid

358

colliding with the unfinished pod at 7 pm the previous evening.

Justin took a deep breath and closed the chronopod door, triggering the anti-gravity unit and negative-energy generator.

'There's no going back now,' he told himself. Then realising that "going back" was the only thing he *could* do, gave a brittle, nervous laugh.

An efficient computerised voice calmly announced: 'TEN SECONDS TO DEPARTURE,' then commenced its countdown ...

Justin's thoughts strayed to that first day in May when he'd wished for an adventure. It seemed incredible, but the adventure of a lifetime lay seconds ahead

'NINE ...'

He was poised on the threshold of a whole new world; a world where the weird would be commonplace and the impossible became possible.

'EIGHT ...'

Primed with an influx of antigravitational exotic matter, the subatomic wormhole-vortex accelerator activated automatically.

'SEVEN ...'

Justin stared at the monitor, watching the computer simulation of a microscopic Planck-sized wormhole inflating to a traversable size.

'SIX ...'

Beneath the centre of the chronopod, a pinprick of purest white light materialised. Then, gleaming with fierce intensity, its shimmering periphery spread slowly outwards.

'FIVE ...'

Mirrored in the pod's convex metallic surface, diaphanous wisps of plasma spiralled upwards like twisted rainbows of liquid smoke.

'FOUR ...'

Dazzling light blurred the edges of reality, and an inferno of snowfire encircled the pod, until it resembled the blazing egg of a gigantic mechanical phoenix.

'THREE ...'

Justin gazed in wide-eyed wonder through the tiny window. It was like being trapped inside a snow-globe surrounded by a lava lamp whirled within a colossal kaleidoscope.

'TWO ...'

On the computer screen, Justin watched the wormhole's virtual geometry configure into a vast inverted vortex of multi-coloured luminosity.

'ONE ...'

The iridescent plasma swirled towards its radiant zenith of singularity – two metres above the pod – and stopped.

'WORMHOLE STABLIZED,' announced the computer, flashing the words onto its monitor. Justin braced himself, knowing his adventure was about to begin.

The singularity winked open – and instantly, the quantum vacuum of the wormhole sucked the pod into its strong gravitational field. Like a mercury bubble it whirled at tachyon speed along a pulsating tunnel of light, spontaneously generating its programmed course through the fourth dimension. Almost immediately, a second singularity formed directly behind the pod, pinching the wormhole closed and plunging the lab into total darkness.

The greatest adventure of all time had begun. But whether it would be the time of Justin's life, or cost the life of Justin Thyme, remained to be seen.

Two things, however, were certain: firstly, a rift in the Tartan of Time had already occurred, the synchronicity of which only Justin could restore. Secondly, the mysterious X remained in the equation and would stop at nothing – even murder – to get the time machine for himself.

Whether you chose to call it a curse or a coincidence – time was running out for someone at Thyme Castle.

APPENDIX

This list gives brief definitions to some of the more complex words in this book, however, if you are anything like Justin, you'll know most of them already! It includes: general vocabulary, Scottish dialect, abbreviations, and greatly simplified explanations of scientific or technical terms.

*If a word has several meanings only the definition appropriate to the context is given.

A

adjacent - near, close or beside.
adrenaline - a hormone that when secreted increases the heart rate.
adverse - bringing misfortune or harm.
akimbo - usually used to describe the position of both hands on hips with elbows sticking outwards, (arms akimbo).
ambigram - a word written in such a way that it looks the same from more than one angle. From *ambi* (both) + *gram* (word).
ambiguous - difficult to understand. Having more than one possible outcome or meaning.
amnesia - loss of memory.
anagram - arranging the letters of a word or phrase to spell another word or phrase.
anti-gravity - a repulsive form of gravitation.
antithesis - the exact opposite of.
apex - the highest point or tip.
apoplectic - *prone to rage - becoming red in the face with anger.
apparition - *the appearance of something remarkable, unexpected or mysterious.
arachnid - class of animals including spiders.
Archimedes – Ancient Greek mathematician and physicist.
asinine - silly.
aspidistra - a houseplant with long evergreen leaves.
assiduously - diligently - without giving up.
astral - anything to do with the stars.

(Robyn uses it to mean "out of this world!")
atom-smasher - the non-technical term for a particle accelerator.
audacity - boldness.
avant-garde - favouring a modern style.

B

bairn - a baby. *(Scottish dialect)*.
balaclava - a woollen helmet covering the head, showing just the eyes.
balefully - dejectedly.
baroque - a style of architecture used between the 16th–18th centuries.
barrage - *rapid fire or continuous bombardment.
bawbee - a Scottish coin no longer in circulation.
BBC - *abbrev*: British Broadcasting Corporation.
Beastie - the Loch Ness Monster, (also known as Nessie).
bemused - bewildered or lost in thought.
binary scale - counting using two figures only, (0 & 1) instead of 10 (0, 1, 2, 3, 4, 5, 6, 7, 8 & 9). Using this scale: $1 = 1, 2 = 10, 3 = 11, 4 = 100$ etc.
binoculars - a magnifying optical device for both eyes. Also known as field glasses.
biodegradable - something that rots naturally.
biscuit - British word for cookie.
black hole - a hypothetical area in space caused by the gravitational collapse of a star.
blether - talk nonsense. *(Scottish dialect)*.
blithering - contemptible.

Appendix

BMW - *abbrev*: Bayerische Motoren Worke, (a German make of car).
bonnet - British word for a car's hood.
boot - British word for a car's trunk.
Botticelli - An Italian artist.
burgeoning - rapidly growing.

C

caber - a roughly hewn tree-trunk used in the Scottish sport of tossing the caber.
cairngorm - yellow or purple gemstones from the Scottish Cairngorm mountains
calibrate - measure.
calibre - *ability.
calligraphy - decorative handwriting.
car park - British term for parking lot.
Casimir effect - negative energy built up between reflective plates inside a quantum vacuum.
cataclysm - catastrophe or a disastrous event.
causal loops - loops in the fabric of time taken at timeforks – the product of cause and effect.
causal/causality - the principle of cause and effect.
cerebrum - the dominant part of a human's brain. The centre of intellect.
cerise - a deep shade of pink.
cerulean - sky-blue.
chagrin - annoyance.
chasmal - as wide as a chasm.
chips - British word for French fries.
chivalry - considerate and polite behaviour to weaker persons.
chloroform - a liquid that gives off a vapour that causes unconsciousness.
chromosomes - microscopic structures that appear in a nucleus during cell division consisting of genes responsible for hereditary characteristics.
chronic - *affecting a person for a long time.
chronology - proper sequence of past times, dates or events.
chrononaut - a time traveller.

circumspect - cautious and watchful.
cliche - an over-used phrase or idea.
coerced - compelled or forced.
cogito - *Latin* for 'I think.'
collywobbles - *intense feeling of nervousness.
compound - a substance made of atoms from two or more chemical elements.
concentric - with a common centre – usually of circles.
conceptual - based on concepts or ideas.
concurrently - at the same time or location.
condescending - in a manner that implies a feeling of superiority.
conductivity - the power of a material to conduct heat or electricity.
configure - the arrangement of external parts or an outline.
conglomeration - a mass of various things.
conniving - secretly plotting or conspiring.
conspiratorial - in the manner of a conspirator - or one that shares a secret.
consternation - anxiety or dismay.
contemptuous - showing contempt - the feeling of despising something.
contraption - a device, often mechanical.
controversial - causing argument or dispute.
convulsive - shaking violently.
Copernicus (Nicolaus) - Polish astronomer who claimed the universe was heliocentric (revolving around the sun.) (1473 – 1543).
corpus callosum - a band of fibres connecting the brain hemispheres.
cortex - the grey matter in the brain covering the cerebrum.
cosmic strings - linear defects in spacetime according to certain theories of cosmology.
counterfeit - fake.
credulity - gullibility.
credulous - gullible, likely to believe

Appendix

easily, with little or no evidence.

crenellated - descriptive of castle walls or battlements with square notches along the top.

criteria - defining characteristics.

cryogenically frozen – frozen rapidly at extremely low temperatures.

crypt - a hidden underground chamber.

cryptic - concealing its meaning in a puzzling way.

cryptid - an enigmatic creature not generally accepted by zoologists, but occasionally claimed to have been seen by witnesses.

cryptozoologist - a person who studies undocumented or puzzling creatures, not generally acknowledged by zoologists.

CT-scan - Computerised Tomography scan.

cumbersome - clumsy or awkward to wear, carry or manage.

curtains - British word for drapes.

cynic - a person who believes that the motives of others are bad.

D

da Vinci (Leonardo) - Italian painter, inventor and genius, fascinated by the science of art and the art of science. (1452 – 1519).

debunker - a person who works to prove that a claim or theory is false.

deja vu - a mysterious feeling that you have already experienced a present event.

derisive - mocking or scornful.

dexter hand - (usually in heraldry). The right hand or side.

dextrous - skilful in handling things.

diaphanous - translucent, see through.

discernible - able to be perceived clearly with the mind or senses.

discompose - to disturb the composure (calmness of the mind).

disconsolate - too sad to be comforted.

disembodied - lacking a body or substance.

disgruntled - discontented or resentful.

dishevelled - untidy.

disillusion - to set free from mistakenly held beliefs.

displacement behaviour - substituting one behaviour for another.

diverging - going in different directions after starting at the same point.

divulge - to make something known or to reveal a secret.

dodecahedron - a solid figure with 12 faces.

dogberry - a dim-witted, interfering official. Named after the character, Dogberry, in Shakespeare's "*Much Ado About Nothing*".

doolally - crazy or insane.

double-helix - two strands coiled around the same axis like the structure of DNA.

dressing-gown - British word for bath robe.

duplicity - double-dealing or deception.

dynamic - usually concerning energy that produces motion.

dysfunction - failure to function normally.

E

E = MC² - energy is equal to mass multiplied by the speed of light squared.

eccentric - *decidedly unusual in behaviour or appearance. **eccentricity** *n.*

Einstein (Albert) - a world-famous physicist who formulated the theories of Special and General Relativity. (1879 – 1955).

elastic band - Bristish term for rubber band.

electro-conductive - capable of conducting electricity.

electroencephalocutor - word invented for this story by combining **encephalo -** indicating the brain, and **electrocute.**

electromagnetic - having both electrical and magnetic properties.

electrophysiological - electrical activity

Appendix

within the body.

emaciated - having become extremely thin from illness or lack of food.

emanating - coming from a source.

embrocation - liquid medication that relieves pain when rubbed on the body.

emporium - *a large shop.

encrypted - encoded.

engender - to give rise to.

enigma - a puzzle. Something mysterious or difficult to understand.

enigmatically *adv.mysteriously.*

enshrouded - *covered completely.

entailed - *property left to a succession of male heirs so that it can neither be sold or given away.

epidural - on the outer side of the dura mater.

Erebus — *n Greek myth.* god of darkness, son of Chaos, brother of Night.

ETA - *abbrev*: Estimated Time of Arrival.

ethereal - delicate.

etiquette - rules of correct behaviour in society.

eureka - an exclamation meaning *I have found it* - believed to have been said by Archimedes on discovering that the weight of an object can be calculated by the water it displaces.

evasive - not straightforward - giving an excuse.

exotic matter – matter with anti-gravitational properties.

exposition - *the part of a story where the main characters and their backgrounds are introduced.

F

facade - a deceptive outer appearance.

fastidious - fussy. Easily disgusted.

feasible - able to be done.

fervently - showing warmth of feeling.

fettle - condition.

fiasco - a humiliating failure.

Fibonacci numbers - a sequence of numbers where each is the sum of the previous two. (0,1,1,2,3,5,8,13, 21 etc.)

fixation - obsession.

flamboyant - *showy appearance or manner.

flatulence - gas generated during digestion.

fluctuations - constant changes or variations.

flux - flow. The rate at which fluid, energy or particles flow. A state of continuous change. Instability. Also a medical term for a particularly nasty bout of diarrhoea.

footling - petty and trivial.

foraging - searching or rummaging - often for food.

foreboding - an uncanny feeling that trouble lies ahead.

Fortean - descriptive of anomalous (unusual, puzzling or unexplained) phenomena – after Charles Fort, who spent his life researching mysteries of the universe, like: cryptozoology, teleportation, coincidence, chance and synchronicity.

Foucault's pendulum - a pendulum named after Jean Bernard Leon Foucault that demonstrates the rotation of earth on its axis.

fractal - a geometric shape that is equally complex and detailed in structure at any level of magnification.

fuchsia - a purplish-pink colour, like that of the fuchsia flower.

fundamental - basic.

fusion - thermonuclear reaction - energy created by the fusing of two nuclei into one nucleus.

G

Galileo (Galilei) - Italian mathematician, physicist and astronomer. (1564 – 1642).

galvanized - *stimulated sudden activity.

genetics – *the study of hereditary.

googol - a large number, written as one

Appendix

followed by a hundred noughts.

googolplex - a very large number, written as one followed by a googol noughts.

gormless - stupid.

goth - short for gothic. descriptive of a style of dress and makeup designed to create a vampire-like appearance.

GPO - *abbrev*: General Post Office.

GPS - *abbrev*: Global Positioning System.

Greenwich Mean Time - the time on the line of longitude that passes through the site of the former Royal observatory in Greenwich - used to calculate time throughout most of the world.

grimace - a facial expression showing embarrassment, pain or disgust.

guttural - harsh sounding.

gyroscope - a device used in navigation instruments aboard spacecraft, consisting of a heavy wheel, which, when spinning fast, keeps the direction of its axis unchanged.

H

haematoma - a swelling caused by internal bleeding.

haemorrhoids - an unpleasant and uncomfortable medical condition involving swollen veins on the rear end.

handbag - British word for purse or pocketbook.

hapless - unlucky.

Harrison chronometer - a priceless timepiece made by master clockmaker and genius John Harrison between 1730-1760.

haver - to talk nonsense. *(Scottish dialect)*.

Heath-Robinson - a ridiculously complicated mechanical device that performs an uncomplicated function.

heliograph to send messages by reflecting flashes of sunlight in a mirror

HG (Herbert George) Wells - English author of science fiction novels including

"The Time Machine". (1886 – 1946).

hiatus - a break or gap.

highland tattoo - a Scottish military display, usually with bagpipes and drums.

hologram/holographic - * three-dimensional images usually produced by lasers.

horologist – watch or clockmaker.

hydraulic - operated by a pressured influx of liquid.

hypodermic - injected beneath the skin.

hypothesis - a suggested explanation.

hypothetical - an explanation that is unproved and may not necessarily be true.

I

illusory - based on illusion - not real.

impassive - calm, not showing any emotion.

impeccable - faultless, without error.

impediment - physical defect.

impending - about to happen shortly.

imperative - *essential or obligatory.

imperceptibly - too gradually to be noticed.

impervious - *cannot be influenced.

impracticable - incapable of being put into practice.

impromptu - done without rehearsal or planning.

inadequacies - failings.

inanimate - lifeless.

incognito - in disguise or using an assumed name.

incomprehensible - unable to be understood.

incongruous - unsuitable. Out of place.

inconsequential - trivial or insignificant.

incriminating - something that proves a person is involved in wrong-doing.

inexorably - relentlessly, unceasingly.

infallible - certain, dependable, not likely to be mistaken.

inferno - a fiery place.

infiltrate - to enter without being noticed

Appendix

- like a spy.

infinitesimal - extremely small.

influx - the act of flowing into.

insidious - behaving harmfully without attracting much attention.

integral - a part needed to complete a whole.

integrity - honesty and loyalty.

interminable - endless - often boring.

intractable - hard to deal with or control.

intrepid - bold and daring.

intuitive - resulting from instinctive knowledge or a hunch.

iridology - the study of patterns in the iris.

irony - an expression that means the opposite of how it sounds. Or, an event so unexpected or badly timed it appears to be meant to annoy. **ironically** - *adv* characterising or using irony.

irrevocably - unalterably *adv*.

J

jeopardise - to risk or put in danger.

jelly - British word for jello.

jovial - jolly. Full of good cheer.

K

kaleidoscope - an optical toy that produces brightly coloured symmetrical patterns.

ken - understand. *(Scottish dialect).*

kilt – a knee-length pleated skirt, usually made of tartan material, (worn by both men and women in Scotland).

kongamato - pterodactyl-like creatures allegedly seen in Zambia.

L

Laird - a Scottish landowner similar to an English Lord. *(Scottish dialect).*

languished - *left under miserable conditions.

LCD - *abbrev*: Liquid Crystal Display.

light-speed - 299,792,458 meters per second, or 186,282 miles per second.

Lipizzaner - an intelligent breed of white or grey horse, often used in circuses.

lithe - supple and agile.

litigation - legal proceedings.

livid - *furiously angry.

loch – lake.

lugubriously - dismally, mournfully.

luminescence - light emitted at low temperatures.

M

M Theory - a comprehensive 'theory of everything.'

malapropism - confusing a word with a similar one with a different meaning – usually with hilarious results. (After Mrs Malaprop in Sheridan's play *The Rivals*). For example: when Mrs Kof confuses "bowls" and "bowels".

malevolent - wishing harm to others.

malicious - showing malice - a desire to harm others.

matriarch - *female head of the family.

mayhem - violent destruction, confusion or chaos.

Medusan - *Greek myth.* Like Medusa, a gorgon, portrayed as a woman with snakes for hair.

mercurial - changeable, volatile - like mercury.

mesmerised - hypnotised.

metabolic rate - the rate at which food is converted to energy.

metamorphose - to change gradually (like a caterpillar into butterfly).

methodology - science of method and procedure.

meticulously - with great attention to detail.

metronome - an adjustable mechanical device that swings to and fro with a clicking noise to indicate the tempo of music.

microbot – microscopic robot.

Appendix

millefiori - colourful patterns often found in glassware. *Italian*: thousand flowers.

minimalist - *a design style which uses the minimum of objects arranged simply.

Minkowski space-time - co-ordinates given in four dimensions. Three indicate spatial position – the fourth a point in time.

minuscule - *very small.

mobius strip - a one-sided surface - made by joining the ends of a rectangular strip after twisting one end 180 degrees.

mokele-mbembe - a plesiosaur-like dinosaur said to still exist in the Congo, but seen only by BaAkan pygmies so far. Its name means: one who stops the flow of rivers.

monochrome - *in shades of black and white.

Moriarty - in fiction, Sherlock Holmes' arch-enemy.

morphine - an opium-based anaesthetic.

morphing - the gradual distortion of one image so that it changes into another.

mortification – a feeling of humiliation.

Mozart (Wolfgang Amadeus) - Austrian composer and genius. (1756 – 1791).

multiplicity - a large number or variety.

multiverse/multiversal a theory including multiple parallel universes as oppose to just a single universe.

Munro - a mountaineering term for any separate peak in Scotland over 3,000 feet high.

myopic - short-sighted.

N

naive - showing lack of experience and poor judgement. **naively** *adv*.

nanosecond - a billionth of a second.

nappy - British word for diaper.

nebulous - vague or not definite.

neep - turnip. *(Scottish dialect)*.

Nessie - Loch Ness Monster.

Nessiteras rhombopteryx - the 'scientific' name given to the Loch Ness Monster by some cryptozoologists.

neurons - nerve cells.

Newton (Isaac) - English mathematician and physicist, remembered for his law of gravitation and three laws of motion. Author of *Principia Mathematica*. (1643 – 1727).

nonchalantly - calmly, without showing anxiety or excitement.

nondisclosure agreement - a legal document that prevents a person from revealing confidential details about their employment.

nuance - a slight or subtle difference.

O

oblivion - *a state of unconsciousness or unawareness.

obsessed/obsessive - confined to one continual thought or behaviour pattern.

och - Scottish interjection like *oh*, often used to preface a remark: 'och, no dear.' Pronounced *ock*. *(Scottish dialect)*.

olfactory - relating to the sense of smell.

opaline – opaque, (not transparent), whitish glass., which captures the light like an opal.

optimum - best.

orienteering - a race on foot through a series of checkpoints, following a map and using a compass only.

ornithology - the scientific study of birds.

oubliette - a dungeon.

overtly - open and clearly visible.

ovoid - egg-shaped.

oxyacetylene - a mixture of oxygen and acetylene used for either welding of cutting.

P

paradox - a puzzle or an odd statement or situation that appears to contradict itself.

paramount - of supreme importance.

Appendix

paranoia - a tendency to mistrust and be wary of others. **paranoid** - behaving this way.

particle accelerator - a machine used for research in nuclear physics that accelerates charged elementary particles.

patently - obviously

patronise - *to buy from or bring trade to.

PC - *abbrev*: Personal Computer.

PDA - *abbrev*: Personal Digital Assistant.

pelmet - British word for valance.

penitentiary - state prison *(U.S)*.

perceptive - having insight and understanding.

periphery - the boundary or edge of something.

petersham - strong corded ribbon.

petrol - British word for gas.

pettifogging - paying too much attention to trivial details.

phenomenological - the science of phenomena.

phenomenon - * a remarkable occurrence or outstanding person.

phonetic - *spelt or written as it is pronounced. **phonetically** *adv*.

pictogram - pictures used to represent written words or phrases.

PIN - *abbrev*: Personal Identification Number.

pivotal - *vitally important.

pizzazz - a combination of vitality and glamour.

Planck-sized - something billions of times smaller than an atomic nucleus.

plasma - *a gas used in modern flat television monitors. Also a hot ionised material consisting of nuclei and electrons present in the sun and fusion reactors.

plausible - believable.

plesiosaur - an aquatic long-necked dinosaur.

pneumatic - an area of physics concerned with the mechanical properties of gases.

poliosis - loss of colour from the hair.

polygraph - a lie detector.

polyphonic - of music, having multiple voices.

potpourri - dried petals used to scent the air.

precipitate - to cause something to happen before it should.

precocious - with abilities developed earlier than usual.

predetermine - to decide in advance.

pretentious - *intended to impress others.

primatologist - a zoologist who specialises in studying primates.

prioritise - *to deal with things in order of their importance.

procrastination - delaying an action until a more convenient time.

prodigious - vast in amount.

promontory - a rocky area of land that juts into the surrounding water.

prosthetics - an artificial replacement for a missing body part.

protestation - the act of protesting.

prototype - a first example upon which others can be modelled.

proximity - nearness.

pseudo- - pretend.

pseudonym - false name.

psittacine - pertaining to parrots.

psychedelic - *having vivid colours and intricate patterns.

psychic - *able to read thoughts telepathically, sometimes known as mind-reading.

psychology – scientific study of methods of thought and behaviour.

psychotic – *mentally unsound.

Q

quantum mechanics - laws of physics governing the realm of the very small, where things happen unpredictably and by apparent chance.

Appendix

quetzal - a bright green South American bird - also a monetary unit in Guatemala.
quirky - a trait or mannerism peculiar to an individual.

R

radioactive - emitting radiation.
raucous - hoarse, harsh or loud.
reconstituted - reformed.
refrigerator - British word for ice box.
regalia - *special clothes.
regressed - *reverted back to.
Relativity - (Justin will look at the theories of Special and General Relativity later in his notebook).
relentless - continuous, without letup.
remote manipulator - a remotely operated device that handles substances dangerous to humans.
rendition - performance.
repertoire - *the complete collection of works/songs etc., that a person can perform.
replicate - to copy or reproduce.
resolute - firm and determined.
reverberate - to resound or re-echo.
reverse psychology - tricking someone into doing what you want by urging them not to!
rhetorical question - a question that doesn't need answering.
rhinencephalon - the part of the brain that contains the olfactory bulb.
Roman a clef - a novel in which real people are depicted with imaginary names. (*French* for novel with a key).
romanticised - *a fictitious account.

S

sack - British term meaning to fire someone, as in *to give someone the sack*.
sanatorium - medical institution or health resort.
sasquatch - a simian-like cryptid usually known as Bigfoot.

scandalised - shocked.
scant - barely sufficient.
scapegoat - an innocent person punished for someone else's crime.
scatty - empty-headed; probably short for scatter-brained.
scenario - summary of a plot or sequence of events.
sceptic - one who doubts what others believe. **sceptical** *adj.* **scepticism** *n.*
Schrodinger's cat - a hypothetical paradox concerning a cat and a radioactive atom. (Justin will deal with this later in his notebook).
scrutinising - examining carefully.
scythe - a tool for cutting grass having a long handle and a long curved blade.
seismic - relating to earthquakes.
sepulchral - gloomy, as if in a sepulchre or tomb.
serendipity - making a fortunate discovery by accident, or being in the right place at the right time.
serendumpity - a word invented to mean the opposite of serendipity - being in the wrong place at the wrong time - or the fact that if something can go wrong it probably will.
serried - in close formation like ranks of soldiers.
SIM - *abbrev*: Subscriber Identity Module.
simultaneously - at the same time.
singularity - a hypothetical point in spacetime at which matter is compressed to infinitesimal volume.
sinister hand - (usually in heraldry). The left hand or side.
smithereens - tiny shattered pieces.
spacetime - the fabric uniting the three dimensions of space and one of and time.
spanner - British word for wrench.
spasmodic - in sudden brief bursts.
spasmodically adv.
speculate - to guess without knowing all the facts. **speculation** *n.*

Appendix

spinster - an unmarried woman.
spontaneously - occurring naturally or without external influence - or arising from impulse.
sporadic - occurring at irregular intervals.
sporran – a pouch, (usually made of fur), worn hanging in front of a kilt.
staccato - *short, abrupt sounds.
staphylococcus - a type of bacterium.
stentorian - loud.
stereotypical - conventional or unoriginal.
stimuli - things that stimulate a response.
subatomic particles - a particle or process occurring within an atom.
subconscious - acting without awareness – or the part of the mind that is on the fringe of consciousness.
subdural - between the dura mater and the arachnoid.
subliminal - without being consciously realised.
subterranean - underground.
succumbing - giving way to.
suitcase - British word for valise.
superfluous – more than is needed.
supernova - an exploding star that for a short time burns millions of times brighter than the sun.
surface tension - the intermolecular force near the surface of a liquid that appears to form a film holding it in a globular shape.
surreal - *dreamlike. **surrealist** - *a painting in this style.
surreptitiously - stealthily.
sycophantic - trying to win favour by flattery.
symmetrically - *matching on both sides.
symmetry - similarity. Balancing perfectly. **synaptic** - descriptive of points at which nerve impulses are relayed through the brain.
synchronicity - two or more causally

unrelated events that appear almost identical.
synchronising - occurring at the same time.
synthesised - produced artificially.
syzygy - *a pair of opposites.

T

tachyon - a hypothetical particle that can travel faster than light.
tam o' shanter - a Scottish beret, often abbreviated to **tammy**.
Tannoy - a public address system.
tarpaulin - waterproof canvas.
tattie - potato. *(Scottish dialect)*.
technophobe - one who fears using technologically advanced devices.
teleportation - a hypothetical method of transporting a person or object from one place to another instantaneously.
temporal - relating to time.
tempus fugit – *Latin* - time flies.
tentative - *hesitant, **tentatively** adv.
tenuously - flimsily.
terminology - specialized words.
terse - curt, abrupt or concise.
thermal - pertaining to heat.
thermodynamics - a branch of physics concerned with the conversion of different forms of energy.
thesaurus - a book containing lists of synonyms (words with similar meanings).
thesis - *a subject for an essay.
thrum - a monotonous sound.
thylacine - also known as the Tasmanian tiger. although thought to be extinct, some people believe a few have survived.
Thymum Sempiternum – *Latin* - Thyme Eternal. (The Thyme Clan motto).
time machine - a machine designed to travel backwards in time.
torch - British word for flashlight.
traipsed - trudged.
trajectory - the path of an object moving through space – usually thrusted.
transfixed - made motionless.

Appendix

traversable - something that can be travelled along.
traversed - *travelled along.
trepidation - a state of nervous fear and anxiety.
triceratops - a dinosaur with 3 horns.
trousers - British word for pants.
tweeny - a maid who helps both up and downstairs - short for *between-maid*.

U

ultimate - *final.
unabashed - unembarrassed.
unceremoniously - without ceremony.
unethical - without ethics (moral principles and values).
unscrupulous - without scruples.
usher - show to an appointed place.
utilise - to make practical use of.

V

velocity - speed.
venison - the edible flesh of a deer.
viable - useful.
viscosity - concerning the thickness or stickiness of liquids.
VIP - *abbrev*: Very Important Person.

volatile - inconsistent, fickle.
vortex - a whirling mass of, gas, liquid or flame shaped like a whirlwind.
vulnerable - *open to attack.
VW - *abbrev*: Volkswagen, (a German car).

W

warp and weft - threads arranged lengthways and widthways on a weaving loom.
wee - small. *(Scottish dialect)*.
whimsical - *quaint or unusual.
whodunit - a mystery story challenging the reader to deduce who commits a crime by finding clues in the text.
witchetty grub - an edible Australian caterpillar.
wormhole - a tunnel through spacetime connecting two different points in either space, time or both.

XYZ

Zeitgeist - the attitude or general outlook of a specific period. German, literally *the spirit of the times*.
zenith - *the highest point.

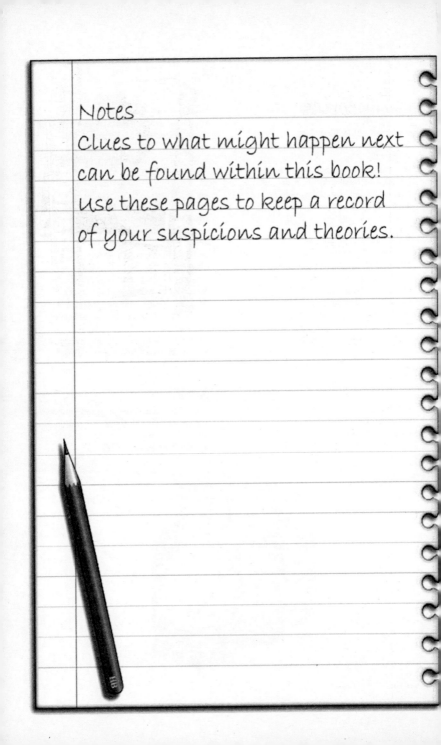

Notes

Clues to what might happen next
can be found within this book!
Use these pages to keep a record
of your suspicions and theories.

Theories

...et,
...forget
...e sea,
...you've married me.

Clues and Suspects

RICARR'S FACE EMPORIUM

Purveyors of Beards, Moustaches
& Facial Prosthetics Since 1989

Puzzling Connections

Everything
is
Connected
to
Everything Else

Thyme Running Out

"The cool, efficient voice of the inbuilt computer commenced its countdown, but Justin wasn't listening. Oblivious to the spirals of plasma swirling round the chronopod, he wondered how many of the *Rules of Time Travel* he'd just broken."

As the threat of the Thyme Curse closes in on Justin's family, his life is once again thrown into complete turmoil. Will he finally unmask Agent X? Has Evelyn Garnet stolen his wristwatch? What's making Eliza act so aggressively? Why is Sir Willoughby planning a secret trip through time? And where has Robyn mysteriously vanished to? Only one person knows the truth – but can Justin find her before it's too late?